HEALER

HAVENHART ACADEMY BOOK ONE

R L MERRILL

To William D. Russell

Thank you for your guidance, your passion, your wisdom, and your search for the truth.

ONE

AN EDUCATION

"I'm sorry, Delaney, but with your health issues, I think this is really for the best. Having subs in here so often has led to an increase in suspensions. Besides all of that, there are more budget cuts being announced for the next year, and we just can't justify keeping your program running."

Nothing like starting your first day back from disability with these words of encouragement from your superior.

"There's a counseling position at the high school I can recommend you for," the director of personnel told me. "With your credentials and experience, you can work anywhere. I know you've loved this job because you were able to teach and counsel your students, but you were also a great counselor before. The high school would be lucky to have you. Think about it over the weekend and let me know what you want to do on Monday."

Just like that, all of my hard work building a program for emotionally disturbed students for the past five years was down the tubes.

Awesome, I thought to myself on the walk to my classroom. *I'm so glad I came back for this!* I coughed so hard, I almost lost my breakfast and rushed to my locked cabinet for my inhaler. My hands shook, and I fumbled with the keys trying to get the damn door open.

Mornings had been particularly rough since I'd suffered a bout of pneumonia last month. My asthma was now set off by anything, whether it was an artificial fragrance, a whiff of fresh-cut grass, or smoke from a neighbor's chimney. My doctor said this was as good as I was going to get for a while, so I'd gone back to work. I'd missed my students, and also dreaded seeing what damage they'd done to each other in my absence.

Two hours later, I was attempting to keep Victor and Clarence from stabbing each other with shanks they'd crafted from the last of my pencils while giving a lesson on genetics. The sub had left safety scissors out last week and that's all they'd needed to craft weapons of potential destruction.

My aide, Norman, took the boys to the office after they refused to quit their dueling. Normally I'd have handled it on my own, but I barely had the energy to stay upright on my stool today.

"Alright, gentlemen. It's time for P.E. Coach Valencia will be waiting for you outside."

My remaining ten students rambunctiously made their way out the door of my portable classroom and onto the blacktop, where they terrorized their P.E. teacher for the next fifty minutes while I tried to literally catch my breath.

I brought out my nebulizer from the cabinet where I kept my personal things locked and poured in the solution. I took my breathing treatment while surfing the net for job postings, trying to find a position where I would hopefully make a positive impact and get healthy in the process. A counseling job in the high school meant sitting at a desk and shuffling papers, which wasn't exactly the hands-on work I lived for.

WANTED: GUIDANCE COUNSELOR TO WORK WITH A UNIQUE GROUP OF YOUNGSTERS at Havenhart Academy. PATIENCE AND AN OPEN MIND IMPERATIVE. MUST BE WILLING TO RELOCATE AND BOARD ON CAMPUS. GENEROUS COMPENSATION OFFERED. Send resume via email nigel at havenhartacademy dot org or by mail to P.O. Box 13, Haven, Arkansas, 90060.

That's different. I'd never thought about relocating from the East Bay, but there's a first for everything. All California had to offer me now was more disappointment and frustration. Patience and an open mind, I had in droves. Health, not so much. Was this the change I needed?

My favorite cousin, James, lived in Arkansas. At least I'd know someone nearby. I'd call him later, but for now, I answered the ad with the resume I'd worked up when I'd heard rumors my middle school behavioral program was being terminated a few weeks before I got sick. It couldn't hurt to see what they had to say.

I loved my students, despite their daily efforts to self-destruct. They loved to brag about their illegal hijinks outside of school. In class, they stole things out of each other's desks, insulted each other, refused to do work, and had major meltdowns worthy of Oscar nominations. But I'd made a connection with each and every one of them, and they'd all made progress this year. I knew that with a little more time most of them would make the transition to high school successfully. Others would require the high school equivalent to my program. Sadly, lack of money and a sick teacher meant they wouldn't get that chance. I'd failed them because my stupid lungs wouldn't cooperate.

The rest of the day went by with more of the usual. Ronnie cut his arms with some glass he found on the playground during their lunch break. Victor and Clarence came back and ended up in a real knockdown, drag-out fight that required a call to the police. Norman and I had been able to separate them before anyone got really hurt, but Victor threw a punch at Norman before all was said and done. He wouldn't be coming back. My heart broke at the thought of him going back to juvenile hall.

Clarence quit struggling as soon as I got my hands on his arms. I made him look at me, and his breathing slowed and the anger bled out of him until he was apologizing to me profusely, begging for a second chance. I hoped he'd get one.

At the end of the day, I just wanted a bath and my bed. I prayed somehow for the strength to keep this up, at least until the end of the year, which was in a few short weeks. These kids needed more than I was able to provide for them in my current condition. I'd lost another one today, something I told myself I wouldn't allow to happen again. I drove home in tears, grateful I had the weekend to recuperate.

A voicemail waited for me on my cell.

"This message is for Delaney Frost. My name is Nigel Hart, headmaster at Havenhart Academy. We've received your resume and would be delighted to make your acquaintance. Our representative, Mr. Preston, will be in your area tomorrow and would like to meet you for lunch, if at all possible. Please connect with him as we are anxious to meet you."

"That was fast," I said aloud as I scribbled down the number.

I was excited at the prospect of meeting with someone from this mysterious place. The only Google links I'd been able to find about Havenhart Academy when I looked further into it at lunch were from another education job site that contained the same posting, and their website, which only had a section for inquiring about enrollment for students and a phone number. No pictures, no other information and nothing written about the school by an outside party.

In this world of Internet interconnectedness, I could find twenty to thirty posts when Googling my own name. It was unnerving to find no information about this school.

What if it was a setup? I'd heard horror stories of predators luring women out for nefarious things. Not that I was paranoid, but human trafficking was a real concern in our current society. The thought of having a fresh start and maybe even getting to counsel kids the way I worked best was so tempting, I had to at least try, right?

I used my inhaler and then called the number while my cat, Ramses, watched with a disinterested look on his face. He wandered off as the third ring sounded. A deep voice answered in a sharp, almost irritated manner.

"Preston."

"Hello? Hi, um, this is Delaney Frost. I received a message from Mr. Hart. He left me your number?" *Nervous much?* My voice sounded hoarse from talking and coughing all day. I just hoped he didn't hear me wheezing through the phone.

"Wonderful, Miss Frost," he said, his voice sliding into a warm, welcoming tone that immediately eased some of my tension. "I'm Damien

Preston, Director of Student Services for Havenhart Academy. Headmaster Hart asked me to interview you for our counseling position. May we meet for lunch tomorrow?"

I filled my lungs with much-needed oxygen as I pondered his accent. British? His voice was smooth and pleasant; the kind that would soothe an infant to sleep…or easily seduce a woman. *Whoa.* That thought didn't help my attempts at breathing.

"Absolutely. Where would you like to meet?"

There was a moment of hesitation on his part. "I'm not really sure," he said with a chuckle. "This is my first time to this part of California. I'm staying in Berkeley and I don't really know the area. Do you know of a place?"

"How does pizza sound? There's a great place called Zachary's. I can meet you there?" I covered my mouth to halt a coughing fit but one slipped out.

"Certainly," he said. His voice lost some of the warmth and the irritation seemed to return. "I'll meet you at noon. Be sure to drink some tea with honey," he said forcefully before hanging up.

Was it that obvious? Then I truly became frantic. I had to come up with something other than jeans and a t-shirt to wear. Tomorrow.

And Zachary's? What was I thinking? I was going to fling sauce and Lord knew what else all over myself. I hoped by some miracle I still had a skirt that would fit and not look too schoolmarm-ish or hippy-dippy. At five feet ten and a size fourteen, my clothing options tended to be limited. My district had a loose dress code, which was great for my fashion disability. I kept telling myself someday I would dress more grown-up, but as I surpassed forty years old, it had yet to happen.

I settled on what I affectionately coined Ye Old Standby: A navy-blue skirt and matching shell with white flowers embroidered on them. I'd worn this same outfit to just about every ceremony in the past ten years, be it wedding, funeral, or graduations. I desperately wanted to make a good impression, especially after hearing his voice.

Something about this whole situation seemed like destiny calling.

THE YOUNG GIRL HID IN THE CLOSET LISTENING TO THE EVENING'S ARGUMENT coming from the next room. She'd spent many nights of her short life hiding. Hiding from his wrath, hiding from his hands, and hiding from the pain.

"I won't do this to her anymore, Gerald! You've lied too many times, and she's too fragile. I won't let you hurt her anymore!" Mother sounded hysterical and the girl was afraid for her. Father never let Mother talk back without reprisal.

"You'll do exactly as I require, Janet. Don't think you can go against me. Do I have to remind you what happened last time you questioned me?"

The girl cringed, remembering the beating Mother took. He managed to make the police go away that time but they'd had to run again the next morning. It was the same routine time and time again, and the girl knew to be prepared. Mother sobbed and pleaded but she had to know it was useless.

Anytime the girl had the Sight, it meant Father was closer to achieving his goals.

The girl hid her Sight from him whenever possible because it usually meant someone would get hurt. They would have to move again, and even though Father would be kinder, it wouldn't last. He'd made a living off of impressionable churchgoers, winning their trust before he robbed them blind and moved on to the next small town. No one could resist his Influence. His dazzling smile and hypnotic eyes stole the breath from the women. The men nearly fell to their knees in worship. They were drawn to him, looking for absolution and affirmation.

No one saw him as she did: a creature out of a nightmare. A man who had the power to slide his Influence past any wards or mental walls without detection. He instinctively knew just what each situation required: finesse, coercion, flirtation, threats or acts of violence.

The young girl never imagined there would be so many opportunities for him, so many small towns. But every time she Saw a new church, they would go, and it would begin again.

TWO
THE INTERVIEW

THE NEXT MORNING, I AWOKE WITH THE PREDICTABLE INTERVIEW ZIT ON MY chin, dark circles under my eyes, and the frightening prospect of having to perform an at-home pedicure on my gnarly feet as well as giving myself a breathing treatment. I had hours to go, so I tried to calm myself and make the best of it.

I arrived at the BART station at eleven, giving myself extra time to wander along College Avenue for a bit before heading to Zachary's, trying to calm my nerves.

I walked through the door and spotted who I assumed to be Damien Preston immediately. He was the most out-of-place person in the joint, wearing a brown suit, cream dress shirt and an olive tie. I noticed a brief-case on the floor next to him, similar to what you'd see a college professor carrying, but we were kind of far from the university for a professor to be hanging out on a lunch break. He had a streak of white running root-to-tip on the right side of his thick, black-brown hair that brushed the top of his shoulders.

I watched him for a moment as he read the local free paper, the *Express*, and drank a cup of tea. He appeared to be in his mid-to-late forties, with shoulders so broad and legs so long, he looked as if he were too big for the table. He smiled, amused at something. I worried I was intruding upon a private moment. His long fingers reached for the teacup again, and I noticed a large gold ring on the middle finger of his left hand.

He was absolutely stunning.

I swallowed hard.

I'd been told I had a staring problem. My mother used to scold me for lingering too long on others in public. I guess I never learned because at that moment, he looked up and caught my eye. Piercing green eyes gazed out from under long eyelashes. He stood and the corners of his mouth turned up slightly. As I navigated my way through the tight space to the tiny table for two, he stepped around to pull out my chair.

"Miss Frost, I presume?" His size was imposing up close. He had to be six and a half feet tall, but his warm smile put me at ease. "Were you waiting there long?"

I caught myself blushing. Definitely British. I took the hand he offered and gazed at the ring he wore on the middle finger of his right hand. It had a large onyx stone and the gold band was engraved with the letter H on either side of the stone. Beautiful. I realized again that I was staring.

I shook his hand awkwardly, internally cursing myself for being creepy, and took my seat.

"Just for a moment," I responded quietly. I struggled to breathe and wasn't sure if it was caused by my asthma or the fact that I'd have to come up with intelligent conversation while sitting across from this impressive man who had me so nervous.

I was such a clod. I was wearing sandals, for crying out loud, and Ye Olde Standby. His brown loafers were some designer brand I wouldn't know and perfectly polished, as was the rest of his appearance. There was no way he would hire me.

Oh well, at least I'd have me some Zachary's on his dime. A server approached and I ordered a Diet Coke.

"Miss Frost, thank you for meeting with me. Forgive me, but I must ask. What drew you to our job posting? We've had it up for months and haven't found the right person. I'm curious."

The voice I'd heard on the phone fit him perfectly. In person it was full of warmth and comfort and any sign of irritation was gone. I forgot for just a moment that I was on an interview and not out for lunch with a treasured friend. Who was still talking.

"Our academy is unique in this country and we don't normally advertise, but we've been without a counselor for some time."

He gazed at me for a long, scrutinizing moment. I hoped he wasn't judging the outfit. His smile eased my nerves.

"I was intrigued by the posting. It didn't sound like your run-of-the-mill school, and I've been looking for a change." That was putting it mildly. I was about to be unemployed, not just soul-searching.

He continued to gaze at me. My face flushed again. How was it that he alternately put me at ease and get me so flustered?

"I can assure you, we are not, as you say, a run-of-the-mill school, Miss Frost. I'd very much like to ask you a few questions and perhaps we can determine if this is that change you've been looking for?"

"Ask away."

"Excellent. I took the liberty of ordering for us. A house salad with vinaigrette followed by a mushroom and pepperoni stuffed pizza. Does that agree with your taste?"

I was stunned. How did he know exactly what I always ordered?

"Yes. Thank you, Mr. Preston."

"Please, call me Damien. I wish for us to become acquainted less formally."

I wasn't sure where he was going with that but I nodded in agreement.

"Our academy employs only the very best candidates. Your resume is exceptional and your experience with diverse groups of students is very appealing to our headmaster. Personality is quite important to us, as well."

I tried to compose myself, suddenly compelled to *not* blow this interview.

"What would you like to ask me, Mr. Preston?"

"Damien," he corrected. "First, when you read our advertisement, how did you interpret our interest in finding someone who was 'patient and open-minded'?"

The smile was gone but there was a curious and inviting expression to replace it. I wanted nothing more than for him to keep looking at me like that. Wherever my professional demeanor was hiding, it was time for it to show up.

"Well, anyone who works with children needs to have those qualities, don't they?"

He didn't smile, so I tried another tactic.

"I don't know much about your students, but the students I've been working with have needed a little something more. I've worked with many kids who were truly broken and traumatized. They've given up hope. They trust no one, so getting them to open up requires sincerity. I model positive interactions with them and earn their trust, but it isn't easy. I've worked with kids who have had major involvement in gangs, committed violent crimes, been abused, had serious drug and alcohol problems…"

I stopped because I realized he was looking at me very intently. I hadn't registered that he'd moved, but he was now leaning over the table with his chin resting on his laced fingers. Long fingers.

I completely lost my train of thought and blushed, yet again. There was a pregnant pause, and then he leaned back in his chair.

"It is apparent from your discourse that you care very much for your students. But tell me, how do *you* fare with this kind of work? It can be quite draining." He looked at me with a skeptical glance, and then looked toward the kitchen to check the status of our food.

My answer was not going to be completely truthful. "I draw strength, I suppose, from watching these kids start to find success."

He seemed pleased with that. *Maybe this isn't going to be so bad.*

"Should I gather, then, that this year you have not seen as much success?"

His question startled me. What, did I have "Loser Teacher" written across my forehead?

"Why would you think that?" I stammered, feeling a tad defensive.

"Please, Delaney, I didn't mean for you to detect any doubt in my voice. I merely asked because I can sense you've been ill."

It was my turn to sit back, but without the confidence he seemed to possess. Our salads arrived, and for a few moments we sat in silence, enjoying the food. I took this opportunity to collect myself and decide how to answer his accusation.

"Excuse me, but how did you know I've been ill? Did you contact my employer? He had no right to tell you my personal business," I finished softly. Matt, my current administrator, wouldn't give anyone that information, would he? How did Havenhart Academy have time to check my references? Didn't they usually wait to check with your current employer until after they'd met you?

My lungs burned, and I struggled to get in enough oxygen.

Damien held up his hand. "Please don't be upset. I spoke with your employer strictly to discuss your resume. I *sensed* that you had been ill. It is something I do. This is where the open-minded part comes into play. We at Havenhart Academy all have a little...how did you put it? Extra, to offer our students who need it desperately. The students you've described sound similar to ours, with some drastic differences. I am not at liberty to discuss that with you at this point in time. My 'extra' is simply that I can detect health issues in others."

"But how did you know? Yes, I'm recovering from pneumonia. I haven't had anything that serious before, but it's been a rather tough year for me."

It saddened me to remember what I was about to lose, and what my life had become. I looked down, hoping the pizza would come soon and rescue me. My lungs were heavy. I debated using my inhaler, but after his comments, I was afraid to show any weakness.

"Not to worry, Delaney. I'm merely curious. Your health will not be an issue, should we determine that you are a good fit for our students. You will likely find that it improves greatly once you arrive. Most of our employees enjoy that perk. Headmaster Hart takes very good care of his staff. We want for nothing. Though we may not have anything as delectable as this pizza I see before us, we manage." And with that, he lightened the mood.

Our server, God bless him, was pierced, tattooed, and had gobs of spiky hair. One of the things I loved about this neighborhood was the eye candy. He smiled at me, looked suspiciously at my companion, and slid our slices onto our plates.

"I have never seen anything quite like this. I assume this is fork-and-knife pizza?" He studied his meal for a moment, like a tactician studying a worthy opponent. "I'm glad you suggested such a wonderful place for our meeting." Damien smiled brightly, and then was lost in his pizza.

I started to blab about coming to Berkeley in high school and on home visits from college, and how much I loved the feel of this town. I gave him a little history of the area in between shoving globules of cheesy, saucy goodness into my mouth. The comfort level was back, and I found myself telling him stories of my first piercings on Telegraph Avenue, and shopping for used CDs and vinyl at Rasputin's. He was beyond a good listener. It was as if he truly absorbed every emotion and nuance in my stories

"If you love this place so much, are you really sure you could leave it?" He asked his question gently, but his concern was evident.

I knew this would come up, and I wanted to answer carefully.

"You're right. I do love it here. But I'm ready to make a change if it means working with the kind of kids who need me most. Can you tell me a bit more about your program? What are the ages? Are you an accredited school? Where do your students come from?" I had so many questions but figured I'd stick with the safe ones.

Damien put his fork down and wiped daintily at his face with a napkin. He raised an eyebrow, and his eyes crinkled a little around the edges.

"Tell me, Delaney. If you were to design the perfect school for students similar to those you've been working with, what would it be like?"

I thought I caught a glimmer in his eyes, as if he were a child with a secret. I enjoyed the way my name rolled off his tongue. He caught me off guard. Who was this guy?

"I've always sort of joked that if I won the lottery, I would open a boarding school for at-risk kids. I would staff it with the most competent teachers and caregivers and give the kids the life they deserved. So many of them have been affected by things completely out of their control and have been dealt a bad hand, you know? It's been my experience that when kids come to school on Monday mornings—especially after a vacation—they're a mess. Not having the structure and nurturing they receive at school, even for two days of a regular weekend, makes them moody, impulsive, and sometimes volatile. Often it takes us a few days to get them back on track. If we could give them a different option, a place where they'd depend on three meals a day, supportive folks…"

I knew I was rattling on again, but this was my dream. Somehow, I thought maybe this man might understand that.

"What you have described is very similar to the principles that Havenhart Academy was founded on. We take in children between the ages of twelve to eighteen from around the world who have suffered terrible trauma, and we try to rehabilitate and educate them to make use of their gifts and talents. Our academy is on a large plot of land complete with horse stables, athletic facilities, and a variety of outlets for creativity. We have state-of-the-art science and technology resources, and our visual and performing arts wing is first rate. We choose only those most damaged, and those we feel truly need our intervention. Our mission is to make them whole again. Does this sound like what you had in mind?"

I fell silent. It was as if he'd heard all my rants over the years about how we should really take care of these kids and in turn created a safe place for them. They even called it Havenhart Academy. It was déjà vu, only someone was explaining my own idea back to me.

We finished our pizza in silence. Amazingly, I only managed to let one rogue tomato land on my lap and the navy-blue material hid the stain expertly. I had no idea what Damien thought about my qualifications for his academy. I was beginning to desperately hope they wanted me.

We left Zachary's, and he asked if I would mind showing him around town. I was leery about getting into a car with him, but my gut told me he was safe. I trusted my feelings and agreed. Damien smiled and held out his arm as a Town Car drove up. I noticed it was registered to a local company I knew of, making me feel more at ease.

"Have your driver drop us off on Telegraph and we can walk. I'll show you why I loved it here as a teen." I smiled, hoping I was making the right move.

Telegraph Avenue, for many years now, had become a home to teenage runaways, and there were usually many of them taking shelter under the eaves and panhandling for spare change. I understood the draw, although the street was not what it used to be. Many of my favorite hangouts had long since closed their doors due to the worsening economy, but I still loved to visit the area. There was so much history, culture, and music in Berkeley. I loved to walk along the avenue, visit the remaining shops, and peer at what the street vendors had to offer.

Damien took in all of the sights as we drove. "The architecture here is fantastic. And the gardens...so beautiful."

I was pleased to see his enjoyment. Sitting next to him in the backseat of the car gave me a further appreciation for his height. He folded himself quite elegantly into the car and, I thought, for a man of his size, his grace was notable. His shoulders were broad underneath his suit coat, like those of a construction worker or professional athlete, but he was much more refined. He rested his hands on his knees and eagerly gazed out the window. He did his best to give me space. He was being careful not to make me uncomfortable. I appreciated that.

We headed up College toward Berkeley, turned left on Ashby and right on Telegraph, and I directed the driver to drop us off as the street became a one way. Damien said he would call when we were ready to be collected.

We set off on foot, and I pointed out some of my favorite spots. As we passed Zebra Tattoo I recalled my first California tattoo. I gave a sideways glance at him while telling him the story.

"Are my tattoos going to be a problem?" I'd adorned myself with quite a bit of ink—at least half of my body was covered by this point—and while I kept most of them hidden at work, invariably the students knew about them and my district didn't have a policy against them.

His amusement turned to a full-blown guffaw. "We have all walks of life at our academy. A few tattoos will not turn many heads." My interest in this place grew as the day went on and he told me more.

"May I ask, is there an expected dress code for teachers? Because I can tell you right now, my wardrobe is not equipped with much more than jeans and tees."

He stopped for a moment and gave me a serious look. "We do have an expectation that our staff will promote a successful lifestyle and model attire for our students of the caliber society expects of them. We offer a clothing allowance and can arrange for a tailor to meet with you, if necessary, to take care of any wardrobe needs you may have." He smiled kindly, assuring me that he meant no offense.

I was not too proud to accept some fashion tips from a professional but I wasn't too sure about having my clothing choices dictated for me.

"Does that mean the students wear uniforms?" I asked, trying not to show my disdain for such an archaic policy. Mind you, sagging pants annoyed me to no end and the clothes my female students wore were better suited to the beach or night clubs, but I was all for freedom of expression and believed that wearing clothes that showed my personality had given me the confidence I needed to make it through high school.

But I would go along with uniforms if it meant I was going to get to do the work I desired.

"They do on class days. The students have not shown any aversion to their uniforms. Many of them come from severe poverty, and they are very appreciative of what we offer them. You asked earlier where our students come from, and I want to be sure I answer all of your questions. It is important to us at Havenhart Academy that our staff makes an informed decision before joining our faculty. We are not fond of attrition. Because of the sensitive backgrounds of many of our students, confidentiality is crucial. Our children come from around the globe. Many have experienced hardships that are difficult for us to relate to. That is where a talented counselor comes in handy." He smiled again. "Are there more questions I can answer for you?"

Since we were on the subject of duties, it seemed the perfect time to ask about their expectations.

"Your ad was for a guidance counselor. Can you give me an idea of the job duties?"

That glimmer was back in his eye. "I'd love to hear what you think a counselor's assignment should entail."

I drew in a breath. *He asked for it.*

"My beliefs about the purpose of counseling haven't always met with favor from my previous employers. I'm a firm believer that in order for a child to learn, they must be treated holistically. You can't teach a student their math facts if they're hungry. You can't expect them to understand the works of Shakespeare if they're worried about going home to their parents and potentially another beating. While I feel guidance toward college and other post-graduation endeavors are important, if a student needs personal counseling, that should come first." I paused to get a reaction.

He looked as though he was taking it all in to process, nodding to himself.

As we passed the old Gap store, I noticed a young girl dressed in black with dyed-black hair. She was pierced in several places and wore a denim jacket with punk band patches all over it. She stood in the doorway of the now-closed clothing giant with a backpack and a scruffy-looking dog on a leash. She was with a boy not much older than her, who mirrored her appearance but was a full head taller. Her head was down as he berated her for something.

My spine stiffened and I tried to make eye contact with her. She looked horrified and embarrassed. I wanted to stop and intervene. But when she caught me staring, she winced and turned and walked away with her scruffy dog.

Damien noticed my concern, and he grunted as if to say he felt the same.

We continued to walk toward the campus without speaking much, crossed the street and entered Sproul Plaza. We walked over to the steps and sat down. A group of musicians were setting up and getting ready to play. Their steel drums and guitars rang out in the afternoon sun. I closed my eyes for a moment, feeling at peace in this city. For any person with a desire for learning and understanding the human animal, it was truly magical.

"You seem very relaxed here."

His words interrupted my inner meditations and all at once I realized that I was still on a job interview. I sat up a little straighter.

"What if I told you that you would have complete freedom to do as you see fit for our students? That besides a few scheduled activities we require, such as faculty meetings, student supervision, and classroom duties as needed, you would be free to meet with students as you like?"

I narrowed my eyes. "What about scheduling?" I asked with trepidation. "And what kind of supervision?" I still had nightmares from my many years supervising the lunchroom. *Ugh.* The conversations I'd been subjected to, the horseplay, policing the lunch line so no one cut. I prayed he didn't have that in mind.

"As Director of Student Services, I decide on the master schedule, and while you may want to discuss individual class choices with students, we have an assistant who handles the data entry. A counselor should be utilized for counseling, don't you agree?" He paused for a moment and watched the musicians as they continued on with their jam session. "As for supervision, we have many activities for students, and we match staff members up with students who have similar interests. For example, one of our instructors enjoys playing basketball with the students in the afternoons. Another formed a musical group, and we have quite a strong spoken-word program overseen by another instructor."

"I taught dance in the past and worked with cheerleaders, dance teams and show choirs. I'd be happy to help out with any of those if there are students who are interested," I offered.

"A dancer. How lovely. Do you still practice?" He glanced down at my legs stretched out in front of me, and then turned to face me to wait for my response.

A wistful smile crossed my face. "I haven't in years. One of my regrets is that when I left home for college, I didn't continue with my studies. I went to a great college, but they didn't have a dance program. In hindsight I wish I'd kept it up. But I still love it and would love to get back into it."

"You are referring to Graceland College in Iowa, correct me if I'm wrong? Did you enjoy your time there? It must have been quite a change from this." Damien gestured at our surroundings.

"You've got that right." I laughed. "In fact, after the first semester, I wanted to head home. I wasn't involved in anything and had few friends, so I joined the cheer squad for basketball season. I embraced the freedom to make friends with people who didn't know me and made a fresh start. I loved the small-town feel and the safety. What else do you know about me?"

"I know that your previous employers have been extremely pleased with you. Former colleagues nominated you for Teacher of the Year, which speaks volumes about their respect. You graduated Cum Laude from college and Magna Cum Laude from your Master's program. I know you are a product of divorced parents and grew up with your mother and stepfather. You have a stepsister and half-brother. You've never been married. You experienced a traumatic event in your early teens, and you have suffered from severe asthma and frequent bouts of illness ever since. You received intensive therapy—"

I jumped up from the steps and glared at him. "How do you...I can't believe... How is that *any* of your business? What kind of place is this that you would dig this deep into my personal life?" I wrapped my arms around myself, suddenly feeling nauseous.

"Delaney, please. Sit down." He reached for my hand, and I shook my head. Damien ran his hand through his hair and took a deep breath. "Perhaps I have not been clear enough about the purpose of our institution. We can only have the best people working for us. Our children have suffered terribly, often at the hands of adults they trusted. We cannot take the chance that we may inadvertently expose them to more trauma by hiring the wrong person. We always do a *very* thorough background investigation before interviewing a candidate to weed out possible problems. Wouldn't you do the same if you were to open your own school, as we discussed over lunch?"

"But within hours? I only applied a day ago!" I sat down away from him. I stared ahead at the musicians who were playing a slow, intoxicating melody on an acoustic guitar, flute and clarinet. My head was spinning. I was not a secretive person, but the idea of my employer, this stranger, knowing intimate details about my life was unnerving.

"I know you have suffered too, Delaney," he said quietly, also watching the musicians. "It is your suffering that has given you the strength and the gifts you use when working with your students. We seek those gifts. They will benefit our students, and you will be safe with us."

I thought about what he said. It was true, my life experience had certainly affected how I interacted with students and drove me to do my best to take care of them. But to leave everything I knew and trust what this stranger promised was a frightening prospect.

He continued. "I know this is a difficult decision, and I know it may be difficult to trust what I say. But as the ad promised, you will be compensated generously, your accommodations will be comfortable, and you can even bring your cats with you."

I laughed at that. "You even know about my cats?"

He smiled. "I heard one yowling in the background when you called me to set up this lunch. I assumed it was a pet and not an animal you were torturing. Am I correct?"

"Yes. That was Ramses. He and Clio, my other cat, have been my companions for many years now." I smiled and thought of how empty my life would be without them, forgetting about how often I had threatened Ramses with the sausage factory after he destroyed yet another item in my house.

"An Egyptian Pharaoh and the Muse of History. How appropriate." He even knew where their names came from. *Eerie.* "Take time, if you need it, to make your decision. I will be in town through the week. I'm actually interviewing a math teacher from Santa Cruz on Monday. Are you familiar with that town as well?"

"Are you kidding? When I wasn't in Berkeley, I was watching the Dawn Patrol." I laughed. I was the only one of my friends whose mother approved of cutting school to go to the beach. Once I proved to her that I was able to drive my 1973 Super Beetle over the mountains on Highway 17 safely, I was given permission to go whenever I wanted.

"I am unfamiliar with this Dawn Patrol." He looked at me quizzically.

I laughed. "The Dawn Patrol consists of those crazy surfers who hit the surf at sunrise to get in a few good waves before starting their day. My friends and I would bring our sleeping bags, watch them surf, then nap until it was warm enough to sunbathe."

Why am I telling him about my high school indiscretions?

"Perhaps this is something I should see while I'm here. Would you mind accompanying me to Santa Cruz for the interview then?"

I was not prepared for this, but forgetting my earlier unease, I agreed.

"As long as I can drive," I said. "I haven't gone out for the Dawn Patrol in a decade, but I'm sure we can catch some sunset surfers. What time is your interview?"

"I'm to meet with this teacher at four p.m. in the university commons. She graduates this June. Her student teaching experience just finished and she comes highly recommended. I would be pleased to have you accompany me and give me your opinion. I assume, in your duties as a counselor, you have had opportunities to observe teachers in action?"

"Sure." I often worked with teachers on problems they were having with specific students, to try to make the relationship work better for both of them. It was actually one of my favorite parts of the job. I especially liked to mentor younger teachers. "I'd be happy to go with you. Can your driver bring you to my school? I'm finished with work at two-thirty. We can leave from there." The thought of spending more time with Damien was a strangely pleasant one. I wanted to find out more about Havenhart Academy and this mysterious man who wanted to whisk me away to a strange but intriguing place.

"Of course. And we can discuss any concerns you have further on our drive." He smiled warmly. I was torn between my misgivings and my excitement. He called for the driver and we walked to the street to meet him. They dropped me off at the BART station on Shattuck and we parted ways.

"I'll look forward to seeing you on Monday, Delaney. It's been a wonderful afternoon. Thank you."

I nodded, thanked him for lunch, and closed the door, turning back once to see that he was watching as I descended the escalator. He smiled at me again before the car pulled out of sight.

I took a deep breath and steadied myself on the railing. I didn't know if I wanted to run screaming from or to embrace this challenge. I had forty-eight hours until I would see him again and I had a lot to think about. The train ride back to the Union City station was the perfect placed to ponder all we had discussed, so I plugged in my earbuds and did just that.

MONTANA WAS PRETTY AND THE PEOPLE WERE NICE. FATHER MET WITH THE *pastor and he immediately invited them to stay in his home. Mother was uncomfortable and the young girl sensed her unease.*

For several weeks Father led the services as a "guest minister" and each night they would meet with congregation members in the social hall of the church. He told them of his mission, that the Maker had tasked him with finding those who were truly worthy of redemption. He assured them that the end of days was growing near and that if they could see the truth in their hearts, and give him the financial resources he needed to build them a community, they would earn a place in the Maker's grace.

The young girl watched, fascinated, as people gave their paychecks, their savings, even the deeds to their homes to Father. He was so powerful. They were completely in awe of him, completely in his thrall.

Each night he would come to the young girl and remind her that it was her duty to them all to show him the things the Maker had planned. She would try very hard, but didn't quite know what she was trying for.

On the fourth Sunday they were in Montana, the young girl sat next to Mother at the front of the congregation. She hadn't slept well and was ill. During Father's sermon, she started shaking uncontrollably and slipped to the floor in front of the altar.

Father ran to her and lifted her in his arms. She began to speak rapidly...

"The fire is so hot. It will burn them all. They will die choking while their clothes melt into their skin. They will scream in pain and scratch at the doors with their nails until they bleed."

Her head fell back and her body went limp. From far off, she heard Father. "She has Seen the truth, brothers and sisters. The end of days draws near. Will you make the sacrifice your Maker has asked of you? Or will you burn with the unworthy He leaves behind. There is no middle ground, friends. Only absolute devotion will earn you a place in Heaven."

THREE

DAMIEN'S STORY

I THOUGHT ABOUT THE DAY'S EVENTS ON THE TRAIN RIDE HOME, BUT CAME to no conclusion. I decided I wouldn't make any decisions until after I spent Monday with Damien.

Damien. What an enigma. I wondered about the white streak in his hair. Often people developed them after a traumatic experience. At least that's what happened in *Poltergeist*.

"Great, Delaney. Using Hollywood as your guide to real life is always a smart move."

I hadn't learned a thing about him other than he worked at the academy and had a foreign accent. And there was his remark about his "gift." He knew I'd been sick. Maybe I looked peaked. It had only been a few weeks since I was well enough to return to work. I hadn't used my inhaler while we were together. I'd heard of people having a "sick" smell. Maybe that was it.

Awesome. I was going to be in a car with him for a total of two hours round trip and I'd smell like a sick chick. How pleasant for him. I couldn't believe my current employer told him. How else would he know? I didn't quite know what to do with this tidbit of knowledge so I filed it away in my "figure it out later" mental bin.

A day later I stood looking over my balcony at the eucalyptus trees behind my apartment and sighed. I'd grown fond of it here, but it was quite a lonely existence. The only visitors I ever had were my parents making pity calls on me, staying only long enough for a glass of water before they came up with an excuse to vacate. I had no mating prospects. All my best friends lived far away. I really was getting dangerously close to becoming a cat lady and that thought scared the crap out of me. What was I waiting for?

Maybe my experience Monday afternoon was a sign. I got a call from the office while teaching my final period of the day, telling me I had a visitor.

"A Mr. Damien Preston is here to see you. He wants to visit your classroom."

I freaked. It was only two. I'd told him to meet me at two-thirty.

"Uh, can you give him a visitor badge and send him over" I asked weakly. I began to sweat, profusely. I hadn't counted on an observation as part of the deal. I shouldn't have been surprised. Didn't mean I would enjoy it.

He came to the door as I was explaining to the students that we were about to watch a film on genetics.

In my planning for the day, I'd forgotten the ever-so-important rule about videos: Always preview a video loaned to you, even if it's from another science teacher. I'd borrowed it from a friend at the comprehensive high school after we'd collaborated and she'd sworn it was appropriate. The students looked bored. Some attempted to text under their desks. I did my whole proximity thing and discouraged them gently from breaking the "off and away" rule.

Damien sat in a chair close to the doorway. I made my way over to him and whispered, "I thought you were going to meet me after school. I wasn't prepared to be observed."

I was only slightly joking. He had that amused grin on his face again, the one that showed off the dimple in his left cheek that I'd been trying to forget about. This only served to make me even more unnerved.

It was at this moment that I heard the squishing, gurgling sound coming from the television. The students had been quiet up to this moment but they immediately lost it.

"Damn, that's hella wrong! Miss Frost what kind of nasty-ass video are you making us watch?"

"Trevor, language please."

As I glanced at the screen, I was horrified to see a farmer, with his arm fully inserted into a cow's vagina, talking to the camera while showing his viewing audience the catheter used to artificially inseminate said cow. The next scene was of a calf dropping from the heifer with a sucking sound that could have been heard across town.

A chorus of "Ews" and "What the fucks?!" echoed throughout the classroom. I hurried over to pause the film and explained to them that this procedure is how they got their hamburgers from McDonald's, so they should be quiet and try to learn something. It was a difficult recovery. The snickering continued through the remainder of the video. Damien, bless him, was doing his best not to fall out of his chair laughing. I didn't know how I was going to explain his visit to my students while he was writhing on the floor in hysterics.

The bell saved me ten minutes later. I excused the students as quickly as possible, listening to them rehash the farmer's activity inside the cow, with their own spin on it of course. I walked back into the class and sat down at my desk chair with my head in my hands.

"I cannot imagine a worse possible time for you to come walking through my door."

Damien let out his laughter now that the coast was clear and came over to perch on my desk. "That was brilliant! Such colorful language they have, and such enthusiasm for the obscene. I knew you'd be perfect for our students." He held his side as if the laughter hurt him. I hoped he got the most painful case of the hiccups in the history of humanity.

"I honestly had no idea it was that graphic. I borrowed it from a friend at the high school. She didn't mention any artificial insemination scenes." I was beyond embarrassed.

Damien put a hand on my shoulder. "Honestly, Delaney, you handled that extremely well. I doubt even our headmaster would have done a better job." He stood up. "Shall we collect your things and head off into the sunset?"

That was an attractive idea. I desperately needed to get out of that classroom. I had to get that visual and the sucking sound out of my brain.

We headed out to my ancient teal Honda Civic hatchback. I had so much fun touring around town blasting my favorite metal band of the day. This morning's theme song was Pantera's "Walk," which I forgot to turn down before starting the car. Damien jumped in his seat and gave me a terrified look.

"What was that?" He rubbed at his ears as if that would restore his hearing. If it wasn't turned up to eleven, it wasn't loud enough for me. I usually spared my guests the ear-splitting, raging guitars and screaming vocals, but I was still distracted by images of the farmer's arm completely ensconced in the cow's nether region.

"Oops," I replied with a shrug. "That's what gets me going in the morning. Some people drink coffee. Some exercise. I rely on my Metal to wake me up and prepare me for the onslaught." I grinned to myself as I pulled out of the parking lot.

He shook his head good-naturedly. "I'll agree that would be an effective wake-up call. Are you sure your hearing hasn't suffered?"

I smirked. "Believe me, I wish it had after hearing that horrific slurping sound on that video." I shuddered while he tried to smother his giggles. I shot him my best teacher look. He bit his lip to calm himself.

"My apologies. Lead on, Miss Frost."

I smiled, relaxing a bit. "It's about an hour drive assuming we don't hit too much traffic. You good or do you need anything?" I thought I should at least attempt to be a good hostess, considering that he'd been a perfect gentleman on Saturday.

"I'm fine, thank you."

I grabbed a bottle of water from my stash in the backseat. "You can never be too prepared, right? You never know if you'll be stuck in an earthquake here and need supplies." I offered him the bottle, and he took it with a nod.

"I've only ever experienced one earthquake. I don't remember being too fond of the feeling, nor of the aftermath." His smile faded a bit and for a minute he seemed far away.

"When was this?" I asked, very curious as he had yet to disclose anything about himself.

"Oh, when I was a boy, in Mexico." When he didn't speak for a moment, I wondered if I should press for more. Then he began again.

"Perhaps I should tell you my story now. It might give you a little more insight into the academy and the students we choose to attend."

I tried to concentrate on my driving, hoping he didn't notice my slight swerve into the lane next to us when he made that last statement. I wanted to hear his story. "Please, go on," I encouraged.

"Very well. My parents were doctors in England. Are you familiar with the organization Doctors Without Borders?" I nodded, and he continued after a long inhale. "They were bitten by the travel bug when I was a boy and decided this organization was the best way for them to have it all: family, travel and helping people. We lived in Mexico City in nineteen eighty-five when an eight-point-one magnitude quake devastated the city. Over ten thousand people died. I was fifteen years old. I couldn't do much, but I helped clean up and sat with patients while they waited to see my parents." He had a faraway look in his eyes as he spoke.

"My mother and father assisted with the search and rescue operations. They wouldn't let me help, said it was too dangerous. They entered a school to try to find some children who they heard crying through the rubble. It happened so fast, I didn't realize what I was seeing. The wall shifted and fell just as my parents entered.

"I knew they were dead immediately. I sensed it. I also knew in that instant that I had to step in and assist the clinicians. I went back to the clinic and held the hands of the children as they came in." He paused and took a long drink of his water.

As a counselor, I was used to people opening up and telling me of their most troublesome thoughts and memories. I was always shaken a bit when it was a grown man. I knew how difficult it was for them to break social norms about showing weakness and, God forbid, shedding a tear in front of another. But Damien seemed to be very together, as thought he'd shared this story many times before.

"Delaney, do you remember what the ad said about being open-minded and patient? We've already discussed the patience part, and after today's performance, I would say you've definitely got that down pat, but how are you in the tolerance department?"

Oh, please don't let him remind me of this afternoon again. I was still trying to get that horrid splattering sound out of my head.

"Well," I began cautiously, "I've always thought that anything is possible. If enough people believe in something, they give it power. Now, do I believe in everything? No. I accept that we all have our own perceptions and so what's true for one person is not necessarily true for another, but it still has deep meaning. My theory was tested once when a student was telling me about brujería. Are you familiar with the term?"

He nodded gravely. "I have seen it at work, and you are correct. When enough people believe in something, it can gain incredible power."

"This student of mine had wronged another female in her gang. I seem to recall it had something to do with a boyfriend, as it usually does. What she didn't know was that the girl's mother was a bruja, and while she was away, the woman broke into her home and spread a white powder around her bedroom and on her clothes. She told me that it caused her to break out in sores all over her face, chest and arms. She didn't come to school for two weeks. When she returned, she said she'd been afraid and embarrassed over the scarring that occurred. I saw some faint red marks, but nothing conclusive. This girl was so spooked, though, that I knew no matter what I said, she believed this had happened to her, and I had to help her move forward."

I continued to drive on, merging in and out of traffic, making my way to the carpool lane.

He stared at me intently, readying himself to speak.

"Delaney, when I spoke of my gift, you didn't have much of a reaction."

"I figured you would explain in more detail if I needed to know. I was sort of in shock, though, as I had never expected you to know about my illness. To be honest, I was hoping I didn't have the 'sick chick stink' or something, and that's how you knew."

He spit out the sip of water he had just taken in reaction to my remark. I giggled and handed him a tissue. "Seriously. I was thinking how awful it was going to be for you to have to ride in my car all the way to Santa Cruz if I had a putrid odor about me."

He laughed heartily, a deep belly laugh.

I was beginning to really enjoy his laugh. *Pull yourself together, Frost.*

"Delaney, you smell delightful." He leaned a little closer when he said that, as if to prove he wasn't offended by my scent.

I took a brief moment to glance over at his attire today. He more than filled the seat of my compact car. He'd traded in the suit and tie for khakis, loafers and a periwinkle blue button-up. He looked as if he'd just stepped out of a J. Crew catalogue. All he was missing was the sweater tied around his shoulders.

I looked down at my teacher garb: knit cargo pants and screen-printed t-shirt, this one with a large anchor on it. I had on my clunky Dansko shoes that were oh so comfortable and oh so unappealing to the opposite sex. I left the Spinal Tap and Metallica shirts in the closet until the weekend and only wore my skeleton Vans on rare occasions, so I figured I was doing okay. It certainly wasn't going to be appropriate for Havenhart Academy.

"If you are finished causing me to splatter saliva all over the interior of your car, may I proceed?"

"Shoot. No, maybe you shouldn't do that. Uh... Go for it." This produced another snicker from us both.

"This gift I speak of," he began with a serious tone that sobered me, "came to me in the moments after I watched my parents enter the collapsing building. It was as if their spirits combined and moved into me, compelling me into action. Mind you, I had spent a lot of time watching them work and had learned basic first-aid techniques. But this was different. My parents were both renowned physicians, and I was often amazed by their ability to diagnose and heal their patients. In the moments after their demise, it was if they shared this gift with me so I would continue their work.

"When I went back into that clinic and sat with the children they had been able to remove from the school building, a powerful energy moved through me. The first child I touched looked at me with blank eyes, obviously in shock. What became apparent to me next was that this child had a broken clavicle and internal bleeding due to a ruptured spleen. I wheeled his gurney into the trauma room and found it empty. The doctors had all left to help bring the children out. I whispered 'Silencio.' I closed my eyes and laid my hands on his abdomen. I had no idea what I was about to do. As I said, I was compelled to heal the child.

"I closed my eyes and concentrated on the energy. It was as if the sun had just come out from behind a cloud and blasted me with light and heat. A sense of calm moved through me, down my arms, and into this boy. He stiffened, and then his entire body relaxed. I held on for a few moments until I heard the others returning with more children. The head surgeon seemed shocked to see me, as if he was waiting for me to break. He told me what I already knew—that my parents were gone—and sent me to speak to Father Diego?'

"But I just looked down at the boy, who was smiling up at me. I asked for a sling brace. The head surgeon looked at me strangely and then pointed to the supply closet. I fetched the brace for the boy I later learned was named Tomas, and placed it around his shoulders. I applied a cold compress and dressed his wounds. He took a lollipop from me, calling out, 'Gracias, Angel' over his shoulder. Somehow, I had healed this boy's spleen. I just knew the bleeding had stopped."

He stopped to take a drink of his water, glancing at me out of the corner of his eye, but I was still processing what he'd just told me. He'd healed a child…with internal injuries…with the touch of his hand. *Insane.*

I had heard of healers before, but I'd never met one. I wasn't sure whether I believed him, but I wouldn't discount what he'd said.

"What happened to you then?" I couldn't fathom the tragedy this man had experienced.

"Father Diego, who ran the clinic, let me stay until the city was functioning again, and that took weeks. In that time, I worked in the clinic and helped as many of the children as possible. I was secretive, but Dr. Barnes, the surgeon, knew something was amiss. Luckily no one had any time to question me as the injured were brought in by the dozens. Ours was the only clinic that didn't suffer structural damage so we treated the majority of the victims."

By this time we were heading into the Santa Cruz Mountains, and while I was very into his story, I had to concentrate a bit harder on the drive. Highway 17 consists of a four-lane road, separated intermittently by a concrete divider. The road is steep, winding, and treacherous. Many people don't respect the danger they're undertaking when they're behind the wheel on this road, and those who don't often end up crossing the divider into oncoming traffic or diving down the deep ravine to the side. I'd been caught in a few traffic jams while the Jaws of Life were used to rescue some kid who was flying down the roadway faster than the posted fifty-mile-per-hour speed limit.

Damien continued with his story. "After two weeks of nonstop work at the clinic, I became fatigued. I knew I was running a low-grade fever, and we had run out of potable water to drink. Father Diego caught my arm as I stumbled through his office to gather more supplies. When he looked into my glassy eyes, he knew it was time for me to grieve. He called to his assistant and said he would be out of the office for the rest of the afternoon. He guided me out the back door and into his beat-up Datsun truck. We drove away from the destruction that had been a thriving city.

"I remember falling asleep, and when we arrived I was carried into a house and someone removed my clothes. I was bathed and wrapped in blankets, then placed on a feather mattress. Sleep had never been so peaceful, so necessary.

"When I awoke in this strange place, it suddenly hit me that I was now an orphan. True, many young men in Mexico had given up school in order to work and support their families, but my work had been part of my education. My parents had home-schooled me since I was a toddler to ensure that I didn't suffer from their need to move from place to place. But being an orphan in a foreign country with no close family ties was a frightening concept for me."

"I can imagine you were terrified."

"Indeed."

He grew quiet and I assumed he would tell me more when he was ready. As we took the Highway 1 North exit and drove to the university, he spoke.

"I apologize for leaving off on such a sad note."

"No," I said, patting his hand. "I figured you'd continue when you were ready. I'm in no hurry."

I offered him a smile and focused on the directions my phone continued to speak to me.

As we crested the hill and turned into the Merrill College parking lot, I laughed and sat back in my seat.

"This place brings back memories." It had been years since I'd been in this parking lot, but I'd never forget the United Spirit Association and their yearly cheer camps.

"I thought you attended school in Iowa. Did I miss something?"

I grinned at him and climbed out of the car. "Hmmm, maybe you're not quite the detective you thought you were. Don't think I'm gonna share this one with you. Not yet. I still haven't recovered from this afternoon's humiliation."

He gave me a look that said we'd revisit this conversation and we walked up the hill to the student commons. The common room was bustling with students eating and chatting excitedly with each other. Damien looked around and spotted his interviewee at a corner table.

"Are you ready?" he asked me with a knowing smirk. I glanced in the direction he had been looking and saw a young woman—very young—with wild hair and glasses, wearing a peasant blouse and skirt with Birkenstocks. She had hemp hair ties with rainbow beads at the ends dangling from the underside of her unkempt 'do and hemp bracelets on both of her wrists. She was oblivious to our approach.

"Miss Livorna? I am Damien Preston and this is Miss Frost. May we sit?"

She held up a hand as she finished what she was writing and then jumped up from her seat, spilling her glass of water in the process. Being somewhat of a klutz myself, I instinctively reached for her things as she grabbed a handful of napkins and began sopping up the mess before it hit the floor.

"Mr. Preston, I am so sorry! I was so engrossed in my work. Thesis time, you know? Please, have a seat while I just throw these away. Oh, I can't believe myself, I'm a disaster." She continued to berate herself as she stomped over to the garbage can to dispose of her trash.

I smiled at Damien and set her things back down, noticing some very sophisticated equations being worked out in her notebooks. "Heavy stuff," I commented, thinking she was out of earshot.

"Yeah, I always carry around too much. You never know when you're going to have that brilliant thought. I'm almost finished with my paper. Once I'm done with that, it will be hallelujah time." She gestured wildly with her hands as she scooped things up and shoved them haphazardly into her bag.

The girl had so much energy that I found myself shrinking back to stay out of the path of this oncoming train. I suppressed a chuckle. I had been referring to the work she was doing, but I didn't think I could derail her with that comment. She was on a roll.

"I'm so excited to finally meet you. Havenhart Academy is all I can think about. I have so many questions for you. I can't believe this is happening! Are you on the staff, too? I'm Skye, Skye Livorna," she said while shaking my hand vigorously.

I felt about ten seconds behind in the conversation. "Actually, I'm in the process of interviewing with Mr. Preston as well." I smiled reassuringly at her to let her know that I, too, had questions and was unsure about this huge leap of faith the academy was asking of us. I still had questions.

Damien spoke up at that moment. "Miss Livorna, thank you for meeting with me. I know this is a busy time for you. If you recall from our phone conversation, I wanted to speak with you about your experiences with the children at the center."

She immediately got serious and settled her hands in her lap. The transformation was astounding. She took a deep breath and got down to business.

"I lived and studied at the Raymark Institution for Disabled Children for twelve years. I was a foster kid, and when my foster parents realized I needed more than they could offer, the state enrolled me there when I was six. I graduated early from high school at age sixteen. I continued my residence and worked at the center with the children for another two years full time until I received a scholarship to this university. I completed my Bachelor degrees in Life Science and Mathematics two years ago, and this year I completed my Master's in Education with certification in Special Education. Concurrently, I've been student teaching back at Raymark two days a week to complete my requirements. As soon as I finish this thesis project, my degree and credentials will all be in place."

She took a deep breath and remained very still.

My mind was spinning with all that she had accomplished at such a young age. I started teaching young as well, but this woman was incredible.

"That's amazing. How did you manage to fit this all in?"

Damien interjected. "Miss Livorna has been a very gifted student and educator for some time now." He smiled warmly at her and she returned it, seeming to relax a bit.

"Thank you, Mr. Preston, for your compliment. I was diagnosed with severe OCD and an anxiety disorder as a child. I had the best tutors and made rapid progress. I was so engrossed with learning and sharing that knowledge with the other children there that I just knew I had to become a teacher. When I made that decision, Headmaster Hart contacted me at Raymark and came to see me, telling me about the academy and offering me a position when I completed my studies. This is what I've been working toward for so long that I can't believe it's finally happening."

She seemed to be gaining momentum, as if her engines were starting up again and soon she would be bursting with energy. I didn't quite know what to make of her, but knew at that moment that she would be a huge asset to her students.

"It is our understanding, Delaney, that Miss Livorna here has an ability to reach the so-called unreachable children who others feel cannot be taught. She can determine the best way to work through their disabilities and help them emerge from their tunnel to be functioning members of our community. We've been following her progress since she arrived at Raymark and are delighted she is now certified, so she may join our staff."

I sensed that the academy had more than a passing interest in this young girl. Their far-reaching "interest" in troubled children was impressive. I also had no doubt that they had many more resources at their disposal.

"Her gift, then?" I asked.

Damien nodded, acknowledging that I was beginning to see the picture a bit more clearly now.

"So, does that mean I get to come work there? Oh, Mr. Preston, I've been waiting for this for so long." She jumped up and hugged him so fast, she knocked her chair backward into a student sitting behind her.

"Omigosh, I am sooo sorry!" She stepped over to right the situation and the other student just shook his head and turned back to his studies. Damien had a look of pride and approval on his face as he laughed heartily, almost like a proud father. Just how long had they been following this girl? It made me start to wonder, with the breadth of knowledge he seemed to have about my background. Had they known about me, too? I was nowhere near as fascinating as this young woman flailing about at my side.

I looked across the table at Damien and he must have caught on to my train of thought. He met my gaze with a serious one of his own and moved to wrap up our visit. "Skye, Miss Frost and I must head back now. Mrs. Sinclair will call you to make all of the arrangements. As soon as it's possible, we will bring you out to Havenhart for your orientation. Do you have any questions for me?"

"No, gosh, I am just so happy to finally be going. Isn't this wonderful? I do hope you'll be joining the faculty as well, Miss Frost. It's really been nice to meet you and I must get back to my dorm and wrap these things up, and of course you need to be going and oh, I'm just so excited!" She was beaming from ear to ear. I was excited for her, and just a little closer to making my own decision. But Damien and I had things to discuss first. I intended for that to happen after we'd had some dinner.

Skye gathered up her things, shook my hand and hugged Damien again, knocking into him with her oversized book bag. She took another student out with her purse and bumped one more with her backpack as she made her way through the sea of tables. I shook my head as I watched her go, laughing to myself.

Damien mirrored my reaction then turned to me. "Are you ready for dinner now? All that energy has left me quite famished."

"I bet. Seems to me Ms. Livorna already knew she was coming. This wasn't much of an interview."

"We've been in contact with her for some time, true. But I had to be sure she was ready and willing to come. I also wanted you to meet her."

I frowned. "But why?"

Damien sighed. "I wanted to show you...there is no way I can adequately prepare you for what we do at the academy. I know I'm asking a lot for you to trust me."

The fact that he understood that made me feel better. I smiled up at him for just a moment. I vowed for the rest of the afternoon I'd try to be more open.

He gestured for me to lead the way. We walked out the doors and into the trees. The afternoon sun was beaming through the canopy above our heads and rays of light splayed out all along the walkway. I looked over my shoulder for a moment to see the length of the athletic fields followed by a drop off and the ocean below. I took in a breath of exquisitely fresh air and smiled.

Damien noticed my pause. He looked as if he were ready to ask me again about my history at this place so I turned and hurried forward to the car. Yeah, I'm sure cheer camp was going to be such an added bonus to my resume.

We drove down the hill toward the downtown area of Santa Cruz. There was a little Hawaiian Restaurant and Tiki Bar there that I just loved. I thought it might lighten the mood a little. I also knew at this hour it would be hopping, and we wouldn't be able to have an in-depth conversation. I wanted time to collect my thoughts and decide just what I really needed to know before I made my decision.

"This is a great place. I hope you like Polynesian/Asian fusion." I gave him a small smile.

"I am, as they say, just along for the ride. I'm sure whatever you choose will be delicious. After Zachary's, how could I doubt your taste?"

I was relieved to see that he seemed just as ready to take a break from the heavy conversation and relax a bit.

I loved how easygoing he was about everything. He took my moods in stride and handled the tornado that was Skye with ease. He never seemed to get flustered.

The wait was short, and by the time we reached the table, I realized just how hungry I was. Everything looked good, but I went for my favorite grilled chicken and mango salad. Damien ordered a rice bowl and a Mai Tai, getting himself into the festive spirit, I suppose, so I did the same. Our drinks arrived in tiki statue mugs. He chuckled at the sight of them.

"What should we drink to?"

Damien held up his mug. "What indeed? A long and prosperous working relationship? An evening of revelations? World peace?"

Thankful that he threw in the last one, I breathed a sigh of relief and suggested, "How about an end to world hunger as well?" We clinked mugs and took a sip. He asked if I'd ever been to Hawaii.

"Sadly, no. My folks were big on family vacations but small on budget. We camped every summer and took a couple of trips to Disneyland. Other than that, the only traveling I've done is back and forth to college in Iowa."

"Hopefully you will find the time to do more traveling. Hawaii is a magical place." He leaned back in the booth and closed his eyes for a moment, savoring his drink.

"Believe it or not, with my blonde hair and pasty skin, I used to be quite the hula dancer when I was a little girl."

I didn't know if it was the beverage or if I'd just given up my attempt at guarding myself with him that led to that particular revelation. There many more humorous stories of our childhoods. He admitted to his extensive stamp and comic book collections, and piano lessons to boot. He recalled his lone piano recital, complete with the visual of his slicked-back hair and tails extending over the piano bench. We laughed and chided each other, attempting to judge who was the bigger nerd.

"Yes, but you got to wear the cute outfits. I had to wear tails."

"Methinks he doth protest too much," I said with a smirk. "I wore braces and various orthodontia. That trumps tails." That led into another round of rehashing our adolescent gawkiness.

Was this really the same man I'd met two days ago and had such reservations about? Was it wise to trust him? Tonight, I wanted to enjoy his company and forget about any reservations I still had.

We finished our meal somehow amidst the laughter. I suggested we see if we could catch any sunset surfing going on. He heartily agreed and we drove to the lighthouse. There was a small surfing museum inside and a walking path along the cliff. A few lone souls were communing with the ocean. Damien watched them with appreciation as they raced against the crushing waves, dipping and swerving, dancing over them until they subsided. Then the youngsters and oldsters alike, clad in black wetsuits, would descend once more into the blue. Several more were in various stages of undress by Jeeps and pickups on the side of the road.

I enjoyed the feel of the ocean spray on my face and closed my eyes for a moment. When I opened them, I glanced at Damien, who appeared lost in thought. The glow of the setting sun did remarkable things to his skin. I hadn't yet noticed the golden-brown tone with just a hint of freckles across the bridge of his nose. His face was smooth except for gentle lines around his eyes and a crease where that damn dimple hid. I wondered if he'd lived his years harder than I had.

"Damien," I said, interrupting his thoughts.

"Hmmm," he breathed and continued to watch the sea.

"What happened to you after you were brought to the house in the country in Mexico? Did you return to England?" I had so many questions.

"I did, for a time. Then I became a student at Havenhart Academy. I had a similar visit from the headmaster that Skye described to you, and I went with him. The academy had only been open for a couple of years at that point. I left for some time to pursue my higher education, but eventually was drawn back there." A shadow crossed his face.

A voice inside me said he was leaving out a very painful part of that story. I reached out my hand and touched his sleeve. He flinched. I started to draw my hand back, but he grabbed it and held it gently.

He looked down at my hand and said quietly, "I guess I'll have to be more careful. Your gift is strong, Delaney. I'm shocked that you didn't know."

I blinked hard and drew my hand away. What was he saying? What had just happened?

"Please don't be concerned for me. It's just that I don't speak of my past often, and here I have opened up to you so very much this day. But then, I'm sure this has happened to you before. Am I correct in my assumption?"

"What are you talking about? Sure, I'm a counselor. I've been trained to be receptive to people's feelings. It's my job to help them deal with difficult emotions, that's all."

"Is that really what you think? Tell me that you don't feel something more when you're with someone who's in pain. Tell me that you haven't had big strong men cry on your shoulders who swore that they'd never cried in front of anyone before."

He stepped closer to me and placed a hand on my shoulder, leaning down to make eye contact. The air was still around us. I held onto the railing to steady myself under his gaze. My skin grew warm and my breath caught in my chest.

His eyelids grew heavy for a moment, and he seemed to sway before he looked away.

"You do have a gift, whether you want to believe it was just part of your training or not. Not all counselors can get through the talk to the root pain and help draw it out so the client can move past it. Your gift allows you to do that, and so much more that you haven't even begun to explore. That is why we want you to join us at the academy. We need you."

I stepped back from him to give us both some space. *What is happening?*

He continued. "I have been instructed to hire you, been given complete discretion. I've been told to offer you whatever it takes to have you come and join our faculty."

He paused to let his words to sink in. They wanted me. They thought I was something special. That was something I hadn't experienced in a long time.

"I don't know what you expect of me, but I'm not a miracle worker. I don't want to let you down if you have some expectations of me that I can't fulfill. What you've told me so far has me intrigued…a bit nervous, but interested. But it scares me to think you believe I have some 'gift' when I'm just a normal person. That's all I've ever been. What if I can't do what you want from me?"

He took another step toward me and touched my shoulder again, his hand gently running down my arm as if he were trying to warm me. My bare skin flushed, and I studied him again, trying to read him. I picked up conflicting feeling from him. Appreciation, desire, and a determination to do what was best for the academy and its students. I wished I knew which was stronger, which would win over the other. I'd known this man for less than seventy-two hours, but he was starting to really affect me.

"I'm sure if we dug a little further you'd see that you've never been just an ordinary person. But I've dug enough...and we have time for that later. Whatever it takes, Delaney. What can I say to convince you to join us?" He was sincere. That much I could tell.

"I'm not sure. But the sun is sinking and when it gets darker, driving the hill will be a more formidable task."

He took my cue and dropped his hand reluctantly as we walked back to the car. I was still shaken from what he'd said to me, curious to know more about that dark shadow that passed across his face while we were talking. My arm was still warm from his touch.

I had more questions about Havenhart. That would make for safe conversation on the ride home.

THE FAMILY DROVE TO KANSAS NEXT IN A BRAND-NEW CADILLAC A MEMBER OF *the Montana congregation had given to Father. The young girl was apprehensive. Greedy anticipation flowed from Father and washed over her in waves. She had Seen a new church for him to spread his Influence upon. The people had no idea what was about to happen. But the young girl knew. It would be just like before. Father's Influence would put them all at ease, including the skeptics, until they were ready to give all of their worldly possessions—everything they had—in order to receive his guarantees of Salvation.*

Little did they know there would be no coming back from his form of Salvation.

Mother sat in the rear with the young girl, her cold, limp hand resting in the girl's. Mother was a broken woman by this point. After years of living under Father's rules and moods, she was barely able to speak any longer. The young girl held back her tears, knowing they would only anger Father.

Kansas wasn't as welcoming as Montana. They weren't willing to let Father step in and take over, so he bided his time, working on the fringe groups within the church membership. *When the pastor discovered his deceit, he told Father to leave or he'd report him to the authorities.*

Instead, Father waited until the next Sunday when they would all be in the sanctuary.

During the pastor's prayer, Father stepped up to the back doors of the church and his voice rang out. "Souls of this community, I weep for you. There will be no Salvation for you. Your Maker is displeased. I pray your suffering is short-lived." He stepped back and all the doors and windows slammed shut. The young girl and Mother were sitting in the car watching in horror at what happened next.

Three men came from around the side of the church with large cans of gasoline. They had poured it around the perimeter of the church.

The young girl watched Father standing on the steps. He closed his eyes, tilted his head back and held out his hands. A small flame ignited on the ground in front of him, and a menacing smile stretched across his face.

Mother rolled up the windows and slid over to the driver's seat. The young girl screamed as the car pulled away. Father stayed remained there, the fire dancing in his gaze, until she and Mother were out of sight, and she swore she saw him laughing.

FOUR

IN ACTION

THERE WAS SOME TRAFFIC GETTING OUT OF TOWN, BUT ONCE WE PASSED THE Highway 1 entrance it was smooth sailing.

"I wanted to ask you a question about Saturday," he began.

"Shoot... Oh wait, you aren't drinking water this time, are you?" We both laughed, but mine was nervous. His was polite.

"Do you remember the young couple we passed on the street in Berkeley?" I looked to see that he had turned himself to face me.

"I'm sorry, are you uncomfortable? I hadn't even thought that my little car might not be comfortable for you on this long ride." Yes, I did recall the couple. I hadn't been able to get the girl's face out of my mind.

"You're changing the subject, Delaney. Tell me what you felt." He wasn't going to let me get out of it. That was obvious.

"An educated guess? They're living together somewhere. He's on the verge of turning her out to supplement their income. She loves him and doesn't have anywhere to go. He loves the control and it gives him the only reason he has to survive. When I tried to make eye contact with her, she looked ashamed. I wanted to..." What did I want to do? Rescue her? Give her a referral?

"You wanted to tell her she didn't have to endure that existence," he said, finishing my sentence. "Delaney, no one else on the street was even paying attention to them. I didn't even notice at first until I saw your look of concern. She looked ashamed but there was a part of her that wanted to run to you for help. I sensed that. She is pregnant, but the fetus will not be viable. She'll miscarry within days."

I gripped the steering wheel hard. "How do you possibly know that? And how can you *handle* knowing?"

"Knowing that someone is ill? That they have terminal cancer and don't even have a clue? That a heart attack is imminent? It's difficult, yes. I struggle with it all the time. But I use my gift whenever I can to help people, whenever it's appropriate. That's how I live with it."

I relaxed my grip and took a deep breath. "Tell me more about the academy. What is it like? What's a typical day look like for you? What are your duties at the school?"

Damien turned back to face forward. "It's not like any other place I've ever lived. It's the safest, most accepting place I've ever known. The campus is extraordinary. The staff is very close-knit and supportive of each other. My duties are to assist the headmaster with whatever he needs. I've already disclosed that I handle the master schedule and I have some responsibilities as far as recruitment of staff are concerned. I'm in charge of student services, which means making sure their basic and academic needs are being met. That's a broad task but I enjoy my job immensely. It's the most satisfying thing I've ever done.

"The staff accommodations consist of cottages adjacent to the school. In the commons, there's a full kitchen and meals are prepared for faculty and students alike. Each of the staff cottages has a kitchenette but most eat together in the commons. There's a staff lounge with workspaces, visual and performing arts and technology buildings, and a well-stocked library.

"Activities that are brought to the campus for the students are open to all staff, and the town itself has some more adult-type diversions when one feels the need to get away. We even get the latest movies and have wireless service in all buildings. The academy owns several cars that can be used at your leisure, and the staff often take group trips into the nearest large towns for shopping or an evening out. I think you would find everything you needed to be comfortable there." I saw him smiling hopefully at me out of the corner of my eye. I laughed.

"And what about pedicures? Do you have a masseuse on staff?"

His laugh told me he was enjoying this type of negotiating.

"No, but I'm sure we could manage. I'll give you a foot massage personally if that's what it takes for you to say yes." He broke off with that statement. A line had been crossed with those words. Something was happening between us, something that seemed to make us both wary.

I slammed on the brakes, bringing us both back to reality, as I noticed two crushed cars ahead on the side of the road. No emergency vehicles were in sight and I didn't hear any coming, so I pulled over. He pulled out his cell phone and I gave him our location. He climbed out of the car first. My heart was beating so fast my breath caught in my lungs. I'd never been a first responder in this type of situation, so I decided to follow his lead.

He approached the first car, an overturned SUV. Two teenage boys had already gotten out of the second car and were leaning up against the barrier shivering. I pulled two blankets from the rear of my car that I carried around in case of emergencies. I brought one to Damien and then wrapped the other around the boys.

"My name is Delaney Frost. I'm a school counselor. We've called for help. Can you tell me your names?"

The smaller of the two boys stared straight ahead. The other glanced nervously in my direction.

"Are the police coming? Is the lady okay? We were just driving home from the beach. I dropped my cell phone and was reaching for it when she just came from out of nowhere..."

I placed my hands on his arms. Tension flowed from him in waves. I tried to make eye contact with him to keep him from going into shock. I sensed he was very afraid of the trouble he was going to be in. If I hadn't been in emergency mode, perhaps I would have noticed that there was nothing ordinary about what was happening.

"Are you hurt at all? There's time for details later. The important thing is to determine if everyone's okay." Again, I asked for his name, which he said was Michael and that the smaller boy was his younger brother, Darrell.

"You two stay here and try to stay warm. I'm going to assist my friend. Just make sure to keep breathing, okay?"

Michael nodded. Something told me this wasn't his first car accident, but that it had never been this serious before. I tried to smile and reassure him that he was going to be fine. Again, how could I have known any of this? I'd never seen this kid in my life.

"Michael, do you know where your license and registration are? I can get those for you for when the authorities arrive. And then I can call your family if you want me to."

"Thank you," he said, his voice cracking. "I didn't think anyone was going to stop."

I hurried over to the other car, where I found Damien bent down next to the driver's side assessing the situation.

"Is she okay? Are there kids in the car?"

He shook his head. "She's unconscious. There's no internal bleeding. She may have broken her wrist, and she's definitely got a knock on her head, but there's no swelling of the brain. I don't want to move her without help so I think if we wait—"

At that moment, we heard the first sirens coming over the hill and saw the fire truck headed our way. I left him to go back to the boys, feeling Damien's eyes on my back as I went.

Michael was in worse shape when I got back. Darrell wasn't much better off. They huddled together under the blanket. I talked to them, hoping it would help keep them from shock all the while wondering how I knew just what to say? I'd responded to emergencies before, traumatic incidents happened frequently in schools, but now that Damien had prodded my self-awareness, I paid attention to every detail. I noticed a varsity jacket in the backseat of the car so I asked which one was the athlete. Michael looked up at me and seemed to collect himself.

"Would you be able to call our parents?"

I stepped away to make the call. I sensed all of the woman's emotions over the phone and felt detached from the situation. I listened to my voice as if it were another person, saying exactly what she needed to hear. She thanked me and said she was on her way.

Michael looked up as I walked back over to him. "Thank you.

They're going to kill me. This is my second accident in a month. Both times I was reaching for my phone. My girlfriend and I had a fight earlier. I needed to talk to her." He looked as if he was going to cry. I sat down cross-legged on the ground next to him and held his hand.

"Whatever the fight was about, the important thing is that you and your brother are okay." As I talked, his clammy skin started to warm to the touch and the color started to come back to his face.

I reached my other hand over and took Darrell's hand. He didn't look at me, but his shaking stopped. He pulled up his knees and rested his head on them. Michael got up and walked to the car, so I moved over to Darrell's side.

"Darrell are you feeling any pain?"

He shook his head no. "Just scared. Is the lady okay?"

I asked him how old he was, and he said thirteen. So young. I was so glad the boys weren't hurt.

"Do you play sports, too?" I knew if I kept him talking maybe he wouldn't go into shock.

"Not for school, but for the city. I play baseball."

I asked him what position and what the name of his team was as the paramedics approached us. They checked out both of the boys. I stepped out of the way and walked back over to my car to wait for Damien. He stayed close while the paramedics extracted the woman from her car, explaining that he was a doctor and what he'd learned from his rudimentary exam. They thanked him gruffly then asked him to step aside so they could do their job.

I thought I caught him smirking to himself at his dismissal as he walked over to join me.

The highway patrol officer had arrived at this point. I gave him my information and Damien gave his. He thanked us for calling. I explained that I'd told the boys' mother I would wait until she arrived.

He shrugged. "If you feel it's necessary."

I confirmed that I did. He walked over to the boys and I caught Darrell looking at me. I smiled and nodded encouragement, and he seemed to straighten up a bit. About ten minutes later, their parents arrived. I introduced myself and gave their mother my card. Damien and I said our goodbyes and got back in the car.

I sat down heavily in my seat and grabbed my purse from behind me. The bottomless pit seemed to have snatched my inhaler and it seemed like forever until my fingers found its familiar shape. I took two puffs off of it and swished water around my mouth. Damien looked at me, concerned.

"Are you okay to drive?" He was cool and collected himself.

"I'm fine." I was surprised to realize that was true. My hands shook slightly—more from my inhaler than anything—as I started the car and pulled away from the shoulder carefully. By this time it was near eight and the traffic had dissipated. We drove in silence for the remainder of the trip. His driver planned to pick him up at my apartment. I pulled into my parking spot and turned off the engine. I sat back in my seat and closed my eyes.

"Are you still going to argue that you're simply a normal person who does what any counselor is trained to do? You were able to keep those frightened boys from going into shock. That's no easy feat. I saw them. They were a mess before you calmed them down. You have a touch, Delaney, can't you see that?" He spoke gently, not wanting to appear confrontational but wanting me to feel what he was trying to convey.

I turned to face him, and he reached over to push a lock of hair behind my ear. The car filled with sweet tension. His eyes gleamed brightly, the streetlight reflected in them. A car passed by and its lights flickered across his jaw, illuminating his full lips. His scent drifted over me and our shoulders brushed. The windows began to fog from our conjoined breaths.

"You know why I'd been at that campus before?"

He looked at me, surprised. It seemed to dawn on him where things were headed, and he moved his shoulder away from mine. He smiled and said, "I haven't the faintest idea. Care to share?"

I took a deep breath as I readied myself to make an important disclosure. "We went there for summer camp. Cheerleading summer camp. All in matching outfits, ponytails so tight you'd never need a facelift, and enough hair gel and spray to fix any leaks in the Great Wall of China. Don't even get me started on pom-poms," I deadpanned.

He studied me with eyebrows drawn together in concentration. "But did you ever drop the Spirit Stick?"

We both laughed out loud and the tension was gone, for a moment at least.

"Do you want to come in and wait for the car?" I asked out of courtesy. Things had been too tumultuous tonight and I didn't thoroughly trust my feelings. There was no doubt I was attracted to Damien, even though I hardly knew the first thing about him. He must have sensed my hesitation.

"I think we've had enough revelations for one night, don't you?" His smile was kind, but tinged with sadness and regret. "However, I'm not ready for the evening to come to a close. How about a cup of coffee at that shop on the corner? I'd love one after our little adventure."

"I assumed you knew I don't drink coffee."

"Delaney, it's not like that, really. We haven't bugged your house or planted hidden cameras. We simply conduct a background investigation into our candidates and it's my duty to be vigilant about that. I'm also very observant, which is another reason why the headmaster sent me. For instance, I noticed the sign said coffee, but also ice cream served twenty-four hours." He wiggled his eyebrows at me and I giggled.

"How can I resist?" *Boy, isn't that a loaded statement.*

I opened the car door and he followed suit. We walked to the coffee shop on the corner of Niles and G. We had to adjust our eyes to the brightly lit room. He ordered cup of tea and I graciously accepted a hot fudge sundae.

"I'll go ahead and reveal this weakness... A sundae can ease my stress any day."

He smiled and raised his cup to me.

"Delaney," he said after we'd sat in silence for a bit. "Have I earned your trust? Can I tell the headmaster he's got his new counselor?"

The hopeful look in his eyes cemented the deal.

"When do we leave?"

THE YOUNG GIRL SPENT THE SPRING AT GRANDFATHER'S FARM IN IOWA, AND SHE had experienced happiness at a level previously unknown. Mother assured her that Father would join them when he could. No one spoke about the fire and the girl was enjoying the peace and tranquility of life in a settled place.

Mother had let her begin attending Sunday School classes and for the first time, she had positive interactions with other children. She was shy, but they were quick to include her in their games. Mother began singing with the choir and Grandpa was teaching her about life on the farm.

At first, Mother was very jumpy, and the girl heard her and Grandfather arguing in the night when they thought she was asleep. Then the dreams started. Fire and smoke so real, she felt the burning and choking. She'd awaken crying and when she told Mother about it, she would look terrified. Grandfather became increasingly distant.

One afternoon, the girl approached him in the parlor. He was holding a picture of Grandmother and crying softly. She touched his arm, and he spun around, angrily pushing her away from him. She cried out and Mother ran into the room.

"Why, Janet? She'd still be with me if you hadn't... Why? Was it worth it?"

Mother cupped her hands to her face and shook her head.

Both Mother and Grandfather turned their heads sharply toward the front of the house.

"Hide the girl," Grandfather said.

Mother pleaded with the girl to hide and closed her in a dark room.

There was shouting and then screams.

The girl smelled the smoke and felt the heat from the fire...and then everything went black.

When she awoke the next morning, she was in a strange place and Father was speaking to the police.

"I'm terribly sorry for your loss. Your father was a good man," a policeman said to Mother, who was sitting in a chair staring off into space, what was left of her sanity holding on by a thread.

Grandfather was dead, burned in the fire.

The young girl spoke, and all those in the room turned to her.

"They will call him leader, and they will welcome him with open arms," she called out loudly, and then began to whisper. Father had a new gleam in his eyes. He was proud of his offspring and glad they were back together. He had such plans. He prayed loudly and fervently to his Maker for Him to bless his daughter and the miracle he had bestowed upon her.

Mother's eyes shone with a new terror, as though everything that had gone before was nothing compared to what was about to occur. She hugged herself and rocked in her chair as Father knelt down beside the young girl in her bed, praying to his Maker for thanks.

FIVE

THE LEAP

SCHOOL ENDED IN JUNE, AND I PREPARED TO MAKE SOME MAJOR CHANGES. I spent the next two months packing and thinking about my future and wondering about my new life. Thoughts of Damien cropped up frequently. We exchanged two emails that were strictly business, more businesslike than our visits had been. I tried to avoid dwelling on thoughts of him, but I had so many questions. Would this tension still be there between us? For all I knew, he had someone in his life. He'd been careful not to divulge too much information about himself. I recalled the moment at the lighthouse, when I touched his arm. What had he been feeling? What had he not wanted me to know?

He was right about the big strong men crying on my shoulder. There had been many. Most were friends, some were students, and a few lovers...It always unnerved me but the situations would usually end with them thanking me, saying they felt better, and then the end of the relationship. It was if they couldn't handle that they'd exposed themselves to me. I always worried I'd done something wrong and would inevitably get the "it's not you, it's me" routine.

How did Damien know these things about me? Maybe it was conjecture on his part, and I was going to drive myself crazy thinking about it. Thinking about *him*. It made things more nerve-racking. I'd even had a conversation with my best friend Cassidy about him when she was in town.

"Do you think anything will happen between you two when you get there?"

"I honestly don't know. We didn't talk much about his circumstances. All I know is the story he shared about how he lost his parents in Mexico, and that he was a student at Havenhart for a time and now works there doing various assignments for the headmaster. I don't know anything else, not his middle name, where in England he was born. I don't even know how much of whatever I felt was happening between us was due to the situation we encountered or even if he felt the same."

Since he'd left, there had been two emails from his office, and both were completely professional. One detailed my flight plans and the other thanked me again for offering to pick up Skye from Santa Cruz before our chartered flight. That email had ended with, "Looking forward to your arrival, Damien." Whatever chemistry we may or may not have had certainly wasn't reflected in our correspondence.

"What do you *hope* is going to happen?" Cassidy asked me with a sly smile. She had such a different life than me as a pilot for a charter airline. She'd been married for several months now to a fellow pilot named Robert Crane. They'd had a whirlwind romance and eloped in Hawaii. I thought perhaps since she was in love she wanted the same for everyone around her. I didn't know if the L word was in my future.

"I can't even think about that. He's beautiful to look at though. Being so close to him in my car...if it hadn't been a job-interview-type occasion, I think I would have wanted him to kiss me."

Cassidy was super excited for me and my new adventure. She was only upset that she wasn't getting to fly me, but said she knew I was making the right choice.

"I just know it. I can't explain it. You know that happens to me sometimes."

She was right. I loved that about her. I promised her I'd keep her posted.

I didn't sleep much the night before we left. I'd picked up Skye and we stayed at my parents' house. They offered to help us ship our things and bring us to the airport, which was a huge help. I got to know her a little better and was glad to not be making this adventure on my own. We shared our concerns, but were both delighted to be getting a fresh start.

Skye told me a little about Headmaster Hart. "From what I remember, it was as if he'd stepped out of some classic novel, like Sir Arthur Conan Doyle. When I met him, he was wearing a tailored suit with an old-fashioned tie, everything pressed perfectly, and he even carried a walking stick with an embossed silver handle."

Funny, she'd just described Damien when I'd met him, sans the walking stick. I chuckled to myself that they must have a traveling uniform. Damien had been dressed down when we went to Santa Cruz. For a moment, I started to imagine him in a pair of black denim jeans and—

"Can you believe it's really happening? I can't believe I'm finally going! It's going to be perfect. I can't wait to see the campus. I wonder where we'll be staying. I wonder what classes I'll be teaching. What will the kids be like?"

She rambled on for most of the flight. Her energy and my fears eventually drained me. I dozed at some point, dreaming about a little girl and a fire...

Skye squealed with delight, pulling me from my slumber. I *never* slept on planes, yet I'd been out almost the entire flight. It may have had something to do with the fact that we were up late the previous night wondering about the academy.

The pilot chose that moment to announce we would be arriving shortly, so Skye and I cleaned up our lunch mess. A caterer had provided sandwiches and salads, and I'd been pleased to see bottles of Diet Coke there as well.

Pleased, yes...but that nagging red flag popped up again. And come to think of it, the sandwiches were turkey with cheese and mayo and lettuce only, and the chips were Fritos. It was as if someone had followed me into Togo's and watched me order.

I shivered. How did they know so many of my likes and dislikes? I was beginning to think that I had better be ready for more of these "coincidences."

I knew I had my out, though. If things got too weird, Favorite Cousin James would rescue me. I'd let him know I was coming and he was "stoked."

I peered out the window of the jet and saw the lush, fertile green of the Northern Arkansas terrain. It really was lovely. I was not, however, looking forward to the thick, muggy air I was going to encounter when we deplaned. I wasn't quite sure how I was going to handle the humidity. I'd never really been a fan of the South for that very reason. But I'd taken this leap and was going to have to get used to it. I just hoped my asthma would be able to cope.

The plane landed at the Fayetteville airport and a driver met us, complete with the black suit and a sign with our names on it. We received the royal treatment for sure. I hadn't been sure what to take, so I'd packed light and shipped a few boxes to the Eureka Springs post office care of Damien Preston. He assured me during our email exchange that he'd collect them. I'd decided on some of my most cherished trinkets, a few of my stand-by favorite books and movies, some pictures of friends and family, and my clothes.

Ramses and Clio had accompanied us on the plane. They had been given sedatives to make the trip less traumatic for them, but they woke when we landed and proceeded to yowl the remainder of the trip to the campus. I apologized to Skye and the driver. They assured me they understood. Hopefully my pets would relax when they saw our new home.

I hoped *I* could relax.

I had asked Damien before he'd left to send me a brochure or something with pictures of the campus. He'd just smiled.

"It's not something we normally do. One cannot fully appreciate the beauty and splendor of our academy unless they see it in person. I'm sure you understand."

I really was going into this blindly.

We wound through trees followed by open spaces with homes sprinkled here and there. I noticed an abundance of churches with billboards out front, sharing some of the most interesting religious views I'd ever encountered. "IF YOU THINK IT'S HOT IN HERE, TRY HELL," or "DUST ON YOUR BIBLE LEADS TO DIRT IN YOUR LIFE, "or "DO

YOU KNOW WHAT HELL IS? COME HEAR OUR PREACHER!" My favorite said, "GOD WILL ACCEPT BROKEN HEARTS, BUT HE MUST HAVE ALL THE PIECES."

I'd grown up going to church, but my mother had encouraged me to decide for myself what I believed in, and our church was very supportive. I'd seen a lot of ugly things done in the name of the Christian god up to this point in my life, but I did believe that a higher power certainly guided folks. Perhaps that's what this so-called gift was all about. Maybe I was just a tool in the overall plan. Anything was possible.

Our driver, Vincent, was quiet during the ride while Skye and I stared out the windows and pointed out interesting landmarks to each other. We passed the town James lived in. I looked forward to seeing him as soon as I got settled.

We neared the town of Eureka Springs and I knew we were close. It was a Sunday afternoon, and our orientation was set to begin on Monday, so I didn't have much time to get myself together before jumping in. That was probably a good idea. Otherwise, I might get to thinking too much and make a mad dash for the first flight back home.

Just past the town, Vincent turned down a heavily wooded private road, stopping at a security point not far off the highway. We drove on for another five minutes or so, and then there was a break in the trees. Before us was a massive, round brick building covered in ivy and surrounded by wrought-iron fencing.

It was breathtaking.

I'd never expected to see something so beautiful out here. Thick groves of pine and oak trees pressed around the edges of the property, making it difficult to determine how far the campus extended. I glanced at Skye, and she had a dreamy, satisfied look on her face. I knew she would be happy here, that she would feel at home.

Upon closer inspection, I noticed security cameras and a security guard at the gates. This served to make me feel both secure and alarmed at the same time, if that was possible. It was nice to know that I wouldn't be threatened by any crazies out here in the middle of nowhere, but also made me curious why there would be a need for all of this security. Sure, Damien had told me that many of the students were high-profile kids who had been through some horrific experiences. If these measures made them feel better about being here, who was I to complain?

We drove through the intricately designed gates and followed a circular drive. Vincent finally broke his silence, pointing out the main offices in the front. He continued on to the left, following a concrete drive that led to a row of adorable cottages. My excitement grew when I realized they were the staff accommodations. Skye and I grabbed each other's hands and giggled with delight.

There were two cul-de-sacs facing each other, with ten cottages of different designs in each one. At the end of the drive was a larger Victorian home, which I imagined might belong to the headmaster. It had a stately carriage house to the rear that looked as if it had apartments on the top floor. The architecture had been preserved so well. It gave me a warm feeling of comfort to see such care had been taken with this place.

The van turned to the right and stopped at the end of the cul-de-sac. He pointed out the two end cottages that had been prepared for Skye and me.

"Yay, we'll be neighbors! Oh, thank goodness you'll be close so I can come over and chat if I can't sleep, and we can have coffee together in the mornings on Sundays and…"

I tuned her out as I looked closer at the home that would be mine for the foreseeable future. All of the cottages had covered front porches with flower boxes on the front railings. My new home had some of my favorite flowers planted in the boxes, and my heart fluttered a bit when I saw a wicker chair on the porch, perfect for afternoon reading sessions. I got out of the van and walked up the steps to look more closely. The smell of the flowers and the weight of the day made me feel a bit dizzy. I allowed myself a moment to space out before I returned to the van.

Skye was talking to Ramses and Clio in their crates and helping the driver remove our belongings. An older woman in overalls with long silver hair and a floppy straw hat rounded the corner of my cottage as I was carrying up the first load.

"Oh, thank goodness. You ladies arrived. We've all been so excited for you to finally be here!" She brushed her hands off on her pants and extended her hand first to Skye and then to me.

"I'm Grace. Grace Walden. My husband George and I run the horticul-
tural and food service programs here. Welcome, welcome. I have your
keys here, so you can get settled in. Thank you, Vincent," she called out to
our driver, and we thanked him as well. He tipped his hat to us and took
off in his van, rounding the main building complex and out of sight.

Grace handed us our sets of keys and continued with her welcome.
"You ladies just let me know if you need anything by way of supplies.
Linens have been stocked, along with some food staples and cleaning
materials. If you need anything else, we usually make a trip about once a
week into town to pick up things needed for the academy, and we can
always add to our list." She seemed very friendly, very businesslike.

I noticed the gardening trowel in her back pocket. "Are you responsible for these beautiful flowers?"

She nodded proudly. "Gardening is my passion, and I guess I have a bit
of a knack for it. I'm glad you like them."

"Very much," I answered. "Perhaps you can show me a thing or two. I
love to work in the garden but my thumbs lean more toward the color
brown than green."

She laughed and said, "There're ways around that. I'd be happy to.
Now you go on and get settled in. Dinner is served daily at five-thirty and
everyone is looking forward to meeting you both."

"Thank you for everything, Mrs. Walden. It's so nice to meet you."

She waved her hand at me. "Just Grace, please, and thank you for
coming, Delaney. We've been short a counselor for too long," she said with
a sad smile on her face. I would have wondered about that look but I was
anxious to see my new digs.

Skye had gathered her things onto her porch and she smiled over at
me. "Well, here we go. Let's see what's inside."

And she was gone.

I stood there for a moment longer, until Ramses started banging on
the gate of his crate.

"Alright, buddy. I'm sorry. Let's do this."

I took the keys Grace had given me and slid the larger one into the lock.
The door opened into a brightly lit sitting room with a small sofa and wing-

backed chair in front of an entertainment unit complete with a TV and DVD player. The furniture was nothing fancy but looked comfortable. The floors were dark hard wood, with a cream rug placed in front of the sofa. I would have picked out similar items myself. I was already beginning to relax.

A desk was set up behind the sofa and beyond that, an island with stools and a small kitchenette. Off the kitchen were three doors, the one on the left leading to a bathroom and the one at the rear, I assumed, led to the bedroom.

The cottage certainly seemed to have everything I'd need to be comfortable. It was decorated in blues and yellows, bright but not over-whelming.

I decided to bring in my things from outside before I did any more exploring and worked quickly to get the litter box set up in the laundry room off the right of the kitchen, which held a stackable washer and dryer and a utility sink. I was surprised and a little relieved to see that someone had left two bags of cat litter for me to use and a bag of Iams—the brand I had been feeding my cats. I'd wondered how I was going to manage all that, since I couldn't really lug those items onto the plane.

I opened the gates of the cats' crates and they darted out, checking out their new territory. I found bowls in the cupboard for water and food and got those arranged so they would feel more at home.

I carried my suitcases to the bedroom, which was roomy and had a queen-size four-poster bed in the middle of the space. One wall was entirely closet space, and I breathed a sigh of relief at that. I unpacked my clothes into the closet and antique dresser that matched the bed. The cherry wood was exquisite. I resisted the urge to dive right in and snuggle down for a nap.

I unpacked my mother's quilt I had brought for comfort and laid it out on the bed, feeling a wave of homesickness. Wear and tear from the past few days was presenting itself, not a good thing, considering I needed to be strong and healthy to face my new circumstances.

I carried my toiletries into the bathroom—and gasped at what I found there.

A huge claw-foot tub rested in the middle, with a shower hookup on one end. A low table sat under the frosted window with candles, vanilla soaps and packets of oatmeal for soaking.

I wanted to cry. It was the most amazing part of this journey so far.

"If I can soak in this tub every day, I can survive anything." I ran my hand along the edge and thought maybe I'd sneak in a soak now, but I knew I'd be worthless for dinner, not to mention the temperature and humidity had me thinking I'd get more relief from a cold shower. I decided that as soon as I'd unpacked the rest of my clothes and toiletries, the other stuff could wait, and I'd take a quick shower to freshen up for dinner. I had an hour and a half to go.

I opened all of the windows in the place. Fresh air was definitely needed. I wondered about the person who'd lived here *before me*. It brought up thoughts of the counselor who had been here *before me*, and I started to think again of all the questions I had about this place. I thought about the students I would get to work with, and it put the spring back into my step.

I finished quickly and checked on the cats. They had already found comfy places to sit. Ramses settled on the top of the wingback chair, basking in the sun, and Clio took the seat. Both watched me as I paced around, putting things in temporary spots, knowing I'd be moving them five more times at least before I was satisfied.

Finally, I stripped off my traveling clothes and threw them in a basket provided for me at the bottom of the closet. I walked into the bathroom and smiled again at my new best friend. I adjusted the water just right and stepped into the stream of refreshing lukewarm water.

The heat hadn't been as bad as I worried it would be, but I had certainly accumulated a layer of sweat. The cool water trickled over my skin, washing away the filth from the day. I drew my fingers through my short, spiky blonde hair, and the tension that had been building seemed to subside. It was soon replaced with a glimmer of anticipation.

I'd see Damien soon. He was here, or at least I assumed he was. It had been a long two months since I'd met him, and I had found myself thinking of him more than I wanted to. I couldn't get those green eyes out of my mind, remembering how difficult it was to read him. I thought of our moment in my car after the harrowing ride home from Santa Cruz.

Had he wanted to kiss me? Had he wanted to come inside with me? And what would have happened if he did?

Those thoughts and the shower were a dangerous combination. I finished and turned the water off before allowing myself to get carried away.

I was startled when I opened the curtain to find Clio looking up at me from the rug. I reached down to scratch her ears, and she closed her eyes and purred.

"Miss Clio, you have always been my rock, and I'm so glad you're here with me." She turned and flicked her tail at me as she sauntered out of the bathroom, rubbing her cheek on the doorjamb.

Before I put on the clothes I'd laid out, there was a knock at my door. Luckily, I had unpacked my short silk robe and hung it conveniently on the back of the bathroom door. I grabbed for it and was just tying the belt as I got to the front door. Assuming it was Skye, I opened without looking.

A lanky, blond, ponytailed man stood there, filling up my doorway.

"It seems you've arrived in one piece," he said with a glowing smile.

I pulled my robe tighter around me, oddly feeling as though this guy saw way more than what was exposed. I stared at him blankly.

"I'm Jackson Howe. I've so been looking forward to seeing you again! Do you remember me from Big G?"

"I...uh... Wow. Was not expecting a visitor. You went to Graceland?" Real slick, but what else was I supposed to say to this guy who was obviously waiting for my recognition?

"Yeah. Orion house? We were brother/sister houses when I was a freshman and you were a sophomore. When I heard you were coming here, I was blown away. Now here you are!" His smile grew very intense.

Still speechless, I clutched even tighter at my robe and stepped a bit behind the door.

He seemed to get that I was a bit uncomfortable having a conversation with a stranger while mostly undressed. He stepped back and put his hands in his back pockets.

"I know you just got here, so I'll let you get ready. I just wanted to see if you wanted me to walk you to the commons for dinner but, uh, I think you're a little underdressed. If you just head up the path there to your right, it's the double doors at the end of the walk. I'll see you inside, okay?" He rubbed at his jaw and grinned. "Damn, I can't believe it's really you." He took another step down the stairs of my porch.

"Thank you, Jackson. I'll be there in a few minutes."

I kind of closed the door on him at that point, probably not the politest maneuver, but how else was I supposed to respond when I had just been presented with someone I was supposed to know and I was half naked? Okay, not half naked, but naked under a robe was still pretty bad.

I waited by the door until I heard his footsteps descending the walk a minute later. I peeked through the curtains and saw him smiling to himself and shaking his head as he shoved his hands farther in his pockets and strolled down the path with a spring in his step.

This day had sure been full of surprises.

I retreated to the bedroom and grabbed a pair of denim capris and a sleeveless t-shirt, slipped on my Dansko sandals and ran the blow dryer through my hair for about two minutes, then massaged some product through to the tips. I used my inhaler and drank some water to try to help clear my lungs. I hoped I didn't have any issues at dinner. My usual makeup routine consisted of eyeliner, mascara and a bit of lip gloss. I had no reason to derail from that.

I took one more look in the mirror and said to myself, "You can't hide here all night, Delaney. Go out and face the music."

Skye was just stepping off her porch as I closed my door, making sure the cats didn't run out. I called out to her and we walked together. Her outfit consisted of rainbow gauchos, a pink tank top and her regulation Birkenstocks. She and I made quite a picture, the California girls. Damien had assured me that my tattoos weren't going to be out of place here, that there were all walks of life. I was about to find out.

"Who was that guy who came to your door a bit ago?" Skye was dying for the details.

"His name is Jackson, and he apparently knows me from college, but I didn't recognize him. Totally embarrassing. I only had my robe on when I answered the door."

"Embarrassing my ass," she scoffed. "He's hot!"

I coughed out a laugh.

"Yeah, not the way I want to start things here, Skye." I shook my head at her, laughing at myself. "But I'm sure he was surprised by my lack of apparel."

She gave me a *tsk tsk* and pointed out that I should have looked out the window first.

We rounded the walkway to the double doors Jackson had pointed out and entered the commons. It was a vintage paradise with a 1950s diner motif: checkered floor, red vinyl booths and a juke box in the corner playing Jackie Wilson. How fun! There was even a section for a dance floor, with a small stage at the rear where I noticed a collection of instruments. Four round tables sat near the service counter, which also had red vinyl stools, and those tables were occupied with folks I assumed were the other staff members. Some looked up when we came in and smiled.

Jackson stood and walked over to greet us.

"Jackson Howe," he said as he extended his hand to Skye. She fluttered her eyelashes at him, graciously returning his handshake. She laid it on a little thick, but it was cute. I scanned the room and was disappointed to see Damien wasn't there. I didn't see anyone resembling the headmaster, either. We followed Jackson back to his table, where he introduced us to Isaac, Jared, and Jared's wife, Moira. They were all teachers at Havenhart and I could totally see why Damien told me my appearance wouldn't raise any eyebrows. There was a lot of ink and metal around that table.

"Don't be concerned if these two gentlemen get a little heated in their arguments, it's just time for their daily current-events smackdown." Jackson gestured his head toward Isaac and Jared. They hardly noticed as they carried on about the latest news.

Moira seemed fed up with the discussion her husband and colleague were having and glad to have a change of scenery. "Welcome to Havenhart. Have you seen the grounds yet?"

"Not yet, we only just arrived this afternoon," Skye answered for us.

Grace came over to our table and greeted us all. "Alright, folks. It's burgers and fries tonight. Skye, I know you're a vegetarian, so I hope veggie burgers will meet with your satisfaction?"

Skye nodded appreciatively.

We all gave our thanks and she headed back to the kitchen to retrieve our meals. She and George, I was told, only served the staff on special occasions. Most nights they would cook and set it up buffet style.

My eyes wandered around the room, looking at the retro posters with vintage ads for Coca-Cola and pin-up girls lounging on classic cars. I loved the feel and knew I would enjoy eating my meals here.

At the other tables, the conversations carried on and, as I glanced at the farthest table, I noticed a woman with shocking red hair watching me. It was a welcoming but somewhat knowing look. I took a chance and smiled. She nodded and said something to her tablemate, a dark-skinned gentleman, who then turned and nodded my way as well. He was older, tall and thin, and had scars on his cheeks and deep-set obsidian eyes.

Something about the way he stared at me was unsettling.

A stocky man with gray, bushy hair emerged from the kitchen carrying trays overflowing with burgers and fries. Jackson jumped up to assist him. Grace brought condiments around to the tables, and I stood to help her. She smiled thoughtfully at me and handed me several bottles. I made my way to the table with the red-haired woman.

"I'm Delaney Frost and here are your condiments," I said, giving them a little curtsy.

The woman laughed heartily. "Such poise. Have you waited on tables long?" She held out her hand. "I'm Morgan, and this is Elijah."

I shook hands with them both. The woman had pale skin and a curvy shape under a black dress. When she smiled, she brought her hand up to her cheek and rested her face in her hand. She wore an identical ring as Damien. I wondered what else the two of them shared in common. I noticed one on Elijah's hand, too.

She continued to speak. "I heard you arrived today. I take it things went smoothly?"

I nodded. "Yes, our travel was pleasant. We're starting to settle in."

"Orientation starts tomorrow morning. I'll be working with you, and Elijah will be working with one other new teacher we've brought on this year. Damien assures me that you're going to be quite an asset to our academy."

I noted a hint of skepticism but I hoped it was just my nerves.

"I certainly hope so. I'm very pleased to be here."

"Pleased. Well, okay. Enjoy your dinner, and I'll see you in the morning after breakfast. We'll meet in the library. I'm sure you'll be able to find it. Just follow the scent of sandalwood." She laughed, and I thanked her again.

I hoped we'd get along well if she were to be my mentor teacher. I assumed she'd be outlining the schedule and giving me some information about the students...but I would soon learn she had other things in mind for me.

I returned to our table and got down to the business of grubbing. The burgers were perfect, and I hadn't realized just how hungry I was. Jackson was poking fun at Isaac and Jared, who seemed heavily into their discussion on the latest influenza outbreak the media had been harping on. Isaac inferred it was a conspiracy and blamed the CDC for covering up details that had led to its development into a near pandemic. Jared was convinced the media was blowing things way out of proportion and we would soon learn it was just another seasonal outbreak, and we would all be fine.

Moira sat and ate quietly, and when she was finished, she excused herself, kissing Jared on top of his head as she left. He reached up to touch her face and then went right back to the argument.

Jackson turned to me at this point. "Do you remember me yet? You used to eat at our table in the dining room."

I choked on my fry and took a long drag of my Diet Coke to wash it down. Skye had gone in search of desserts, which were on a tray on the counter, leaving me alone with Jackson and his questions.

"You okay?" Jackson patted me on the back.

I pulled away from him. "I'm fine. Yeah. I remember those dinners. We had some fun conversations. Who was your roommate?" I had to ask him something that might trigger a memory. I always remembered people's faces; I was kind of known for my great memory. I had no clue who this guy was.

"I had a couple of different roommates. You roomed with that chick with the curly hair. Marjory? Wasn't that her name?"

I shivered. He gave me no information, and yet knew so much about me.

"Yeah. Marjory. What did you major in? Did we have classes together?"

Jackson took the opportunity to drape his arm around the back of my chair and lean in to speak. "I can see the wheels turning. I'm sorry if I upset you, Delaney. I seem to be doing this all wrong. I was just really excited to see you," Jackson said in a humble tone.

I smiled back at him. "It's fine, really. I just haven't thought about those days in a long time. Anyway, we used to have some laughs, didn't we?"

I hoped he wouldn't catch the fact that I didn't say I remembered him, specifically. I wanted to be polite. He seemed willing to let it go and tried a different route when he spoke again.

"What do you think so far? I've been teaching art here for two years and I love it. It's such a nice home away from home, very much like Graceland was. Did you feel that way about Big G?"

"I was very comfortable at Graceland. The dorms were great. Even after I moved off campus, I always found it inviting there."

"That's right, didn't you live in the apartments above the video store on Main Street?"

Another shock. He remembered so much about me. I guess I'd always been that way about the students who were older than me, too; interested in their comings and goings as I tried to make my own way.

"Oh yeah, that place. It was so hot in the summer, and we would always get wasps flying in through the ripped screens. How about you? Did you stay in the dorms or move off campus?" I hoped that by changing the subject from myself, I might figure out who this guy was and whether I should remember anything specific about him.

"I moved into the Units, the apartments on campus for older students, when I was a junior. It was nice to have my own space by then. I was really into painting and had enough room finally to do my work." He went back to his hamburger.

I had a vague memory of attending some art shows at the gallery on campus, but still nothing was ringing any bells about him.

Jackson and I caught up on what we'd been doing since Graceland. He told me he had joined the Army after graduating and spent his career in a specialized unit. He enjoyed the service, but his first love was always art. He decided to go ahead and become a teacher after he did his twenty years. He was vague about how he'd been introduced to the headmaster, but said Havenhart intrigued him and he decided it would be a nice change of pace. His eyes seemed far away when he spoke of his deployments, so I figured now wasn't the time to pry.

He asked about my teaching career, and I gave him the quick rundown. Whether I remembered him or not, he might be a friend, and I certainly needed those. He was so charismatic and excitable, and really animated in his speech and gestures. He kept Skye and I laughing the entire meal. I was grateful for that, given how nervous I was to be there.

Skye returned, having found herself a piece of apple pie, but my attention drifted to the ice cream counter.

"Hot fudge sundae, here I come," I said to my tablemates, and they all laughed. Hey, I needed to bolster my strength, right?

We all finished eating and headed back to our cottages. Skye interjected her thoughts into the influenza discussion, giving them statistical and scientific data to back up the actions of the CDC and government agencies. Isaac and Jared listened to her intently, asking questions she was able to answer with ease. I hung back with Jackson and laughed at their debate.

"I hope you like it here, Delaney. Let me know if you ever need anything. Are you settled in yet? I'm happy to help if you need me to." He looked hopeful.

I smiled back warmly. "Thanks, Jackson, but I really didn't bring much with me. I'll let you know though."

We approached the two cul-de-sacs, and I halted at the intersection. I noticed a dark figure on my porch. My heat stuttered in my chest when I recognized Damien's profile.

I noticed Jackson's smile drop. "I guess you have a visitor. See you tomorrow, Delaney." He turned quickly and headed back toward the dormitory, stopping to chat with Jared and Isaac on the way. They turned and waved as well.

I tried to keep my excitement in check as I walked up to my porch.

"Hello, Delaney." He stood from the wicker chair where he'd been waiting with one foot propped up on the base of the railing.

I paused, taking in the sight. He was once again in what I thought of as his traveling uniform of a formal-looking suit, his dark hair messier—and a little longer—than I remembered. My cheeks hurt from smiling so widely.

"If you're the welcoming committee, you're a few hours late," I joked.

He smiled, but didn't laugh. "I apologize that I wasn't here to greet you. I was away on academy business. I wanted to make certain that you had everything you needed in your bungalow. I asked the Waldens if they would bring supplies for your cats. Were they acceptable?"

"Absolutely, and thank you for that." I stared up at him and tried to get a sense of his intentions or his feelings about seeing me again. Those green eyes continued to keep me in the dark. He was so guarded. I doubted I would ever truly know where I stood with this man.

"It was no problem whatsoever. I want you to be comfortable here."

"Are you here in one of these cottages?" I asked, looking around. Some of them were lit up, and what I assumed were some of the other staff sat on their porches talking.

He shook his head. "I live in one of the apartments above the carriage house. They're quite nice. Not as cozy as these, but it suits me just fine so long as the horses aren't too riled up. The smell isn't too bad, but for the very humid days," he said with a laugh. The conversation was light, but there was a tension in the air.

"I should probably let you get to sleep," he said, as though he was uncomfortable. "You've had a long day." He looked down at his feet for a moment, as if there was something else he wanted to say. "I meant what I said. I want you to be comfortable here. If there's anything you need, I'll do everything in my power to assist you." He looked up again with a pained look on his face, but I couldn't pick up on what he was thinking or feeling.

"Thank you, Damien. I'm happy to finally be here." I spoke in a quiet voice. "I've thought a lot about Havenhart in the past couple of months. It's nice to finally see it for myself. And you were right. Pictures wouldn't have done it justice."

He smiled and took another backward step down my porch stairs looking thoughtfully at the fading sun in the sky. "I'm glad. I'll bid you good night, then. Sleep well," he said. He walked to the end of my path and then turned back to face me. "I hope you find the orientation to be helpful. Morgan is looking forward to working with you. There is much you can learn from her." He hesitated yet again, then smiled at me and nodded. And he walked away.

I stood on the edge of my porch, watching him go. *What a weird interaction.*

Not what I'd expected, but then, I hadn't known *what* to expect when I saw him again. Part of me wanted to dissect the entire conversation, and I probably would have, but I heard my phone ringing inside. I fumbled with my keys and made a mad dash inside.

"DELANEY! YOU PROMISED ME YOU WOULD CALL THE SECOND YOU LANDED!"

I swallowed hard and realized that moms will always worry, no matter how old you are.

"I'm here and I'm fine, Mom. I just got back from dinner." I assured her the place was fine, the people were nice, it wasn't too hot, and that I would call her after my orientation.

"Well, just don't melt. I love you, Laney."

"I love you too, Mom." I was a little tearful when I hung up. The length and breadth of the day had me feeling emotional. My lungs were heavy, too. I used my inhaler again and dragged myself into bed. My head barely hit the pillow before I was out.

THE YOUNG GIRL AWOKE THE NIGHT AFTER YET ANOTHER FIRE, THIS ONE IN THE hotel room where they'd been living. The girl had been too close and had suffered from smoke inhalation. Father appeared late in the night and ripped the hospital blankets off her. He berated her for not being ready to leave. "We have much to accomplish and Mother doesn't seem to be of much use."

Father turned off the hospital machines and unhooked her IV.

The young girl asked where Mother was. Father muttered, mostly to himself, and the young girl became increasingly alarmed. The last thing she'd remembered was her mother begging for forgiveness and then everything went black.

"It's a blessing we have that El Camino from Flagstaff, otherwise she'd have suffered even more."

He wanted the girl to believe Mother had left of her own volition but she had Seen the blood, the torn clothes, the dirt. Father had finally grown tired of Mother's questions and he'd taken matters into his own hands.

She tried to keep her wits about her, knowing weakness of any kind set Father off. Sometimes what she Saw did not come to pass, the chain of events was never guaranteed, but she didn't think that was the case for her mother. She would have to buy his story and show no fear.

"Salvation will come only for those who BELIEVE. Believe in your Maker and let Him into your life. Your Maker works through me. Let me be your guide."

The congregation rose to its feet, singing his praise. Father was raising them higher and higher in ecstasy and as the young girl looked at him, all she saw were the dollar signs in his eyes. The offertory plate was passed around and the parishioners gave everything they had, even writing checks equal to their mortgage payments. Some who had heard Father before brought deeds to automobiles and stock certificates.

The young girl looked on in awe and fear. When she was a child, his words soothed her and she'd believed in him. Her father had the power to Influence all he came in contact with to give him whatever he desired. But he couldn't use his power on her, not his Influence. On her he used his love, until she grew wise. Then he used his fists. She told him of all she'd Seen, guiding him to the places he was most likely to be successful. In those places the congregations were ripe for the taking. She knew not of his Maker, or any plans for the End of Days. She wanted no part of it. She merely wanted to survive.

Mother never joined them, and the young girl knew, despite his excuses, that she never would.

She did her best to keep him appeased, as he'd begun to get even more agitated and impatient. There were nights when he would wake her up, shaking her.

"Daughter, have you Seen? You must tell me! Our Maker is not a patient one. He needs us to do his work!" He'd struck her repeatedly, begging and pleading and screaming at her to give him a sign.

The young girl knew the truth. There were angry men in the small towns they passed through. They came for Father with threats. Then they'd leave abruptly, as though Father's influence compelled them. She would tell him when she'd Seen a new place to go. She tried to feed him false information or to hide the truth from him, but she'd paid dearly for it.

Not all of her Sight did she share with him.

She'd begun to See a woman...one who would save her from him, put an end to the violence.

It was in Texas when the young girl knew she had little time left. Father had grown increasingly violent, beating her when she failed to See where they should go next. He withheld food and kept her awake for days at a time. When she finally Saw where they would go next, he'd hold her close and say it was the will of the Maker. He'd cry and promise her things would be different this time. After they earned enough money, they would settle somewhere and she could go to school.

She'd learned by now not to trust him. They moved from motel to motel. New cars were brought to him each week by the men he'd Influenced to work for him. She didn't know where they came from or what happened to the old ones. Her clothes were in tatters, her hair in mats. Some of the church ladies she met tried to help her but Father would not allow any others to touch her. They listened to him. They always did, because they believed in the Word he brought them. They all wanted to ensure their place with the Maker when the end of days came.

SIX

DIFFICULT LESSONS

I SLEPT FITFULLY THAT NIGHT, PLAGUED WITH STRANGE DREAMS. THE FIRST one was a visceral memory. I was in our old church building, and I smelled smoke and heard the children crying. I woke myself up wheezing and coughing. I got up to get a drink of water, trying to put the ugly thoughts out of my head.

The second dream, though, was different, disturbing. I was no stranger to those types of dreams. Eerily, sometimes they came true. I tried to pay attention.

In this dream, I was running through the woods, trying to get away from something or someone. I heard someone behind me, yelling for me to stop, but I keep running, tearing up my legs on the brambles. I entered a small, mist-filled circle in the trees, with benches around a campfire, and saw a shadowy figure entering the circle. I hesitated as the figure came toward me. I couldn't see the face, but for some reason I knew it was a man, and one I needed to avoid but was drawn to at the same time.

I slowed to a walk and raised my arms as if to embrace him.

As he grew closer, I was pulled away. I turned to look back and saw Damien. He opened his mouth to speak, but I turned back to face the shadow man. This time I saw only a bright light. Pain slammed into my chest, knocking the wind out of me.

I woke with a start, unsure what to make of it.

I stumbled out of bed and looked in the mirror. My face was a little pale but I was otherwise okay. My lungs were less tight this morning. I ran a hand through my hair and decided to go straight to my lesson with Morgan. I didn't feel much like company, so I broke open a box of Multigrain Cheerios—again with the favorite brands. This was getting too spooky—and found milk in the fridge. I sat at the counter and looked out the window to my side yard. An empty cottage sat next to mine, and behind it was a vegetable garden bursting with plants of all sizes. Mr. and Mrs. Walden worked together with loving smiles on their faces. It was nice to see such harmony. I hoped I would continue to see that in the other staff.

I thought about the people I'd met last night. Isaac and Jared cracked me up with their diatribes. It made me miss my colleagues at my former school. We used to sit around at lunch and have those great debates. It made our work seem less draining. Moira seemed a bit distant but nice.

Elijah intrigued me. I looked forward to speaking with him again and hoped whatever strangeness I'd felt was just my imagination.

That left Morgan. I had the distinct feeling she wasn't too sure about me. The feeling was mutual. My impression of her was that she possessed powers I would never comprehend. She had presence. Women like her were to be treated with respect. And caution.

I dressed in light cotton capris and a knit tank. I wanted to be ready for the hot Arkansas summer air. I knew I'd have to address my wardrobe issues soon. Just not today. I patted both the cats, who seemed thoroughly uninterested, and stepped out into the sunshine.

Morgan had said to follow the scent of sandalwood, so I walked toward the main building, through the doors into the courtyard and across to the left, where a set of double doors were marked "LIBRARY." They were propped open, emitting a faint scent I assumed to be said sandalwood.

The library was dark, yet inviting. It reminded me of an old university library. Deep mahogany shelves were set in a circular pattern inside the dome-like part of the building. Four steps down led to a seating area with black leather couches and heavy wood tables with lamps for studying. The chairs were upholstered with dark green material that looked velvety soft. Past the seating area, four steps led up to more stacks and an office door which stood open. I took the stairs up to the stacks and wandered toward the office, enjoying the artwork and rare first editions on the shelves. The library was magnificent, and I intended to spend some quality time there. That is, if its mistress would allow it.

Inside the office was a desk and computer and at the rear was another doorway. I called out and received no response but I heard someone moving around. I passed through the office and into a small hallway that wound around to the left and the floor slanted downward. Music similar to Gregorian chants played softly, and I saw a huge candelabra at the end of the hall. The practical side of me thought fire near all these books was not a good idea. That caused me to shiver.

Too close to home.

I called out a weak "hello" and was answered by more chanting.

To the right of the candelabra, there was a large wooden desk covered with leather-bound books and scrolls. To the left was a passage lined with more candles. It was from here where the scent and sounds were coming. I called out again, not expecting an answer as the music was quite loud. I let my footfalls carry and cleared my throat.

The passage opened to a room with a large fireplace and stone walls with no windows. The décor was Gothic, the candles plentiful, and in the center of the room, amidst bay leaves and rose petals, stood Morgan, deep in meditation with her arms raised, her mouth moving silently. She wore a black velvet robe, her feet were bare, and her wild red hair splayed out upon her shoulders. In one hand, she held what appeared to be a ceremonial dagger with a ruby hilt; in the other was a leather-bound book.

I stood motionless, mystified by what I was witnessing.

Minutes went by, and then she lowered her arms and turned to me with a solemn look on her face.

"It's necessary to perform a blessing ceremony prior to our first lesson. I assume Damien didn't tell you what to expect today?"

I shook my head, not trusting myself to speak.

"Cryptic, that man. Always thinking people need to seek and decide for themselves. So be it. Come into the circle, please."

I hesitated. Never before had I taken part in any sort of witchcraft, and I knew that's what she was practicing. Not that I didn't believe; on the contrary. But I wasn't sure if I was ready to take part. I guess there was a first time for everything.

I stepped forward into the stone room. I noticed against one wall there was an altar with various artifacts and beautiful pieces upon it. Morgan waited patiently, and then reached out her hand as I stepped forward, the dagger having been placed into a fold in her robes.

"Native Americans used white sage to purify. In the ancient ways of the Pagans, rose petals symbolize healing, and as you are to be our emotional healer, I thought it important to include them. At the five points, you will find representations of the elements: fire, air, water, earth, and aether, the spirit. All of these elements must be present, and we draw upon their strengths in our work here."

She closed her eyes and began to whisper. I took in everything that was around me and breathed in the scents hanging heavily in the air.

"Delaney, it is important that you be of pure mind during our session today. Is there anything that you need to get off your chest before we begin?"

My voice didn't want to work for me.

"Uh...I'm really not sure. I've never been a part of anything like this before. I'm willing to learn, and I'm trying to keep an open mind, but I'm not a witch." I hoped that wouldn't offend, but I wanted to be honest. If this was my fresh start, then that's what I needed to do.

"Of course you aren't. And if you didn't have an open mind, Damien wouldn't have brought you here. I'm only expecting you to listen and learn today. Take with you what you want from this, but you must at least be open to our ways. Otherwise, I don't see that you will be open to our students. Shall we continue?"

I nodded. Her voice was calm, but I heard skepticism rooted deeply in her tone. There was a part of me that was very interested in what she had to teach. I didn't want to disappoint.

Over the next four hours, she continued her cleansing rituals and explained to me that Havenhart called upon all forces at its power to bring healing and safety to its students and staff. Morgan, I learned, was the librarian and a mystic, who used her powers to help make decisions for the good of the academy. Her "gift" was the power to See many things, including others in pain. She sensed it and their location, including the likely outcome of a situation. Never referring to herself as psychic or a witch, she claimed only to know things and to use that knowledge to help people. She had studied the many religions of the world and used that knowledge to further her cause.

I respected where she was coming from. I could see why Damien insisted on her having an open mind part. Anyone else might have made a run for it after walking in on Morgan's ritual. Instead, I was curious. I hoped to learn much from her. Her main instruction of the day consisted of an explanation of the school calendar, including the important rituals and celebrations observed, the roles we take as faculty members with the students, and again, she impressed upon me the need for confidentiality and security for our students. Restating that they have suffered things humans aren't ever meant to endure and that it is our duty to help them rebuild their lives.

A familiar fire rekindled my passion for working with broken students.

"Morgan, I've been wondering about something ever since Damien first talked to me about 'gifts.' What do you suppose causes these to surface? I mean, I've read about psychic powers being possible when people learn to access more of their brain function or from abnormalities in the brain. I guess that's the scientific explanation. But what role does magic play in all of this?" I hoped she wasn't offended by my question but I needed to know.

I must have piqued her interest because she leaned closer to me. I noted a sparkle in her eye as she spoke.

"Does it have to be one or the other? The mind is fascinating on its own, but when you combine the two, the possibilities are endless. Magic is just really being able to tap into the energy around you. Some can do it, while others don't have or don't recognize the ability."

I really thought about what she said. "It's similar to the Nature versus Nurture debate, then, isn't it? Like, are we capable of certain things instinctually or are they a result of our experiences?"

"Exactly!" she exclaimed. "Take our 'circle of power,' if you want to call it that. Elijah and I derive our power from nature and from calling upon various entities. Damien's powers are mostly organic, intrinsic. I think the way he's able to seek out illnesses in someone is a higher brain functioning, but then when he actually heals, he's able to draw energy from life around him. Nigel," she paused and then laughed, "well, he's an entirely different matter. He's never shared with us how he came to know of his power, and he's not very forthcoming about it in general. He just knows things.

"And you...your energy is similar to Damien's, but since you have no idea when it started or even how to wield it, it's a mystery."

Things were starting to make a bit more sense, the secrecy and security. I was a little unsure about the witchcraft element, but I was willing to give it a chance. I'd done enough reading on my own to understand there was a difference between what you see in the movies and how it was used in real life. I wanted to learn more and hoped Morgan would teach me. As we wrapped up, I asked her a question that had been bothering me.

"Morgan, thank you everything you've taught me today, and I hope to continue learning from you. But I have the sense that you doubt me, or feel as though I'm not meant to be here. Am I correct in this assumption, and if so, how can we get past it?"

She frowned at me and turned away, busying herself tidying up the place. I waited patiently, wondering if this was the right time to have asked her. After a long silence, she put down a stack of books on a table at the back of the circular room.

"I've been at Havenhart Academy for twenty years. It's my home, and I guard my wards and my brethren fiercely. I don't know you," she turned to face me at this point. When she continued, her tone was less harsh. "But I have Seen you. I know you've suffered, but you don't know what to do with your gifts. Damien has faith in you, so I'll take that...for now." She stopped for a moment, putting her hands to her hips. "Has anyone told you what happened to our last guidance counselor?"

"No. Mrs. Walden just mentioned it had been some time since you had someone in that capacity."

She raised an eyebrow. "It is not my story to tell, but I'm sure you'll learn of it soon. Mrs. Sinclair, the headmaster's assistant, will meet you tomorrow morning after breakfast to show you to your office and go over your schedule for the week. I suggest you get some rest before then." She turned away again, and I assumed that was my dismissal. I turned to go, but paused at the entrance to the passage leading out of the room.

"I've taken a huge leap of faith in coming here, to the middle of nowhere, to a job in which I'm dealing with a whole new clientele and I have no idea what to expect. I'm a good counselor, and yes, I have suffered, but no more than anyone else. I have no idea how much spying you guys have done on me, but it appears you know a lot, so you probably know that I give my all to my students—and I'll be damned if I do any less here." I paused, hoping my tone wasn't insolent. I simply wanted to set things straight with Morgan. I respected her, but I wasn't going to be intimidated.

She gave me a reluctant smile. "I don't know anything about spies, Delaney. And yes, I do know you give your all and that's what I'm expecting of you. Get some rest. You will need it. The students arrive in two days." With that, she turned back to her work, and I hurried out of her office and out of the library, feeling a little less welcome.

My energy was nearly drained as I trudged up the steps to my cottage. I walked straight to my bed, where I flopped down, fully clothed, and took a much-needed nap. At some point, Ramses had climbed up next to me to nuzzle my neck, but I didn't move. At a much later point, I rolled over and realized that the grumbling I was hearing wasn't him purring, it was my stomach telling me I hadn't eaten lunch and needed nourishment.

I took a quick shower to wake myself up and slid into a light sundress. My summer tan remained, and I wasn't too concerned about my tattoos showing after what I'd seen in the dining room the previous night. Isaac had wide-gauge holes in both ears and wore a thick coat of guyliner. Jared had full sleeves and wore huge silver rings on both hands. Definitely not a crowd I worried about standing out in.

Dinner that night featured a repeat of the Isaac and Jared show, with Moira sitting there patiently, listening and eating quietly. Skye and Jackson conversed about the importance of art education for students who've experienced trauma. Jackson, I learned, had completed coursework in art therapy, and I looked forward to speaking to him more about that in the future, but I remained quiet throughout dinner. He looked at me with that intense gaze several times during the meal, but Skye kept his attention for the most part, and I was able to get by with a few "aha, you don't says".

I looked over to Morgan's table and saw that Damien had joined her and Elijah. My mood lifted a bit...until I looked closer. The three of them were deep in conversation. Damien appeared to be disagreeing with Morgan, shaking his head and gesturing angrily with his hands.

When she noticed I was looking, she touched his hand and he fell silent. She nodded at me, and then turned to speak to Elijah.

So much for confidentiality, I thought. I was sure she was telling him about my comments earlier, and he probably thought I had been rude and arrogant with her. I got busy with my food, wanting nothing more than to be out of that room.

I excused myself, bussed my utensils, and walked out the doors.

It was twilight, and the insect population of the campus was singing their hearts out to each other. I remembered hearing the cicadas in Iowa in the summertime and how it took a while to get used to the sound at night when I was trying to go to sleep. I hadn't noticed it the night before, probably because I had been exhausted from traveling, but was sure tonight I wouldn't fare so well.

Everyone else was still eating dinner, and I walked slowly to my cabin, smelling Mrs. Walden's flowers as I walked, trying to clear my head of all the accusatory thoughts: Why didn't I keep my mouth shut with Morgan? Why did I have to blow it on my second day? When were they going to ask me to leave?

I entered my cottage but felt restless. I called James and arranged to meet him on Friday night, giving me something to look forward to at the end of my first week. I put on some Bob Dylan and tried to finish putting away my things. Really, I was just moving about aimlessly.

After a couple of hours, I gave up. I grabbed a Diet Coke out of the fridge and stepped out onto my back step. It was near eight o'clock and starting to get dark. The lights were out next door at Skye's. I wondered how her day had gone. She'd met with Justin, the tech guy, for her orientation. I doubted there were any candles and bay leaves in her lessons. I chuckled to myself at that thought.

I glanced the other direction, toward the carriage house. One of the bays was open and a light was on. I hadn't been over to see the horses yet, and I didn't see anything wrong with taking a stroll. I stepped off my porch and onto the path.

The carriage house was about two hundred yards from my cottage and to the right rear of the headmaster's house. I had an appointment with him tomorrow after lunch, and I looked forward to finally meeting this mystery man. The insect brigade was growing louder and louder as the evening turned to night. I neared the carriage house and heard metal tinkering and horses shuffling and whinnying softly in their stalls. A male voice cursed colorfully just as I was about to turn the corner. I giggled in surprise.

The surprise turned to shock at what I saw inside.

Part of the stables had been converted to a garage. Hay was stacked against one corner and a classic 1965 Mustang, fully restored, was parked in the rear. Leaning over a black Indian motorcycle was a tall, well-built man in a tight black t-shirt and frayed Levi's, with black motorcycle boots rounding out the attire. His back was to me, his muscles outlined clearly under the shirt, and his dark wavy hair was pulled back in a ponytail. He had grease on his arms and was bleeding from a cut on his elbow. As I was about to turn the corner and sneak out, he cursed again and threw down a wrench. I barked out a laugh.

"Your bike not cooperating with you?" I asked in a joking tone.

The man ran his hand back over his hair before turning to face me. When he did, my knees about collapsed under me, and I had to steady myself against the doorway.

It was Damien, minus the tweed and tie for sure, but those bold green eyes left no question. He didn't seem too pleased to have company. I immediately regretted my snooping.

"I'm sorry. I didn't mean to interrupt. I saw the light and just wanted to visit the horses. I'll leave you alone." I turned to leave but he called out to me.

"Wait. I thought everyone had turned in for the night. I wasn't expecting company. You're correct, however. This is quite an uncooperative motorbike. I'm about to chuck it in for the night. Come in. Let me show you around." While his words were polite, there was nothing inviting in his tone.

"Are you sure? I really didn't mean to bother you," I said before entering the garage.

"No, no, it's fine. Come in. I'll show you the horses." He closed up his toolbox and placed it on the shelf inside the doorway. He picked up a bandanna and wiped off his hands.

"You're bleeding, there on your elbow. Is there a first-aid kit in here? I'll clean it for you."

He grimaced and threw the bandanna down. He reached up on a higher shelf and pulled down a white box with a red cross on the front. I approached him and started to reach for the box.

"I'm fine, it's just a scratch," he said impatiently.

"It is, but it's in an awkward spot. Let me clean it and put a Band-Aid on it. It won't hurt a bit." I smiled weakly, hoping he wouldn't be too pissed off I'd interrupted his temper tantrum. He handed me the box and turned around to lean back on the workbench, offering me his elbow.

I took out an alcohol pad and removed it from the package. The cut was about two inches long and was still seeping a bit of blood. He flinched when I touched his arm and then inhaled deeply, closing his eyes. I wiped off the blood with the alcohol pad then cleaned the wound as best I could. I found a large Band-Aid and covered it up.

"There. Delaney Nightingale, at your service." I smiled as I gathered up the wrappings and looked for a garbage can. I found one on the floor next to the shelves. When I turned back to face him, he was looking at me seriously.

"I'm sorry you had to witness my little conniption fit. I've been having trouble with this bike for a while is all. Vincent will have to have a look. He can fix anything." He looked back at the bike and shook his head. "What are you doing out? You should be getting your rest." He seemed irritated and I sensed that there was something more to his foul mood than a broken motorbike. His brow furrowed deeply. I didn't care for his tone.

"I was just a bit restless, that's all. I'll go and let you have your peace. Sorry to disturb you." I turned to go, but he grabbed my arm.

"Delaney," he said sternly. He turned me to face him, his expression intense. I didn't know if he was going to pull me to him or push me away. I don't think *he* knew which he wanted to do more. He just stood there holding my arm for a moment, and then released me to take a step back. He ran his hands over his hair again.

"I don't mean to be rude. It's just that I…"

He paused and took a step toward me again.

I stood there uncertain, wanting desperately to time warp back to my porch and forget this whole thing had ever happened.

He brought his hand up to my face and hesitated, then touched my hair. He frowned, his jaw muscle working as he clenched his teeth together.

"Damien, what is it?"

I wished I had a damn decoder ring for those eyes. If only I knew what he was thinking, how he was feeling. Was it anger? And if so, was it directed at me or himself…or something or someone else?

His hand lowered and his knuckles brushed my cheek. "Delaney, I want you to know that I am very glad you're here. You are going to do great things for our students. Our staff is going to benefit from having an experienced counselor to guide them in their endeavors with the students. I pray you'll come to understand and accept our ways." His voice was steady and calm, giving away nothing of his feelings.

It was my turn to frown now. My hands came to my hips, my ire growing. "Did Morgan tell you something about our session, is that why you're angry with me? Because I'm sorry if you're disappointed, but you didn't give me much to work with before I arrived. I'm doing the best I can." Here they wanted me to have an open mind, but they sure as hell didn't seem willing to give me a chance.

He reached out with his other hand and took hold of my right one. "Delaney, I am not angry with you. If anything, I'm angry with myself for not seeing things clearly. Having you here is a blessing for the school, but a bit of a complication for me."

I pulled out of his grasp at that statement.

"A complication? Is this why I hardly heard from you after your visit?" I shook my head. "I'm sorry if you're having regrets, but you brought me out here, and I intend to do my job. If that's a problem for you—"

I broke off when he winced. He turned and sat down on a hay bale, dropping his head in his hands.

I was frozen to my spot.

He lifted his head and locked those green eyes on me as if urging me to take him deadly serious. "I have no regrets about bringing you here, Delaney. Understand that right now. My only regret is that my time with you has been brief, and not spent in a manner in which I would prefer."

He stood and walked toward me again. His movements backed me up until I bumped into the workbench. He placed his hands on the bench on either side of me, getting all up in my space.

"I want your presence here to be a benefit to the students and staff. I want you to use your gift to heal people." He leaned closer, his face softening. "The difficulty, for me, is realizing that I really want to have you all to myself."

It was my turn to flinch. I searched his face for his intentions, not believing what I'd just heard.

"But...you never called. And since I've been here, you've been so—"

"Formal. Precisely. I don't know whether it's wise to proceed with you. So I've kept my distance, even though it's pained me to do so."

My lungs tightened, but the lack of oxygen wasn't from asthma. He stood so close. A bead of sweat dripped down the back of my dress, pooling at my lower back. My skin felt awake, alive, as though every particle of energy that passed between us danced across my flesh.

"So, what now?"

He had been ever present in my mind, true, but I didn't want this to be a problem. A relationship gone sour would be just the thing to do it. "I don't want to cause problems for you, and I certainly don't want them myself. This is my chance to make things right in my life."

We stood there looking at each other, and then he pulled me into an embrace, breathing in the scent of my hair as if I were a scintillating meal. I rested my head on his chest and was consumed by the power emanating from him. Not just physical power, which he had plenty of, based on the feel of him under his shirt. But his spiritual energy flowed through his body.

I thought back to the rituals Morgan had done that morning. I shivered, and he pulled me in closer, his fingers digging into my back.

I didn't want the embrace to end. When he spoke, his voice was husky.

"I want you to be happy here and to have everything you require. I will not let my feelings for you interfere with that." He pulled back and looked down at me.

I wanted to protest. I wanted him to hold me like that forever. I wanted him to kiss me, dammit. But I knew this had to stop, for both of our sakes.

I took a deep breath and narrowed my eyes at him. "Well, don't stay away from me. I would hate that. Do what you need to do, but don't stay away." I didn't know what else to say. He was already slipping away from me, closing that door.

He smiled a sad smile. "If you hadn't noticed, it's quite a small affair here. I won't be far. Our paths will cross."

I tried to return his smile but it just didn't want to come. Why was I mourning the loss of something I never had?

"Let me walk you back," he said softly.

"Actually, I think it's better if I go alone. Good night, Damien."

He nodded in understanding. If he walked me back, it would have been even harder to separate. I turned and walked out the door and kept going straight up the path to my house, only looking back when I reached my rear door. His silhouette in the doorway of the garage had my resolve fading fast. His gaze was all that had followed me home.

Why did I have to walk away? Why couldn't I have had my cake and eat it, too? The perfect job? A new love interest?

As I stepped inside and closed the door behind me, I knew that I had to accept the truth. I was here to do a job. The kids were going to need my full attention. I couldn't afford to be distracted and lovesick after Damien.

God, I hated making the smart choice. Especially after seeing him in those jeans. Ugh. I needed another cold shower. There's something about seeing a man out of his element that just...

I had the same nightmare again that night, but this time I saw Damien as he was dressed last night in the woods before the bright light hit me in the chest. I awoke drenched in sweat and wheezing.

I grabbed for my inhaler and took two puffs. I closed my eyes and counted to five before blowing each of them out slowly. It took a good five minutes for me to catch my breath. I sipped water from the glass next to my bed and thankfully the coughing fit stopped. I knew I wouldn't be asthma-free forever, but anytime I had an episode it worried me that I would sink down into that hole again; the hole filled with drugs, nebulizers, and misery.

THE NEXT STOP WAS FLORIDA, ANOTHER SMALL TOWN WITH ANOTHER congregation to be Influenced by Father. The young girl was growing increasingly weary, and she feared she wouldn't have the strength to wait for her Protector. Father pushed her for details of what she Saw, threatening to hurt her if she didn't tell him something.

"There's no one left to save you now, girl. You must put your faith in the Maker to guide you." His eerie preacher voice made her cringe, inwardly of course, or there'd be another beating. Father was handy with a belt.

Finally she Saw the moment of her own salvation. She only needed to hang on a little longer...and give Father enough rope to hang himself with. When the police were just about to catch up to them, Father lost it and beat her unconscious. Thankfully she knew it would be the last time...

SEVEN

RESPONSIBILITIES

AFTER A SHOWER AND A GOOD DOSE OF METAL TO START MY MORNING, I decided to join the others for breakfast, thinking some company would take my mind off things. My lungs hurt and I was still coughing, but no wheezing. After putting on another sundress, I left for the commons. Either I was late or early, or the other staff wasn't much for breakfast. Jackson sat alone, deeply engrossed in his scrambled eggs and bacon. I smiled and thought now was as good a time as any to get some answers from this guy who seemed to know so much about me.

After serving myself, I headed over to his table. "Mind if I join you and your breakfast?"

He jumped at the sound of my voice, and then a huge grin spread across his face. He stood up, grabbing a swig of OJ to wash down a huge mouthful of eggs.

"Delaney. I'm so glad you're here. Sit down."

This was a much more pleasant invitation than I'd received last night in the barn.

"Thank you. Did I miss the morning rush? I thought seven-thirty would be a busy time here."

He smiled, trying to finish chewing before speaking. I appreciated that. I wasn't quite ready to see eggs fly while he spoke.

"Actually, we're still on summer hours, I reckon. Most of the others are still in bed. We had a late-night jam session. Jared, Isaac and I have a little thing going. You'll have to come hear us sometime." He smiled hopefully.

"I love live music. What do you play?"

"I'm a keyboard man, myself. Took piano lessons as a boy. I play a little guitar. Jared plays bass and Isaac plays drums. Damien sits in on guitar sometimes when he's not busy with academy business." He said the last with a hint of disdain. I wondered what he might have against Damien.

"How 'bout you, Counselor? Are you a passive or active listener?"

I laughed at his counselor humor. "I love to sing, but I'm not very good. Maybe a step above shower singer, one step below karaoke? I know a lot of songs. Where do you guys play?"

"In here, over there." He pointed to the little stage where I had seen instruments set up before. I looked forward to hearing them play. It would be a welcome distraction.

"A few of us were headed into town tonight for some drinks. Think you might want to come? There's a great bar in Eureka Springs with tapas and dancing if you're up for it." Again with the hopeful smile. I wanted to be friends with Jackson, but certainly didn't want him to think there was more to it.

"I'll see if Skye wants to join us, too, if you don't mind. She could probably use the distraction as well. Orientation was a bit heavy yesterday. It would be nice to blow off some steam."

"Ah, you mean your session with Morgan the Mystical. Don't let that bog you down too much. She's a bit heavy, but she means well. She was really close to our last counselor."

He lost a bit of his smile and his face went dark. I remembered Morgan told me the previous counselor's story wasn't hers to tell. Who was I going to get a straight answer from about anything around here?

"She mentioned it had been a while since there was a counselor here. What happened?" I hoped I didn't sound too eager, but I wanted to know

"Turner left last fall, uh...after some incidents happened on campus. So, we're leaving around seven tonight. You in?" He started to gather up his plates. "Sorry to run off but I've got to inventory my art supplies so I can head into Fayetteville tomorrow to restock. The van will meet us right outside the gates, so don't be late." He paused as if he wanted to say more, then ducked his head with a frown and headed for the door, calling over his shoulder. "Have a good one, Delaney. See you later."

Well, damn. More mysteries.

"Enjoy your breakfast, Delaney?" I turned to see Mr. Walden coming out of the kitchen with a towel in his hands.

"Yes, thank you. I'm so spoiled here. If I'm not careful I'm going to gain fifty pounds." We both laughed at that, and he came over to the table.

"It's so good to have you here. You off to meet with Mrs. Sinclair? She's no-nonsense, that one, but you'll never find a better assistant." He started cleaning the tables. I saw the care he had put into this place.

"Mr. Walden you've done an amazing job with this place. I feel as if I'm back in the fifties. And thanks again for breakfast."

"Please, call me George. You're makin' me feel like an old fart."

We both laughed. "Old? No way. I bet you could take any of these young guys."

He flexed a biceps at me and I cracked up.

I cleared my dishes and walked out of the cool commons into the muggy August morning. I was proud of myself that I hadn't fallen apart over the heat. No one was going to call me a California weather wimp.

The campus seemed to have much more life to it today. Workmen prepared the classrooms for the students, waxing the floors and dusting the furniture. Mrs. Walden worked in the courtyard, planting some new flowers to welcome the students.

"Mrs. Walden, you need a hand?"

She looked up from her work and smiled warmly. "Thank you, Delaney, but I believe you have a busy couple of days ahead of you. Perhaps Saturday, you and I could work on the flower beds behind the student dormitory?"

"Sounds great. I want to get busy with my green thumb lessons."

The thought of having something to occupy my weekend made me feel better. Busy was good. It kept me from thinking too much. I waved to her as I walked into the front offices of the building.

Student Affairs was located in the main building across the courtyard from the library. All student services were located here, including

Damien's office. Upstairs, I found Mrs. Sinclair at a workstation in front of a huge picture window that looked out onto the front of the property. She appeared to be in her mid-fifties, with shiny black hair streaked with gray and cut into a smart bob, wearing a businesslike skirt suit in eggplant. No-nonsense was definitely the impression I got from her, and I did not want to disappoint. I stepped up to her desk and waited while she finished a phone call.

"Hello, Miss Frost. It is so nice to finally meet you." She had a warm voice, which soothed my nerves immediately. I offered my hand, and she took it in both of hers, giving it a squeeze. I had a feeling I had just met an ally.

"We have a lot to cover today, but I wanted to make sure that your arrival has been smooth so far?"

There was a part of me that wanted to hug her and reveal all my insecurities and worries. She had that fix-it mom vibe going on, and all at once I missed my own mother desperately.

"It's been...fine. I feel a little foreign here. I'll be better once I get to work."

She smiled knowingly. "I know this was a big step for you, coming all the way across country to a place you'd never even seen. All that can be discombobulating. I'm here to make this comfortable for you, so whatever I can do, please tell me. I took the liberty of unpacking the boxes you sent for your office. I hope you like the way I've set up the space. Feel free to make any changes you want, and I can certainly get you anything you need." She led the way and we walked down a hallway and turned into the first doorway on the right.

My office, at last. A genuinely satisfied grin spread across my face. Like Mrs. Sinclair's workstation, I, too, had a large picture window that looked out over the courtyard of the building. Natural light was plentiful. There was a couch along one wall with a low table in front of it, and a big comfy chair directly across. My desk had a computer and space for files. A bookcase next to the couch held my tools of the trade—reference books meant to guide the practitioner in helping folks with any number of ailments to the soul—along with a few tomes I didn't recognize.

Mrs. Sinclair gave me space to take it all in. I realized she was still holding my hand, and I looked down at her and smiled. Just like my mom, she was a good six inches shorter than me, maybe more without those heels on. But I had no doubt she was able to hold her own.

"It's absolutely perfect. Did you decorate this yourself?"

She nodded proudly. "I knew you would want to make your students feel comfortable and what better way than with a big cozy couch? Our last counselor was very formal, but I get a much more personal feeling from you."

She'd just given me an opening I couldn't resist.

"Mrs. Sinclair, can you tell me why the previous counselor left?"

She smiled sadly and walked over to sit in the chair.

"It was a rather unfortunate turn of events that led to Mr. Chance's departure. He'd been with us for about five years, but had never truly been satisfied here. This past school year, he had some unsettling interactions with a student and determined he was no longer an asset to the academy. He left after the first semester, and we've been without a counselor ever since. He was a very nice man, but I don't think he quite accepted what it is we do here. Mr. Preston has been trying to cover his duties," and here she winked at me conspiratorially, "but I don't think he's quite comfortable dealing with all the needs of the students, particularly the young ladies with boy troubles."

We both chuckled at that. She ran her hand absently along the arm of the chair.

I was tickled that this wonderful space was all mine. I crossed the room and came to a halt in front of the bookcase. I looked at the titles there, including those that weren't from my collection, and noticed a few that looked similar to the books I'd seen in Morgan's office.

Before I had a chance to ask, Mrs. Sinclair rose from her seat and joined me. "Yes, Mr. Chance was a mystic as well. He came from powerful magic, but even that cannot always prepare you for what you'll face in life. He was a good healer, and we all miss him." She smiled at me. "But I think you're exactly what we need."

I appreciated her acceptance and confidence. Again, I wanted to do my best.

"I hope you're right. So, this is the place where it all happens. Do the students have to make appointments or can they just come in as needed? And how about other duties? Damien…er, Mr. Preston told me there might be other assignments?"

She laughed. "You're welcome to set up appointments however you prefer. I understand you're a hands-on professional. I assume you'll want to be open to students however they need. As for other duties, we're also in need of an elective teacher, and I noticed in your resume that you've taught both Sociology and Psychology before. Are you open to teaching a class?"

I beamed at her. "Absolutely. I love teaching those subjects. I even packed my materials."

She seemed just as pleased. "I knew you were perfect for us. Your class will be on Wednesdays and Fridays, then, in the classroom adjacent to the library. Miss Forrester, the librarian, has some textbooks in her depository. If you choose to use them, you can get those from her later. Now, let's go over your caseload, shall we?"

She had brought a file folder with her containing a list of the students and pulled up an additional chair to the desk. I put out my hand to touch hers.

"Mrs. Sinclair, I don't mean to be rude, but I really prefer to not go over my students' files before I meet them. I prefer to form my own relationships with them, if you don't mind."

She nodded affirmatively. "I only wanted to offer. Of course, you may choose to look at whatever information you want. I have a list of students who need counseling services, but I took care not to include any of their personal information. Will that suffice?"

"That sounds good. I just want to start off without any preconceived notions of why they're here. They'll tell me when they're ready."

Once again, she smiled at me like a proud soccer mom, and I was nearly convinced I could do this.

"All one hundred and fifty students have files in your cabinets, and Mr. Chance left his notes from their meetings. You may find that you need the information down the line, but I understand your wish for a clean slate. The list I have here is simply names, contact information and schedules for all of our students.

"We have children here from ages twelve to eighteen. They all take courses in Language Arts, Mathematics, Science, Technology, Physical Education and Social Studies. They may also choose courses in the Arts and Music building, or to work on various projects. Some of the older students participate in work-study with the academy. Students are all expected to put in time each week cleaning the dorm, the cafeteria, or working on grounds-keeping tasks. How about a quick tour of the student facilities before lunch? The headmaster has requested that you join him for a private lunch in his office, will that work for you?"

My head was spinning with all of the information she'd just shared. She smiled that knowing smile again and took my hand.

"Come, let's see the rest the academy has to offer."

We visited the classrooms in the main building, and then passed through the gateway opposite the dining room toward the Tech Lab. The Math, Science and Technology courses were taught there. Skye worked in this building and, sure enough, we saw her setting up her classroom. She was working with a man whom I assumed was Justin, her orientation partner. Mrs. Sinclair informed me that Justin, or Mr. Chan, was the department chair. They smiled and waved at us as we passed. Three teachers made up the science department, and she said I would meet them Friday. Students began arriving tomorrow for orientation and classes would begin the following Monday.

I smiled as we entered the Arts building and immediately noticed all of the student work posted in the entry hall. I'd seen galleries back home that were much less sophisticated than the work here. The students had completed miraculous pieces of art. I was beyond impressed. The Arts building included a gallery, and a theater used for performances as well as to show cinema releases for the staff and students, Mrs. Sinclair explained. She was quite the tour guide. Elijah Black, she told me, was the chair of the Arts department, teaching music lessons to the students.

There were classrooms and labs for each of the mediums, including a ceramics studio, in which we found a shirtless Jackson working a pottery wheel. My jaw dropped as I watched him work from the doorway. Clay was splattered on his chest and abdomen. He didn't hear our approach over the din of his music. I approved of the choice. *Appetite for Destruction*, however, was not your typical art school soundtrack.

Mrs. Sinclair was still talking, and I realized I had missed the last few sentences. Jackson looked up at that moment, and my face flushed as I realized that I had been admiring more than his pottery skills.

"Hello, ladies. Care to get your hands dirty?" He was all smiles as he wiped his hands on his jeans and came over to us.

"Jackson, I'm really impressed with the work your students have displayed. You've set up quite a program here."

He seemed genuinely pleased with my compliment and, as he approached, I was embarrassed to see Mrs. Sinclair looking intently at both of us.

"Good morning, Mrs. Sinclair. Did Delaney tell you we went to college together?"

She nodded and smiled. "I remember you sharing that. Did you two know each other?" she asked me, smiling again.

"Um, we had friends in common and shared some dining experiences…" Jackson cut in, laughing. "Yeah, she doesn't remember me. Upper classman and all. You know how it is." He actually winked at Mrs. Sinclair, and she laughed up at him. It seemed his charm worked on all the ladies.

"We'll let you get back to work, Mr. Howe. Shall we?" She gestured for me to walk ahead of her. I smiled back at Jackson.

"See you tonight, Delaney."

His anticipation and excitement were evident in his smile. I needed to be careful around him, especially after that display. I had one thing to say for Havenhart Academy, it certainly wasn't lacking in the attractive male department.

We left the Arts building and continued in a loop. The student dormitories were housed in a large brick building with an activity center in the middle and two blocks of rooms on either side. Mrs. Sinclair informed me that a woman named Marcia Gray was in charge of the girls' dorm, and that Jackson was the Head Resident of the male dorm. He assisted Miss Gray with student activities. Marcia also taught dance in the Arts building. I looked forward to meeting her and intended to offer my assistance.

That completed our tour, with the exception of the athletic facilities, which I figured I'd check out at a later date. I knew there was a weight room with fitness equipment that was open for students and staff to use. There was even an indoor pool. I looked forward to starting an exercise routine. My body craved it.

We walked back to the Student Affairs office and I felt overwhelmed but pleased.

"Miss Frost, I know this has been a lot to process, but I want you to know that I'm here to help you in whatever way I can. The headmaster has put me at your disposal for the time being while you get your bearings, and I'm glad to assist. As I said before, you're just what we need here at Havenhart."

"Thank you, Mrs. Sinclair, for everything. You have really put me at ease."

She smiled at me. "I would prefer you to call me Diana, if that's okay. We'll be working closely together, and I feel no need for the formality."

"Thank you, Diana. Then it's Delaney, please. You've been so kind to me today. I really appreciate all of your support. I hope I live up to your expectations."

She patted my shoulder and we headed back up the stairs.

"I have no doubt you will. It's in the cards." She left me with a knowing look. I smiled suspiciously at her, and she laughed as she walked away. Guess I didn't have to wonder what her gift was.

I looked forward to having some time in my office before my lunch date with the headmaster. I needed to let the morning's events sink in.

I stepped out of my office and saw a women's lounge two doors down, so I went in there to freshen up. I splashed some cold water on my face and ran my fingers through my hair. I looked at myself in the mirror...and paused.

Ever since I'd been ill, the dark circles under my eyes had been prominent and my skin had a yellowish cast. Even with a summer tan, I'd looked rough. But now, looking at myself in the mirror, my skin was clear and there was only the faintest trace of darkness around my eyes.

I thought back to my conversation with Damien before I came. He said I would likely notice that my health improved when I arrived. Come to think of it, I hadn't had to use my inhaler quite as much over the past two days as I had been the past few months, with the exception of after those horrible dreams. I felt stronger than I had in years. I don't know if it was the academy, or just the prospect of doing the work I'd always wanted to do, but I felt great. I needed that to continue.

I heard Diana laughing with someone when I left the lounge. I turned the corner and smiled when I saw a dapper-looking gentleman standing with her. She looked over his shoulder and smiled back at me. When he turned around, I was delighted to see he had a bushy moustache and circular glasses. He truly could have stepped out of a Victorian novel, complete with a gold pocket watch attached to his vest. He bowed to me as I approached and spoke in a thick British accent.

"Miss Frost, I presume. How delightful to finally make your acquaintance in person." He took my hand and kissed the back of it, making me blush.

"Headmaster, thank you so much for bringing me here to your academy. I'm so excited for this opportunity."

He offered his arm, and I took it as he led me the opposite way down the hall to a set of double doors I presumed was his office. He was taller than me, and quite stout with a round belly. His skin looked as though it had spent too much time in the sun unprotected and his hair was a bit unruly.

"Please come in and make yourself comfortable. Violet will pour you a drink. It's Diet Coke you prefer, isn't it?" He was such a gentleman.

A woman came forward wearing a uniform and carrying a tray with two salads and fresh-baked bread and oil. There was a table and chairs to one side, and a sitting area with huge leather couches to the other. His desk was at the rear of the office in front of a large window. It faced toward the front of the building, as Diana's did. The décor was sophisticated art collector meets hunter with trophies. All that was missing was the bearskin rug and rifle over the fireplace. There were black-and-white photographs adorning the walls, along with antique weapons from around the world. A large oil painting of the main building of the academy was mounted above the table. I was admiring it when he came to join me at the table.

He took his cloth napkin and placed it daintily in his lap, motioning for me to dig into my salad. My mouth watered, and I realized I was quite hungry after the tour we'd taken that morning.

"I take it you enjoyed your morning with Diana? She's priceless, is she not?"

I nodded in agreement and reached for my drink as he raised his in a toast.

"Here's to a bright new addition to our family. May you find peace and fulfillment here with us." We clinked glasses, and he had a twinkle in his eye as he took a drink.

"So please tell me what you think so far. Have you been provided with everything you need? Do you have any questions of me?" His smile was inviting, so I took him up on his offer.

"Everything has been wonderful so far, and yes I do have some questions. I was wondering if you'd tell me just what was involved in your background check? I'm finding that you folks know a lot more about me than what was on my resume." I took a deep breath, hoping I hadn't overstepped my bounds.

The twinkle in his eye remained as he removed his napkin and wiped at his moustache. "Miss Frost, tell me, have you ever believed in something so strongly that you were willing to sacrifice everything to see it come to fruition? I ask that knowing the answer, but I want to hear it from you."

I put down my fork to steady myself.

"I felt that way about my former school. I gave everything to that program because I believed so strongly in what we were doing. Unfortunately, those in charge didn't support our mission. And yes, you do already know this." I looked over at him, waiting for his response.

"And tell me, Miss Frost. How did you feel when you learned they were considering closing your program?"

I froze, my hands sitting clammy in my lap. How was I supposed to answer that?

"I believe you lost a piece of your soul," he continued. "That's why you have been ill, is it not? When you pledge your entire being to helping those in need, it takes its toll. If you are not supported, there is no way you can remain whole."

I stared in disbelief. He was right. I wondered exactly how much he knew about my life. When I spoke, I didn't trust my voice. "This past year has been difficult. They warned me in September that budget cuts likely meant the program would be closed. I was devastated." I looked down at the table, feeling way more vulnerable than I wanted.

I began again. "Headmaster, how is it that you seem to know so much about my personal life?" I was afraid to know the answers, but I felt compelled to put it all on the table.

"Please, Miss Frost, join me in the sitting area. You have met with Miss Forrester, correct? How was your experience with her?"

I rose and walked over to the couches, sitting across from him. "She told me that she can see and feel peoples' pain." While I told myself I was open to all that she had shared with me, I remained somewhat skeptical. "Wait—are you telling me that she literally *saw* me?"

He nodded, waiting for my reaction.

"How can that be? I'm trying to be open to all of this, I really am, but how did she know about me?"

The headmaster smiled affectionately and leaned across to place a hand on top of mine. "Delaney, do you remember back in school being part of a program called 'peer counseling'?"

I nodded, my unease growing.

"Your instructor, Mr. Rodriguez, was a dear friend of mine, may he rest in peace. I have a network of contacts all over the world who connect me with promising young people who may either make good candidates for students or for my staff. Mr. Rodriguez spoke highly of your skills, including sharing some stories of students you helped…as well as details about the fire you survived as a young teenager."

He paused to let that sink in.

Hearing him speak of the fire gave me chills. I avoided thinking about it. It was still too painful after all these years. Although the room temperature was comfortable, I shivered.

The headmaster continued. "There were numerous stories from your school years that led us to keep an eye on you. We worked with our contacts at Graceland, as well, to observe from afar how you were progressing. Miss Forrester's mother, who was here before her, had been made aware of you after the fire. It was through Morgan's gift that we learned of the closing of your program and the pain it was causing you.

"It is our policy that we can never intervene in situations, only be there to assist in the recovery. You showed such strength and resiliency, completing your studies and then becoming a competent teacher and then a highly skilled counselor. We watched as you did your internship at the children's burn unit as well..."

He handed me a tissue and continued speaking. I didn't even realize I had been crying softly while listening to him detail my history of misery.

"Delaney, I am so very proud of all that you accomplished and grateful that fate has brought you to us. We were deathly afraid that we might lose you if things continued to deteriorate with your health. I hope you will view our watching from afar as coming from a place of admiration, and nothing sinister. I would truly understand if you were angry. Please know that we never intend to invade one's privacy. On the contrary, confidentiality is a principle we hold in the highest esteem. The only members of the academy who know these details of your life are myself, Miss Forrester, Mr. Black, Mr. Howe because he was in college around the same time, and Mr. Preston."

My heart sank as he added Damien's name to the list. Strangely, I was all right with the others knowing, even Morgan. But for Damien to be aware of my failure...

"The five of us make up a sort of spiritual guidance team for the academy. Our gifts are used to create a conduit from which we can do the work we're so desperately needed for. With Morgan's sight, Damien's ability to heal, Elijah's gift of harmony, Jackson's connections, and my networking, we've been able to bring people here who can benefit from what we do.

"That is my life's work. I am pleased with all that we have accomplished, but there is always work to be done, always children who need saving and rebuilding. That's why we've watched you, and that is why we have brought you here now. I hope you will see our actions as needed for this end result. We don't use our knowledge for ill-gotten gains. Please trust me on that. Our integrity is what we stand on."

I was speechless. Of course I was uneasy with the knowledge and power they had over me. I was completely vulnerable in his presence, and though my instincts told me he could be trusted, I had experienced too much negativity in my life to be able to accept it without suspicion.

"I understand why you've done what you have. But my business is mine. I just want to do my job, do good work with the kids. That's why I'm here, not because of any 'gift' you believe I have. I don't know what you expect me to think about all this." My hands shook in my lap.

He leaned back on the couch and crossed an ankle over his knee. "I accept that it will take time for you to fully realize the powers you possess. I understand completely if you feel betrayed by our practices, and would also understand if you choose to leave. But you and I both know how wonderful you are with children, how gifted a counselor you are. I would do *anything* to care for my students here." I saw the determination in his face but didn't sense any menace or ulterior motives.

I stood and walked to the doorway, needing some space.

"Take the rest of the afternoon to think about what you want, Miss Frost. We are here to teach you, coach you, support you and guide you as to how to use your gift to further your purposes. I am patient, and you will come to me when you are ready, of that I am sure. But know this— you will do great things here at Havenhart. It is your destiny. Do not fear what you have been given. It's a gift from the gods."

He smiled gently. He seemed pretty confident I wasn't going anywhere.

"Can you feel the peace here, Miss Frost? I have worked my entire life to create a safe place for the world's broken children. It is my calling, and I take that very seriously. I have never let anything or anyone get in my way, and I never intend to." He smiled another fatherly smile.

After all that we had just discussed, the rational side of me said I should leave, that I shouldn't be so comfortable with this man. But deep inside, I knew he was exactly what he said...and I was going to trust him, even if that meant the possibility of getting hurt. If I didn't, there was no way this was going to work—and in that moment, I was determined for all I was worth that this *was* going to work.

THEY TRAVELED BY NIGHT AND DURING THE DAY THEY STAYED IN SEEDY MOTELS. There were constantly shady characters in and out of the room, most of them eyeing her hungrily, but Father assured he was the only one to touch her.

Money was exchanged, deals made, all in the hopes of getting Father's debts paid off. But it was never enough. Father could never have enough money or power. He was sending all of it...somewhere. The girl wasn't able to See whatever Father was planning after Florida. He had something big in the works, but he no longer shared any details with her.

"One day, I will have them all at my feet. I will have them all begging for my mercies. You and I, girl, will lead them into the Light."

There was an ominous tone to his plans, and the young girl could no longer See what was to come for him. She was more determined than ever to get away from him and longed to reach out to her Protector. If only she could draw people to her as Father could. But her gift was only that of Sight. She Saw what was to come but was powerless to influence it.

EIGHT

DISTRACTIONS

I FELT RAW WHEN I LEFT THE HEADMASTER'S OFFICE. I ASSURED HIM I WAS fine, but too many truths from my past were laid out for me to deal with in one meeting. I was disturbed by how much they knew about me.

I walked back to my cottage in a daze. I passed the Waldens and gave them a quick wave, hoping they wouldn't stop to chat. When I got inside, I closed the door quickly behind me and pulled the shades down. I sat on my sofa and hugged my knees to my chest and just rocked. A dull ache grew in my chest and chewed on my lungs, trying to get out. I had no time for a breakdown now.

Ramses meowed loudly, pulling me from my thoughts. I don't know how long I sat there. Eventually I got up and went into the bathroom. My eyes were bloodshot and any makeup I had put on that morning was gone. I washed my face and then stepped out into the kitchen. There was a knock on my door and a voice called out.

"Delaney, it's Skye. Open up. I know you're in there. It's almost time to go to town."

I trudged over and opened the door. The bright afternoon sun hurt my eyes and my attempt to smile appeared to be a grimace. Based on Skye's reaction, I must have looked like shit.

"Delaney, are you okay? What happened? I thought you were just checking out your office today and having a meeting with the— Ohhhh. You met the headmaster. Was it not a good meeting?"

Her genuine concerned touched me. I opened the door wider to let her inside. We sat down on the sofa and she turned to face me.

"Tell me it wasn't horrible. He's such a nice man."

"No, you're right, he's very nice. He just…" How much did I want to tell her? We had sort of struck up a friendship. She was so much younger than me, but she knew how the academy worked. They had been watching her, too, for a long time. The difference was that she had known about them and that made it easier to accept, I thought. She had seemed so pleased to be coming…

"Skye, what did you think about them watching you for all this time? Weren't you curious? Didn't you feel as if you were being spied on?"

"I'm not going to lie. I often wondered why they never brought me here to be a student. The center was good for me, but I never felt as if I had a family. I knew I would here. But it wasn't time. I needed my training to be complete before I was going to be helpful here, and I accepted that. How long had they known about you?"

"Apparently since high school. The headmaster knew one of my teachers. And I knew nothing about this. Maybe that was better, I may have been too leery to come. But I'm spooked now. Skye, they know *so* much about me and it's hard for me to trust them with that knowledge."

"Delaney, I know it's hard for you. You seem like a really private person. Maybe that's why this is the time for you to be here. Maybe it's time for you to let down that guard a little and let people in, people you know you can trust. I know you felt comfortable with Damien, right?"

"Ugh, don't bring him up. That's even worse." I dropped my head into my hands and she put her hand on my shoulder.

"What happened? I thought there was some serious chemistry there. It certainly seemed that way when you guys came to see me in Santa Cruz."

I turned to her and made a face.

She giggled. "What? You guys seemed as if you'd known each other forever. He couldn't stop staring at you. I thought you were already a team."

I shook my head and laughed. "Well, you don't have to worry about that now. He made it clear that nothing is going to happen, so no complications there."

"He's crazy to let you go, but I'm sure that will make Jackson happy." Then she burst out laughing—and I realized she was laughing at my reaction. "You should see your face; you're killing me."

I smacked her thigh and got up to get a tissue. "It's not nice to laugh at the disaster, Skye." But I laughed, too. "I guess I just spent so much time thinking about this place over the summer. Thinking about possibilities with Damien had me intrigued. It was silly, I know, but there just seemed to be something there. And I think there is, but he doesn't need the complication, and apparently neither do I. And Jackson is out, too, for that matter. I'm going to be complication-free from now on."

She snorted at me. "Yeah, sure. I'll believe it when I see it. Besides, complications are the spice of life...aren't they?" We both fell apart laughing at that point, till I looked at the clock.

"Holy underwear! We're supposed to meet in thirty minutes. I look like I got run over by a truck. What the hell am I going to wear?"

Skye got real businesslike in a hurry.

"You get in the shower while I find you something hot to wear. Complication-Free Frost is going out on the town and damn, she's going to make them work for it." We both cracked up, and I did as I was instructed.

Twenty-nine minutes later we stood out in front of the gates with Isaac, Jared, Justin, and a science teacher named Margaret, whom I hadn't met yet but Skye was already tight with. Vincent pulled up in the van and Jackson came jogging up.

"Phew, thought I was going to be late. I got carried away in the studio and before I knew it, it was six-thirty and I was covered in clay."

I remembered him covered in clay. Damn. I shut that memory down with a quickness. I missed part of the conversation.

"Glad you made it, Delaney. I wasn't sure if you'd come. You had a lot going on today." His look told me he knew exactly what I had been through today. I was too tired to get upset again. I told myself I was going to have fun tonight if it killed me.

"Today was a lot, but I'm ready to rock. Let's blow this joint, shall we?"

He smiled and gestured for me to climb into the van ahead of him.

The ride to Eureka Springs took about fifteen minutes. I relaxed as I listened to Jackson sing along with the radio and Jared and Isaac arguing today's topic, which apparently had something to do with pitchers in major league baseball. I wasn't up to following that conversation so I tuned into Skye and Margaret talking about their classrooms and new equipment. Margaret taught Biology, which threatened to bring back memories of slurp and suck sounds...and Damien and...*shudder.* She and Skye seemed to share a love of technology. Those people were important to have in your life. The next time my computer crashed I'd know who to run to.

We pulled up in front of a brew pub called Shenanigans, which was already hoppin' on a Tuesday evening. A row of Harleys out front spoke volumes about the clientele. I was anxious to do a little recon of the local population.

Jackson got us a table in the rear next to the dance floor. The house band was playing Southern Rock with a side of the Blues and the patrons were drinking and dancing with abandon already. Isaac brought over a pitcher of beer and a pitcher of something pink that smelled delicious.

"For the ladies," he said with a smile and poured us all drinks. Jared toasted to a good opening week of school and that the Mets would win the pennant. This caused the argument to flare up again with Isaac, so the girls and I turned to each other to toast again. Whatever was in the drink warmed me to my toes instantly, and I smiled broadly.

The band started in on a new song, and Justin jumped up and asked Skye to dance. She gladly accepted, and the two of them skipped out onto the floor and started gyrating wildly.

"So how was today? You holding up well?" Jackson asked me seriously, leaning in close so I would hear him over the music.

"I'm okay. I really just want to forget about it. How 'bout you ask me to dance?"

So much for no complications...

Jackson stood up and held out his hand. I took it, and he spun me out onto the floor. I knew he was enjoying being close to me, and for tonight, I was going to enjoy being enjoyed.

The music slowed, and he put a hand on the back of my neck to pull me in closer. I went with it. The band was good, the drinks were flowing, and I was determined to have some fun. He smelled really good, like a fresh-peeled orange. I closed my eyes and placed my hands around his broad shoulders. When I opened my eyes and glanced at him, he had a very serious look on his face.

"You seem different tonight, Delaney. Your clothes are different. Your eyes are different. Even your laugh is different. I can't tell if you're opening up or moving further away from me."

I wasn't sure where this was going, so I tried to lighten the conversation.

"Skye picked out my clothes. Maybe that has something to do with it."

She'd chosen a knee-length layered skirt and a tank that dipped down low in the back for me. I was definitely showing a little more flesh than I was used to, but no more than the majority of women in the place. Skye was wearing an even shorter skirt and a top that showed off a pierced navel. Her hair was pulled back into a loop, and when I glanced in her direction, it appeared that Justin was enjoying her neck.

I looked back up at Jackson to find him scrutinizing me still.

"Jackson, lighten up. I did have a rough day, okay? I don't want to talk about it. Can't we just have a few drinks and a few laughs tonight and pretend like tomorrow isn't a really big day?"

He turned me around in a circle and looked away, a smile starting to turn up his mouth.

"Well, if fun is what you want, fun is what you'll get. I'm the King of Fun around here, and all are my subjects. Worship me, and you will have all you desire." He did a very kingly bow, and I curtsied in reply.

"If you think I'm kissing your ring, though, you are sorely mistaken." We both laughed and headed back to the table for another drink.

I'd never been much of a drinker. Isaac had been refilling the glasses while we were all talking, and I realized I'd kind of lost track of how much I'd had. I wasn't too far gone, but my upper lip was a little numb and the desire to giggle was too strong for my taste. It was time to stop. I also needed to go outside and get some fresh air to clear my head.

I went past the restrooms, through the back door, and out into the night. A few couples lingered anonymously in the dark. I stayed under the light, just breathing and trying not to think.

A hand gripped my waist, and I spun to find Jackson looking down at me. His smile was playful but the look in his eyes was way more engaged.

I took a step back, and he pulled me in closer.

"Delaney, I want to dance with you some more." But he didn't move. His eyes were smoldering. I took another step back and my heel scraped the wall. He moved in closer, his lower lip pushed out. He was really beautiful under the light, but I quickly shook myself and realized what was about to happen. Complication-Free Frost was about to let a man kiss her. And it wasn't the man she dreamed about.

"Jackson, let's go dance. C'mon, I'm going to get mosquito bites all over out here." I tugged at his arm but he wasn't budging. *Damn.* "Jackson, I'm not ready to go there with you. Please don't let this get weird? You're serious-friend material. I really need that right now." I hoped he understood where I was coming from. I really didn't want to turn him away.

He winced, and then he smiled gently.

"Friend material. Ouch. I guess I can live with that. As long as I get to dance with you tonight. I'll just have to work on my game, I suppose." He smiled and the awkward moment passed. He pulled me in and gave me a hug, smelling my hair. I shivered, remembering the last man I was in this position with. He started to lead me back inside, but he turned to face me first.

"I'd never hurt you, Delaney. I'll wait. But I'm not Damien...so don't expect me to be a *total* gentleman."

I didn't know how to read the look that came over his face at that moment. Was it a challenge? Did he think Damien and I had something going on? I gathered that he was certainly going to pursue more than a friendship with me. That was definitely going to be a complication.

I sighed and pulled his hand to lead him inside the bar. Skye and Justin were still dancing with Margaret and Isaac. I looked around for Jared—and froze when I located him at a table across from us...a table where Morgan and Damien were sitting drinking beer. Damien's green eyes pierced me from across the room. He simply tipped his bottle toward me, and then went back to his conversation with Jared and Morgan. He kept one eye on me as Jackson and I returned to the dance floor.

Jackson pulled me in close for another slow song and turned my back to Damien. I assumed he was looking over my shoulder at him and gloating.

How did I end up in this situation? Now I had not one, but two distractions to contend with, and tomorrow the students were arriving.

The counselor in me said I had set good boundaries. I had been clear about my feelings with both of them and I should feel content with that. The reality was, I was in the arms of a gorgeous man who had almost kissed me, and all the while I felt a pair of the most heavenly green eyes boring a hole through my back.

Some women would have been flattered by the attention, would've eaten it up. Me, I just wanted simplicity. Never having been the object of two men's affections, I had no idea how to proceed. So being the efficient counselor, I decided that I would extricate myself from said gorgeous man and head back to the table.

That was a great plan until someone tapped on my shoulder.

A huge, burly biker with a thick beard and wild eyes said to Jackson, "I want my turn with this little lady. You've been hoggin' her all night."

He tried to pull me away from Jackson, but the look in my eye told Jackson I wasn't okay with this turn of events.

Jackson smiled calmly at the guy and said, "Afraid I can't let you do that, friend. I'm the only name on her dance card tonight. So thanks, but no thanks."

Of course that wasn't the end of it. No, not on this night.

The guy pulled back a beefy fist and let it rip, nailing Jackson right on the jaw.

He barely flinched, to my surprise, seeing as this guy probably had about sixty pounds on him. Instead, Jackson pushed me gently to the side. He turned to face his attacker—my failed suitor—and addressed him calmly.

"You want to try that again, friend? You've got my undivided attention now."

It had all happened so fast, no one had even noticed there was a problem yet.

"Jackson," I said, keeping the fear out of my voice. "Jackson, let's just go."

But before I got the words out, Biker Dude hauled off and let one swing again. Only this time, Jackson caught his fist in midair and stopped it.

A menacing smile spread across his face as he proceeded to squeeze that fist into a pulp.

The biker's eyes got wide and his mouth fell open as he dropped to one knee, letting out a shriek and a string of curses.

"I believe you owe this lady an apology for your rude behavior," Jackson growled through clenched teeth.

The biker grimaced in pain. Jackson squeezed once more and the guy stammered what sounded vaguely like an apology. He planted his boot in the guy's chest, knocking him back across the floor. The guy stood slowly and shook his fist out, looking scared. He turned and fled for the door.

"Jackson," I said again, the look on his face filling me with dread. He was smiling but his eyes looked deadly. I backed away from him, and his expression immediately changed.

Damien was at my side in a second. "Are you alright, Delaney?"

"I'm fine. That guy, uh, wouldn't take no for an answer." I doubt either of them heard me over their glaring match. It was a long moment before either of them spoke. Jackson broke the silence.

"What's the matter, Preston? You wanted in on the action?" He laughed but there was no humor there. The two stared at each other like animals ready to attack.

"I simply wanted to ensure Delaney's safety, Jackson. I'm sure that was your main interest as well." He placed his hands on my shoulders. "Are you sure you're alright?"

"I'm fine, thank you. Jackson, what time was Vincent returning? I'm ready to go."

I went back to the table, unable to look at either of them. Skye and

Margaret had seen the whole thing and looked ready to intervene. I grabbed my purse and the three of us went to the ladies' room. I didn't even look back to see if the animals were still circling. Neither of the girls said anything while I splashed some water on my face, a habit I seemed to have adopted this week. I took a minute to use my inhaler, then worked on slowing my heart rate.

Damien and Morgan were gone when we returned. Isaac approached us to say Vincent was waiting for us with the van. The group was quiet during the drive back to the academy. Jackson sat in the front with Vincent, staring out the window with an unreadable expression on his face. My stomach was still in knots after watching him hurt that man with such a cool air about him. His reflexes had been quick, and could have been deadly. I knew that in my heart.

Jackson was capable of inflicting serious pain, and that scared me.

When we returned, I broke for my cottage. Jackson followed and caught up to me at my porch.

"Delaney, I'm sorry you had to see that. Are you okay?" He seemed completely calm, no trace of the violence he'd reeked of in the bar.

I turned to face him. "You know, I don't think I can trust myself to evaluate what just happened. Thank you for the dance, Jackson. I'll see you tomorrow, okay? I've really got to go to bed."

I let myself in the door and stood in the dark for a moment, letting my eyes adjust. Before stepping away though I looked out my peephole. He was still standing on my porch, his eyes looking toward the carriage house, almost as if he sensed his competitor across the field. I watched as he smiled to himself and then walked back toward the dorms.

The tears I had held back all afternoon would no longer be denied.

FATHER HAD RECEIVED PERMISSION FROM THE PREACHER OUTSIDE OF *Jacksonville to preside over services. They'd been there for several weeks, and Father was having more success than ever.*

He'd hired two men to travel with them, and they carried guns under their coats. The young girl didn't trust either of them and kept the door locked whenever they were around. They did bring her food, which she gratefully accepted.

Father was elated at the cooperation of the congregation and had even begun to talk about setting up a permanent base of operations. He felt that time was growing nearer for the end of days he'd been teaching about.

The young girl knew differently. She had Seen that the only end near was the end to his criminal activity—and thankfully, her participation in it.

NINE

NEW ARRIVALS

It was another fitful night of sleep. The dreams returned. The fire first, and then the woods. This time, though, I knew it was Damien chasing after me, and when I turned to face him in the mist-filled circle, he spoke but I couldn't understand him. The ending was the same, the bright light and pain in my chest.

When I woke, I had to reach for my inhaler, as I was about to have a full-blown asthma attack. I stood up shakily and stumbled toward the bathroom. Clio came in to check on me and I assured her I was fine, and the wheezing passed soon after. She rubbed on my legs to be sure and then sauntered out to wait for her breakfast.

I lingered in the shower, not really knowing what to expect of my first official day of work. Diana had told me Damien would meet me first thing this morning to give me a schedule of intake appointments. After the events of last night, I wasn't sure how to feel about seeing him. Even though it had been Damien who'd put on the brakes, the look on his face told me he wasn't pleased with what he saw on the dance floor. I wasn't wrong to spend time with Jackson, and it wasn't as if I was hanging all over him. I shouldn't be uncomfortable, right?

And what about Jackson? I wasn't ready to get close to him after his display in the bar. He did some major damage to the guy who wanted to dance with me, and while I appreciated his intervention, he'd looked as if he would have enjoyed doing more. I didn't want to be around that kind of violence.

I dressed in my last sundress and thought perhaps this weekend would be a good time to improve my wardrobe. Diana seemed to have the style thing down, perhaps I'd ask her for some suggestions. A little product in the hair, a little eyeliner, and I was ready to face my first day. My Cheerios threatened to make another visit, I was so nervous. I prayed for strength and grabbed my purse before heading out.

The morning was overcast and muggy, threatening a warm summer thunderstorm in the coming hours, and the birds and insects were quiet. I took a deep breath and walked down the path toward the main building.

I noticed through the dining room window that the staff seemed to be enjoying a leisurely breakfast, but that was not what I needed this morning. I needed to stay focused. I walked through the archway into the courtyard. The flowers Mrs. Walden had planted were breathtaking. Zinnias, Columbine, Snapdragons, and even my home state flower, Poppies, were nestled in between some deep green leafy plants. In the center of the plantings was a fountain I hadn't noticed before. The sound of the water trickling was soothing.

I looked up and knew that my office window looked out over the courtyard. I thought about how nice it would be to open my window and listen to the water throughout the day. This thought filled me with calm, so much so that I didn't hear Damien approach me.

"Good morning, Delaney."

Startled, I turned to face him. The warmth on his face eased the rest of the tension from me. He was absolutely beaming. His dark wavy hair was shining, his green eyes were radiant, and his tanned skin contrasted with the mint-green shirt he had on. He was positively glowing.

I breathed a little easier, discerning that there wasn't a trace of anger or disappointment from last night. He truly seemed happy to see me.

"Delaney Frost, reporting for duty, sir." I gave a mock salute.

He took me gently by the arm and led me over to a bench in the courtyard. We sat down, and he continued to smile at me for a moment. Positive energy flowed from him in waves. What an incredible man he was.

How fortunate the students were that he was looking after their best interests.

"Glad to see you're up for the challenge today. I trust you slept well?"

I hoped he didn't notice that the circles had returned under my eyes and that my smile dropped a little.

"I'm great. I'm ready. What's the plan?"

He frowned for a moment. "You used your inhaler this morning. Are you feeling alright?"

Damn, I forgot about that. "I'm fine. Really. It's just nerves. What've we got today?" I smiled hopefully at him, praying he would let it go and get back to our business at hand. I could handle his gift better if I knew he wasn't using it on me.

He drew out a manila folder from his satchel. "I took the liberty of printing out a schedule for you. Tomorrow and Friday, you will be working with Isaac and Jared on the orientation for our returning students. They're planning to meet with the staff after dinner tonight to plan. Diana has arranged four intake appointments for you this morning. The purpose of these meetings is simply to get to know the students and their needs. I've already met with their families in their homes." His voice became solemn. "I'm afraid we have some particularly heartbreaking cases joining us this year. I have no doubt you'll be able to guide them through their journey here. I'm confident we can heal them."

The warm smile was back. He certainly had faith in my abilities. I just hoped he was right.

"And this afternoon, I've asked Diana to take you out for some shopping and a bit of pampering. I hope that meets with your approval? Actually, I don't really care if it does. As your superior, I am *ordering* you to enjoy yourself."

He was quite proud of himself. I wasn't going to argue, but I did want to get one thing clear.

"Just how often do you plan to pull this superior crap?" I squinted my eyes and tried to sound angry. We both knew it wasn't going to work.

"Whenever I see that you need taking care of and you refuse to do it yourself." His tone wasn't condescending, only concerned. I thought back to the first night here, when he came to my porch and said he wanted to be sure I was comfortable and had everything I needed. Why did he have such a need to take care of me? Was I broadcasting *I'm a wreck. Please save me?*

"Damien," I said seriously. "All joking aside, I do appreciate all you have done to make this move go smoothly for me. But contrary to popular belief, I can take care of myself, and while I'm not one to turn down a pampering session, you don't have to go out of your way to dote on me. Frankly, it makes me uncomfortable."

He continued to frown. "I do not believe for one moment that you're incapable of taking care of yourself. I do, however, think that you don't always take it one step further and do what's necessary to soothe yourself. I'm therefore taking it upon myself to assist with this necessary act." His half smile was back, indicating he was about to get difficult. "I can't have my counselor getting too drained. I need her in good shape. If that requires a manicure, pedicure, and massage, so be it." He chuckled to himself. "It's worth the investment."

I sighed. "Very well then. Bring it on. I'll suffer through it somehow. I won't enjoy it one bit, just so you know."

This was getting dangerously close to flirting. There was a new glimmer in his eyes, and I realized with a shock that he was leaning in close to me, his hand on the bench perilously close to my thigh.

As if he read my mind, he pulled back and cleared his throat.

"Well, it's, ah, seven forty-five. Your first appointment is at nine with Hazel Ward. Her older brother is bringing her and her things here. You'll meet with them, and then I would appreciate it if you'd take her over to the dorm to meet with Marcia. Then at ten, you'll meet with a young man from your neck of the woods."

I looked down at the list he'd given me. Sure enough, Nathan Calendar, twelve years old, was from Oakland.

"Cool! How fun to have someone from home. Who's next?"

"At eleven, you'll see Matteo Cabral, from Spain. He flew into Little Rock last night and is staying with a friend of the headmaster's. He lost his family in the train station bombings in Madrid in 2004, when he was only a year old. He's been living with an aunt and uncle and has had some difficulties with school. Since we heard of him through one of our contacts, we've been working on getting his student visa arranged. He is very excited but will need some help with English, for certain.

"At noon, we have a readmit. Raven Parsons was with us for part of last year, but she left us at the semester. Her guardians have asked that we take her back."

He paused to run his hand down his face.

"Delaney, just so you know, Raven had some negative encounters with our previous counselor, Turner Chance. She may be reluctant to speak with you. I'm hoping that a new face will help her to turn over a new leaf. She's an extremely intelligent and articulate young lady. Also quite powerful."

I wanted to know more. I'd been getting pieces of information about the counselor I was replacing but never the whole story. I decided, though, that it was best I learned for myself what occurred. I would try my best to earn the girl's trust.

"They sound interesting. I can't wait to meet them."

I was genuinely thrilled to be getting back to work. All of the stress of the past couple of days, all of my worries, seemed to disappear as I focused on the work ahead. It would be tough, true, but it would feel good to be doing what I was meant to do.

Damien seemed to sense my resolve. "You're going to be great. So this afternoon, enjoy yourself. Diana has been given a clothing allowance for you. I hope you will find the spa to your liking as well." He leaned toward me again, his arm pressing against mine, with that intense look on his face. "I shall see you at dinner when you return." He smiled and stood up. He gestured toward the door leading to the Student Affairs office. "Shall we face the day?"

"We shall." I smiled up at him and led the way into the foyer. We split off at the stairs and he paused before entering his office.

"Have a good morning, Delaney. You're going to be great."

My breath caught in my chest as I nodded and ascended the stairs.

I closed the door to my office behind me, taking a deep breath.

Morgan was standing in the middle of the room, burning some kind leaves and chanting softly.

I was surprised to find her in my office, but more surprised that I wasn't upset she was there. And the smoke wasn't bothering my asthma. I was comforted by the knowledge that she was blessing the place where I would be doing my work. It made me feel even more positive about the day. I stepped back out into the hall so she could finish.

"I'm going to be great," I repeated to myself.

Next to my office was a sitting area in front of another bank of windows. I walked over and opened a window. The sound of the water fountain drifted up, and I inhaled, smelling the flowers planted below. Yes, this was perfect.

I settled down on one of the sofas and sighed. The campus was just starting to come to life. I saw some of the teachers heading into the classrooms in the building across the courtyard. Classes wouldn't begin until Monday, but they all wanted to set things up to welcome their new students for sure. I really hoped that these people, my new colleagues, would accept me and my work, and that I could make things run more smoothly for them. This place was so important. These kids needed to have a taste of the power they would gain with the knowledge we provided.

At that moment, Morgan stepped out of my office with a smile. "All set."

"Thank you, Morgan. I feel a lot better knowing you've blessed my space."

She nodded and turned to leave.

It was now eight-fifteen, so I walked out into the hall to see if Diana had arrived. She was just setting down her purse and turning on the computer when I leaned over her workstation.

"Ready for today?"

"A-ffirmative," she said with a smile. "And I brought chocolate." We both laughed as she handed me a secret stash.

"How did you know I'd need it?"

She simply smiled a devious smile. "What woman doesn't need some medicinal chocolate in her drawer?"

I knew I was going to love this woman.

"Do you have everything you need for the intakes?" She sat down in her chair, smoothing her skirt.

"Yes. Damien gave me the list and we went over the appointments, including ours this afternoon. You could have warned me." My voice was serious, but I was holding in a laugh. She returned my attempt at serious-ness with a scolding tone of her own.

"Delaney, the Orchid Day Spa is necessary." Her stern face completely relaxed and she closed her eyes. "They do the best hot stone massage there. You're going to love it." We both sighed, thinking of how inviting it sounded.

"Very well. If I have to. Damien instructed me to enjoy it. Does he pull that 'I'm your superior' crap with you, too?"

She didn't laugh this time. "It's important to him that you are well. If he's ordering you around, it's only because he's concerned about you." She paused, choosing her words carefully. "You are very important to him, Delaney. To all of us. This may be a difficult and strenuous year. It would serve you well to listen to him. He has your best interests at heart."

I was shocked. I hadn't meant to offend her. I was going to have to be more careful with my sarcasm.

"I'm sorry, Diana. I didn't mean to sound ungrateful. I'm just not used to it, that's all."

She smiled back at me. "Not to worry. We're going to have a delectable afternoon. Now you go get ready for the onslaught. You'll need to have your game face on."

I appreciated her pep talk and thanked her for it.

I returned to my office and booted up the computer. I had brought some files with me that I wanted to upload, so I plugged in my memory stick. I noticed that they hadn't wiped the computer after Turner had left. I put his files into a folder in case I needed them, though I was a little leery of reading his personal files.

I spent some time reading over the notes Damien included with my schedule so I'd know how to answer any questions the students might have.

Ten minutes to go. I was making sure I was still put together when there was a knock on my door.

"Not disturbing you, am I?" Jackson asked as he opened the door. He rested his hands on the doorjamb and leaned his head in. "Place looks good. Mmmm, I can smell that Morgan has been here." His smile was tentative, perhaps sensing that all was not well after last night.

I wasn't going to let anything get to me this morning, so I smiled brightly at him.

"Just getting ready to meet with the new students. What are you up to today?"

He didn't come in, and I didn't invite him.

"Setting up the art studios, helping Elijah inventory the instruments in the music lab. Going to run into Fayetteville later to pick up my art supplies. Care to join me for the ride?" He looked so hopeful. I hated to say no, but I had my orders.

"Can't. I've been ordered to get pampered. Apparently, the big wigs want me to be relaxed or something." I hoped making light of the situation would work.

He shook his head and laughed. "Well, orders are orders, I suppose. Catch you at dinner? I hear we've got orientation run-through tonight afterwards. Should be interesting."

"Yes, I'll be there. Possibly I'll be a lump of Jell-O, but I'll be there."

He let out a big chuckle and slapped his hands on the doorframe. "Yum, dessert." He winked at me, but I had a suspicion it was only partly a joke.

"I hope your day goes well. Just wanted to say good morning. And thanks for the dances last night. I certainly slept well." He had a dreamy expression on his face. I grabbed a pillow off the chair and threw it at him. He caught it and laughed, throwing it down to the couch. "Be seeing you, Delaney." And with that, he sauntered off.

Oh boy. I shook myself as my phone rang.

"Delaney, your nine o'clock appointment is here. You want me to bring them in?"

"No, thank you, Diana. I'll come and meet them." I gave myself another mental shake and stepped out to meet my first student at Havenhart Academy.

Hazel Ward and her brother were waiting for me next to Diana's desk. She looked to be about sixteen years old, short and thin, with long, straight brown hair. She was wearing a traditional Amish dress. Her brother was also dressed in traditional clothing. He looked nervous.

"Good morning. I'm Miss Frost," I said kindly as I walked toward them and extended my hand first to Hazel and then to her brother. They both shook my hand weakly, not making eye contact. "Shall we go into my office?"

We entered my office and they sat next to each other on my couch. He looked to be in his early twenties, with a strong build and hands that looked as though he had spent years working outdoors. "I trust your travels went smoothly?"

Her brother nodded.

"Can I get you some water to drink?"

Diana had thought brilliantly to put a water cooler in my office. Not only did I drink like a fish, I was sure it would come in handy with my visitors.

"Thank you, no," said Hazel's brother. He fidgeted on my couch next to his sister, his shoulders hunched and his hands bound tightly together.

I wondered just how much contact they'd had with the outside world. I knew some Amish traded with secular communities and entertained tourists, but there were some groups who kept to themselves.

"Okay. Well. We're meeting this morning so we can get to know each other a bit and so I can answer any questions you may have about the academy. I understand you met previously with Mr. Preston?"

They both nodded. Hazel had her hands folded in her lap and her head down, only looking up briefly when I spoke.

"Hazel, just so you know, I'm new here, too. In fact, today's my first day and you are my first appointment. We're going to be learning together."

She gave me a weak smile and then looked at her brother.

He frowned and then spoke up. "I'm Jeremiah. Our parents asked me to bring Hazel here. She has had a difficult time with our people since her accident."

"Do you want to tell me what's been happening, Hazel?"

She looked up with wide eyes and again deferred to her brother.

"I'm assuming Mr. Preston told you why she's here," Jeremiah answered curtly.

I shook my head. "I prefer to meet my students before reading their files. I think it's only fair that neither of us knows the other, so we can form our own opinions." I tried to catch Hazel's eye but she was still staring down at her hands. "Hazel, do you want to tell me what happened?"

She looked at me and shook her head. "I'd rather Jeremiah told you." She looked away toward the window and tilted her head as if she heard something.

"You can open the window. We have a nice water feature in the court-yard. I meant to open it myself but I hadn't gotten around to it." She looked at me, then to her brother, as if she were getting his permission. "It's alright, go ahead." I smiled at her and tried to send her some reassurance.

She walked to the window, hesitated, and then opened the lock, pushing the window out. Her eyes lit up at what they beheld. I saw the corners of her mouth turn up as if she wanted to smile but was still afraid, that maybe she would be punished for enjoying herself.

"Hazel's accident happened at the fall harvest. She was in the barn preparing to milk the cows when one of the horses got loose and knocked her over, kicking her in the side of the head on the way down. We weren't sure she would make it, but she woke up the next day just fine. Well, phys-ically she was fine. But then she started having dreams. And these dreams were about the people in our community.

"They weren't happy about it. They said that evil had entered her when she was unconscious. Our parents tried to protect her, but the others said she was a danger to us all, and that she had to be cast out. When Mr. Preston came to see us, we were ready to send her to a chil-dren's home."

I hid my shock at what this poor girl had gone through. Her brother was only doing what he thought was best for her, but the intolerance she had faced infuriated me. I looked over at her, still standing by the window, and she had a faraway look in her eyes. I thought of all the misery she'd experienced, and I hoped desperately things would be better for her here.

There would be a major adjustment period, but I was determined she would be safe and welcome.

"Hazel, do you know our mission here at Havenhart?"

She shrugged, still not looking my way.

"We bring children here from all over the world to offer them a second chance, and to help them bring their gifts to fruition. I believe these dreams may be *your* gift. Maybe we can learn how to use them to do good things. Would you like that?"

She continued to look out the window, but then she nodded and began to speak in a frail voice. "I tried to help them. I told them what I dreamed. I thought they would be happy to know, so they'd be prepared. But they said I was bad, and that I was going to bring evil upon us all."

She looked over to Jeremiah, and the gaze she met was one of love and anguish. He didn't want to give her up, but knew that she wouldn't be safe at home any longer.

I stood and walked over the window. I reached my hand out and placed it on her shoulder. She looked up at me, startled. Then she smiled shyly. "I dreamt of you, too. You were standing on the side of the road with two boys. They were afraid. You made them warm."

"That's incredible. Do you know that actually happened, Hazel? I was with Mr. Preston and we passed a car accident. We stopped because no emergency personnel were there. One of the cars had two brothers in it. I wrapped them in a blanket from my car to keep them from going into shock."

It was true. I guess I hadn't known what it would be like experiencing the gifts the students had. It was one thing having Damien explain it, but here she was in the flesh, retelling my past that she had no way of knowing.

"Hazel, what you have is a remarkable gift. There are people here who can help you learn how to come to terms with it. How does that sound?"

She looked at Jeremiah and then back at me. She nodded, the shy smile appearing once again.

I took her hand and led her back over to the couch. She sat next to her brother, who looked desperate. "I don't know what to say, Miss Frost. Can you help her? Can you make her well?"

"Jeremiah, I think all she needs is acceptance and a place to learn and thrive. We can provide that here, and we are happy to have her. Do you have any questions for me?"

"Well, um, I told Mr. Preston that we can't pay."

I shook my head. "There's no fee for this academy. Hazel will be provided with room and board at no charge, and she will work toward earning her high school diploma. We'll also assist her in deciding where she wants to go when she graduates. We have a scholarship program as well."

Hazel seemed to brighten at that.

"Now, I understand that Hazel is used to her world, and ours may be a bit of a shock. I will do whatever I can to help her with the transition. How do your parents feel about this?"

He shrugged and looked down at his hands. "They had no other choice. It was here or the children's home. They thought at least here, she would get a good education and have more options. She can't come back to our community. They'll drive her out." He looked so sad, as though he blamed himself for failing to protect her.

"She will be well cared for here, Jeremiah. You've done the best thing possible by bringing her here. We may even be able to arrange for you and your family to visit."

He seemed relieved. He took one of her hands. "Sister, will you fare well here?"

She nodded enthusiastically. "Brother, I want this. I want to be with people who know what I am and accept me for it. I think they'll do that here. Please let me stay." She looked pleadingly into his eyes.

He smiled and leaned over, kissing her on the forehead. "Of course, Hazel. I want you to be happy."

"Well, how about I take you both over to the girls' dormitory? Hazel can settle her things and I can introduce you both to Marcia Gray, the head resident? Maybe that would make you feel a little more comfortable entrusting her to us?" I smiled at Jeremiah, and he looked grateful.

"Thank you, Miss Frost. Really, I couldn't bear the thought of her staying in that awful children's home."

Hazel's smiled a little more boldly now as we walked out the door, down the stairs and across the campus to the dormitory. Hazel looked around excitedly while I pointed out the buildings and gave her a brief tour. Jeremiah looked nervous but he held his head high.

When we reached the dorm, I led them to Marcia's apartment on the bottom floor. I hadn't met her in person yet and therefore didn't know what to expect.

What I got was so much more than I'd hoped for.

The woman who answered the door had the most genuine and contagious energy, with round cheeks and eyes that nearly disappeared when she smiled.. She was short and plump, with a real mom vibe. She was perfect. She was wearing a pair of comfortable sweats and looked as if she had just been working out. I smiled at her and stuck out my hand.

"Ms. Gray, I'm Delaney Frost, the new counselor, and this is Hazel Ward and her brother, Jeremiah."

She leapt at me and gave me a warm hug. I wasn't expecting it, but returned the hug with pleasure.

"Oh, I am so glad to finally meet you! This is so great." She then took Hazel's hands.

"My first new student. Aren't you beautiful! Please, come in, come in." She shook hands with Jeremiah, who seemed more and more comfortable as our morning went on.

I left them in her capable hands to head back for my next meeting with a promise that I would check in with Hazel at dinnertime. I reassured Jeremiah that he could contact me anytime and was welcome to visit.

My next appointment was with Nathan Calendar from Oakland. Was he ever a trip! Nathan was a talkative, funny kid who exuded confidence. He was going to be a big hit on campus. Mom wanted to get him out of town after his brother had been killed by street violence. Nate had shown amazing promise in school in both his academics and athletics, and was a natural leader. That was apparently his gift, and we intended to nurture it. His mother was so grateful that we were taking him on. She was especially happy that I was 'from home.' Nate would have someone to relate with.

We instantly hit it off, and I decided I would arrange a work-study assignment in my building for him, so I could spend as much time with him as possible.

I felt really good after my first two appointments, and the third, with the exception of the language issues that we skirted well, continued my streak. Matteo was very excited to be in America. He was a bit shy, most likely due to his language barrier, but ready to learn.

Matteo's gift was the ability to sense danger. Sadly, his gift came too late to save his parents and sister, who were victims of terrorism when a van ran into pedestrians on Las Ramblas in Barcelona. He was determined to learn to use his gift to help people and had a desire to work in law enforcement. I figured Jackson would be a great mentor for him with his military experience.

I escorted Matteo over to the dorms after we'd gotten acquainted and found Jackson singing loudly along with Led Zeppelin in his apartment with the door opened. Matteo and I both snickered as we watched him without his notice. He was hanging a painting in his hallway, using the hammer as an impromptu microphone.

"You know, for a soldier, you're easy to sneak up on," I joked.

We apparently startled him, because he fell off the stepladder he was standing on. He laughed as he sat on his ass on the floor. "I wasn't expecting you guys for a bit. Uh, the music was a little loud." He grinned sheepishly.

I introduced him to his charge, and they both began to speak rapidly in Spanish. I smiled warmly at Jackson and left the dudes to talk dude stuff. Matteo hugged me as I turned to leave. I assured him he'd see a lot of me over the coming days. He seemed happy about that.

I walked slowly back to my office, smiling to myself and feeling recharged. It had been so long since I had been a part of something I really believed in. These kids I'd met this morning had lived through such horrific events. They were all ready to put the past behind them and embrace what we had to offer. This was what I had been working toward my whole career.

I ascended the steps back up to my office and found a young girl waiting for me in the sitting area. She had her arms crossed over her chest and looked quite irritated.

"Hi, I'm Miss Frost. Were you waiting to see me?"

She looked over at me coldly and said in her most annoyed voice, "Uh, yeah, if you're the counselor lady."

I gestured for her to follow me into my office. She rolled her eyes at me while making a show of how irritated she really was to be here. I braced myself for an end to my winning streak of the morning and shut the door behind us.

"You must be Raven. Would you like something to drink or eat? Did you travel far today?" I served myself a glass of water while she continued to glare at me from the couch with her arms crossed.

"I don't want anything from you. Do I really have to be here or can I just go to the dorm and see my room?"

Okay, this definitely put an end to the kumbaya feeling of the morning.

"No, you don't have to stay. I did want to introduce myself and let you know that I'm here if you need anything. I don't know you, and you don't know me. I'm not expecting your trust just yet, but I hope to earn it eventually. I don't know what your experience was here last year. Frankly, it's only my business if you choose to tell me. I'm a whole different ballgame than your previous counselor. I haven't read your file, and I don't intend to unless you think I need to."

I paused for a moment and noticed that her arms had uncrossed and were now resting on her lap. She still glared at me. I figured I'd made headway.

"Do you have any questions for me, Raven?" She shook her head. I smiled at her. "Okay. Want me to walk you over to the dorm?"

"I can find my own way, thank you. And Miss Frost? You don't need to be afraid of things here, at least not now. Just thought you should know that since you're so worried about how *effective* you're going to be." She even used finger quotes on the "effective."

I kept my game face on and watched her as she stood and looked around. I assumed this was part of her guard; by shocking people, she'd have the upper hand in conversations. If she needed that, I'd let her have it for now.

"Well, thank you for your observation. I think it's my job to be effective here, don't you think? If I wasn't worried about it, then I probably wouldn't be the best person for the job." I chose my words carefully, trying not to sound defensive or angry. I wanted to approach the line she'd drawn and not cross it. Not yet.

She smirked at me and turned to leave the office. "Does orientation start tomorrow?"

"Yes, although I don't have the schedule yet. I'm sure Miss Gray will go over it with you tonight."

"Fine. See you around, I guess."

"Nice to meet you," I said to her back as she walked out.

Wow, I saw why Damien had warned me. She presented a challenge, sure. I'd do my best to rise to the occasion.

It was time to meet Diana for our adventure. I approached her workstation and she looked at me with concern, that mom vibe popping up again.

"How did that go?" she asked warily.

I lifted my chin. "She scored first, but I answered her. I'll give her space. Eventually she's going to have to deal with me."

Diana smiled approvingly. I asked her if Damien was in. That approving smile continued as she nodded toward the stairs. I told her I'd meet her out front in ten.

I knocked softly on the door. He opened it with his cell phone to his ear. He smiled brightly when he saw me and waved me in. I sat in a comfortable chair in front of his desk. He sat back down behind his desk and I watched him while he finished his conversation. His eyes never left mine. His smile continued to blind me.

"Aren't you a sight for sore eyes," he said as he ended the call. "I take it your morning went well?"

"Wonderful. For the most part," I answered.

"My morning has been full of difficult people being difficult while I have to be the nice guy. Sometimes I get tired of being the nice guy."

I laughed as he raised an eyebrow at me.

"I get what you mean. Being nice is highly overrated."

We were walking that line again. I quickly got to my purpose for coming to see him. "Just wanted to let you know my meetings went very well. Hazel should be settled in by now, as well as Nathan and Matteo. Matteo hit it off very well with Jackson. I didn't know he was bilingual."

Damien nodded. "Jackson is multitalented. I know he at least speaks Spanish, Arabic, and I believe he even knows some Russian dialects. His military service was eventful, to say the least." He genuinely admired Jackson. That was evident.

"Do you speak other languages?" I asked him, taking the opportunity to try to learn more about my mysterious boss.

"Spanish, some Mandarin, some Thai and Cantonese, and Japanese. During my time with my parents, we lived mostly in South America and Asia. Later, I spent time in Japan and learned as much as possible. Amazing cultures." He looked wistful.

"How does one settle in Arkansas, of all places, after the places you've been? It was hard enough for me to leave California, and I'd only lived in Iowa previously." I hoped my teasing would open him up more, but he was on to me.

"Other places don't contain such a facility as this. Honestly, why would I want more?"

I didn't believe him, but I let him win.

He leaned across his desk toward me. "Er, how did it go with Raven?"

"We met. She glared. I let her know what to expect of me. She rolled her eyes. I asked if she had questions. She threw down the psychic gauntlet. I didn't flinch. I think we came out even. How's that for success?"

We both laughed at that one. He seemed impressed that I'd survived unscathed.

"That young lady is definitely a force to be reckoned with. When I first met her, she assured me I wasn't going to end up alone."

Our laughter died down at that. He grew serious again. "Her gift, if you caught on, is to sense the fear in others. I'd love for her to learn to use that as a way to ease others, almost like what you do. Instead, she chooses to shock people." He paused. "What did she sense in you?"

"She told me not to be afraid of things here, that worrying about being effective was useless. I thanked her and assured her I would do my best, regardless. I'm used to meeting resistant kids, but she definitely takes it to a new level. Difficult girls have always been my Achilles' heel. As you pointed out when we went to Santa Cruz, I have a way with men and their tears, but adolescent girls are scary as hell."

He burst out laughing at that proclamation and came around the desk. He sat down in the chair next to mine and turned me to face him. Our knees touched. He leaned toward me with his hands laced together.

"Delaney, if I had any doubts about you, you wouldn't be here. But if you doubt *yourself*, you'll find yourself not well again. I don't want to see that happen."

I inhaled deeply and sat back in my chair, my lungs feeling tight. "I don't ever want to feel as I did this past year. I was devastated when I heard they were closing my program. I felt impotent, as if everything I had done was for nothing. I fought so hard to keep the program open. All for nothing. I don't want to be in that position again. Kids are too important to me."

The conversation had gotten serious all of a sudden. Instead of learning more about him, I spilled my guts. Again. I couldn't help myself. I was drowning in those green eyes. It was as if he was pulling my pain out by the roots, and I was powerless to stop it.

He leaned toward me, placing a hand on my knee.

"I didn't mean to upset you, Delaney. Forgive me. You don't need to worry about that anymore. You are safe here. Havenhart isn't going anywhere, and as I've told you before, you wouldn't be here if I didn't think you were right for our students. They mean everything to me as well." He lifted my chin with a long, strong finger. "I only choose the best. *You* are the best for our students. I just want you to feel what it's like to be living your calling. I know you're up to it." His smile was so kind.

A wave of energy passed through me, and I gasped slightly.

His eyes held mine for a minute more, and then he stood and held out a hand to me.

"I seem to recall you have important business in town to attend to, so I am ordering you to be on your way."

His attempt at bossing me around worked. I stood up, surprised at how close he was. His unique scent woke all of my senses. A hint of bergamot, tea tree, and something...primal. I didn't know how else to describe it.

He brought one hand up around the back of my neck and pulled me closer. My heart jumped. I thought he was going to kiss me. But then my brain kicked in and remembered his spiel about not getting close.

He must have sensed my confusion.

"Delaney...I am so drawn to you. I'm sorry. I know in my head that this shouldn't happen. I just can't seem to convince my heart. I desperately want to kiss you."

He held my face in both of his hands for a moment, and I stopped breathing. Everything in my being wanted him to touch me. His hands were so strong and warm. We both trembled. My pulse quickened to the point I thought he must be able to hear it.

Then his phone rang.

He took a deep breath. So did I. He stepped toward his desk, but slid one hand down to hold mine.

"Preston," he answered. He sighed and squeezed my hand. "She'll be right out. Sorry for the wait, Diana."

"Saved by the bell," I choked out.

A pained look crossed his face, and he let go of my hand. The hand that had been holding mine went to his chest and he began to rub it absently. "I'm afraid we've kept our dear Diana waiting. You need to go. I'm sorry I..." He trailed off.

I shook my head. "I'm not. I'll see you later."

I turned and walked out with a spring in my step.

He may have been conflicted, but I wasn't. It may have been wrong for us to start something, but it was becoming unavoidable.

Diana waited for me by her car, smiling. "Sorry for the interruption, but we do have a schedule to keep."

Did she know what she had interrupted? I didn't dare ask. While I was comfortable with her, I wasn't ready to confide in her about things with Damien. I didn't want to put either of us in a difficult position.

EUREKA SPRINGS DID INDEED HAVE SOME WONDERFUL BOUTIQUES. IT WAS SO nice to browse knowing I could actually afford what I thought would look good on me. Diana helped me with my selections and before long, we had several shopping bags to load in her car.

Next stop was the Orchid Day Spa. As we walked through the door, the air conditioning cooled us and the aroma and trickling water soothed us. A woman led us to a locker room, and we changed into fluffy bathrobes. Our nails were taken care of first. We were each doted on by no fewer than four workers at a time. They treated us so graciously and were highly skilled.

Diana told me a little about her family and what it was like growing up in Arkansas. Her children were grown and navigating their way through the post-baccalaureate world of interviews and internships. I thought to myself how lucky her children were to have such a loving mother.

When it was time for our massages, we were taken to separate rooms. The hot stone treatment *was* heavenly. I closed my eyes and dozed off, thinking the heavy air in the spa was eerily similar to the feeling I'd had while in Damien's office. His hands on my skin had been such a revelation. His energy and warmth had traveled up my arms and down my spine. I imagined that was his healing gift, but I also sensed his longing and his conflicted feelings.

I knew he thought a relationship with me was not in my best interest, but I wondered if there were other factors involved. Whatever Damien and I felt for each other, we'd have to be very careful.

I was so relaxed when the massage concluded that I barely remembered getting dressed. When I came out, Diana was waiting for me with a glass of water. We drank in silence, both of us sighing in appreciation of the spa's good work. We'd already had a fight about paying for the services. She assured me it was taken care of, but I insisted on leaving the tip. We dressed and walked back out into the humid afternoon. There was a school van waiting for us out front.

"They'll take you and your things back to campus. I've got a hot date with my husband."

We giggled, and I gave her a hug. "Thank you, for everything Diana. This was a wonderful afternoon. You think my new outfits will suffice?"

She nodded and stuck out her chin. "Of course they will. I helped pick them out. They're perfect."

I rolled my eyes at her, causing me to think of Raven again. I wondered how she was settling in, and how she and her roommate would fare. I hoped Raven would behave herself. I didn't want anyone getting hurt. Either way, I'd hear about it.

"And Damien will definitely approve." She dropped that bomb as she sauntered away to her car.

I stared after her and then grabbed my bags to load into the van.

"Why don't you let me get those for you?"

Standing in front of me, stunning in the afternoon sunlight, was Jackson.

I blinked and made sure my mouth wasn't gaping. He was dressed in his usual jeans and work boots but was wearing a tight white tank, leaving nothing to the imagination. I noticed for the first time a series of scars across his shoulder blades as he was loading my bags in the back.

"I thought you were getting art supplies?" I asked him, suspicious of why he was here to pick me up.

"I was just on my way back. I called Diana and let her know I was coming through to save her a trip back out to the campus. How was your massage?"

"Delectable. I am officially Jell-O." I rested my head on the seat back and closed my eyes, hoping to relax on the drive back.

He smiled and began to sing to himself as he put the van in gear and sped off.

"Is that the same song you were singing when we snuck up on you this morning?" I knew he was irked that we'd caught him, and I had to rub it in.

"I was fully aware you two were there. Don't think for a moment that you're ever stealthy enough sneak up on a Ranger," he said smugly.

I scoffed at him, and he didn't dare to give me another look.

Pretty soon, we were both singing along to *Led Zeppelin II*. "This is definitely their best album," I declared.

He nodded in agreement. "But each of their albums has something a little different. I love them all." The trip back was quick and when we returned to campus, Jackson pulled up to the walkway in front of my cottage.

"I'll help you bring these inside," he said, grabbing an armful. "Damn, woman, what did you buy? A whole wardrobe?"

"Apparently, my jeans-and-tees repertoire was not suitable for this establishment," I said in my best British accent.

He laughed. "Yeah, I get away with a bit more because of the whole messy art studio thing, but I still wear my khakis and button-ups. They just have their share of paint and glaze on them."

"That's not fair. Counseling is messy, too. There's all the blood, sweat and tears…and snot."

We got all of my bags inside, and he stood for a moment in the doorway, his hands in his back pockets. "Are you ready for dinner or did you need some time?" He looked hopeful.

I told him to take a seat and grab a drink if he wanted while I freshened up, though I was conflicted with him in my place. The concern I had after our experience in the bar had dissipated some. He seemed like a guy friend who was fun to hang out with, and he'd turned down the charm to an acceptable level, as though he'd accepted being friend zoned. I could certainly get used to hanging out with him.

I just hoped he realized that's what it was. Friends hanging out.

I went into my room and pulled on some shorts and a tank, as it was sweltering this evening. When I came out, Jackson was sprawled on my couch, bottled water in hand, and he'd turned on my iPod. His head bobbed gently to the music, and he took a long pull on his water. He really was handsome; fairly tall, curly blond hair pulled back in his usual ponytail, broad, muscular shoulders and narrow hips leading to slender legs.

His boyish charm was misleading though. Looking at him there, with his eyes closed, I felt he was anything but carefree. I sensed an old soul behind his "king of fun" exterior. He'd been through a lot, seen more devastation than any human should see and lived to tell about it.

And there was a darkness lurking there. I wasn't afraid of him. I knew he wouldn't hurt me, but it was unsettling. I hoped I'd never see that dark side again. He was good at keeping it hidden, but it was there.

"You gonna keep staring or come over and sit by me?" He hadn't even opened an eye but his eyebrows were raised.

"Funny guy. We need to get to dinner. We've got orientation run-through, remember?"

He groaned and made a production out of rising from the couch.

"If we have to…" He trudged over to the front door and stuck out his lower lip in a pout.

"Come on, big boy. Let's get you fed before your poor, weary self keels over."

He laughed and threw an arm around my shoulder. I turned to lock the door. I took one look back and saw the door was open to the bay where Damien had been working on his motorcycle. I had a fleeting thought about this morning.

Not the time to dwell on that. I had to have faith it would work itself out.

Jackson looked down at me and smiled, apparently unaware of my distraction. "I'll race ya."

He took off running while I laughed at him. "Nice try, Howe. I don't run."

We got to the dining hall and the gang was already eating. Skye jumped up when I came in and gave me a huge hug.

"How was your day? Did you meet your new students? Are you all ready for orientation? Oh! And how about your trip to shop for clothes? How exciting and…"

She was on one of her energy kicks again. I really had no idea where it came from. If I could bottle her essence, I'd be a billionaire.

Jackson and I joined her and Margaret at the table. Justin sat on the other side of Skye, looking at her like a lost puppy. I sure hoped he was able to keep up with her.

I glanced around and saw Damien sitting with Morgan and Elijah. I tried to catch his eye but he was once again deep in conversation with Morgan.

I wondered about their relationship. Every time he was with her, he seemed so serious. I knew they worked together to seek out students and staff for the school, but there was something more to it.

Morgan looked over at me at the same moment I was wondering these things, almost as if she'd heard my thoughts. Her stare penetrated.

A chill ran down my spine. I hadn't reconciled my feelings for her. I respected her, but I was intimidated. I think she enjoyed having that edge. It kept ordinary people at bay.

My eyes wandered over the students' tables. I saw Nathan and Matteo eating together. Raven sat at the end of a table where four other girls chatted happily. She didn't look upset, but hadn't joined in their conversation. A group of boys sauntered over to her, and she went from withdrawn to coy in an instant. The boys were hanging on her every word.

I excused myself from my table, ignoring Jackson's questioning look, and I headed over to a table to sit down with Hazel. She looked up, surprised when she saw my approach.

"Enjoy your dinner?"

She nodded. I noticed a bit of a spark in her that I hadn't seen earlier. "Dinner was very nice. And I really like my room." She sounded as if she was afraid to be happy and excited.

"I'm sure this will all be a change for you. I know you'll be just fine. Tell me, Hazel, have you ever used a computer? Listened to popular music?" She shook her head, her eyes wide. "Well, you have a bit to catch up on. Take it slow, it will come. There are many folks here who will walk you through it all."

Some of the other girls scooted closer and listened in on our conversation. I introduced myself, and they whispered to each other. One girl with short hair, ebony skin and a foreign accent spoke up for the others.

"We're really happy to have a woman for a counselor this year. Thank you for coming."

"I'm glad to be here. Some folks prefer one or the other. I think all counselors have something to offer. I just hope you guys will come to me if you need anything."

They all nodded enthusiastically.

"We didn't mean to eavesdrop, but we heard you say you've never used a computer or listened to music. Not to worry. I come from a small village in Rwanda. I had never even seen a computer before coming here. We will help you, and the teachers here are very, very nice. You'll like it here. My name is Winny."

The other girls introduced themselves. Jasmine was from Taiwan originally but had been in the states since she'd started school. Kat was from Bosnia and had been at Havenhart for four years as well. She and Winny were roommates. Tara was from here in Arkansas and seemed right at home with her expat dorm mates. Tara and Hazel were roommates. I hoped it would be a good match.

I sat with the girls for a bit longer, listening to them all fuss over Hazel and reassure her about the big step she'd taken.

I left them chatting and headed over to the table where Matteo and Nate were sitting. The two of them were rapping along to Kendrick Lamar. It was good to see they'd found some things in common. Jackson had told me on the way home from town that they'd been paired up with current students but were next door to each other. I was glad to see them hitting it off so well.

Dinner wrapped up and the students went with Marcia and Jackson back to the dorms.

The staff lingered while we waited to hear what our tasks were for the following two days of orientation. Damien stood and handed out a schedule to everyone.

Isaac and Jared high-fived each other when they saw they'd be handling the games and challenge portion of the program. This was a time when the students would learn to work together and trust each other to achieve a common goal. Moira, Skye and Margaret would be doing ice-breakers with the kids throughout the day. Marcia and Jackson would be doing a dramatic interpretation of dorm life, complete with costuming, which I knew would be quite entertaining.

My job, it turned out, would be to hang out watching the events and to mingle, just getting to know the kids. I would also be handing out class schedules and talking to the older students about preparing for post-Havenhart life. Sounded easy enough.

Damien gave us a brief pep talk, and then he left the room. The effects of the day wore me out, so I decided to turn in. Starting a new school year was always exciting to me. This was going to be a year like no other I'd ever experienced before.

I floated as I walked along the path back to my new home, anxious to sleep so it would be tomorrow.

THE YOUNG GIRL DECIDED TO TRY TO REACH OUT AND CONNECT WITH HER *Protector*. She'd never been very successful. She didn't have Father's Influence. She also didn't have much time. His next plans for the Florida people were terrifying.

He meant to make examples of them. Once he had procured a large enough place, he planned to bring them all to him and keep them until the End of Days. The young girl was starting to wonder just what this End of Days was going to entail, because all she Saw from Father was his greed, and more death.

She wasn't sure if she would make it out of this one.

Father's powers were so strong. He affected people in person, but also from far away if he had enough information about them or knew where they were. He'd even begun planting ideas about the importance of letting him speak into the minds of the pastors of the churches they visited without even having met them. Something had shifted and he was growing stronger.

The young girl closed her eyes and pictured the hazel eyes, the blonde hair, the warm and loving smile. That vision was all that kept her from succumbing to Father.

She'd awakened that morning with a new vision—the one she'd been waiting for.

Outside the hotel room, she heard men's voices before the door was busted in. Father jumped out of his bed, but she just lay there still. She tried to listen but she was so very tired.

She drifted off to the sound of Father shouting.

TEN

RESCUE MISSION

Rest was not in store for me when I returned to my cottage. Headmaster Hart was waiting on my porch.

"Good evening, Delaney. I'm sorry to disturb you, but it's crucial that I speak with you.."

I was a bit startled by his presence. I opened the door and gestured for him to enter.

"Thank you. I know you've had a really long day, but I received a disturbing phone call this afternoon, and I'm afraid I'm going to need to ask you to pack your things and come with me."

My heart dropped to the floor. "Am I being fired already? This has got to be some sort of record." I was perilously close to tears.

"Heavens no, my dear! Of course you're not being fired. Whatever would give you that idea?" He took my hands and led me over to sit on the couch. Good timing, too, because my legs gave out. I reached frantically for the inhaler I'd left on the coffee table. "Delaney, have we not made you feel welcome here?"

I cleared my throat and looked at the floor. "It's not that. I'm afraid this is all too good to be true."

"You must let go of previous disappointments. They were cases of others letting *you* down, not the reverse. I came to you tonight because I must ask you to accompany Damien on a sensitive mission. We've received word from colleagues in Florida that a young girl was brought to a Jacksonville hospital for treatment this afternoon, a young girl who we have recently learned is meant to be here. The truly sensitive part of this is that her father is the cause of her injuries. My connections in social services have agreed to grant me guardianship of her, but we must go and collect her. She will be too weak to travel without healing from Damien and your influence. If you leave tonight, we can have her back here by tomorrow and we can move on with our orientation."

I felt his growing concern for the girl. "I'll go, Headmaster. When do we leave?"

"Damien will collect you in one of the school's automobiles. You will take our private plane to Sarasota as soon as possible. Damien has further instructions and will phone me with your status." He stood to leave, then paused. "Delaney, this young woman is extremely fragile. She needs you. I have the utmost faith in your abilities, and I am incredibly grateful that you're here. Thank you."

I jumped up to pack an overnight bag. I made sure the cats had enough food and water for the day and called and asked Skye to come over to check on them if I wasn't back by tomorrow. She must have sensed something in my voice because she didn't question me, just agreed to do whatever I needed.

I stepped out onto the porch and saw Damien climbing out of a car at the curb. I jogged over and opened the rear door to throw in my bag.

"Thank you for accompanying me, Delaney. I'm sorry for the late evening. I'll make sure you get some rest once we board the plane."

We both climbed into the front, buckled up, and Damien drove off into the night. I remembered the airport was about thirty minutes away, so I sat back and kicked my sandals off.

"Is there anything you can tell me about the girl?" I pulled my legs up under me on the seat and turned toward him.

"All I know is that Morgan had a vision of her about six months ago. She and her father live alone and move around frequently, which is why we hadn't located her sooner. She has the gift of Sight. She's capable of seeing what's to come. It's an undeveloped skill and we hoped to intervene and bring her here. But then we learned of the reason her father has been moving her. He's become increasingly violent, and has been trying to use her visions for his financial gain. After this latest incident, he's been placed in police custody. We've been given guardianship of her temporarily. A judge will have to approve it, but we at least have ninety days." Damien took a drink of aromatic tea from a Thermos.

"What's the plan, boss? Do we hide her in the laundry basket and sneak her out the back?" He looked at me, shocked, and then rolled his eyes at me when he saw I was teasing. "Sorry, gallows humor gets me through tough times like this. Hope you don't mind."

"Actually, I brought you along to flirt with hospital security while I sneak her out. Did you bring anything more revealing?"

It was my turn to be shocked as he looked down at the outfit I'd put on, one of the new ones I'd bought. He grinned triumphantly. I slugged him a good one in the biceps.

"Hey! You're stronger than you look. I'll have to watch myself." The tension bled out as we laughed together.

"In all seriousness, I'll take my cues from you." I wanted him to trust me.

As if he'd read my mind, he said, "Delaney, I have no doubt you will handle yourself well. The headmaster has no doubts about you, either. He suggested I take you as soon as we heard. And in answer to your previous question, her name is Joanna, and she's fourteen. Her mother disappeared some time ago, and her father is under suspicion for possible foul play."

"They've moved from New York to Montana to California, and now they're in Florida. He's got warrants out for his arrest in Nevada and Texas, as well. The U.S. Marshals have taken him into custody and will be transporting him back to Texas. We're hoping to get her to Havenhart without any trouble, but if we have any, Headmaster Hart has some law enforcement connections in Florida that will be at our disposal."

"Good. And the hospital staff knows we're coming?"

"The hospital administrator has been informed that Joanna will be coming with us as soon as she is stable."

I raised a brow at that. "I'm guessing he hasn't been informed that *you* will be stabilizing her?"

Damien looked at me sideways and grinned. "I'm sure that part was left out. Once she's awake and feeling better, I'll need for you to break the news to her that we'll be taking her with us. From what I know of her Sight, she probably already knows we're coming. I don't know what her response will be, as we haven't been able to reach out to her without going through her father. I can only hope that she'll be cooperative and realize that we're looking out for her best interests."

He seemed in a sharing mood. I took a chance. "Who are you people that you can just waltz across state lines and take a young, abused girl into your custody and fly her out of state? How the heck does the headmaster get away with this stuff?"

Damien chuckled to himself and then tilted his head in thought, almost as if he was thinking of the best way to explain this without me freaking out. "I know you've been concerned about us and our reach. Yes, the headmaster has obtained great power and influence with many nations in the world. Some of this has to do with the power of the visions that Morgan has. He also has an uncanny knack for reading people and discovering their deepest, darkest secrets and wishes. He knows who he can bribe, who he can coax, and who will go along with his program simply because they can feel his power when he enters a room."

He grew serious again. "Delaney...he *knew* me. When he found me in Mexico, he knew me, knew so many things about me. He promised me an education and a life of purpose if I joined him in creating this place. How could I turn that down? I know you had to have had the same feeling when I explained to you what we're all about at Havenhart. Being able to do the work you want, the work you know is so necessary, without the limits of others' fears and expectations?

"I have since learned to accept many, many things I either had no understanding of or lacked a comfort with. Never have I been pushed into anything I didn't want to do, nor have I had to compromise what I thought was right. I've had everything I could need or want here." With that, he looked over and gave me a glance.

A rush of heat flowed between us without him so much as laying a finger on me. His power amazed me. It was hard to believe it was real, but I wouldn't deny it anymore after the things I'd seen so far.

We rode the rest of the way in silence. When we reached the airport, Damien grabbed our bags and carried them onto the private plane, handing an envelope to the pilot as we climbed aboard. Once inside, we made ourselves comfortable. Damien plugged in his iPod to a docking station and put on some instrumental guitar music. It was beautiful. The music soothed my joints and muscles as though the fingers on the strings were caressing me. I leaned back in the seat and closed my eyes.

I felt Damien looking at me.

I opened one eye. "Does this music have any otherworldly powers? Because it's doing a heck of a job putting me to sleep."

He reached over and grabbed my hand in both of his. "Yes, it's magic, now get some rest."

I wasn't sure if he was teasing again or not, but I followed his instructions. The warmth from his hands spread through my arm and up the back of my neck, over the top of my head and made my eyelids even heavier. It continued to move throughout my body, heating me like the sun and sand back home on a California beach.

I wasn't aware that I had fallen asleep until the nightmare began.

I was running through the woods again, Damien in pursuit, the Shadow Man in front of me, bright light, pain in my chest—

"Delaney, breathe! Breathe for me. It's okay, I'm here with you."

I was on the floor in front of my seat, wheezing and coughing. I pointed at my purse. Damien reached inside and grabbed my inhaler for me. I used it, and he handed me a glass of water. I drank slowly and the coughing fit eased.

"You were gasping for air, and then you slumped onto the floor. I thought you were having a heart attack. Has this happened to you before?" The worry was very apparent in his eyes.

I took one more moment to collect myself before I tried to speak. "I've been having this nightmare since right after I arrived at the academy. I don't know what to make of it. Every time, it seems to knock the air out of me."

Damien had been kneeling next to me on the floor of the plane but now he sat back on his heels and gave me a stern look. "I wish you would have told me. Can you remember what it was about?"

I was a bit unnerved at the prospect of letting him into this particular slice of hell.

"I'm not sure I want to tell you, Damien. It's probably nothing, just my nerves or something." Yeah, I knew I wasn't going to get away with that.

Sure enough, he raised an eyebrow. "I seem to recall, my dear, that you have a tendency toward premonitions, am I correct?"

He had me there.

"Not all of my freaky dreams come true. We haven't had a Neanderthal be elected president or anything— Oh my God! It's true, Damien. I can predict the future!"

I tried to get him laughing, but he was having none of it.

"No? All right." I shook my head. "Sometimes I dream things and then they happen. Big deal. They don't *always* happen. I had a particularly disturbing recurring dream while in college of being attacked on a snow-covered walkway outside at night. That never happened. So this dream is probably nothing."

He didn't buy that, either. I sighed dramatically.

"*Fine.* I keep having a dream I'm running through the woods, you're running behind me, some dude is in the shadows in front of me, I see a bright light, something hits me in the chest, I wake up wheezing. Okay? Satisfied?"

His look assured me he wasn't pleased at all with my admission. He stood up and helped me back into my seat. He placed his hands on my arms and closed his eyes.

The warmth I'd felt before was mild compared to the rush of heat I experienced now. Waves of heat flooded my chest. The pressure built until I thought I was going to pass out. He finally pulled me into his arms, and my breath came in deep gasps.

Miraculously, the tightness in my chest was gone.

I looked up into his eyes and saw concern there. I smiled weakly and reached up to smooth the crease in his forehead. "If you keep looking at me like that, this is never going to go away."

"Are you breathing better now?"

I nodded sleepily and he lay me back against my seat.

"We'll be arriving in Florida in about two hours. You should rest." He still looked worried, though.

I closed my eyes to appease him, but I couldn't go back to sleep. I heard him get up and step to the back of the plane. After a few moments, I heard him whispering urgently on the phone.

"She's been having nightmares followed by asthma attacks. ... No, she's resting now in the front cabin. ... I'm not sure but I'm worried. I'll keep her close. ... No, I won't let her out of my sight. I realize how important she is. ... I'm going to let her rest for a bit before we go over to the hospital. She needs to have all her faculties when she meets Joanna. ... Yes, the marshal is supposed to have him out of the area before we arrive. ... I will protect them both and bring them back safely to you, but when we return, I want her to have a full exam. ... I'm not sure, but something about these attacks concerns me. I can't quite get a reading on what's causing them. ... Yes. Of course. I'll call you when we have her with us. Good night, Headmaster."

He hung up the phone and sat back down next to me. His fingers tousling my hair gently did wonders.

Before I knew it, we were landing in Florida. It was still dark outside. I wondered if we would even be allowed in to see Joanna at this time of night.

Damien gathered up our things from the plane and put on a light coat. "Are you awake?"

I nodded and stretched my arms and legs before trying to stand. I felt amazingly good for going on no sleep. His healing touch must have given me energy as well.

"There's a car waiting outside to take us to the hospital. Our driver is a detective with the local police department. Headmaster Hart has been in touch with them since Joanna Rains was admitted this morning. He'll be taking us there and assisting us with her release."

I really hoped this was going to go smoothly, however, I was worried.

The detective was all business. He shook hands with Damien and opened the door for me to his Lincoln Town Car. The hospital was only ten minutes from the airfield. When we arrived, Damien came around to help me out of the car.

"Are you ready for this?"

I nodded, and he took my hand, leading me into the building. We followed the detective to the admissions desk. He showed the nurse his badge, and she gave us directions to Joanna's room.

My heart stopped when I saw her frail body laid out on the bed. I had to collect myself.

Damien gave my hand a squeeze and then left my side to approach her. "Joanna, can you hear me?"

She blinked a few times and opened her eyes. She looked from Damien to the detective to me. At my face, she stopped. She tried to smile but her upper lip had been split. The movement caused her to wince. She was bruised extensively on her face and had defensive wounds on her arms and hands.

Damien looked grim.

She opened her mouth to speak, and she managed a hoarse whisper. "I knew you would come, Miss Frost. It looks worse than it is."

Startled, I moved to her side and took her hand in mine. "Joanna, I am so glad to meet you. Do you know why we're here?"

She nodded and looked to the detective, and then to Damien.

"Can I talk to you alone, Miss Frost?"

"We'll be right outside," Damien said.

I smiled to reassure him. Once they left the room, Joanna whispered to me again.

"They have my father. They said they're going to take him back to Texas. I know that they can't hold him there. Will I really be safe with you? Because if he finds me, he will finish this." She sounded way too mature for her years.

"Joanna, we want to take you back with us to our academy. Do you know about us?"

She nodded. "I know that you work for people who help kids like me. I want to come with you, but the doctor said I can't leave my bed."

I looked to the door, and then she pulled on my hand to bring me nearer. "Ms. Frost, you can trust your dreams. You will see the light." She lay back and closed her eyes for a minute.

A jolt hit me in my chest, almost like what I felt in my nightmare.

"You know about my dream?"

She didn't answer.

I couldn't be distracted from our task. This girl was too important.

"Damien, can you come back in here?"

He entered tentatively, and we exchanged a look. I wanted him to know we had to move on this quickly. She was so weak, and I felt compelled to act, as though something or someone was coming to do her harm.

"Joanna, do you trust us?"

She nodded at me weakly and tried to smile again. I knew we didn't have much time.

"Mr. Preston can make it so that you can travel with us."

She didn't open her eyes but she nodded again. "It's okay, Mr. Preston. I know what you can do. You'll need your powers again for Miss Frost. She will see the light."

Damien looked shaken by her pronouncement. He stood next to me on the side of the bed and took a deep breath. He laid his hands on her stomach and closed his eyes.

Joanna sucked in a breath. I stepped back from the bed and watched in fascination as the bruises faded noticeably from her face. Some of her color returned.

Damien stepped back and stumbled a bit, reaching for the chair behind him. I hurried to his side.

"What can I do? What do you need?"

He opened his eyes and looked at me. He had a fine layer of sweat on his face and when I touched his chest, I felt his heart racing.

"I'm fine, I'm fine. That was just…she needed a lot from me."

I reached for a glass of water for him and he drank.

He looked up at me and said, "I'm just glad you're here."

Joanna sat up on the bed and looked over at us. "We need to go. My father has sent his associates to find me. They'll be here soon."

I called for the detective and he came into the room. He helped me get Joanna out of bed. Miraculously, she was able to walk despite her injuries. I stepped back around the bed to give Damien a hand. He draped an arm around my shoulders, and we hurried out to the car. I got Damien to the passenger seat while the detective put Joanna into the rear. I joined her there.

I leaned forward and placed my hands on Damien's shoulders. "Are you okay?"

He reached up and grabbed one of my hands, giving it a squeeze. "Yes, thank you, Delaney."

Just then, a huge F-150 pulled into the parking lot. Joanna lay herself across my lap and gestured with her eyes toward the truck.

"Damien, do you see—"

The detective got on his radio and called for backup just as I pointed out the men to them. Two burly guys climbed out of the truck dressed in awful Hawaiian shirts and khakis like something out of a detective show on TV, and they had holsters strapped over their shoulders, guns visible under their arms.

They quickly walked toward the entrance and entered the lobby of the hospital without noticing us.

I sat back, breathed a sigh of relief, and looked down at Joanna. She took my hand and sat back against her seat.

"Arkansas is beautiful. We drove through there on the way to Florida. I knew I would be going back there. There are others like me at your academy?"

I nodded and smiled shakily. The past twenty-four hours had been so tumultuous that I didn't know how I'd recover. I wanted to get both of our minds off the fact that we almost ran into those two thugs, and that we hadn't made it back to Havenhart unscathed as of yet. I looked at Joanna and brushed her hair from her forehead. It was damp with the sweat of her exertion, but she seemed better.

"I haven't met everyone yet, as I just arrived myself, but I have met some amazing people with talents I've never imagined. I'm in such awe of all of the children. I hope you'll feel as comfortable as I do there, Joanna. I want you to have a fresh start."

"Like you," she said quietly.

I placed my other hand over hers and nodded. "Like me. We all have to follow the path laid out for us. I'm just glad it's led me here and to you. We'll make sure you have everything you need, but was there anything you're leaving behind?"

She looked out the window and thought for a moment. "I think a fresh start needs to be just that. I don't want anything to remind me of…my past." A single tear ran down her cheek.

I leaned closer to her, and she lay back against me. I held her close and tried to concentrate on making her feel safe.

"It's working, Miss Frost. Thank you."

Was I ever going to get used to these little surprises?

The detective turned onto the road for the airstrip. We boarded the plane and he made sure we were all on and seated before he left. There was a pull-out bed in the rear cabin, so I readied that for Joanna. Her brief burst of energy seemed to have burned out. She lay down and smiled at me before closing her eyes and falling deep asleep.

Back in the front cabin, Damien was just coming out of the restroom. He apparently needed to do my trick with the whole face-splashing thing. He looked pale as he passed me. I followed him to our seats. We sat down, and I turned to face him.

"Damien, I'm worried. Does this usually take so much out of you?"

He took a long drink on his orange juice before he answered. "Occasionally. If the person I'm healing has as much emotional damage as physical pain, it's more draining. That is another reason I wanted you to be here. I knew you would make her feel comfortable. There was a lot of physical and emotional pain within her. She's been through a tremendous amount of abuse. It about broke my heart to feel all of her pain."

I pulled him into my arms, and he rested his head on my shoulder. I closed my eyes, wishing I could take the strain from him.

"She knew all about us, Damien. She was ready to come with us. I didn't do much."

He actually growled at me. "Do I really have to argue this with you again? She was ready because you calmed her. Your presence washed over all of us in that room. You really don't comprehend the effect you have on those around you, do you? I don't know how else to explain it to you. When you touch me, I can feel your energy like a fire in my veins, and then alternately like a gentle wave washing over me. You ignite me and calm me simultaneously. It's…intoxicating." He placed his hand on my thigh and traced an infinity symbol repeatedly, absently.

"Okay, obviously you've had just a little too much fun today, good sir. Just close your eyes and relax before you start hallucinating."

The hand on my thigh made a fist, and then relaxed. I swear I heard him mumble "impossible" under his breath before he, too, fell asleep.

I closed my eyes and drifted off, enjoying the feel of him against me, his dark hair tickling my cheek like silk.

When the plane landed in Arkansas three hours later, Vincent was there to help with Joanna, who was still sleeping peacefully. We rode in silence back to the school. Joanna was taken to the infirmary adjacent to the girls' dormitory. There was a nurses' station fully stocked with first-aid supplies, an exam room, and what appeared to be a patient room. Joanna woke up briefly and was placed in the care of Mrs. Walden, who I learned was a registered nurse and ran the infirmary when necessary. Joanna smiled at me and told me to get some rest, that I'd need it in the days to come. Again with the maturity.

Damien walked me back to my cottage. Sleep was coming on like a freight train. I barely made it in the door and back to my bedroom. I fell on the bed fully clothed and didn't even feel Damien remove my sandals and tuck me in.

I awoke the next morning with sunlight pouring in through the window. I sat up with a start, not remembering how I'd gotten home. Then I heard someone in my kitchen and smelled bacon frying. I stumbled through the doorway and smiled when I saw Damien there. I greedily drank in the sight of him.

He stood in front of the stove in his khakis and just a white t-shirt, his dress shirt draped carefully over the back of one of the barstools. He had the perfect build for a tall man, with just enough muscle tone to fill out his large frame. His broad shoulders and back tapered down to a narrow waist. He filled out his pants nicely. As he stepped over to the sink, his thighs strained against the fabric.

He had a fine covering of black hair down his arms and onto the backs of his hands. His wavy hair was pulled back, and in the sunlight, I saw gray hairs dappled throughout, in addition to the white streak. I'd heard people say that gray hair made a man look distinguished. On Damien, it showed the heaviness of the years he'd lived. While his face was still youthful, he had seen more than his share of tragedy.

He was absolutely sexy as hell.

He seemed very comfortable in the kitchen. As someone who hates to cook, it was intriguing to watch. Every once in a while he'd look out the window, resting his palms on the counter. I could watch him for hours. My satisfied sigh caught his attention.

"Good morning, sunshine. I waited to wake you, but duty calls—" He turned around and stopped to stare.

"I know. I'm a mess. You're really brave, you know. I'm not a morning person."

He put the utensils down on the counter and approached me, taking in the sight before him. "I don't think I've ever seen anything more adorable." He ruffled my hair and pulled me into a hug. My arms circled his waist as if it were the most natural move. I enjoyed the feel of his body against mine.

"How are you up and chipper so early? Did you go home?"

He laughed. "Delaney, its one in the afternoon. I went back to my place to shower and change, checked in with the headmaster, and then came back here to wait for you. I enjoyed watching you sleep. You were so peaceful."

I groaned and pulled away from him. "Not fair. You got a shower and I haven't even brushed my teeth."

He laughed again and went back to his breakfast-making while I got in the shower. I replayed the last twenty-four hours in my mind and felt strangely satisfied with our mission. Joanna was here and safe. Damien trusted me with his gift. He was even making me breakfast. The last part made me smile mischievously to myself. I wondered if that meant I got to keep him.

The cats came barreling into the bathroom, yowling at me simultaneously, my punishment for being gone, I assumed.

"Oh, lay off, you two. I was just doing my job." I gathered they didn't approve. If I wasn't at their beck and call, I wasn't truly working.

When I was presentable, I went back out to the kitchen. Damien was telling someone on the phone that I was up and around and that he would be feeding me before we headed over to the orientation.

"Am I in trouble for oversleeping?" I got myself a glass of juice and sat down at the island to watch him cook. He seemed to know his way around the kitchen competently.

"Actually, that was Diana just checking on you. She and the headmaster took care of your appointments for this morning, and this afternoon they just want you to observe the festivities. We've got a meeting with the students at three, then dinner, then the staff are doing their 'dramatic presentation' for the students this evening, followed by some music I'm sure."

"Sounds like fun. I'll be ready for anything after this breakfast. Thank you so much for this."

He smiled and gave me a nod. "Anything for you after what you did last night." Those green eyes locked on me. "I really want to thank you for going with me to get Joanna. I couldn't have done it without you."

"I'm glad I got to meet her. And I'll go anywhere with you if it means you'll cook for me." I was only mostly teasing.

He gave me a satisfied smirk and served me a plate of fried eggs, bacon and biscuits. Another one of my favorite meals.

"You guys keep getting this stuff right. How do you do it? Spy cam in the purse? Bugs in the bedroom? What's your trick?"

He looked at me seriously and said, "All of the above."

I stopped mid-bite. "You aren't serious. Damien, how do you guys know all of this about me? It's eerie, right down to my favorite type of cereal."

He stepped over to the sink and washed his hands. After drying them off, he walked around me to the living room and started to gather his things. "We have someone here who knows that kind of thing, so we use it. It's nothing nefarious. Now eat up, and I'll see you in the Media Center at three."

He started to leave but stopped in the doorway, rubbing the back of his neck. "I really do want to thank you. I also want to make a request."

I nodded to him, encouraging him to continue.

"If you have any more of those nightmares, any more asthma attacks, I want you to tell me immediately. I told you I'm worried about putting too much stress on you. Don't wait until it gets bad before we take care of it. Do you promise me?"

I shrugged my shoulders. "Won't you know if I'm not well?"

His look told me he wasn't going to joke about this.

"Delaney, you must promise me. You will come to me if you have any more problems."

I stood from the island and walked over to him in the doorway.

"I promise. But you must promise *me* something. Don't keep things from me. Even if you think I need protecting, don't. I would really hate that."

He nodded and took my hand gently. He looked down at our hands together for a moment, gave mine a squeeze, and then turned to leave.

I watched him walk down my path and was even more confused. I had thought the events of the night before had made him feel more comfortable with me, but it appeared he still had reservations.

"Guess I better finish my breakfast. Lord knows what I'm up against tonight."

Ramses and Clio were back in position on the wingback chair and just looked at me blankly.

"You two are no help at all. What am I going to do about him?" The answer was nothing. I could do nothing but sit back and wait.

ELEVEN

ORIENTATION

I WENT TO CHECK ON JOANNA BEFORE BEGINNING MY ORIENTATION DUTIES, but she was resting. Grace assured me she would stay with her until dinner and I assured her I'd be back.

I took my time wandering over to the Media Center. The heat sapped the little energy I'd received from Damien's breakfast. Strangely, it wasn't as oppressive as I was afraid it would be, and it was August, the hottest month of the year.

I noticed a group of students playing volleyball in a sand pit at the rear of the student commons. I stopped to watch for a bit, this being my first chance to really see the students in action. There were about ten boys and girls playing and another thirty or so students watching. Jared refereed with his shirt off and a hat on backward. Moira sat on the grass with some of the girls who were braiding each other's hair. I saw Hazel in that group, sitting with her new dorm mates. It made me smile to see her laughing and enjoying herself with her peers, probably a huge change from where she had come from, where all children were expected to be reserved.

The students didn't resemble a typical high school group of kids. They looked like kids who were having the time of their lives. Kinda like a group at summer camp. No feigned boredom or apathy. The kids playing were giving it their all and being good sports. Some of the kids in the observing group were talking to each other but there were several students sitting alone, talking to various staff members or just watching the others with varying degrees of interest. I wondered if there were language barriers or if they just hadn't met anyone yet.

I noticed one emo-looking couple sitting under a tree away from the others. We used to call them Mods, then they were Goths, and now, emo or scene kids... Names change but things stay the same, I supposed. They faced each other, sitting cross-legged, and the girl read something from a journal to the boy. He looked at her with adoration and it made me smile. Young love, whatever the guise, always tugged at my heartstrings. I so looked forward to meeting all of these kids. They were all mine now.

I walked along farther and heard music playing in the commons. Some of the kids were listening to the jukebox. Jackson sat on the makeshift stage at the piano, with Isaac, Elijah and four kids with various instruments. The students admired the equipment, and I looked forward to hearing some live music. Perhaps they'd play tonight after the performance. I worried that I might be expected to do something.

I was lost deep in the chasm of my thoughts, looking around at the trees and flowers and wandering aimlessly, when I ran into something solid. Startled, I found myself face to face with a boy in his late teens with a muscular build and deep-set almost-black eyes. He glared at me.

I blurted out, "See what happens when you think and walk at the same time?"

He tilted his head to the side, frowned and then started laughing. "I understand. You are making joke. I am laughing at this joke. Very funny."

I breathed a sigh of relief and stuck out my hand. "I'm Miss Frost, your counselor. If I'm not mistaken, you're Sergei? I saw we had a student from Russia. I'm pretty sure you're not from Arkansas."

He laughed again. "I am Sergei. It is pleasure meeting you. I am still learning English. I practice with you?"

I nodded. "You're doing just fine, Sergei. Are you heading over to the orientation? Want to walk with me? Maybe you can keep me from running into anyone else."

He actually bent over laughing this time. "You are comedy maker, not counselor. Maybe they hire you for wrong job."

"Funny guy. So how long have you been in America, Sergei? Did you live in another city before coming here?"

He stopped laughing and became more solemn. I worried I was going to lose him, but then he lifted his chin and swallowed hard.

"I am living in this country for three years. I live with American family in Detroit, Michigan, before meeting the headmaster. He bring me to live here with other children. He says I have gift. I think other people different from me."

I thought about that for a minute. "That may be true, but different can be a great thing. Some people dress different, like different music or sports, some people have special talents that set them apart from other people. I think all of those make for interesting friends, don't you?" He nodded and smiled again. "Personally, Sergei, I like different. Different is good." He looked at me, uncertain, and I winked at him. He started to laugh again.

"That because you different. I never met lady who run into people while thinking. You must have heavy brain."

Now it was my turn to laugh. "Heavy thoughts, yes. Thinking about the people here. I'm new, too. This is my first time meeting the students. I'm a little nervous myself."

"You meet me and you do fine. You not cause me to bleed. That is good start, yah?"

"Okay, you. Let's get going before we're both late." I grabbed his arm in mine and we hurried into the Media Center just as the other students were filing in.

Damien and Morgan were down in front, along with Justin, Marcia and Jackson. There were ten tables set up with eight students at each. I was amazed that they were all here, all together in one room. My heart pounded with excitement. I hurriedly scanned the crowd. I recognized the students I had met the previous day (had it only been a day?) in my office. Nate and Matteo were sitting close to the front. Raven sat alone with the sullen expression. I really hoped that she and I could get past the crossed-arm scowl. I knew I wouldn't win them all. If it wasn't me, though, I hoped she'd find some adult to connect with.

Damien motioned to me to come forward while the students were still chatting away at their tables. When I approached, he smiled kindly and handed me an outline for the session. I had a few minutes to prepare what I would say. I didn't always do well on the fly. After my introduction, Diana and I would hand out schedules.

Earlier in the day, the new students toured the campus and all of the kids received their uniforms, which they would begin wearing on the first day of class on Monday. They'd also received their work-study assignments. Each student was required to do five hours of work per week in various capacities on campus. Some jobs were chosen and some were assigned, based on pairing them up with certain staff members.

I read over the list and was pleased to see Nate would be working in the office two hours a week, along with three students I hadn't met yet, and Raven. I sucked in some air when I read her name and braced myself for the work ahead. In my papers was also a list of students who would be taking Sociology with me, and I snickered when I saw Sergei's name on the list. I would certainly have more fun with him. He had a great sense of humor.

Damien quieted the room down. I took a seat to the side of the tables next to Skye and Justin. I noticed a change in temperature when he began to speak, or maybe it was just me remembering the heat from the night before. The students paid close attention to him. I surmised there weren't too many discipline problems, although they'd apparently needed me.

"Welcome to Havenhart Academy. I am Mr. Preston, your Director of Student Services. I am so very pleased to see all of you sitting here today. Some of you have come from faraway places, and some are close to home. But all of you have come a long way *personally* to be here." His eyes traveled the room, making contact with many of the students directly.

"We have chosen you to attend this academy because all of you possess unique and powerful qualities. We want to help you learn to use them to their full potential. Many of you have faced obstacles and skeptics in your lives. Many of you have suffered tragedies and losses. Many of you are away from family for the first time, or have not *had* family for a very long time. My staff and I want to provide that family for you.

"The headmaster, who will address you tonight at dinner, has hand-chosen the best and most qualified teachers and specialists to work with you. The education you receive will be superior to that of your peers all over the world. In return, all we ask of you is that you keep an open and tolerant mind, be respectful of *all* persons on our campus, and utilize this gift of education that has been bestowed upon you. We expect great things from you, and will provide you with all the tools necessary for your success."

The students began to applaud nervously. They looked at each other, trying to read the situation. The psychic energy in the room was humming. So many of these children were powerful beings. It was overwhelming to have them all in the same place.

Damien called them to attention again. "I would now like to introduce you to our staff." He began calling out the teachers one by one: Morgan and Elijah, the Waldens, Vincent and various other staff, including Marcia and Jackson. Lastly, he called my name and told the students I would be saying a few words.

Nervously, I stepped to the front. I looked around for a moment and drank in the silence. The hair on my arms stood at attention, the energy swirling around me like static electricity. I cleared my throat before speaking.

"How many of you have ever had to see a counselor or a therapist?" A few raised their hands, a few more looked around nervously, afraid to admit it, and others crossed their arms and grimaced.

"Okay, thanks to those who responded. How many of you had a positive experience?" A few hands went up, not many.

"Great. Now how many of you think all shrinks and counselors are full of crap?"

Nervous laughter sprung up and more hands were raised. "Alright, now we're talking. I'm a firm believer that counseling never works if there's not a relationship between the two people involved, and if one of those is a quack, then no one is going to benefit. Am I right?" There was a murmur of agreement, so I went on.

"Now, as a counselor, you might assume that I think I can fix people, or that I think everyone needs therapy. I'm here to tell you that that's not the case. I absolutely think counseling can be helpful. I think everyone needs someone to talk to from time to time. But counseling with the wrong person or for the wrong reasons can be very detrimental. And most of all, if someone is forced to go to counseling, or has been told 'you've got a problem so you *will* go to counseling,' it ain't gonna work, right?"

Heads nodded, and I stopped to smile at them.

"The way I see it, it's my job to be what you need me to be. Whether it's a tutor, a sounding board when you've got to make a tough decision, or a shoulder to cry on, I'm here for you. If you just need a place to hide or to yell and scream until your voice gives out, that's what my office is for. Come and see me whenever you need me, grab me when I'm out and about, or even come for a walk with me. But don't stay away because of previous experiences with counselors. I don't know you, you don't know me, so we have a clean slate. Got it? Good."

I smiled and stepped back over to my seat. Jackson shook his head at me and chuckled to himself as I passed. Skye high-fived me as I took my chair.

When I found Damien's eyes, they were focused intently on me. I saw approval there, and something else...admiration? I blushed and looked away first.

Morgan spoke next about the Media Center and the services she would provide there. She then said a blessing for the school year. Many of the students gazed inquisitively at her. Others were moved by her words. I wondered if the students would be open to her teachings and figured many probably would. The young are usually more open to the other side of life than some of us older folks.

I sat back and watched as Skye and Margaret led the students through some ice-breaker activities, including person bingo. Several of the students approached me shyly to ask questions such as could I roll my tongue, how many foreign countries had I visited, and whether I was an only child. The rest were all excited and competitive, climbing over each other to be the first to get a bingo, which meant all of their squares were filled in. Nate was the winner, and he took a bow in front of the other students.

When the session was over, Morgan excused the students to dinner and they all rushed out excitedly. I trailed behind the emo couple I had seen earlier. They held hands and walked quietly next to each other. I made a mental note to keep an eye on them, and to be sure I gave the sex talk to the girls...soon. I figured I'd rope Jackson into having the talk with the boys. It's was sometimes easier for the kids to ask questions of a same-gendered presenter.

I checked on Joanna, but she was sleeping again. Grace let me know she'd been awake, she'd been fine and had drank some broth before falling back to sleep. Grace let me know she'd be staying nearby tonight in case Joanna woke up so I could focus on the rest of the students.

Lost in my thoughts, I hadn't noticed Jackson catching up to me.

"Earth to Delaney, you there?"

I cocked my hand back to give him smack to the back of the head but he hopped out of my reach.

"Don't even think about it, woman. I got moves."

I failed to suppress an eye roll at that statement.

"Seriously though, I wanted to ask you about tonight. We could use some help with the skits. How's your acting ability?"

"You doubt my mad skillz?" He gestured his apology. "I'm up for it. What do I have to do?" We conspired for the duration of the walk to the commons. "I think I've got it. Do I need a costume?"

"Nah, I've got you covered. But I was wondering, do you have plans for Friday?" He looked hopeful. I was really glad I had made other arrangements. I didn't want to hurt his feelings, but I also didn't want to go there with him.

"Actually, my cousin James is driving over from Bella Vista to visit me. I'm really excited to see him. We've lived apart for a long time."

Jackson frowned.

I'd hoped he wouldn't have this reaction. If he knew the extent of the situation between Damien and I, he'd probably *really* lose it. I wasn't sure what to do with this situation. I grew uncomfortable the longer I walked with him, which sucked, because I really thought we'd be able to be friends.

"Any visitors have to be cleared by the headmaster. You need to get the visit approved. Otherwise, you'll need to meet him in town. I'll see you after dinner." And with that, he stomped off to join the other teachers.

"Jackson. Wait."

But he was already gone. I really didn't have the time or the energy to deal with a temper tantrum. A part of me—not the counselor part obviously, because that part knew better—wanted to take care of his feelings, wanted to be sure he didn't get hurt.

The delectable scent wafting from the commons pulled me out of my rut. If I wasn't mistaken, the Waldens had prepared some mouthwateringly delicious fried chicken. I held my breath until I verified that *yes!* We were having my favorite tonight.

I heaped my plate with a breast and drumstick, some mashed potatoes and corn on the cob. Comfort food for the masses. What a great way to ease any nerves after the previous session. I looked around and spotted Skye sitting with some students I hadn't met yet, so I joined them for our meal.

Skye was apparently having a conversation with the kids about California. They wanted to know if it was true that everyone there, including me, modeled, surfed, and ate granola? I assured them that while I was once a Little Miss Valentine pageant runner-up and had boogie boarded and enjoyed the occasional bowl of granola, everyone was quite diverse in California. Skye and I told them about the different kinds of people you can find in our home state and the kids fired question after question at us.

The other teachers were also spread out and visiting with the students, which warmed my heart. I knew I was working with some really special people.

Everyone's heads turned as Headmaster Hart took the stage. He welcomed everyone again and let the students know how delighted he was to see them all looking well and prepared for the term to begin. He told them he would have some surprises in store for them, so they should work hard and get acclimated. The students watched him in awe, as his presence was quite intimidating. I had yet to detect anything sinister from him, despite my earlier misgivings.

Plates were cleared and the staff began their skits. We were all rolling in the aisles at their attempts to look and sound like the students. When it was my turn to act out the proper behavior in the Media Center, I was ready to be the bad example. Morgan scolded me properly, and while the kids found it hilarious, I hoped this wasn't a place I would find myself in often. She was scary.

When the skits were finished, the guys set up their instruments and began to play. Jackson manned the keyboards, Justin banged the drums, Jared played guitar and Isaac strummed the bass.

"How you doin' tonight, Havenhart Academy?" Jackson shouted into the mic. "We're That One Band, and we're going to do our best to entertain you with a few songs you may or may not know. Rules are that you have a good time, dance if you feel like it, and please, no heckling."

They played a few alternative tunes from the likes of The Killers, Neon Trees, and Muse, all with Jackson doing a fantastic job on the vocals. Damien was deep in conversation with the headmaster when Jared called out to him from behind the microphone to come pick up the guitar.

I held my breath in anticipation. I really had a weakness for guitar players, and dammit if his whole aura didn't change when he slung that guitar over his shoulder and started to tune. He pulled his hair back into a low ponytail, leaving one curly strand hanging in his face. He rolled up the sleeves of his button-down Brooks Brothers shirt and then turned to face the rest of the band.

I was sitting toward the back of the commons, so I couldn't hear their planning session. Mr. Walden had turned down the lights and I noticed for the first time they had actual stage lights. There was even a disco ball, for goodness sake. The lights danced over the players and Jackson leaned into the mic. Justin tapped out a "1, 2, 3, 4" on the sticks and Damien played the opening chords of Lynyrd Skynyrd's "Gimme Three Steps." A group of kids jumped up to dance.

Skye grabbed my hand and pulled me out to the center of the floor. We flailed about with abandon. Jackson smiled at us and pounded away on the keyboards. His voice was gravelly. He had the Southern Rock vibe down. He seemed very at home as the band leader.

I tried my best not to look at Damien, but when he went into a guitar solo, I had to take a peek. His usual proper demeanor was absent. He closed his eyes and pursed his lips in concentration. When he finished the solo, he opened his eyes and immediately caught my gaze.

He smiled wickedly and pointed to me, mouthing, "You're up next."

I shook my head vigorously, but as soon as the song was over and the whole room applauded, Jared had ahold of my arm. There was no sense in fighting him.

"Well lookey here, folks. Miss Frost is going to sing one for us. Let's give her a hand." Jackson was having way too much fun with this as I was pushed up to the front. I was as mortified as if I were standing up there naked. I looked to Damien desperately for help, and he just gave his usual chuckle.

"I can't do this," I whispered to them.

Jackson wasn't going to let me get away that easy. He stepped up and placed his mic in my hands.

"Sure you can, Counselor. What do you sing in the shower?" He was truly eating this all up.

"Fine, you guys know 'Bobby McGee' by Janis Joplin? No? I didn't think so." I turned to run from the stage as Damien grabbed an acoustic guitar and played the opening chords. I turned around and found him staring me down with hooded eyes, nodding at me in reassurance.

The kids were all watching and smiling. I knew I couldn't expect them to be strong and face their demons if I couldn't even sing a silly song.

I cleared my throat and closed my eyes, figuring I'd just dive right in.

I started to sway along and loosen up a little. The kids mimicked me and listened to the music intently. Some of the adults raised their cell phones in lieu of lighters. I smiled and felt my voice growing stronger. I'd loved this song since I was a kid. My mom played it a lot.

I was really enjoying myself and started to lose myself in the moment. I smiled at Jackson, who stared at me with wide eyes and an encouraging grin. The others in the band were having a great time as well.

I finally gathered up what was left of my courage and looked over to Damien as I began singing the last chorus. His gaze burned a hole right through me.

My heart was on fire. The joy of the day's events, my favorite song, and this fascinating man energized me. I stepped up to the front of the stage to finish the song and saw Hazel standing to the side of the stage, smiling brightly. I knew she had probably never heard songs like this. It was so wonderful to see her having fun.

When the song ended, the crowd burst into cheers for me. I curtsied and handed the mic back to Jackson with an evil glint in my eye.

"I will get you for this, Howe. I already have payback in mind. You are in so much trouble."

He grabbed his chest in mock pain. Brat. He'd be sorry when I roped him into doing the boys' session of Sex Ed 101.

The band broke into a jam session as I walked over to the counter to grab a glass of water. I was a little shaky but exhilarated. I didn't have a future as a rock star, but damn that was fun.

I hadn't noticed the absence of a second guitar in the music, so when Damien took me by the elbow and guided me toward the back doors, I almost spit my water out in surprise.

"I never knew water was lethal," I joked, referring to him spitting it out in my car, was that months ago?

He paid no attention to my feeble attempts at humor. His eyes were wild. Energy rippled off his skin.

The night air was cool, but still muggy. I immediately began to perspire but I didn't know whether to attribute that to the humid night, exertion, or present company. Still holding my elbow, Damien led me around the back of the commons to a path heading into the woods.

"Where are you taking me? Is it Human Sacrifice time?"

"I really hope that's a joke, Delaney. I told you we don't do anything particularly out of the ordinary here, none of the really evil stuff." If he was trying to appease me, it wasn't working.

"Okay, but I'm warning you. I don't taste very good, so if you're serving me up to the Forest Monsters, I don't think they'll be satisfied."

At that statement, he backed me up against a trunk just inside the tree line.

"On the contrary, I'm sure you taste delicious. I can't wait another minute to test that theory."

Before I came up with another smart-assed comment, his lips were on mine, insistently. His long fingers gripped my shoulders, pushing me firmly but not painfully against the tree. The kiss was so unexpected, as most of his actions were, but certainly not unwelcome.

I melted into his body and grabbed his hips to steady myself. I'd say it was hard to imagine this level of passion coming from such a prim and proper man, but I'd sensed this feeling from him in glimpses before, and had hoped desperately that if he ever let it surface, I'd be on the receiving end.

He pulled away from me slightly, panting, the waves of energy pulsating around us. "God, Delaney, I've wanted to do that for so long. The day we sat on the steps on Sproul Plaza as you closed your eyes and listened to the music. When we watched the sun set over the ocean in Santa Cruz. When we spoke in your car after our harrowing journey home... Every minute I've spent with you here has been an exercise in restraint. But watching you sing tonight proved to be my breaking point. You're extraordinary. I want—"

I grabbed the sides of his face and rose up on my toes to kiss him again. His groan rumbled against me. I pressed myself to his chest and his arms wrapped around me, pulling me tighter. It was difficult to breathe... for so many reasons. But I didn't want it to end. His lips were so strong, yet soft. He held me firmly yet tenderly. The intensity built and built until I cried out.

My fingers dove into his hair, damp with sweat and soft as silk. I held on for dear life as his energy and excitement lifted me off my feet. Literally.

I pulled away, gasping, and I realized he was supporting my entire weight. I wrapped my legs around his waist. His strong hands grasped my thighs, and I felt his lips and teeth drag down my neck. He pressed kisses into the hollow of my throat and to the tops of my shoulders.

"If we keep this up, I'm going to need my inhaler."

He looked up at me with alarm. I smiled slyly at him. He lowered my legs and my feet hit the ground. He slid his knee between my thighs, he rested his hands on either side of my neck, and he pressed his forehead against mine.

We stood there breathing heavily. His scent filled me with desire for more of him. I wanted to stay in this moment with him forever. But then we heard the kids coming out of the commons, heading for their dorms for the night. They couldn't see us from the path, but it served to cool us down.

"Delaney," he whispered into my hair.

I smiled and rested my head on his chest. His heart beat rapidly and so strong, I felt it. Any question I had about his attraction to me was gone, however I didn't know what that meant, either. I knew things had changed between us. I was just going to have to patiently see how it played out. Because I was so good at that.

"Okay, so we've determined that we can do some things well together. I thought we sounded great up there onstage. And we both enjoy nature walks at night."

His husky laughter tickled me as he kissed the top of my head, rubbing his chin along my scalp.

"And that you will joke to deal with just about any serious moment."

I looked up into his eyes and found peace there, understanding. He knew that I was uncomfortable with intensity and wouldn't force me to deal with it, yet. Funny how I gave the best advice to people about intimacy issues, but when it came to my own, I was clueless.

"Hey, it's common knowledge that most counselors are more screwed up than their clients. You were warned."

He stepped back a bit and coolness hit me where his body was now absent. I wanted to pull him back and hold him there, never let him go.

"Someday, you are going to let me in there," he pressed a finger into my breastbone. "All kidding aside, Delaney. I can't stay away from you. I know this is a fine line we walk here. I'm not quite sure how to proceed, but I refuse to deny this anymore."

He leaned in and kissed me, lightly this time, just faintly touching his tongue to mine with feather-like strokes. He brushed his cheek against mine and then looked into my eyes again.

"I'm not sure what my boss is going to think about this. He might not approve." I brought his hand up to my mouth and kissed his knuckles gently.

He groaned deep in his chest and let his head fall back, closing his eyes.

"Woman, you are too much. Your boss is just going to have to deal with me."

He began to lead me back toward campus. "I'm going to see you home now before we discover just what else we do well together." The smile that followed knocked me out. I figured him for passionate, but this smile was all male and cocky. It left me weak and without a comeback.

We walked side by side without speaking. When we reached my porch, he gave me one last kiss.

"Get some rest, beautiful. Tomorrow's Friday, and we've got some last-minute bits to go over before school starts on Monday. Then I plan on testing my theories a bit more. One can never stop an experiment after the first trial, am I wrong?"

"Hmmmm..." I said into his shoulder as he held me close for a moment. I jolted away then. "Friday. Oh. Um, I guess I should tell you that I have plans with another man tomorrow night. I meant to tell you before we had this, er, discussion."

His expression was priceless. I couldn't help but let him suffer a bit for teasing me earlier and making me sing.

Damien stepped onto a lower step and cleared his throat. "Do you mean Jackson, Delaney?" He looked really hurt. I instantly felt horrible.

"Oh, no. Damien! No, ugh, I am so sorry. I just meant to tease you a little. My cousin James wanted to see me. Nothing shady, I promise."

He smiled a little at that and squeezed my hand.

"I suppose I deserve that. Is he going to come and see you?"

"We hadn't worked out the particulars yet. I wasn't sure if it was okay for him to come here. Jackson said I needed to have the visit approved by the headmaster and with all of the excitement, I totally forgot."

"It's no problem. I'm delighted you'll be seeing your cousin. Would you permit me to take you into Eureka Springs so you can meet him for dinner? It would be no trouble. I have some business in town anyway, and then I could collect you later in the evening. What do you say?"

"That sounds great, Damien, really. I've wanted to see James for a long time. I really miss him. He's been going through a difficult time. His ex-wife is keeping his daughters from him and he's heartbroken about it."

Damien's face turned dark for a moment. "Being kept from your children is the worst pain anyone can visit upon a person. I am sorry for him."

"Something tells me this is familiar territory for you. You know...I never even asked. God—are you married? Do you have any children?" I held my breath in anticipation of his answer. I really hoped this thing between us hadn't just crossed over into ugly territory.

"No, I don't have any children. Nor am I married anymore." He looked away from me toward the trees, and it appeared he was collecting his thoughts. "I *was* married, but it was a long time ago. Someday I'll tell you about it, but if it's alright with you, I'd rather put that off for another time."

"Absolutely, I'm sorry. Counselor thing. Can't help but pry a bit."

He shook his head. "No, it's fine, really. You have a right to know after I just mauled you in the forest. I *will* tell you, Delaney, but tonight, I just want to think of how much I really enjoyed the feel of you against me. Is that alright with you?"

His voice dropped an octave at that last statement, and he drew closer to me again. He wrapped an arm around my lower back and his other hand grabbed my neck. He held me close while his lips performed their magic once more.

This time when he pulled back, I saw sadness in his eyes. I tilted my head in question, and he smiled.

"Nope, no more counselor magic tonight. I shall see you in the morning, my lady. Go say goodnight to those cats and get some rest. Until then..." He bent down and kissed my hand.

I stepped inside and watched him walk to the carriage house through the window. His silhouette in the moonlight was breathtaking. I swore I saw energy glowing around him.

If all that was from a kiss, then what would happen if...

TWELVE

COMPLICATIONS

I ENTERED MY COTTAGE AND LEANED AGAINST THE DOOR. I COULD STILL smell Damien on me. His scent had permeated my skin and hair. I smiled to myself and closed my eyes. I heard my cell phone buzzing on the counter where I'd left it this morning. I sauntered over to check it out. There were three messages.

"Delaney, it's your mom. I just wanted to hear your voice. I really hope things are going good for you out there. I miss you. Call me when you can. I love you."

"I miss you too, Maw." Being away from home was difficult, but there was so much going on that it didn't affect me as much. I knew this move was going to be tougher on her because of the potential permanence.

"Favorite cousin. It's your favorite cousin. Call me."

James and I had a lot of catching up to do. I had so much to tell him about this place.

"I hope you're okay. You shouldn't be alone with him. Did he tell you about his wife? I bet he didn't. Delaney, I don't want to see you get burned, and you will with him. I just wish... Never mind. Be careful. Don't play with fire."

The layer of sweat on me turned ice cold. Jackson. He must have seen us leave together. How dare he leave me a message like that? What did he mean?

I don't know how long I stood there, but both Ramses and Clio had come over to either side of me. They nudged me with their noses and climbed up to bat at my knees with their paws. They had always been able to read me and knew when I was upset.

I went to the bathroom and washed my face and then fell into bed with my clothes still on. I proceeded to sleep fitfully.

This time when I dreamed, there was fire all around me. Just like before, I was covered in flames, but I didn't burn. I heard screams from the children and I fought desperately to reach the voices. Suddenly, I was running through the forest toward the circle. He was there. The blinding light—

When I woke around six, my chest was full of goo. I coughed and coughed but my lungs wouldn't clear, even after using my inhaler. I made some tea and let it steep while I showered. Afterwards, I sat down at the island in the kitchen and sipped my tea, grateful that my coughing fit had ceased and my eyes weren't as puffy. An hour later, Skye knocked on my door.

"Delaney? I just wanted to see if you were coming to breakfast."

I called out to her that I'd see her later. She hesitated, then asked if I was sure. I told her I'd meet her for lunch. When I was sure she'd left, I stepped out and went straight to my office. I wanted to organize things a bit and put some ideas together for my Sociology class that would be starting the following week. Anything to avoid thinking about the previous night.

I called James and told him I'd meet him in town at six. He suggested a diner and then drinks at Shenanigans. I prayed it would be less eventful than my previous visit.

The next time I looked up, it was eleven and I'd worked myself into a massive headache. Diana was at her station when I stepped out of my office coughing. I apparently startled her.

"I didn't know you were in. You've been so quiet." When she got a closer look, she stepped out from around her workstation. "Are you all right, Delaney? Do you want me to call Damien?"

I shook my head vigorously. "No. I don't want to see him this morning," I blurted out.

Diana frowned. "You don't have to tell me what happened if you don't want to, but I know he'd be very concerned if he knew you weren't well. Did something happen last night?"

I thought about what was safe to tell her. "Just didn't sleep well." I tried a smile. She didn't buy it.

"I still think I should have him come see you." She started back for her phone.

I touched her hand gently as she picked up the receiver. "Please, Diana. I don't want him to see me like this. I need to get my head together before I see him, okay? Please? I promise if my breathing gets worse, I'll go see him."

She wasn't happy but she acquiesced. I wondered if she would call him anyway.

More good news was waiting for me after I used the restroom.

"Raven. Hi. Is there something I can do for you?" I wasn't sure I had enough strength for another go 'round with her. She had a sour face on and a "whatever" posture. I made sure I had my best smile and my most gracious voice ready for my response.

"Ms. Frost, I wanted to talk to you about my work study. Do I really have to work here? I think I've had enough of the counseling office. No offense." Maybe I would have bought that last statement if it weren't dripping with sarcasm.

"I didn't assign the work study. You'll have to speak with Mr. Preston about that. I *will* tell you that working here doesn't mean you have to have anything to do with counseling. I'd love some help getting set up for my Sociology class. Would you be interested in doing a little research, stapling and grading papers, stuff like that?" I sensed interest, but she had to continue to front with me.

"Whatever. I guess that wouldn't be as bad. I can always talk to Mr. Preston later. Do I have to start today?"

"When did your schedule say you started?" I figured it would be next week before the kids had to start working, but then Damien and I hadn't had enough time to discuss it.

"It said Monday. But I'm not doing anything, not like there's anything *to* do around here. What do you need researched?"

Yes! Success.

"Well, I need to talk to Miss Forrester for a bit. How about we walk over to the library and I can explain it to you on the way?"

She shrugged. I took that as a yes. I grabbed my work I'd been busy with that morning and told Diana where we'd be. She nodded, watching Raven and I with eyebrows raised.

On the way over, I told Raven that I'd taught the class before and I planned to cover a wide range of topics, that perhaps each week we'd discuss an article dealing with topics such as education, religion, and the institution of family as a way to kick it off. I showed her my outline and she looked it over intently.

"I can find you some articles that go along with these, that's no problem. I'm great with Google." She was still trying to sound as though this was all beneath her, but I detected a definite interest.

"That would be a huge help. After I see Ms. Forrester, I'm going to head back to my office. You want to bring me what you have when you're finished?"

She nodded without making eye contact and plopped down at the nearest computer, eyes already fixed to the screen.

I let myself feel a small dose of triumph as I walked past the stacks to Morgan's office. She was reading and bobbing her head to some ethereal-sounding Gaelic music. I hated to disturb her, but of course at that moment, I had a coughing fit and had to grab my inhaler from my bag.

"What can I do for you, Delaney?" she asked without looking up from her book.

"I left Raven out front to work on some research for me. I hope that's okay."

She nodded as her eyes continued to scan the page in front of her. "And what can I do for *you*?" At this, she turned to look at me, her expression concerned. "You don't exactly seem up for working today. What happened?"

I didn't know if I was doing the right thing but I had to ask. I had no idea why I'd come to her, other than she seemed to know more about the staff than anyone, including Damien. And beneath her slight hostility, I thought she respected me. Perhaps she was trustworthy.

"What do you know about Jackson? I mean, has he given you any reason to think he's not, how do I put this delicately…"

"Stable?" She stood up from her desk and motioned for me to join her on the couch. "Headmaster Hart and I have differed in our opinion about the propriety of him being here. I know he loves the kids, so I keep my mouth shut. What do you want to know?"

"Well, when I first met him, he went on and on about knowing me at Graceland. Honestly, I don't remember him, and I don't think I was so self-centered that I'd forget someone like him. And his mood swings around me are a little freaky. I didn't want to say anything to Damien because, well, there seemed to be some tension there, especially after the bar incident. I've been very clear with Jackson that I'm only interested in being friends with him. I'm just not sure if he gets it." I stopped for a moment and took a swig off my water bottle to stave off a coughing fit. Talking set me off easily.

"From what I know about Jackson," she began, "he was in the military after a short time in college in Iowa. I know he had some hairy experiences in Iraq and Afghanistan. He's only been out for the two years he's been here. He's intense about his art and the kids. He spends some time hanging out with the guys, playing ball and jamming, but he keeps to himself a lot. Maybe you don't remember him from school because he wasn't there very long? I don't know. Only Damien and the headmaster have detailed personnel information like that."

She tilted her head and looked at me with squinted eyes. "You're not well. Can I do a blessing for you? You might find it helps. It's not the same as Damien's touch, but it should suffice."

I wanted to trust her. I needed to.

She stood and went to her table and began to gather some ingredients. She motioned for me to sit on the floor. She joined me, and as we sat facing each other, she lit some incense and put her ingredients into a bowl. Once again, I was surprised the incense didn't bother my lungs.

She ran her hand over the top of the bowl and closed her eyes. She whispered some words in a foreign language and I closed my eyes, too. Flashes of my nightmare and my memories of the fire intertwined for a few seconds, and then everything went black.

After a moment, I opened my eyes.

Morgan was looking at me, concerned.

"Delaney, you are carrying some heavy baggage. For a counselor, I would think you'd know better than that. You certainly won't be able to fully care for our students here with that stuff hanging around."

Great, called out by the witch. "I'm all ears if you have ideas." I tried not to sound sarcastic, but it was as if she'd cut me open and was slipping her fingers around in my guts for fun.

"Nothing worthwhile is painless, you know that. I think a regression and some trancing would help. But you've got to be open to it. I'm not sure you're ready, but I'll be here when you are. In the meantime, I really think you should talk to Damien. I know something is trying to happen there, and you'd be stupid to screw it up over this."

I was shocked at her candor, not to mention the fact that she knew about us.

"How did you... Did you see us, or did you *See* us?"

She laughed as she gathered up her tools.

"You really think I'm going to give up trade secrets? Forget it. But then, you'd have to be blind not to see the way he looks at you. He does confide in me from time to time, Delaney, and I wouldn't betray a confidence from either of you. But he didn't need to tell me. And yes, being a Seer does have its advantages. The Fates haven't made any predictions about the two of you at this point. You both have a lot of unfinished business, and before you ask, no, I will not tell you about his. You both need to be open with each other, and I realize that's difficult when you're in a fish bowl."

She paused for a minute. "But this business with Jackson does bother me."

"Yes. It's almost like he knows things he shouldn't know. He left me a really cryptic message on my answering machine last night about Damien and me, and the fire—"

"I know about the fire, Delaney."

I didn't want to go there. I really didn't. My hands start to go clammy again.

"I'll do what I can. I will see what I can See, without letting him know. If I discover anything disturbing, I'll certainly let the headmaster know."

I was still unsure how to approach Damien about this.

"Thank you so much, Morgan. I'm sorry to burden you with this."

She held up a hand in protest. "Just as Damien told you he wanted you to be well for our students, I want the same. I've Seen how important you'll be to us. We can't lose you over something so insignificant. You are stronger than you know, Delaney, but you need to let go of these things that haunt you. I'll help however I can."

She stepped over to me and pulled me into an embrace. I couldn't have been more surprised if she'd handed me her winning lottery ticket. I hugged her back, and instantly some of the tension eased.

I left Morgan's study feeling a little woozy, but breathing much better. Raven was still huddled in front of the computer so I left her to her work, pleased at her diligence.

I wasn't ready to go back to my office and counseling matters. My feet led me in an entirely different direction. Before I knew it, I was in front of the infirmary. I stalled out in front of the door, not ready to see Damien yet but concerned about Joanna. At that moment, Mrs. Walden stepped out of the door.

"Hey, Delaney. We still on for planting in the morning?"

I nodded enthusiastically. Gardening would surely ease my troubled mind. "I'm very much looking forward to it. How's Joanna today?"

She nodded gravely. "Physically, she's better. Emotionally, she's stronger...but psychically, she's all over the place. She said some disturbing things during our visit, but didn't elaborate. The headmaster is in with her right now. Damien should be back to see her this afternoon."

I was grateful that I still had some time before I had to see him. "Thanks. There's something wonderful about her, isn't there?"

She smiled affectionately at me, patted my shoulder and headed off toward her cottage.

"Ms. Frost, how delightful to see you this afternoon. Have you come to see our Joanna?"

The headmaster, looking dapper as ever, but he had a disturbed look in his eyes. I gathered from others that he too had a gift of Sight, and I wondered just what he knew. He was kind of an enigma. He'd drop psychic bombs on you after making you feel settled, like a bucket of cold water dropped from a window above.

"I was coming to see Joanna. But first, is everything set for classes to begin on Monday? I'm afraid I missed the briefing this morning. I was a bit lost in my own preparations."

He smiled kindly, knowingly. "Yes, of course, dear. No worries whatsoever. Damien has this place running like clockwork. Between he, Morgan, Vincent, and Elijah, I don't even need to be here." At this, he chuckled heartily.

I knew his statement to be false. His spirit was ever present, no matter where he might physically be. The school had his imprint all over it, from the buildings to the staff, the students to the atmosphere. It was almost like a security blanket. Knowing he had the vision to bring us all together felt like divine intervention.

He bid me farewell and stepped out into the warm summer afternoon. I entered Joanna's room quietly. She appeared to be sleeping, so I sat down in the chair next to her bed. I figured she might want something to entertain her and wondered what she liked to read.

"Anne Rice is my favorite. I found her books in my grandfather's library. I had to leave all my books behind when we moved around. I hid them under the mattresses so Father wouldn't find them." She opened one eye and smiled at me. Her talents extended to full-on mind reading. Yikes. I was going to have to be careful around her. Or not. She seemed so knowing, almost omniscient.

"You don't have to hide from me, Miss Frost. I don't want you to be afraid of what I know. Some things are inevitable. The light will come, and bring with it pain, but it will also bring you together." She closed her eyes again, almost as if talking was causing her strain.

"Joanna, can you turn it off? I mean, it appears to be draining you." I smoothed her hair back from her face.

"I don't know. I've never been able to try."

I hated that she'd been through so much.

"Thank you for your words. I won't hide from you. I want you to trust me, and I know you will doubt me if you can read one thing and I say another. I want to help you heal, not just from your injuries, but from your past and the pain that you're still experiencing."

She nodded, still with her eyes closed. She looked almost ethereal lying there on the bed. Her hair was jet black, long and straight with little-girl bangs. Her skin was so pale it was almost translucent. It barely covered frail bones. When she did open her lids, long lashes swept back to reveal ice-blue eyes. She was chronologically a child, yet experience and knowledge gave her an old soul. It would be easy to treat her like an adult, but she still needed nurturing.

"Mr. Preston was here this morning. He's worried my father will find us. My father is already making a plan to come here. I dreamed he escaped from the marshals and showed up here. When he does... I can't see what will happen."

"Joanna, we will move Heaven and Earth to keep you from him. Tell me about him. What can you tell me that will help me protect you? Because I'm not giving you back to him."

She smiled at my determination.

"He's the source of my conditions...all of them. He has some of the Sight but his true power comes from his Influence. We are linked. He can always see me, which is why I never tried to leave him before. He made me weak. He wanted to use me for...his gain. But our connection is limited. He can only sense me. He was the same with my mother until he...until she disappeared."

After all she'd been through, she was still afraid of outing him for all of his crimes. I took her hand in mine, closed my eyes and tried to ease her.

She smiled peacefully and sighed. "That's so nice. I feel like my body is mine, like I have it all to myself when you do that. Is it true you didn't know you could do that before you came here?"

"I never realized I did anything other than what any ordinary counselor would do. I've just always tried to use my intuition about where someone's pain came from and tried to draw it out. Of course, sometimes I don't even think I was trying, but my presence seemed to have the same effect." I chuckled to myself, thinking of big overgrown dudes crying on my shoulder.

"Yes, there were many, weren't there? And they weren't just giving you a line, they were crying for the first time. Except for one, he just wanted to, um..." She blushed at that, afraid to tell me what I had already gathered.

"Ah, yeah. Consider that a warning to you. Although you'll always know what their intentions are, won't you?" We both laughed at that. I leaned over to brush her hair back once again, the strands sliding through my fingers. "I've got to run out for a while tonight, but I promise I'll bring you a treat from town. I'm guessing you'll be out of here in a day or two."

She frowned for a minute, contemplating what I'd said. "You know, Miss Frost, I've never really spent much time with my peers. We were always on the move, my whole life. My mom home schooled me because she didn't want me to get hurt at school, and then when she left, well, there wasn't much academic schooling going on anymore. I don't know how to be around other kids. How do I handle it? Will my roommate be mad at me when I tell her what she's going to do the next day?"

"In a regular school, I'd say yes. Definitely people will never be satisfied with you. Either they'll want to know more and more, or they'll be mad that you told them anything, especially when things don't turn out the way they wanted. Here, however, everyone has a little something special. I have a feeling you'll find more empathy than anger. How does that sound?"

"Like you're the perfect counselor."

I was glad she had a sense of humor about this. "Har-har. You get some rest, got it? When I come back tomorrow, you'd better be feeling better. I'm beginning to think you're going to fade away from me."

She smiled up at me brightly. I had hope that she would get past this and have a full life. Maybe not one that others might call normal, but good for *her*.

"Thanks, Miss Frost, and have fun with your cousin tonight. He's worried about you, so make him feel better, kay?"

I smiled at her and leaned over to give her a hug as I left, kissing her once on the forehead. She closed her eyes again and drifted back off to sleep. I really prayed she'd have pleasant dreams.

I checked the clock on my way out and saw it was already five. I hurried back to my cottage to freshen up for the evening. There was a message on my machine from Vincent stating that Damien was running late, and that he would be driving me into town to see James instead. Damien would meet me later.

I sighed in relief, changed out of my new "work attire" and back into a maxi skirt and tank top. I was at the front gates by five twenty-five and found Vincent waiting with the school car. A man of few words, he tipped his head to me and opened the door.

I looked back at the school—and flinched at the sight of Jackson watching me from the commons doorway. He wore a grim expression.

I was borderline creeped out by his behavior, and it was getting worse.

I closed the car door and tried to relax for the ride.

I asked Vincent to drop me off near the bookstore. I had about ten minutes until James arrived, and since he tended to run about ten minutes late as a rule (his little rebellion against his military service and years with his dad), I figured I actually had about twenty minutes before I met him at the diner. The bookstore was a hole in the wall on the backside of the street where we were going to meet. I browsed the cramped stacks for a few minutes and emerged with a copy of *The Witching Hour* for Joanna, some romance and Sociology books for me, and a book on dream interpretation for Hazel.

As I left the store, I was deep in thought about Joanna and Hazel, knowing I needed to watch both of them carefully this year. They were out of their element, somewhat like me, and would really need support.

I walked outside just as James parked his bike on the street. A victim of premature hair loss, he'd been shaving his head since his late teens. His goatee hung down about eight inches from his chin and was sprinkled with brown, red, and gray hair. Now in his late forties, James had led a colorful life first in the military and then doing shit he wasn't allowed to discuss before returning to Arkansas a few years ago and settling down. His usual look was biker regulation, and he was owning it right now as he swung a muscular leg over his bike to dismount. He whipped off his sunglasses and his intense blue eyes scanned the street. His devilish grin let me know he'd spotted me. He approached me with open arms. I ran and jumped on him. He staggered a bit under my weight as he spun me around.

"Damn, girl, you just get better with age." James kissed me on the cheek and led me toward the diner.

"Yes, like a fine wine. Or more like moldy cheese."

He pushed me away at that, and I grabbed him and smooched him hard on the cheek.

"Always a smart-ass. Who the hell taught you to be like that?"

"That'd be you, FC," I said with a smile. We stepped inside and were taken right to a table in the back. We passed a jukebox so I bummed some change off him and went over to select some appropriate dinner music. I smiled when I scrolled past Lynyrd Skynyrd, and then settled on some Tom Petty, Steve Miller Band, and E.L.O.

"What's the dealio? Folks sure got stories about that school. They got you worshipping Lucifer, sacrificing cows or anything yet?"

"Nah, just a couple of goats. Seriously though, I cannot even begin to express to you how much energy there is at that place. I've met some truly remarkable people with amazing gifts, Favorite Cousin. Things I'd never thought possible before. The place is wonderful. I can't believe I'm actually here, though, and here with *you*. What the hell is going on with you these days?"

We spent the next two hours gabbing about our jobs, his kids, my mom, and his time following the Dead. We laughed and ate so much, I thought I'd burst for sure. I needed to be careful or my new wardrobe was likely to split.

When it was clear the waitress was fed up with my requests for more Diet Coke and we'd had our appetizers, main course, seconds, dessert, and James had coffee, we decided to head over to Shenanigans.

On the walk over, I told him that my supervisor, Damien, was going to be coming to pick me up and I wanted them to meet.

"What's my role here, Del? Big brother, scary ex-military, or just coolest guy he'll ever meet?" I pretended to gag but then had to laugh.

"How 'bout a combination of them all? Speaking of which, were you able to find out anything about Jackson Howe? Something spooks me about him. I wanted to be friends with the guy, but he's seriously creeping me out. He knows way too much about me. It's just weird."

James had led a short but colorful military service and still had connections all over the planet, maybe even the universe. I had sent him an email earlier in the day asking him to check into Jackson, thinking maybe he could at least get a timeline on when he was at Graceland, or something about his military service.

"My buddy hasn't gotten back to me, but as soon as he does I'll call you, got me?" I nodded and felt a little better. He grabbed my hand and looked serious for a minute. "What about your boss, Preston? Want me to find out about him, too? What's the deal with him?

How much did I tell him? "No, I don't want you to do any digging on him. If I decide I'm not going to get answers from him, I'll do it myself. But James, I'm…"

"Ahhh, I see. This guy has you dazzled. Well, you keep a good head about you, dig? Because I won't just sit back and let you get hurt. I'll be through those gates in a hot minute."

"James, it's not like that. Although Jackson seems to want me to believe it is. I think he has ulterior motives, though. Damien hasn't done anything for me to not trust him."

We entered the bar and found a booth. A server appeared right away and took our drink orders. James sat with his back to the wall and gazed around the bar before he spoke again.

"Tell me about it, FC. I don't think I'll ever be able to let another person put their grubby paws on my heart ever again. Dana killed that for me." He accepted a bottle from the server and waved away the glass. The server sat my water down and left us, so James continued. "She fucking ripped my heart out, and if that wasn't enough, she took my damn kids." His eyes teared up, and he downed a few gulps of his Shiner Bock.

"Babe, I'm so sorry. I know you miss the girls. I miss them, too. When I figure out what the hell I'm doing here, you and me are going to work this out, okay? I'm here now. You're not alone anymore."

"Don't start that shit with me, Del. I'm not here for counseling." He bristled at my words. James frequently opened up to me, but if I used any "counselor lingo" he'd shut down. I guess it was my gift that made him comfortable, but he hated it. I never would have known there was something "other" about me if I'd never met Damien or come to Havenhart. I would have likely spent the rest of my life not knowing…

And just as if he knew my thoughts, Damien entered the bar in his motorcycle gear. He shook hands with the bartender, who pointed us out. He nodded his thanks and walked over to us.

All my resolve disintegrated, my fears morphed to some serious anxiety, and my breath caught in my chest as I watched him approach, a look of concern on his beautiful face.

His hair was pulled back again with that same stubborn piece falling in his face. His jeans were quite worn, boots broken in, jacket sufficiently beaten up. The clothes and boots had obviously gotten a lot of wear and tear.

"Pick up jaw from table, FC. I take it this is boss-man."

I looked helplessly at James. I had no idea what to say or how to behave. I was truly happy to see Damien. Ecstatic was more like it. But Jackson's weird message played over in my mind, leaving me unsettled. I shifted in my seat as he got close.

He sat in the chair next to me and took my hand, kissing it, all the while looking into my eyes. The events of the night before came back all at once. The feel of his lips on the back of my hand caused goose bumps as far south as my shins.

"Ah, Damien, this is my cousin, James Morton. James, this is Damien Preston."

Damien stood to reach across and shake hands with James, who also stood to measure him up. Damien had a good three to four inches on James, but my cousin was not intimidated.

"James, I'm glad to make your acquaintance. Delaney told me much about you, especially how pleased she was that the two of you would live close together again. I think that may have been the main selling point in her agreement to work for us, so for that, I thank you."

James looked sternly at Damien from across the table, arms folded on his chest, leaning back in the chair. "I'm just glad I can be close if she needs me. You're going to be sure she's taken care of, aren't you, Preston? Because I'd really hate to learn that she's not." Okay, he had decided to go with big brother first. I admired the move, but Damien was just as intense.

"Undoubtedly. We want the same for Delaney." He placed his arm around the back of my chair without breaking eye contact. "She's quite valuable to our academy, and especially to me. I'll see to it that she's not harmed in any way. You can be assured of that."

I looked back and forth between the two as if they were having some demented tennis match. I wasn't sure who was the victor, but the intensity was too much.

"Ahem… Is it just me or is the testosterone getting deep in here?" I raised my eyebrows at James. Damien chuckled and brushed his fingers across the top of my shoulder, sending a shiver through me.

James leaned back on two legs of the chair, still with arms crossed, and tried to look hard for a minute. Then he let the chair's legs fall forward and started into the really important stuff.

"So, what kind of ride you got?"

This led into a detailed discussion of the anatomy and physiology of various motorcycle brands. I was soon lost. My gaze followed Damien's lips as he spoke. He continued to brush his fingers along my shoulder, but he was deep into his conversation with James, who had given up his big brother act. It turned out they had both been at Sturgis two years previously. Before I knew it, they were discussing tattoos they'd received there. James had a Ghostrider on his left pec, while Damien apparently had the logo of his Indian on the back of his left shoulder.

I reached back to run a finger across his shirt without thinking of James…who went back to playing big brother long enough to embarrass me for a while.

"I know our tats can't compare to yours, FC… Tell him the story about the mermaid with six fingers." He had to choose my most embarrassing story.

"Fine. I went to Des Moines to get my first tattoo at age twenty and ended up getting the 'apprentice.' He had some issues with dimensions, I guess." I lifted the bottom of my tank to show them the tattoo just under my ribs, and this time it was Damien who traced a finger across my skin. He looked up at me with a heated glance.

James took that moment to head over to the bar for more drinks.

I smiled tentatively at Damien, and then I thought about Jackson's message again. I flinched a bit and sat back in my chair. He looked at me questioningly, and then also leaned back in his chair. James arrived with fresh beers and sat down.

"She tell you about her weird message yet? I hope you guys don't have a bunch of freaks working at that place."

Damien frowned at me and I knew I had to tell him about Jackson.

"I hadn't seen you to tell you today. When I got back last night, I had a message from Jackson in my voicemail. He said some things about my past that I don't know how he would know…"

I paused for a minute, deciding whether or not I should go deeper. I felt safe enough with James there that I continued. "And he said some things about you."

Damien crossed his arms and looked at me thoughtfully. "I guess that means he's not going to be a good sport about this. What precisely did he say about your past that has you concerned?"

I looked to James for a rescue, and he nodded. I looked down at my hands, which were now shaking like a 7.0 earthquake. I knew I needed to tell him about the fire, but the thought of reliving it had me terrified. I'd done a thorough job of burying those memories, or so I'd thought until I showed up at the academy…Or maybe it was meeting Damien that unlocked the door I'd secured the memories behind.

Damien took my hands in his. I started to feel warmth move through my fingers, encircling my wrists and swirling through my forearms. I smiled at him appreciatively, but my chest still started to tighten. I was beyond his touch at that moment.

I excused myself and ran to the bathroom, grabbing my purse before I left. I closed myself into the farthest stall and took two puffs from my inhaler. I still couldn't catch my breath at all. I started to panic.

Before I lost it completely, I closed my eyes. I willed myself back to the library and my session with Morgan. I smelled the incense she used and when I opened my eyes, the tightness was gone and I breathed freely. I splashed some water on my face—to hell with my makeup—and rubbed some along the back of my neck. I stepped out the door and looked over to the table.

James was talking heatedly, and Damien had his head down, nodding, deep in thought with his brows pulled together in a worried frown.

"Somehow I don't think the world's problems will be solved by two bikers in a bar in Arkansas, but go ahead and keep trying."

Damien looked up and held out a hand for me, pulling my chair closer to him at the same time. I sat down, and he wrapped his arms around me, resting his chin on top of my head.

"It's not the world's problems I'm concerned about just now."

I looked over at James, and he had a grim look about him.

"I told him about the fire, Del. He has to know."

My eyes grew wide, and I started to pull away but Damien just pulled me closer.

"Delaney, it's nothing I hadn't already imagined you had locked away in there. I'm just... I'm just so sorry you had to go through that. And I'm angry that Jackson would stoop so low as to mention it to you. He's got to be reprimanded for this. I will be discussing it with the headmaster."

When I began to protest, he would not be deterred. "I will not divulge the details, Delaney, although you can be sure he probably already knows more than he'll let on. But he needs to know about Jackson."

James had slid his chair around to my other side, and he took my hand in his. "Cousin, you deserve some peace. That fire was a long time ago. Nobody blames you. No one expected you to singlehandedly save six children. You were a child yourself. You've paid for it long enough. Maybe now you can deal. Damien here seems to have your best interests at heart, and if he doesn't..."

I had to laugh at that. He really played the big brother role well. Who needed a real brother when you had a cousin as awesome as James?

"Be assured that I do, James. Delaney, are you ready to head back?"

I nodded and reached out to hug James. He held me close for a minute, and then pulled back and took hold of my face.

"You call me if you need me, got it? And I'll be in touch when I hear something. Love you."

"I love you too, James. Sorry tonight ended on a bit of a downer. Hey, maybe next time we can relive *your* past few years for kicks and giggles."

He snorted at that and fake-flicked me on my nose. He looked over at Damien and held out his hand, which was taken firmly.

"I'll look after her, James. Thanks for meeting us and, well...thanks."

James nodded and turned to go. I had a feeling he wouldn't sleep well tonight and hoped he didn't head home and down more beers to self-medicate.

Damien placed his hands on my cheeks and asked quietly, "Would you like some water before we go?"

I nodded. "And how about a pound of something chocolate?"

He laughed and squeezed my hand.

"We might make the Fudge Shoppe before they close their doors for the evening. We can take some to go. Before it gets too late, I'd like to take you somewhere. Are you comfortable with a bike ride in the moonlight?"

My heart jumped a little. This time it was with excitement and not fear. He held up his jacket for me to put on and I slid inside the silky sleeves, inhaling deeply to smell his scent clinging to the leather.

"Fudge and a ride in the moonlight... That's a recipe for disaster, you know. Sticky fingers, curves ahead, beware or we'll both end up...naked?"

He spit out his last chug of beer and we both fell apart, hysterical.

"You have a penchant for madness." He led me out of the bar and we walked a block over to the Fudge Shoppe. The owner was just turning the Open sign over when we arrived, still giggling, and she opened her door with a smile.

"And what can I get you lovebirds this evening?"

Damien asked her for her best fudge, no nuts. I was pleased to hear that he didn't like nuts either. She packaged a pound for us, and two additional half pound packages for Diana and Mrs. Walden. We settled the bill and stepped out into the moonlight. There were a billion stars out and the air was heavy and warm around us. His bike was parked in the alley behind the bar. He turned to me and placed his hands on my face.

"Are you ready to see something truly beautiful?" He bent down to kiss me softly on the lips. He had such a playful look in his eyes. I could only guess what he had in store for me.

THIRTEEN
MOONLIGHT DRIVE

DAMIEN STRADDLED THE BIKE AND GAVE IT A KICK TO START IT UP. THE muscles in his shoulders bunched and his quadriceps flexed beneath the denim of his jeans. The engine started and he sat back, his body fitting perfectly against the seat. He strapped on his helmet and held a second out to me. I lifted my skirt just a bit and Damien looked away with an anticipatory smile to give me some privacy as I, too, straddled the seat and pressed myself against his back. He took a moment to lace his fingers through the hand that gripped his abdomen. He turned his head to the side, his profile irresistible in the failing light.

"I won't ride too fast. Where we're going is near the campus. Are you comfortable?"

I wiggled a little closer to him on the seat and squeezed him a bit with my arms and thighs.

"Aye aye, Captain. Give her all she's got," I answered in my best Scotty impersonation. I felt more than heard his chuckle. I rested my head against his back. I had a feeling that this ride would be sensational in more ways than one.

He turned us back onto the highway and we soon left Eureka Springs behind. The trees passed by not quite at a blur. The breeze carried the scent of night-blooming jasmine and the various species of trees. My senses were close to overload.

The bike beneath me rumbled, yet it was a smooth ride. The road was dark but for the moonlight and the bike's headlight. We passed a car every so often but it was fairly empty at this time of night. Being so close to Damien allowed me to really get a sense of how much power was held in his frame. His lats were taut and triceps flexed, keeping the bike in line. I felt safe enough, although I knew one false move and I'd need a major skin graft.

But Damien was in control, as he seemed to be with everything in his life. I wondered just what it was that drove him, and why he'd chosen to spend his time with me.

About ten minutes later, he pulled off onto a gravel road and slowed down quite a bit. We followed this path for another ten minutes or so, and as I looked off to the left, I saw lights beyond the trees.

"That's the academy out there. We're almost to our destination," he voiced over the motor. He pulled to a stop shortly after and we both took off our helmets.

We were parked beside a reservoir with a breathtaking view. The moon was reflected in the still waters before us, its path stopping just in front of the bike. I climbed off the back, trying not to get too indecent with my skirt, and quickly slipped off my shoes. I dipped a toe in the fairly warm waters.

Damien remained perched on the bike, his green eyes sparkling. He swung his leg over and took down his hair. As he walked toward me, I wished I could stop time and just keep looping his walk across the short distance. He carried himself so self-assured and professional when we were on campus, but here in the woods, he was almost predatory.

Before he reached me at the water's edge, he veered to the right, not taking his eyes off me. He stopped at a large boulder and began removing his boots... followed by his t-shirt...followed by his JEANS...

I turned my back on him quickly before I'd have the ability to answer boxers or briefs.

"And just what happens now, Mr. Preston?" I asked nervously. After tonight's sharing of scary stuff, I wasn't sure I was ready to take things anywhere near the next level with him. He must have noticed, because now it was his turn to make the smart-assed remarks.

"It's customary that all new staff complete an examination of their swimming ability." I still had my back to him and heard him entering the water. "We need to be sure that all members are adept at water safety instruction. Since your resume states that you were once, in fact, a certified Water Safety Instructor, I thought I'd test your skills personally. Now disrobe and enter the water, please."

He seriously just told me to disrobe.

I turned toward the water, ready to lay into him...and found him submerged chest deep with a shit-eating grin on his face.

"I hope your medical training has prepared you for water moccasin bites or snapping turtle-itis. Are you completely insane?"

Obviously sensing he might be pushing me a bit too far, Damien stepped closer to the edge, revealing more of his torso. The water glistened on his skin in the moonlight. My breath quickened in response, much to my chagrin.

"Delaney," he said in a softer voice. "I'm sorry if you feel I'm being presumptuous. I only thought you might enjoy the water. This is a Water Department reservoir with a cemented bottom and the generators keep the wildlife from the water. Nothing can harm you here, not even me. I will not come within four feet of you. As I'm a complete gentleman, most of the time, I will gladly turn my back while you undress."

And with that, he turned his back. I watched him make waves in the water with his hands as he moved back to the deeper water.

He called out over his shoulder, "You can trust me, Delaney. This is not an elaborate attempt to seduce you." And with that, he dove under the surface. I was captivated by his movements. He surfaced moments later and his skin glistened in the moonlight, and shook out his thick hair.

With a deep breath for confidence, I slid out of my skirt and lifted my tank over my head. I left my undergarments on, content to ride home in wet ones. I made a run for it before I chickened out and dove in, swimming out toward where I'd last seen him surface.

The water was exhilarating. My stress from the past couple of days just slipped away. I swam with a strength and grace I'd forgotten I possessed.

Before I realized it, I'd passed Damien. The bike was a gleaming speck in the distance.

Damien caught up to me and surfaced several feet away. "This must have some healing effects on you. Your stroke looks unencumbered. How do you feel?"

"This feels amazing. Thank you for bringing me. I really needed this." We treaded water for several minutes in silence. The moon was just short of full and the stars were breathtaking.

"I must confess this is the first time I've ever done this at night. I can't believe how much better I feel."

Damien was looking at me intently, waiting for me to *talk*. I took a big breath, dipped my head under the water and smoothed my hair back.

"The water has always been my safe zone. Ever since the fire. I was fourteen when it happened. I was assisting in the nursery during Sunday service. They believe it was faulty wiring that caused the fire, but they never determined a source. I was the only one of the children who escaped without major burns. Three of them died. The flames were all over me, I remember that...but for some reason, I didn't burn."

The story was strange every time I told it. I wasn't sure what his reaction would be, but I felt as if I should continue.

"I started swimming shortly after to help strengthen my lungs at the doctor's advice. Nothing else was really working. While I didn't suffer any external injuries, my lungs were really damaged."

I dove below the surface again, taking a minute to center myself. When I came up for air, he was still there, his patience reassuring. There was no judgment, no pity, just concern.

"Everyone and their brother tells me it's time to let it go, to heal my scars. I guess now you see the limit to my healing ability. I can't get past it. I just can't stop shaming myself for not being able to save the rest of the children. I'm so afraid of letting people down again. Those parents trusted me with their children, and I couldn't save them. There was too much smoke, too fast."

Tears rolled down my face. I felt naked before him. My only saving grace was that my voice hadn't broken once in telling him the tale.

Damien closed his eyes for a moment and when he opened them, they were filled with pain and sadness. "I, too, know about shame and regret, Delaney. I have extensive experience with both." We sat there in silence again. This time it was my turn to be patient.

"Those who have told you to let go are right, it *is* time. However, I know that pain doesn't come with an instruction manual or a map to help you navigate. I promise you that I'll hold your hand through it. I intend to show you just how deserving you truly are, and I hope that you'll trust yourself to know when you're ready to let me in."

I wanted desperately to cross the four feet between us, but I held back. There was still something I needed to know.

"In Jackson's message, he mentioned your wife. I know I can trust you to tell me the truth. Can you trust me to listen? I can be patient, but if there's something I need to know before we go further..."

I didn't want to pry, but the rules of quid pro quo state you get something in return.

He nodded solemnly. "You will forgive me for not being forthcoming. I've always found it necessary to keep the past compartmentalized so that I may function appropriately in my capacity as director." He paused, gathering his thoughts. I was afraid he would stop, but then he lifted his chin and looked up at the moon.

"She was quite unlike you, Delaney. At that time in my life, ordinary was what I needed. I wasn't ready to embrace the path that Headmaster Hart laid for me. Instead, I wanted to pursue my medical career at a prestigious facility. Siobhan was in my medical program, and we were both headed for great success. We were quite competitive with each other. Of course, she knew nothing of my gift, and she would get really frustrated when I was promoted over her. Eventually, she agreed to marry me. She came from a wealthy family, and they thought I was a great catch, although they were suspicious of my background.

"They wanted grandchildren right away, but she didn't want it to interfere with her career. When she got pregnant by accident, she became bitter and withdrawn. It was a difficult pregnancy. I tried to be supportive. She didn't want anyone to know. I thought I could provide enough of my gift to keep her and the baby stable. I was working double shifts at the hospital and coming home to try to give her what she needed. It was draining me. I barely kept it all together.

"Then it got so bad that her pain was intolerable. I told her she needed to go to the hospital for tests, that something wasn't right. She still refused. She said it was fine and didn't want anyone to know because pregnancy was "viewed as a sign of weakness by the patriarchy" at our hospital. She was convinced she could hide it. So I took her to the hospital, and she refused to get out of the car. I tried to make her well...I tried to heal her myself."

He looked away from me, and his chin quivered. I knew this story would not end well. I wanted to comfort him, but I kept our boundary between us. He seemed to need the space as well.

After a moment, he went on. "I came home one night to find her unconscious. She was hemorrhaging. I tried one last time to heal her, but I couldn't pinpoint what the problem was. I was completely weak from lack of sleep and nutrition. I rushed her to the hospital, but it was too late. She was already in a coma and the baby was only twenty-three weeks along. They did an emergency C-section, but he didn't survive. She passed away shortly after they completed the operation."

His voice was monotone, and he looked just as he must have then, helpless and empty. My heart was breaking for him. How had he managed to survive this awful tragedy?

"My arrogance directly resulted in their deaths. I resigned from the facility and left our home. I traveled alone for quite some time after that, until Headmaster Hart found me in Japan. He told me it was time to come home. He pestered me until I agreed."

He turned and offered me a weak smile. "I've been here since. Morgan, Elijah and Hart have all attempted to help heal my emotional wounds, and they have to an extent. I can now accept that I had no control over Siobhan's health, nor the baby's. She didn't want to get well, didn't want to have anyone know, she was so stubborn. I don't know why she was so opposed to our having a child together. We didn't talk much at that stage in our relationship. I know that at that point, there was nothing else I could have done to save them, and I'm at peace with their deaths as much as I can be.

"I did love her, but we were constantly at odds. I don't know what kind of a life we would have had, nor what kind of parents we would have been. I have accepted it was not meant to be. Never since have I assumed that I hold all the answers for anyone's health. That is not what my purpose here is."

He sounded so sure of himself. I wondered what he'd had to go through to get to this point. I admired him for the strength it must have taken, and was grateful he had the others at Havenhart to support him.

"I became a teacher and then a counselor, I guess, so that somehow I might earn redemption. Maybe if I can help enough kids, I'll be able to forgive myself. I've driven myself so hard all these years that I've ended up pushing everyone close to me away. Well, everyone except my family and my best friend, Cassidy. I've never done much more than casual dating because I worried that if I had to tell them what happened, that they would judge me, or ask questions I wasn't able to answer. Now? I want to…"

"I'm glad you want to," he said when I couldn't quite get the words out. "And I should get you back on my bike before you become a human prune."

He took off quickly for the shore but he was no match for me. I beat him by about three strokes. We both got to our feet at the edge of the water. Panting, I sat by my clothes, not wanting to leave just yet, enjoying the view of him shaking out his hair and using his shirt to dry off.

Boxer briefs was the answer.

"You keep swimming with that strength and your asthma will cease and desist in no time. As your temporary physician, I order you to continue these nightly swims…at least until the weather cools. Then you'll have to use the indoor pool at the academy. Either way…" He sat down next to me and shook more of the water out of his hair in my direction. I laughed and swatted at him, showering him back. "Either way, I shall consider it my duty to personally supervise these swims. Do you object?"

I shook my head. "But will you keep your boundary in place, Dr. Preston?" I asked coyly.

He scooped me onto his lap and held me close. "Only if you require. If I had my druthers, I'd never take my hands off you." He kissed me playfully, then deeply, until I began to shiver as much from the cold as from his touch.

I reached up and cupped his face in my hands. "Thank you, Damien. I appreciate your patience and understanding, as well as your trust. I am *so* sorry for your loss."

"Thank you," he murmured.

"And thanks for not running when James told you the truth about my past. I know you probably knew about it—"

"I knew some."

I nodded and exhaled. "If you would have run, that might have been too much for me."

He placed his hands over mine and said, "Delaney, nothing could make me run from you now. I am right where I want to be, and I intend to prove that to you. We'll have our own obstacles to face, so let's leave our previous ones out there in that water and move forward, shall we?"

I wrapped my arms around him and held him close. Whatever I had done to deserve this man's attentions, I was truly grateful.

We dressed and mounted the bike together. My heart was lighter and I couldn't stop smiling. The ride back to the school was short. Damien drove through the front gates and followed the road to the carriage house, pulling into an open bay in the garage.

I had no idea what time it was, but I was sad our evening was ending. I'd learned so much about him, shared so much with him, and I felt we were coming away with a better understanding of each other. He held out his hand to walk me to my cottage. The sound of the cicadas lulled my senses, preparing me for a good night's sleep.

Unfortunately, the visitor on my porch destroyed any hopes for that.

Jackson waited in the shadows. "Headmaster Hart told me to wait here for you and tell you to come at once to the infirmary. It's Joanna."

Damien and I shared a troubled look. "We'll be right there, thank you, Jackson," I said. He turned to leave without a response and Damien followed me inside. I needed to change into something dry. He had grabbed a dry flannel from the garage.

"I meant to tell you about the conversation I had with her earlier. She believes her father is going to be released and will be here soon. I don't see how that's possible. You said he's in prison, right?"

He looked grim and nodded. "What else did she tell you?"

I racked my brain trying to remember our conversation details. "She said he can sense her, and that he's connected to her psychically, that he had caused her harm…" I drifted off as I remembered what she'd said about me. I turned to Damien and repeated her warning. "'The light will come for you, and it will bring you pain, but it will also bring you together.' I don't have a clue what that means, except for the dream I've been having."

Damien pulled me forward and kissed me on the forehead. "We'll figure this out, I promise. Now let's go see our tough little patient and find out what's happened."

"Oh wait. Let me grab the book I bought for her."

I tucked it under my arm and he took my other hand. We hurried through the darkened campus to the infirmary.

Jackson was there ahead of us. He had brought his acoustic guitar and was playing a classical piece softly in the hall outside her room. He didn't look up as we approached. "She seems to be eased by the music. It was the least I could do. She's been calling for you, Delaney. Mrs. Walden is with her, tending to her as best she can." That last sentence had an accusatory tone.

"Thank you, Jackson, for letting us know," Damien said. "My cell phone has been turned off for the past couple of hours. My apologies." He kept his cool so well under Jackson's scrutiny.

Candles bathed the infirmary in a soft, dim glow. "She said the lights hurt her eyes," Mrs. Walden murmured as we entered. "Her vitals are fine, but she's not able to keep down much food or liquid tonight. She wanted to speak to both of you."

Damien thanked her and told her we'd take over. She nodded and took Jackson with her when she left. Damien and I took chairs on either side of Joanna's bed. She seemed paler than this afternoon, and her skin was damp with sweat. I took her hand, and she smiled weakly at me.

"His people will arrive some time tomorrow afternoon. His men will be alone but not without power. If he fails in his attempt to retrieve me, Father has planned another way."

I held a glass of water out for her. She took it and sipped at it with her eyes closed. Damien looked deep in thought.

"Joanna, when you say he will have power, do you perchance mean legal power?"

She nodded. He must have found a judge who could be bought and forced to overlook the warrants out for his arrest and grant him a custody order.

"No need to worry about that, my dear. Headmaster Hart has a greater reach. Legally, we've ensured that your father cannot touch you. If he attempts by other means… Well, we shall have to ready ourselves for that as well." I sensed the wheels turning in Damien's head. He stood and headed for the door.

"Delaney, can you stay with Joanna? I need to make a call." I nodded and he stepped out, closing the door behind him.

"I knew you'd come tonight. I knew he'd bring you, and I knew you'd feel better."

I blushed, wondering just how much she knew about the events earlier this evening. I patted her hand and straightened her blankets absently.

"His energy is completely surrounding you, Miss Frost. Almost like he's claimed you for his own." She giggled, and my blush darkened.

Suddenly, she closed her eyes tightly and her back arched off the mattress. She spoke in a strained voice.

"She will bring down fire upon them and an end to their wrongdoing."

It was over quickly, and she slumped back onto the bed.

I fell back in my chair as a familiar fear crawled up my neck. I peeked into the hallway, and Damien was still on his call. I sat back down and felt the weight of her last words heavily, lost in thought and fear.

First the nightmare, and then Joanna's visions. Were they connected? What was going to happen next?

I reached over and took her hand. She was breathing heavy and thrashing around on the bed. I closed my eyes and tried to concentrate. I made a conscious effort to calm her, taking a deep breath, I thought about all Joanna had been through. I knew she had painful memories about her father. I thought to myself that I would take it all away from her, all of her pain.

A sensation almost like a limb falling asleep stirred in my hands, and I focused on it. The tingling traveled up my arms and into my shoulders, then flowed down my spine and settled at my tailbone. My head felt airy, like the feeling of lying on the beach and listening to the waves. I remained quiet for a few minutes, and when I opened my eyes, Joanna had stilled and was breathing peacefully. She had fallen into a deep sleep.

I leaned forward and rested my chin on my hands on the side of the bed and watched her for a while. At some point I must have drifted off, because the next thing I knew, Damien was carrying me to my bed.

"Where's Joanna? What happened?"

He lay me down, shushing me and smoothing my hair.

"Morgan is with her for the remainder of the night. You fell asleep, and I brought you back here."

He tried to soothe me back to sleep, but I shot up.

"Damien, she had a vision, a warning."

My heart pounded in my chest, and he coaxed me back down to my pillow. He whispered in my ear that it was okay, that I should rest. He wasn't going anywhere.

I curled up as close to him as I could and he held me, soothing me back to sleep.

Waking up next to Damien in the morning was truly a sight to behold. His eyelashes rested peacefully above his pronounced cheekbones. I ran my fingers through that silky hair, tousled and a mess from last night's activities. His face was covered with light stubble. I drew my finger along his jawline, letting the hairs tickle as I went.

He was lying on top of the covers, fully clothed with the exception of his boots, which I could see near the door. The flannel shirt he'd thrown on last night had raised a few inches above the waistline of his pants. I hadn't noticed the night before—probably because I was trying really hard not to look—that his stomach was lightly covered with black hairs. Hairs that met in the middle of his abdomen and traveled down in a thin line...

He was truly breathtaking. I watched him for a minute and when he didn't stir, I slipped into the bathroom to freshen up.

It was early yet, not quite seven o'clock, so I made some tea for him and crawled back onto the bed to watch him sleep. How had I gone from perpetually single to having such an amazing man in my bed?

He rolled over onto his side and a slight snore escaped. I giggled, and he opened one eye.

"Not fair. You got cleaned up already. I bet you even brushed your teeth." His gravelly voice made my toes curl.

"Guilty. I didn't want you dying from my dragon breath. But I did make you some tea. I think it's the kind you prefer, if I remember correctly from our lunch in Berkeley."

That had been three months ago, and now look where we were. Him waking up in my bed.

"You are an angel, thank you. I'll be out of your hair shortly. I know you have a date with Grace Walden, and I have some checking to do on Joanna's father. But really, I wish we could stay right here." He grabbed me and pulled me close, burying his face in my neck and then kissing me gently.

"Hmmmm, we'll just have to try this again on a morning when we can actually sleep in. Although, what will the neighbors say when they see you leave?"

"The neighbors will approve and think I am one lucky fellow. Now the students, on the other hand, I hate to give them a bad impression. They'll soon know we're together, of course, but we should probably institute a level of decorum with our actions befitting our standing here on campus. Headmaster Hart will be pleased. I think he had ulterior motives when he sent me to interview, you rather than coming himself." His large hands caressed my back as we lay there looking into each other's eyes. I was relieved to hear him speaking so calmly about this.

"Why would you think that? I thought you did all of the interviews away from campus?"

He grazed his fingers along my hip, letting them slip slightly below the line of my shorts overalls. His gaze was hungry. I doubted it was for breakfast. I thought perhaps he wanted something a bit more physical.

"Actually, you were the first staff member I'd traveled to interview." I think my shocked look amused him. "Usually I only assist him with student interviews. He had been telling me for a long time that I needed to think about what I wanted for my future, that the Fates didn't mean for me to remain a bachelor like him for the rest of my life. Then when he decided it was time to make contact with you, he insisted I needed to go."

He looked away for a minute with a smirk on his face. "I actually resisted for quite some time. I was perfectly happy here and had no desire to travel. I definitely had no interest in meeting a woman from California who was a Heavy Metal-loving, denim-worshipping, tattooed stubborn teacher who had *no* clue what we were about."

He looked at me out of the corner of his eye to gauge my response. My raised eyebrows were enough. He rolled over and pulled my hips into him, kissing me seductively. I gasped, and he laughed. Then he got serious.

"It proved to be the best trip I'd ever taken. You were more than I ever dreamed I would find."

The look on his face melted my heart. He reached up to cup my cheek, and I smiled back.

"Well, I'll do my best not to embarrass you." He frowned at that. "Seriously," I continued. "You've only seen some of my nuttiness, and you're so proper all the time. I just don't want to offend you or cause you to regret any of this."

Now he pulled back and sat up. "Delaney Rae Frost, of all the nonsense. I would never be embarrassed by you. You are a beautiful and talented woman with amazing skills. Don't ever let me hear you say that again, are we clear?" He seemed genuinely bothered.

I did my best to get him into a better frame of mind.

"What'll happen if I do? Will you give me detention?"

"Most assuredly," he said with a twinkle in his eye. "I'll give you detention and confine you to quarters. I'll have to personally oversee all punishments, can't have you getting off easy…"

He moved to pin me under him. His hair fell into his face and I pushed it back as he leaned in to kiss me. It started slow, and then he melted into me, one thigh falling between my legs. I arched my back to deepen the kiss, and he moaned softly, crushing me with his weight. I slid my hands under his shirt. His skin was like velvet.

"God, Delaney, you feel so good," he whispered against my neck as he kissed his way down my collarbone to the edge of my tank.

I desperately wished we had an infinite amount of time to continue this nonverbal conversation but at any minute, Mrs. Walden would be outside waiting for me.

"Damien, as much as I hate to say this, we'll have company if we take any more time. Can we make an appointment to continue this?"

He smiled and kissed me once more before rolling over onto his back, rubbing his face with his hands. "A postponement. Let's see where things lie this afternoon, shall we? I believe Mr. Walden is showing a film for the students in the commons after dinner. Would you care to accompany me?"

I nodded and kissed his chin. "Will there be popcorn? Can we sit in the back and hold hands?"

He chuckled and kissed me one last time before climbing off the bed. He pulled his boots on while I walked around in front of him.

"I know things are a little crazy with Joanna, her dad, the dream… But I just want you to know that I feel a lot better after we talked. Thank you."

He grabbed me around my waist and pulled me in close.

"It was completely my pleasure. Now run along and find your green thumb, love." He took my hand in his and kissed my thumb, nibbling a little before looking up at me.

"You sure know how to leave on a fantastic note."

He smiled and walked out the back door. I watched him from my back porch as he trudged sleepily toward the carriage house. I never thought dragging one's feet could be considered sexy.

FOURTEEN

CONFESSIONS

"I THINK I WOULD'VE STAYED IN BED IF I WOKE UP TO THAT."

I jumped at the voice right behind me. Mrs. Walden had a mischievous smile on her face. I'm sure I turned ten shades of red before I thought of something to say.

"Yeah, but you know what they say about those who overindulge…" I winked at her.

"They have the right idea?"

We both fell apart at that one. I had already thrown on my shorts overalls with a tank top underneath and plenty of sunscreen to battle the elements. I stepped out to join her in the garden.

"And it's about time for him, I may add. He's been alone for a long time. I knew he'd choose well."

I blushed again and muttered thanks. "I'm the fortunate one, Mrs. Walden. He's really a wonderful man."

She nodded enthusiastically and we got down to work. I hoped I'd have this positive of a reaction from everyone, although I knew I'd have to face Jackson at some point. I just hoped he would be content with our friendship.

"Have you known Damien for a long time?"

"Off and on, yes. We knew him when he was a student here and since he's been back. He was gone for many years in between..." She let that drift off.

"We talked about that last night. I know about his time away."

She nodded sadly. "It was tragic. It has taken him a really long time to regain his smile, however it's been nonstop since he met you."

I gave her a play shove and we both giggled like schoolgirls.

I gathered Grace was in her mid-to-late fifties, a bit my senior, but she had a young heart and a carefree way about her. She was full of life and being around her was infectious.

We weeded and pruned for about an hour, and then Mr. Walden wheeled out a couple of carts with new plants for the vegetable garden. We talked while we worked and time seemed to go by fast.

"I really can't believe you get such a tremendous turnout without using steroids. I kid you not, these are the hugest tomatoes I've ever seen. They look like something out of a magazine."

She took the praise well and divulged a few of her trade secrets.

"Fish emulsion, chicken manure, and a blessing from Morgan do the trick."

I was skeptical of her story. "Grace, magazine vegetables don't even look as perfect as these."

I assured her that anytime she needed assistance I'd be happy to help. She told me she had a couple of students who did work-study with her as well. I thought that was a great option for them.

"So how long has George been working for Havenhart?"

Now that I'd settled in, I really wanted to make some deeper connections, and Grace had been so friendly from the beginning.

"Actually, my husband was a student here. The headmaster brought him here when he was young, about twelve I think? That seems to be the age when most of our young discover their talents."

I hadn't known that Mr. Walden was "gifted." Intrigued, I pressed on. "How did he find him, the headmaster that is?"

Grace sat back on her heels and wiped some sweat from her brow. "Morgan's mother found him. She was a Seer like her daughter, who is much more powerful... Anyway, my husband grew up in Modesto, California, and his grandfather restored old cars. He lived with his grandparents because his father was killed in the Korean War. After that, his mother was institutionalized. Her grief turned into complete despondency and she stopped taking care of herself, and her child. George was only two when this happened, so he doesn't remember his parents. He was very close to his grandfather. They used to work together in the garage every day after school and weekends."

She stood up to gather more mulch, and I thought to myself that I had sure heard a lot of tragic stories since coming here. Damien had explained that traumatic events had a way of bringing out these dormant abilities.

"Phew, I'm getting sweaty. How about we finish this row of lettuce and then stop for the day?"

I hoped that I wasn't making her uncomfortable but I was growing more and more intrigued. I nodded in agreement and asked her to continue, if she didn't mind.

"Sure. You're easy to talk to. One afternoon while George was working with his grandfather, the jack slipped and pinned his grandfather under the car. He experienced some burst of strength. You know how folks say that adrenaline can do that? Well, he lifted the car off of him with one hand, and somehow managed to get the dolly his grandfather was lying on out from underneath. Later, he surmised that the dolly had moved because he'd wished it to move.

"Sadly, by that point, his grandfather had already gone into cardiac arrest. By the time paramedics arrived, he'd passed. George was devastated. His grandmother received a call from the headmaster after that, and he came out to meet George. George listened to his pitch, but really didn't want to come. He actually ran away from home to avoid being sent to Havenhart, if you can believe that." She laughed to herself. "He was frightened by his new strength, and the discovery that he could move things by wishing them to move.

"Crazy things started happening around him, and he couldn't control it. He even tipped over a chair his grandmother was sitting in, frightening her. They had been arguing about whether he should come to the academy or not. He didn't want to hurt anyone, so he took the headmaster up on his offer." She stood up and wiped her hands on her overalls at that point.

"That must have been terrifying for him." George had grown into a confident and friendly man. She hated that he'd gone through such a traumatic event. "So how did the two of you meet?" I asked.

She blushed. "Why, here of course. You didn't really think I learned how to grow these veggies from a book, now, did you?"

I was stunned. "That totally makes me feel better. No one is *that* amazing without a little help," I teased.

She and I laughed at that. My admiration of her grew exponentially.

"What, were you two like high school sweethearts?"

She got a dreamy look on her face as she gazed toward the commons. George was out back cleaning the barbeque without his shirt on. For a man in his later years, he had an amazing physique. There was not an ounce of fat on him. His muscle tone rivaled that of any of the younger men on campus. I shivered as I remembered watching Damien in the moonlight the night before.

I must have sighed, because when I looked over at Grace, she was shaking her head and laughing at me.

"Yeah, I definitely would have stayed in bed."

I threw a handful of weeds at her and she ducked expertly.

I took a nice, long cold shower after being out in the heat. I was shocked to realize that I was actually getting used to the weather.

As the water trickled down over me, I thought back again to the night before. While I was glad that we had talked about such serious matters, and I was grateful that he had accepted everything about me without reservations, I wondered how things might have ended up if there was no "four-foot boundary" between Damien and I.

I closed my eyes and focused on the memory of him standing waist deep in the water. I licked my lips thinking of the way his tasted on me. I ran my hands over my shoulders and imagined they were his. I started to imagine what would happen next, but that proved dangerous when I slipped and had to grab the wall to keep from falling. I begrudgingly finished my shower with a sigh.

After I dried off, I grabbed a protein bar from the kitchen and, what else, a Diet Coke. I decided to boot up my computer and see if there was any business to attend to. I turned on my tunes and danced a little around my cottage while I waited, singing loudly along to Janis. I opened up my personal email first and sent check-in notes to Mom and Cassidy. I had so much to catch them up on about school. I wasn't ready to put into words what had transpired between Damien and I, so I left them on a cliffhanger. I knew they'd be mad.

I signed off that email account and pulled up my work email. Diana had showed me how to access all of the school files on the server so I could work from home. I had several emails from Diana adding things to my schedule, including a few more intakes. Nate Calendar's mom emailed me to get an update. I answered her note first, letting her know that Nate had met his match in a young man from Spain and that they were really hitting it off.

Lastly, there was an email from James. The subject line said, "background check." I guessed he had heard from his friend about Jackson, and I was almost afraid to look.

Favorite Cousin. My buddy got back to me. Call me.

That was just like James to leave me hanging. Probably he didn't want to put anything in writing. I grabbed my phone, shaking my head, and dialed his number. His voice mail picked up.

"Yo FC, it's your FC. Got your email. Call me back at this number when you get a chance. Love you. Out."

I figured he might be out for a ride so I went back to work. I decided I should finalize my outline for Sociology, so I worked on that. Hazel had left a bunch of work for me with Diana that gave me a great start. She had really gotten into it. I decided to propose to Damien that she become my research assistant. I hoped she'd agree. I wanted the majority of my time to be available for seeing students. I needed to order textbooks, too. Diana assured me we'd get them within a week, so I sent her an email with the ISBN number of the text I preferred. I was excited to be teaching as well as counseling.

I started to feel restless, so I decided to go for a walk. I walked past the girls' dorm toward the infirmary to see if Joanna was up and around.

When I entered, Elijah was sitting outside her room looking over the newspaper. He looked up and nodded at me.

"Good afternoon," I said. He didn't say anything, so I cleared my throat a little nervously, realizing I had yet to have a conversation with him. "Is Joanna feeling better today?"

He nodded. I thought that would be it, but then he rose to his feet. I looked up at him, and a surge of power hit me like a blast of cold water.

"You did a good thing for her last night. You'll need to do it again. Heed her words. She is very powerful, that one." He turned and picked up his newspaper and then walked out the door.

I wasn't quite sure what to make of the mysterious man. I made a mental note to ask Damien more about him tonight after the movie.

I pushed open Joanna's door slowly and saw that she was reading the book I brought her the previous night. She was so engrossed that I didn't think she heard me enter the room.

"I'm just to the part when Rowan and Michael discover their connection. Those two are so romantic, don't you think?" She looked over the top of the book and smiled at me.

I sat down next to her on the mattress and smoothed her hair back from her forehead. "I bet you're ready to get out of here, aren't you? See your room? Meet some of the kids?"

She nodded but looked nervous. "I guess I have to get it over with sometime. Do you think I can leave?"

I held up a finger and stepped out of the room and found Grace in the nurses' station.

"Grace? I was wondering if I could take Joanna to her room, let her take a shower and get settled in?"

Grace agreed that was a great idea. "Let me just take her temperature."

Joanna's vitals all looked good so Grace sent us on our way.

"Come on, let's get you out of this sick place and ready for some fun. We can sneak down this hallway, which leads to the dorms, and go up the stairs to your floor."

Both dorms had three floors, and Joanna's room was on the third floor. We climbed the steps cautiously, me supporting her left arm while she gripped the handrail with her right. She looked inquisitive, but not afraid. I was glad for that. I hoped she Saw that things were going to be okay.

When we finally reached her room and stepped inside, she looked around eagerly. Marcia had obviously been busy. She had decorated the room with bright colors and had opened the large windows to let in some fresh air. The ceilings were vaulted and the floors were tile. A twin bed was in one corner with a rainbow comforter on top. Colorful throw pillows adorned the bed and the opposite corner, where there was also a beanbag chair and a reading lamp. There were school supplies and a laptop on the desk and a small Internet radio on the bedside table.

Joanna's eyes were huge when she turned around excitedly to look at me. "Is this really for me?"

I nodded and gave her arm a squeeze. "Go on, check out the closet." Damien had told me that Marcia would pick up some outfits for her to wear during off hours. Joanna squealed when she opened the door and saw clothes hanging up and brand-new shoes on the floor, all in her sizes. This time when she turned to face me, she had gracious tears in her eyes.

I pulled her into a hug, and she began to sob. I held her for a while and stroked her long silky black hair.

"Miss Frost, I've never seen such beautiful things. I can't believe this is really happening. I promise I'm going to do good things for the school. You won't be sorry you brought me here."

I lifted her chin and smiled. "Joanna, the only good things you need to do are for yourself. You've done for others long enough. Now it's time to take care of you. Get an education. Make some friends. And heaven forbid, have some fun."

She smiled and wiped the tears away. I gestured toward the door to the bathroom. Each of the rooms had a bathroom that adjoined to another room.

"And one other thing. We will *never* be sorry we brought you here. Now, why don't you grab the cutest outfit and go take a shower. The bathroom should be stocked with all the toiletries you need. Take your time getting ready. Try to just relax."

"Will you stay for a bit?" she asked nervously. "I'm not sure I'm ready to be alone here."

"Sure. I'll just wander outside in the hall and see what the other gals are up to. I'll come back in a few minutes, okay?"

She hugged me quickly and then grabbed a robe from the closet. "Maybe you could help me pick out what to wear? I don't really have much experience with that."

Her smile dropped. I imagine she was likely thinking about being with her father. He'd kept her in a dingy dress that was too small and from probably a century ago. After she closed the bathroom door I let my shoulders drop. I'd really have to help create a support network for her. She'd need more than I could give her myself.

On the third floor, the rooms were single occupancy. I guess the headmaster thought Joanna could use some privacy, and I agreed that was wise. She needed to be with her peers, but also was going to need some time to herself to process all she was learning and Seeing. I hoped she had a work-study set up with Morgan. I thought she would make a great apprentice, and that Morgan would teach her many things to make her more comfortable with her tremendous power.

I heard laughing and music coming from various doorways down the hall. The girls all smiled as I passed and then went back to their chatter. There was a common room at the end of the hall, and I saw Marcia sitting there with some girls. She called me over and introduced me. Some of the girls looked at me wide-eyed.

"Did those hurt?" one girl asked me, pointing to the tattoos on my lower leg.

"It doesn't feel nice, that's for sure, but it's not the worst pain ever. It kind of feels like you have a really bad sunburn and someone is running their fingernail over it…for three or four hours."

They all shrieked, and I winked at Marcia.

"You shouldn't get one until you're eighteen. And then you should really know what you want." I tried to have a stern tone but Marcia's look said it wasn't working.

One girl got to her knees and pulled her hair away from her ear. She had a semicolon tattooed behind her ear. "I got this one with my friend, and I'm going to get a portrait to memorialize my little sister on my shoulder when I turn eighteen."

The other girls ooooed and aahhed at her and I took my leave, making a mental note to check in with that young lady.

Past the common room there was a hall leading to another set of stairs. I meandered down the stairs following the sounds of muffled music on the other side of the wall. It was an acoustic guitar. At the bottom of the steps, I turned to the left and saw a doorway leading to another stairway going back up. I'd reached the midway point between the girls' and boys' dorms.

I crept up a few steps, listening to the soulful music. I didn't want to come upon any naked boys, so I only went as far as the first landing. The music was coming from Jackson. I listened intently while he played. I wasn't sure if he knew I was there but I didn't try to hide either. When he finished, he looked in my direction.

"I told you, you can't sneak up on a Ranger." He didn't sound humorous, in fact he sounded sad. He started to put his guitar back into the case.

"You've got great acoustics in here. It sounded lovely." I leaned against the wall with my arms crossed, unsure of what to say.

He looked down at his hands and then let them hang between his knees. "What are you doing here, Delaney?"

The tone of his voice gave me pause. There was none of his usual playfulness.

"I took Joanna up to her room and I was just wandering around, checking in on the students, when I heard you playing."

"Oh yeah," he said. "I forgot. The guitar is your weakness. Funny though, it only seems to work in someone else's hands."

His words stung and sent a jolt through my gut.

"Jackson," I started. "I don't know how to respond to that."

He sighed and stood. He picked up his case and slung it over his shoulder. He walked toward me without looking at me and brushed against my shoulder as he passed. He stopped for a moment and then spoke.

"I thought you were the counselor. The healer. Aren't you supposed to know things?" He sounded bitter.

I fought to keep the same sound out of my voice. "Apparently that's not part of my package. If you're angry at me and choose not to discuss it with me, then I can't do anything to remedy the situation."

"You can't do anything anyway. You've made your choice, just like before. I'll get over it, I always do. Just don't expect me to be chummy right now."

"Jackson." I reached out and touched his arm, and he flinched away. He turned and got right in my face.

"You don't get to do that. Not to me. Not anymore." He looked surprised at himself for a minute, and it took me that same minute to realize that I was shaking and pressed against the wall.

I took a deep breath to even my voice. "What do you mean, 'just like before'? Jackson, I'm really good with faces and names. How is it that I don't remember you from Graceland? You need to fess up here, because you're really starting to creep me out."

"I'm sorry. I didn't mean it like that." He ran his hand over his head and took a deep breath. When he spoke, I heard sadness and regret in his words. "I shouldn't have had any expectations when you came. I'm just disappointed. But I know now that you were meant to be here for Damien. It's not that I wish him any ill will, I just need to get used to the idea." A sad smile touched his face, and I relaxed a little.

"I actually only saw you once, at Rimfire's. You were watching the band play...and I'd never seen a woman so captivating. When I saw you there, you were wearing a Guatemalan sundress...blues and reds and teals. You had on a pair of green Birkenstocks and your hair was long and loose, down past your waist. You were dancing to the band with another girl, and I started to go and talk to you but one of my buddies held me back. He said, 'Don't do it man. She's taken.' So I stayed away. But once I'd made that connection, just that once, you were always with me after that."

I felt a pain in my arms and realized that I was hugging myself so hard, my fingernails had dug into my biceps. This conversation wasn't making me feel any better.

"What kind of a connection are we talking about here, like you cutting out pictures of me for your wall, stealing my underwear, secret cameras, what?"

His expression was horrified.

"God, it's not like that! See, that's my gift, as they call it around here. To me, it's mostly a curse. Once someone makes an impression on me—

either like you did, or maybe a guy I served with, a friend from elementary school—it's like they're always with me, you know? Like some kind of freaky link. I can always see them, hear them, feel what they're feeling. I can turn it off if I'm in a good place but when I'm not..." He gulped and put his head down for a minute.

"I was already in contact with the headmaster. He'd found me out in high school in Virginia but I told him I wasn't ready to come here. Too much of the world to see, you know? Went to college, finished early and joined the Army, the Rangers. Operation Iraqi Freedom and all that bullshit. I saw some horrible things there that will haunt me forever. Literally. Try making a connection with some kid whose family you just killed in an artillery attack.

"I was injured a few times, the last time was in Afghanistan. Hart came and picked me up from the Walter Reed Center and brought me here. It's been two years, and I'm learning to shut it off. Finally. After all these years." He smiled a pathetic smile and shook his head.

I touched his arm. He looked at me and then looked away, wiping angrily at his eyes.

"Jackson, I didn't mean to hurt you. I tried to be honest and up front with you from the beginning. I want us to be friends, and I don't want any bitterness between us. What can I do?" I reached my hand out and he took it gingerly.

"Can you clone yourself?"

We both laughed softly. I wanted to take his pain from him. I didn't want to see him hurt.

"I wish I could. But what I *can* do is put in an order for you with the headmaster for the woman of your dreams. Just give me the details and I'll be sure he gets it right." I hoped making light of the situation would work.

He squeezed my hand and his smile looked less pained.

"I guess that's the next best thing. I'm just tired of being alone. It's just not my turn yet."

I decided to get it all out there. "So over the years, were you, like, checking up on me?" I was almost afraid of the answer. I hoped whatever it was, we could both live with it.

"Glimpses, flashes...mostly just pictures when I was feeling down. I'd see you eating breakfast, playing with your cats. I never wanted to invade anyone's privacy, so when I'd realize what was happening, I'd shut it off. It's kind of like other people who daydream? Except the things I daydream about are actually happening somewhere. I saw you and Damien together in Berkeley when he was interviewing you, and I got really excited. I went to Hart and told him I'd known you at college. He asked me what I knew about you."

My eyebrows shot up at that piece of information. He was quick to reassure me.

"No, Del, I didn't tell him anything really personal. He already knew about the fire. He knew more of what happened than I did because I'd pull back anytime you were thinking about it. It was too painful. You were always so alone, never letting anyone get close to you."

"Huh. Try living it." It was his turn to hug me that time. He'd seen some of my most private moments. But instead of feeling weird about it, it was kind of soothing. Like my own kind of guardian angel, and I told him so.

"I guess." He laughed sarcastically. "Angel of Doom maybe."

We'd reached an understanding. Hopefully. With that, he let go and gestured for me to step out of the stairway in front of him.

"I still have that sundress, you know. It's one of my favorites. Sadly, the Birks were a victim of one of my cats. He chewed them all up the first time I left him out free in the house. I still miss those Birkenstocks."

Jackson put his arm around me and gave me a squeeze. "The most important thing is that you're still here. And I'm really glad for that."

I looked up at him and kissed him on the cheek. "Thanks. Me, too."

"If it can't be me, then Preston is the next best thing. I hate to begrudge him the happiness he deserves. He needs it more than I do. He's older, he should get first dibs." He gave me a light punch on the shoulder. I crinkled my nose at him and gave him a real slug back.

"As long as you aren't *bitter* about it."

We laughed, and it was so good to hear him happy again.

"In all seriousness, Jackson. Are we okay? Because I meant it when I said you were much-needed friend material."

He shrugged and smiled. "At your service, Counselor." He turned and waved as he headed back toward his apartment.

"That went completely different than I thought," I said to myself. I hurried back up the steps and hoped Joanna hadn't missed me. When I got to her room, I heard music playing inside. I tapped on the door before pushing it open, and she pulled the doorknob from the inside, almost yanking me off my feet.

"Hurry, come in. You have to help me pick out the right clothes." Her wet hair was wrapped in a purple towel and she was wearing a matching purple chenille robe and slippers. She hopped around excitedly and snapped her fingers along with the music. "I'm glad you talked to Mr. Howe. I felt his sadness. He was meant for another. He just doesn't know it yet."

Her off-the-cuff remarks were still shocking. I tried to just go with it.

"What's the plan for tonight?" she asked.

"Hmmm, well, we're having dinner in the commons and then a movie. Wanna be my date?"

She squealed and spun around in a circle.

"Yes, I'll be your date. Oh, but what about Mr. Preston?"

I raised an eyebrow at her and said, "He'll just have to share me, won't he?"

We settled on a sundress and sandals for her since it was still muggy. I braided her hair in two French braids.

"How'd you learn to do that?" she asked from the bathroom while she admired my handiwork.

"I didn't always have short hair. I used to have hair longer than yours."

She turned around in shock. "Really? But it looks so good the way you wear it now."

I shrugged. "Different hairstyles for different seasons of life, I suppose. I miss it sometimes, but I wouldn't grow it out again for all the money in the world." Dramatic, I know, but any woman who has braved the in-between stage can relate.

It was a self-preservation method as well. It's not as easy to catch in a fire.

"It'll be long again. Definitely by your wedding."

Um, another bomb dropped.

"Uh, Joanna? You might want to take care when you make those kinds of predictions. Not that you're doing anything wrong; remember, we talked about this before. People will never be satisfied. I don't want to see you get hurt. By all means, keep blasting *me* with them, but when you're with the other students, try to put a filter on it, okay? I can help with that, too."

She gave me a grateful smile and slipped on her sandals.

"How do I look?"

She was positively glowing. I gave her a thumbs-up and she beamed.

It was close to five o'clock by this time so we walked leisurely back down the stairs and over toward the commons. Several of the other girls were going that way as well, and I spotted Hazel up ahead. She, too, had had a wardrobe makeover. She was still dressed conservative, but a little more up to date. She looked happy. I thought she and Joanna would get along great so I pulled Joanna's arm to catch up. I introduced the girls, and they smiled shyly at each other. I decided we'd all sit together for dinner and wondered if Damien would join us.

We arrived at the commons and '50s music was blaring. Kids had piled into the booths and were sitting around the tables. Vincent, Elijah, Grace and George passed out meals. The energy was exhilarating. I took the girls' hands and we grabbed seats at the counter. Soon, George was there with a smile.

"I bet you gals could use a good 'ol fashion milkshake. What flavor can I get ya?"

My stomach perked up at that. "Is there really any flavor other than chocolate? I mean seriously."

The girls tried to suppress a giggle.

A decidedly sexy voice boomed from behind me, "Actually, I'm quite fond of strawberry, so I must beg to differ."

I turned to find my current favorite flavor behind me, and he leaned down to kiss me on the cheek. My face flushed, and I grinned.

"I guess we'll have to agree to disagree then." I beamed up at him. "I'm glad you made it. Please join us. These are our dates for the evening, Miss Hazel and Miss Joanna."

The girls blushed and then leaned into the counter to start sipping their chocolate shakes. By the look on Joanna's face, this was likely her first shake ever. A huge grin spread across her face.

"This is fantastic!" she exclaimed.

I leaned in to her and said, "Wait 'til you try a hot fudge sundae." She looked as if I'd opened her door to a whole new world of heaven. "Everything in moderation, though. Otherwise I'd weigh five hundred pounds."

The girls snickered and assured me that would never happen.

I turned and looked at Damien again, and he had that same look on his face he did at the orientation meeting after I'd talked to the whole group. I took another sip of my shake and winked at him.

Damien motioned to me that he wanted to speak to me outside for a moment and we excused ourselves. He took my hand, and we stepped out the door. Once outside, he turned to look at me and smiled excitedly.

"I've been looking forward to seeing you all day. I'd really like to show you just how much I've missed you, however, I don't think that would be appropriate for our audience."

We stood about three feet apart, not touching, but his energy was all over me.

"I'm glad to hear it. I'd really hate to hear you'd gotten over me so quickly." I grinned at him fiendishly and cocked an eyebrow. "So just how much did you miss me?" I clasped my hands behind my back and rocked back and forth on the balls of my feet.

Damien put his hands on his hips and shifted his weight. "Are we really going to do this?"

I tried to look innocent.

"Very well then. Do you want me to *tell* you how much I missed you, or can I show you just as soon as we're finished here?"

Demurely, I replied, "I can't have both?"

Damien lowered his voice to the husky tone I'd heard him use this morning. "I thought about all of your places I want to touch with my hands and my lips. Is that what you want to know?"

He'd totally disarmed me with that confession. I tried to think of a comeback and all I could do was clear my throat.

Damien chuckled. "No jokes? Did I finally make the counselor speechless? Hmmm, maybe I should tell you a bit more." He took a step closer, trying to call my bluff. It worked.

"Mr. Preston, I do believe our dates will wonder where we've gone off to. Perhaps we should explore this matter further after the movie?"

"Oh, there is no doubt about that. I plan to explore matters much further this night. But you're right, and I did call you out here on official business. I'm afraid the headmaster needs me to travel, so I'll be missing the first week of school. I really hate to be gone, for several reasons..."

His lids lowered at that point, and then he visibly shook himself. "Unfortunately, this cannot be avoided. I have full faith in your leadership abilities, and Morgan and Elijah will assist with all day-to-day issues while I'm away."

I was shocked at how sad I was to hear this news. It was almost going to feel like losing a limb. "So, you will be back, though. This isn't like relocation, is it? And wait. Hold it! Did you just say you were putting *me* in charge?"

He actually bent over and grabbed his stomach, he laughed so heartily. "You really are easy to fluster, aren't you?"

I frowned at him sternly. "I'm so glad you think this is amusing."

"I'm sorry, really, but your expression was priceless. Yes, I do intend to leave you in charge of the students. I have no qualms about that. I know at your previous sites you were left in charge quite often."

I sighed in resignation. "You're right. But that wasn't in Arkansas at a site where I'd only been working for a week," I said with absolutely no pouting.

"Delaney, I completely trust you when it comes to the well-being of the students. I do hate to leave, but the students will be well cared for in my absence." He looked off into the distance for just a moment. "I just wish I didn't have to leave now. This doesn't feel right."

"Whatever. We'll make it work. Where do you have to go, or is it like double-o-seven, top-secret stuff?"

He laughed at that. "No spying, not for me. I actually have two new students to pick up from out of state. I'll have my cell with me at all times though, and I can get back quickly if I'm needed. The headmaster should be here at least for the first couple of days, before he has to leave also. He's still working with the authorities on Joanna's guardianship."

"Do you think she's safe?"

"Absolutely. Rains is in high-risk custody, from what I understand. I highly doubt he could make any plan work. Vincent and Elijah will staff the gatehouse, along with George in his off hours, and the security cameras are also monitored twenty-four hours a day by an off-site security company who can be here on a moment's notice. Everyone will be safe. I wouldn't leave if I didn't feel as though you'd all be protected." Somehow, he didn't look totally convinced.

"Alright then. I guess I'll just have to survive somehow. Maybe we'll have a slumber party in the girls' dorm and see what trouble we can get into. You know, when the cat's away…"

"Now, no mischief, Miss Frost, or I'll see you reprimanded."

"Oooo, I might enjoy that." I was shocked by what I'd just said.

Damien looked pleasantly surprised.

"Uh, on that note," I backpedaled, "we'd better get back."

"Oh, yes. Saved this time. My dear, you are courting danger." He moved closer still.

I turned away from him and headed back inside, smiling coyly over my shoulder. "Better hurry up, Mr. Preston, there won't be any of your favorite flavor left."

He growled at me. "Just you wait until after the movie. We *are* going to finish this conversation."

We got back to our seats on either side of the girls. They barely noticed our return, they were so deep in conversation. The burgers served made my mouth water. I'd forgotten to eat lunch, so I was more than ready.

I was also anxious to see something…

"Mr. Preston, since you hail from the most proper place on Earth, how do you intend to eat this tasty cuisine in a sophisticated manner?"

The girls giggled and looked over at him wide-eyed.

"Miss Frost, I'll have you know that I have resided in America long enough to conquer eating even the unruliest foods this country has to offer. Just watch the master at work." He proceeded to load his burger with an alarming amount of condiments: pickles, lettuce, tomatoes (I was glad to see he left off the onions) and more. He smashed the sandwich down with one hand, looked over at Joanna and winked. "Observe."

We all leaned in to watch as he gracefully picked up the massive burger and proceeded to take a dainty bite without a fleck of ketchup landing anywhere.

I was shocked. I thought for sure he'd be trashed after that.

"Wow, that's pretty impressive. Girls, can you believe it?"

They shook their heads and dug into their burgers. I kept an eye on Damien and was beyond satisfied when I saw a pickle slowly sliding out the bottom, catching him unawares.

"Mr. Preston, care to make a wager? The person who gets food on them first has to dance the Hokey Pokey."

"I'm afraid I'm not familiar with that number, but I'll take your wager." With that, he took another giant bite—and the pickle squished out of his burger and slid down his arm, leaving a stripe of yellow and red in its wake, and then it plopped onto the bottom of his white dress shirt.

The girls stared at him—and then burst out laughing. I'm sure the satisfied look on my face was the clincher.

"I reckon you'll need to be teaching me that dance now."

I grinned in triumph and put down my burger. I hopped off my stool and pulled him reluctantly from his. "Come on, let's see what kind of moves you've got, Limey."

He tried dabbing at the stain on his shirt with a wet napkin. "Limey, huh? Alright. You win. How does this work?"

"Oh Mr. Walden," I called, smiling at the girls. They were having a difficult time controlling their giggles.

"You rang?" George approached us in an apron and paper hat, completely looking the part of diner owner.

"I was curious as to whether your extensive music collection here contains the old classic 'The Hokey Pokey'?"

He smiled conspiratorially. "I do believe I have that selection. Be right back."

Damien went along with it, but he definitely had an expression that said, "I will get you back."

A moment later, the first notes of the song came pouring out of the speakers. I took Damien's hand and led him to the area in front of the stage.

"Just follow along with me and you'll be fine," I promised. He really was being a good sport but he looked just a tad mortified

"You put your right foot in, you put your right foot out, you put your right foot in and you shake it all about. You do the Hokey Pokey and you turn yourself around. That's what it's all about!"

The kids clapped along and laughed as Damien and I did the classic dance. His gaze caught me off guard. Forget the fact that we were making fools of ourselves, his expression was full of admiration...and love. I realized in that moment that I'd fallen really hard for this man.

He must have seen a change in my demeanor, because he reached over and took my hand as we continued to be silly.

Some of the other staff joined us, and the kids started to get up as well. Pretty soon, the whole room was doing the Hokey Pokey, and I thought to myself that this place was truly magical. We had amazing kids, a tremendous staff, and I was standing next to one of the most incredible men I had ever known...and he'd stolen my heart.

It scared me to death but I had no choice. I had to hang on and trust.

When the song was over, George announced that we needed to set up the chairs because it was movie time. Damien and I helped move chairs into rows and Jared and Isaac set up the projector. The wall behind the stage was painted white to display the film. It was just about as cool as going to a real theater. Some of our students stared in wonder as they had yet to experience a movie on the big screen. I was proud of our school and the opportunities we were providing for the kids.

Our school. My school, now.

The movie showing was my absolute favorite, *The Princess Bride*. I did my best to not shout out all of the dialogue, although Jackson and Skye were doing a pretty good job of narrating the movie line by line. I laughed to myself and looked over at Damien.

He was deep in discussion with Elijah, and he'd lost the carefree appearance of earlier. Concerned, I walked over to the two of them.

"Call the local authorities and meet me at the gatehouse." Damien turned to head out the door as I reached him.

"What's going on?"

He looked quite grim. "It appears we have an unwanted guest. I want you to stay here and make sure none of the students leave. I've let George know, and he's locking all of the doors. Quietly let the others know and ask Jackson to join me, please."

"Hey," I said, touching his back. He turned to face me, and I grabbed his hand. "Be safe, okay?"

He gave my hand a squeeze and stepped out the door, pulling it shut and checking the lock.

I quietly moved over to the counter where Jackson and Skye were challenging each other in a dialogue duel, and I tapped him on the shoulder. His smile melted when he saw the concern on my face.

"Damien needs you at the gatehouse. He said we have an unwanted visitor."

Jackson nodded and went through the swinging doors to the kitchen. I saw him meet up with George, who handed him one of two shotguns he was carrying. They both checked their weapons and ran out the back of the kitchen. Through the side door, I watched them circle around the building toward the front of the school.

I looked around to see if the students had noticed anything, but they all seemed engrossed in the film. I worked my way around the crowd to Morgan, who was sitting in one of the booths with Grace.

She looked up as I got there, and I realized that she hadn't been watching the movie. "It's a private investigator looking for Joanna. Vincent let Elijah know he was coming up the drive so they could all go out to meet him." She closed her eyes in concentration, and I moved to block her from the view of the students.

"Jackson and George split off and are covering each side of the woods. Damien is talking to the man. He's arguing that he has a court order to have her returned to Florida. Damien is explaining that the headmaster has legal guardianship, and that he refuses to heed this court order."

She jerked, and I touched her arm to steady her. A major dose of static electricity zapped me, and she jerked again. I could barely see the whites of her eyes for a moment, they were so dark.

A wave of energy burst from her, and Grace took her hand. She jerked again, and then was back to herself.

"Grace, go to the infirmary. We have an injury. Delaney, get Marcia and lead the students back to the dorm. If you go through the back door behind the stage, it leads directly into the girls' lobby. Jared and Isaac need to lead the boys back to their rooms and get them locked in."

I nodded and looked up to see the movie was just finishing. I glanced over to the other staff, who were already gathering up the students and leading them toward the back doors.

Some of the students looked concerned, and my heart thumped wildly in my chest when I thought about who may have been injured and what was happening, as well as trying to see above the sea of heads to find Joanna and Hazel. I saw them with Marcia, and while Joanna looked alarmed, she was not frightened. I caught up to them at the rear and put my arms around the girls.

"How'd you like the movie?"

The girls smiled but it was obvious they knew something was wrong. I let Marcia lead Hazel ahead, and I stayed behind with Joanna.

"He sent someone for me."

I knew she had to have had a sense of what was going on.

"Don't worry, Mr. Preston is fine, just angry. It was Mr. Howe who was hurt. I'm so sorry, Miss Frost. I didn't mean for this to happen."

She teared up, and I stopped her, grabbing her by the arms and forcing her to look at me. "Joanna, we knew there might be problems. That's why everyone here is prepared to do whatever it takes to keep you and all of the other students safe. You are not the cause of this. It's your father, and he'll be dealt with. He *will* see that he can't hurt you anymore, do you understand me?"

She nodded, but she wouldn't look at me.

I pulled her into my arms and held her close, taking a deep breath and letting it out. She finally relaxed a bit in my arms.

"I just don't want anyone else to get hurt, Miss Frost."

I smiled down at her. "I know, sweetie. But we all understood when we came here that we're responsible for precious cargo that must be protected at all costs. Okay? We chose this knowing full well what we were getting into. Besides, it just adds to the excitement. You know I'm right. Who'd want to work at some boring 'ol safe school?"

She snorted. "Miss Frost, you're going to have to do better than that if you want me to believe you."

But she smiled, and we started walking again. I took her up to her room and rubbed her back until she fell asleep. When I was sure she was out, I left quietly, locking the door behind me. I hurried down the stairs to the lobby. Marcia and Moira were camped out there, and through the doorway, I saw Jared and Isaac in the boys' lobby talking quietly with each other.

"Are the rest of the girls settled in?"

Marcia nodded, and Moira said, "We did a head count and made sure all of their doors were locked."

"Thanks, ladies. Is there anything else I can do?"

Marcia stood up to hug me, and Moira gave me a weak smile. "I think we're okay here, Delaney. Why don't you go check in with Damien? They brought Jackson into the infirmary."

I said my good nights and hurried over to the infirmary door that was down the hall from the girls' lobby. I now understood the reason for the compound-like structure of the school. All of the main buildings were connected and the dorms could easily be sealed off. Great for bad weather, but also for emergencies like this.

When I stepped into the hallway, I heard Jackson yelling.

"Fuck, that hurts! What the hell kind of nurse are you, George?"

From the sound of his voice, I gathered that he wasn't in any imminent danger. George's laughter and chiding made me relax a bit more.

I rounded the corner and found Elijah and George stitching up a rather nasty cut on Jackson's shoulder. Another bandage was wrapped around his midsection, and there was a pile of bloody rags on the floor. Damien was in the corner on the phone.

"Who forgot to invite me to the party? I'm crushed."

Jackson grimaced, and then yelled a few more profanities at George, criticizing his stitching job.

"Shut your pansy-ass up, Howe. I thought the Army made them tougher these days."

Elijah even chuckled at that one.

"Oh fine, Jarhead. You try getting a slug of lead in your gut and a swipe from a hunting knife across the shoulder and see how happy *you* are about getting stabbed in the ass with a huge fucking needle."

George laughed and slapped him on his good shoulder. Jackson tried to smack him back but winced and grabbed onto his side.

Elijah nodded to me and took a load of soiled laundry with him as he stepped out into the hall. Jackson lay back, and I walked over and sat on the foot of the bed.

"I thought no one could sneak up on you, dude. What the heck happened?"

He scoffed at that. "The guy had obviously set up recon before we got out there and knew where our cameras were. He got the drop on me, but I shared the hurt with him. He won't be walking right for a very long time."

I held his hand, and while he was talking big talk, he was obviously in pain. I saw that Grace had returned and was getting an IV ready for him.

"Alright, big man, I need your hand. I'm going to hook up some pain meds and an IV. George already gave you an antibiotic in the injection to avoid infection. Now just relax."

Grace put the needle in like a pro. Jackson stared straight ahead and then shut his eyes with a wince. I held his hand for a few more moments, and then he smiled.

"I said you couldn't do that anymore to me. I'm not going to fight it, though. It feels really nice."

His words slurred. Obviously the pain meds were kicking in. The grooves in his forehead smoothed out and soon he was breathing steadily. I took a deep breath and stretched my back as I heard Damien finishing up his call. He came up behind me and put his hands on my shoulders, letting out a huge sigh.

"Are the kids all settled in?"

I nodded and stood from the bed. Damien pulled me into an embrace. Immediately, I sensed weakness in him.

"You healed him, didn't you?"

Damien buried his face in my hair.

"I'm worried, Damien. Does it always take this much out of you when you heal someone?"

He shook his head. "He'd lost a lot of blood. He took that bullet for me, Delaney. I didn't even sense the guy approaching us, but Jackson did. The private investigator had brought a couple of goons with him. One attacked Jackson in the woods with a knife. Once that man was subdued, Jackson came over to assist me just as the second one stepped out from behind the vehicle and fired. George tackled him from behind after that, and Elijah disarmed the investigator. We called the local authorities. Nigel is talking to them now."

His voice sounded off. I sensed he was going into shock. I walked him back over to the chair in the corner and knelt in front of him, holding his hands in mine.

"We've called in our private security to patrol the grounds so the children and staff will be safe. I don't think we'll be having any more visitors soon. But I'm concerned that they were armed and so aggressive. I thought Joanna's father would be smarter than that..." He continued to speak, but his voice grew fainter, until he finally trailed off.

"He's desperate to get her back," I said, taking a deep breath. "She was his means to an end. I don't think this will be the last we hear from him." I closed my eyes and concentrated on finding his pain. Soon, some sort of energy flowed between us. I relaxed my shoulders and took some more deep breaths. His skin warmed under my touch, and he relaxed.

Damien opened his eyes and looked down at me with a soft smile. "See, I knew that you could learn to focus. Thank you."

I stood and held out my hand. "I think we should get you to your apartment. You need to rest." I helped him up. He spoke to Grace and told her to call if there was any change with Jackson. She assured him she'd stay with him until the morning.

"I'll come and sit with him later so you can get some rest," I said as we left the room. She thanked me and said that wasn't necessary, that she didn't require much sleep and knew I had a few heavy days ahead.

We said good night and with Damien leaning slightly against me, we walked across campus. When we got close to my cottage, I looked up at

Damien. "I don't think you should be alone tonight, and I also don't think you'll make it up to your place."

"Actually, I don't want to be alone. I just want to hold you, Delaney. Would that be alright?"

I turned his face to mine and kissed him gently on the lips. "As you wish, Mr. Preston."

Once inside, he sat down heavily on my bed. I pulled off his shoes and got him under the covers. He was asleep almost as soon as his head hit the pillow, so I crawled around him and curled up to his side. I'd never tire of watching him sleep, though I soon dozed off as well.

FIFTEEN

A NEW BOND

I woke myself up at five after having the damn nightmare again and quietly slipped out of bed. I left Damien a note telling him I went to check on Jackson. I glanced back at his sleeping form and prayed a thank you that he was okay.

The morning light was emerging. The sky was gray and foggy. I hurried over the wet grass to the infirmary and tried not to let my shoes squeak too loudly on the tile floor.

Jackson was just as I'd left him, resting peacefully. Grace dozed in the corner chair with a book in her lap. She looked awfully uncomfortable. I nudged her gently and she opened one eye.

I whispered, "Go get some rest, Grace. I'll stay with him 'til he wakes." She smiled up at me and gave my hand a squeeze. She stretched her arms over her head and gave Jackson a motherly look as she stepped out the door.

I took a seat and tried to take advantage of the quiet time to think about the events of last night. To what lengths would Joanna's father go to get her back? If her powers were this strong, what were his like?

"His powers are very strong, Miss Frost." Joanna's quiet voice startled me, and I sat up quickly. I looked at the clock and realized I'd been here for two hours already.

"What are you doing out of bed, little lady?"

She stood at the end of the bed and looked thoughtfully at Jackson. "I Saw you were here and I couldn't sleep anymore. Is it okay that I'm here?"

I stood up and gave her a hug. "Of course it is. I'm sure Mr. Howe would be happy to see you, but you need your rest. Why don't you go on up to bed for a bit longer and then I can meet you for breakfast? What do you say?"

"I'll go. But I wanted you to know that my father will not stop at this. He won't be intimidated by Mr. Hart. He has a way of making people do what he wants. If he gets free and comes here, no one will be able to stop him. I just don't want to see anyone else get hurt."

"Joanna, we'll use all of our resources here to make sure neither of those things happen. Now go on…"

"Yeah, go on. You yappy females are keeping me awake." Jackson still had his eyes closed but obviously had heard our conversation.

"Oh look, Sleeping Beauty awakens."

Joanna smiled at him and touched his arm. "Mr. Howe, I am so sorry for what happened. I'm sorry Father sent those bad men."

"Aw shucks, this is just a flesh wound. I'll be fine in a day or so. Thanks for coming to check on me."

He winked at her and she blushed, saying a quiet goodbye to me on her way out. I walked over to the bed and ruffled Jackson's hair.

"Yeah, I'm awake. And I feel like shit, too. I thought getting hit with shrapnel hurt, but damn that knife wound sucks ass."

"I don't think I've ever heard you use so much colorful language. And the headmaster thought you would be a great influence with the boys in the dorm."

He snickered at that. "Fooled 'em, didn't I?" He sat up some more in bed and fidgeted. "Did you come to play nursemaid? I think I need a sponge bath." He waggled his eyebrows at me.

I raised one back at him, crossing my arms in my best impression of my mother. "Har har. I just wanted to make sure that you had a reality check. You were feeling so good when Grace gave you those drugs last night, I hoped you didn't leap out of bed thinking you were Superman or something. I mean, any more than usual."

He laughed at that but it didn't feel good, going by the look on his face.

"Uh, I don't think you should laugh. Perhaps I should stick to knock-knock jokes?"

"Yeah. That was a bad one. I've never been shot before. I've had many bumps, bruises and broken bones… Even a run-in with an IED, but never shot. Guess I've really done it all now, eh?"

"Nah, there's always napalm and electrocution."

He laughed again, and then cursed. "I love your morbid sense of humor, Counselor. It takes skill to perfect one's gallows humor."

I shrugged. "Gets me through. Seriously though, you need to take it easy. Jared is taking over your duties in the dorm and your classes will be covered this week. Morgan will come over and do her thing and hopefully you'll be up and around in a few days."

He sulked at that. "Do I look like the kind of guy who can sit around and be a good patient? Hell NO. And damn, I'm hungry. When can I eat?"

"Slow down, Soldier. I'll check with Grace." I grew serious and put my hand on his cheek. "I'm just really glad you're okay, and I'm glad we had our talk yesterday."

He put his hand over mine and closed his eyes. "Thank you, Delaney. For understanding and, well…just for being you." He looked up at me with the bluest eyes, and we stayed that way until a cough from the doorway caught my attention.

"Damien, you're up. I was just checking on our patient here."

Damien looked wrecked, still in his rumpled clothes with his hair everywhere.

His hair.

A new white streak adorned the left side of his face, to match the one on the right.

He was truly not well. I hadn't realized just how much last night had taken out of him.

He looked at me without a smile and came around the other side of the bed. "Jackson, I…" He struggled to get the words out. He took a deep breath and started again. "I truly owe you a debt of gratitude. You saved my life last night."

Jackson dropped his hand from mine and shrugged. "It was nothing you wouldn't have done for me, or for anyone else here. I owe you just as much for what you did." They looked at each other with a new understanding.

I glanced back and forth between them and was amazed at how much both of them had come to mean to me in such a short time. I refused to lose either one of them. I was even more grateful that they were both okay.

"Anyway, you need to take Delaney and go back and get some rest. You both look like shit."

I laughed at that, and Damien just smiled sadly. "It's a good thing you don't have a mirror in here, Howe. You just described yourself perfectly."

They shook hands, and a look passed between them that seemed like an agreement. Perhaps it was about me. Perhaps it was just what occurs between two people who share a traumatic experience. I knew what I was seeing was powerful.

"We really should get you back to bed, Damien. But first I'm going to talk to Grace and George about getting you some food, Jackson." I stepped out and walked through the halls toward the commons. I smelled the delicious breakfast food before I even entered the hall, but for once I wasn't hungry. The effects of the night before were closing in and my chest started to feel a little tight.

George was behind the counter when I arrived, looking about as good as I felt.

"Good morning, Nurse Walden. Did you get any sleep?"

He nodded and ran his hand over his chin, which he'd neglected to shave this morning. "I did, a little. But duty calls. What can I get you?"

"I was going to grab breakfast for Jackson? He's up and ornery as all get out. Maybe some food will put him in a better mood."

George snorted. "I doubt it. I was actually going to take him some myself. Tell him to give me a few and I'll be right over. Most of the kids have already eaten and Skye and Justin are helping me clean up." I realized I hadn't talked to Skye since before things got hairy last night. I made a mental note to stop by her place later today.

"Great, I'll go tell him. And thanks. Thanks for taking care of him last night and for everything you did to protect the kids."

George nodded solemnly and returned to his work.

I walked back over to the infirmary and into Jackson's room, catching the tail end of their conversation.

"I will. You just be careful with her, feel me? And watch yourself out there. I don't like this one bit..." Jackson trailed off as he realized I had arrived. They both looked as if I'd caught them with their hands in the cookie jar.

"Where's my food, woman? I'm starving."

I rolled my eyes at him and said, "Nurse Walden will be in shortly with your rations and hopefully another 'huge fucking needle' to stick you with." I smiled sweetly and went to stand next to Damien. He let out a huge yawn, so I tugged on him. "Come on, sleepyhead. You need some food and some more rest."

"Yes, ma'am. Jackson, I'll come by before I leave."

Jackson nodded grimly, and we left.

Damien and I walked back toward my cottage. I was deep in thought. I didn't want him to leave but didn't know how to broach the subject without sounding needy.

"It seemed like I was interrupting when I came back to the room. What was that all about?"

"He was telling me that the two of you had quite a conversation yesterday. I had no idea that he knew you like that. That he had Connected with you so deeply. I'm afraid he kept a lot of it to himself. Though his gift has been very helpful over the last two years. He's been able to tell us about people who belong with us."

"Would it have made a difference to you? Would you have stayed away from me if you knew?"

He frowned down at me. "I'm sorry, did I not make myself clear to you in the woods the other night?"

"Well, I guess you kind of like me a little bit." I bumped him with my hip, and he put his arm around my shoulder. "I knew there was something going on with Jackson, something different. It bothered me that I didn't remember him. To know that he'd been seeing images of my life this whole time really explained a lot...the foods, the Diet Coke... You got that information from him, didn't you?"

He looked ahead as we walked. "Does that bother you?"

I shook my head. "I kind of figured it out after he told me. Now it doesn't bother me, but I had been ready to bring y'all up on charges for stalking."

He chuckled at that. "You've handled all of this really well, Delaney. I'm so happy. And grateful. I don't know what I would have done if you'd walked away from all of this. From me."

"Yeah, like that was going to happen. You really could have been doing animal or human sacrifice in the woods and I would have found a way to accept it. I love it here." I smiled brightly at him. He seemed to have a way of bringing it out of me no matter what the situation. I grew serious for a moment.

"You're not still leaving tomorrow, are you? Are you sure you're up to traveling?"

He kept walking, still looking straight ahead. "Unfortunately, I don't have much of a choice. I've got to collect the children and take care of some business." He smiled sleepily at me. "But I'm not leaving until tomorrow morning, and *we* still have some unfinished business, don't we?"

We stepped onto my porch and I opened the front door. "Do we? I don't know. I'm not sure you're up for anything strenuous," I teased.

He snapped out of his sleepiness, pulling me into him. He looked down at me hungrily. "I always keep my promises, love, and I promised we'd do some more exploring." He kissed me greedily, and I melted against him. A weak-kneed feeling hit me hard as we stumbled back to my bed.

"Why, sir, I'd say you've gotten your second wind."

He smiled against my lips and lay me down gently, spreading his body over mine. His breath was hot against my neck as he slid his hands up my rib cage, his thumbs passing lightly over the underside of my bra.

I groaned and pulled him closer, digging my nails into his back as I traced his muscles through his shirt.

"I like your idea of exploring, Mr. Preston. You're a very hands-on type of learner, aren't you?"

He laughed softly against my neck and ran his tongue up the side to my earlobe, which he captured between his perfect lips. I gasped, and then his thumbs found my nipples, which were straining against the fabric.

"Mmmm, and it's fascinating, the kind of response one can get when you use your hands. For example, if I just move right there…" He took my nipples gently between his forefinger and thumb and squeezed, just a little.

I cried out and arched into him, feeling him harden against me.

"That *is* quite nice. Maybe I should give it a try and see what kind of response I get." I ran my hands down his sides and underneath him, grasping his erection in my hand.

"God…oh, Delaney. Yes, I think you've gotten the hang of it." He thrust his hips slowly against my palm, panting. I felt his erection through his jeans. I brought my legs up and wrapped my heels around his hips.

Every inch of my skin was alive. Every fiber of my being ignited with his touch. I breathed him in, desperate to get something of him inside me. He kissed me harder, his tongue seeking mine out and stroking it gently. He pulled back, and I opened my eyes to find him looking down at me adoringly.

"You are incredible, Delaney. You feel so good."

I smiled up at him and kissed him on his chin, nibbling a little before I pulled back.

He pulled me closer and kissed my shoulder before rolling off me. We lay there breathing heavily for a few minutes, our feet entangled, our fingers entwined. He brought my hand up and kissed each fingertip and then rested it on his chest.

His eyes closed, and he had a satisfied smile on his face. His voice was low when he said, "What's going on over there? I can feel those wheels turning in that head of yours." He opened one eye and looked over at me.

"Just taking this all in. I can't believe I'm here, I can't believe *you're* here. And I can't believe how good it feels to be this close to you."

He turned to face me and propped his head up with his hand. "Well, believe it. And yes, it does feel good. Too good." He ran his fingertips up and down my arm, giving me chills.

"How so?" I faced him then, mirroring his pose. "Is there really such a thing as 'too good'?"

He laughed and grabbed my hip, pulling me closer to him.

"There is when one is trying to maintain some sort of propriety. Delaney, I want more of you. I want *all* of you. I'm just not sure where we are, and I'd rather not rush things. We have all the time in the world. I am so enjoying getting to know you." He smiled and kissed me again.

"Thank you. For not rushing, I mean. My body doesn't want to put on the breaks *at all*. But my head is appreciating the pace. I'm not afraid. I trust you. It's just—"

"We both have reasons to take it slow. I haven't been involved with anyone since my wife died ten years ago. I was more concerned about figuring out whether to keep hiding or to do something positive with my life. When I came here, I spent a lot of time talking with Morgan and Elijah. They helped me come to terms with what happened and taught me to use my gift to help others while taking care of myself." He held me tight and kissed the top of my head.

"I haven't been with anyone in a long time. It's been hard, you know? I would start to get close to someone and then think, 'what if?' What if I can't be there? What if I get sick again?' But it also never felt right. I always thought that if I was meant to be with someone...I think I just hadn't found that person."

After I met Damien, though, I think I knew.

"I think I knew before I met you. Nigel had talked to me about you several months before I came to see you. We had just lost Turner, and he told me he had the perfect candidate for us. When he described you, I was intrigued but still resistant to becoming involved. I was pretty closed off with everyone. I was a bit of a recluse. Nigel kept telling me it was time, and like a petulant child, I refused to listen."

"So what changed your mind? I know! It was the cow insemination video in my classroom. That's it. That's the key to seduction. Man, I'll make millions selling that one. 'Women, get the man of your dreams to fall madly in love. Just have him watch this video, and he's yours forever.'"

Damien pulled me tighter and rolled me underneath him again. He kissed me intently. "You're correct, you have me all figured out. The sucking sound and all that afterbirth did it for me. That's all it took to get me to fall in love with you."

My eyes popped open wide but he just smiled back.

"You heard correct. What do you think about that?"

I frowned for a minute while he waited patiently for me to answer. My voice came out in a whisper. "It should scare the hell out of me...but for some reason, it doesn't."

I kissed him long and slow, memorizing the way he followed a caress of his lips with a swirl of his tongue.

"For me, though, it was definitely your Hokey Pokey. When you put your backside in, I was done."

"It was my backside that did it? If I would've known that, I would have shown it to you sooner."

He kissed me lightly, and then with feeling. I tangled my fingers in his hair and cradled his head as he kissed down my neck. My heart beat rapidly from the kissing, but also from the confessions we'd just made to each other.

He was falling in love with me. I pushed all my worries and fears aside and held on tightly. I never wanted to let go.

Our touching escalated to a more intense level. I rolled him to his back and straddled him. My skirt rode up on my legs, and he caressed my thighs before gripping my hips firmly. His chest rose and fell with his breathing and his sultry look had me eager to remove some of the barriers between us. I ran my hands along the hem of his shirt, slipping my fingers underneath to graze those tantalizing hairs I'd glimpsed before. I lifted the shirt a few inches and bent down to kiss his taut muscles. He squirmed underneath me and slid his hands up and down my arms, and then to my waist. As his hands started to roam under my shirt, I closed my eyes and leaned my head back and—

The phone rang.

We both laughed. "Saved by the bell," I said sarcastically. "Don't get up." I reluctantly got off of him and grabbed for the phone on the side of the bed.

"Whoever this is, you've got impeccable timing," I answered, then squealed when I heard who it was. "Cassidy! Oh, it's so great to hear your voice. Where the hell are you? Oh wait, hold on." I covered the phone and looked over at the heavenly body on my bed. "Is it okay if I take this? I'll only be a little while."

He sat up and kissed me on the forehead. "Take your time. I'm going to run back to my place and get cleaned up. I need to pack for my trip tomorrow, and then I have something I want to show you. I'll come back to pick you up for dinner, sound good?"

"Mmm, as long as we schedule in some more exploration time soon."

He gave me a heated look and adjusted himself before he stood up. "You're dangerous." He winked at me before he walked out the back door.

I fell back on the bed and let out a huge sigh before picking up the phone.

"Uh, what did I just interrupt, girl? You sound extremely satisfied, and you weren't alone. Hmmmm… Could it be?"

"Oh Cassidy. I cannot *believe* what just happened. For that matter, I can't believe what's happened since I arrived."

She wanted the details, so I started from the moment I got off the plane to just before she'd called, leaving out the more sensitive details.

"So he actually said he was falling in love with you?" She sounded so happy for me.

"I know. And he was so patient with me. We've talked about so much, and I really feel as though I can trust him. We've both really been through it, you know? I don't want to mess things up, and I know I have a job to do here. And the kids are great, Cass. You wouldn't believe the things they can do." I hadn't told anyone about the "specialness" of Havenhart. I needed to keep confidentiality about the kids, but they were extraordinary with or without their talents. I also left out the visitors from last night because I didn't want Cassidy to worry.

"I don't know of a more deserving person, Del. You had a lot of good karma built up. This is exactly what you should be doing. I'm so happy for you." There was an odd note in her voice at the end.

"Listen to me rambling on. What's going on with you? Do I detect a note of uncoolness?"

She started to cry—and I immediately felt horrible.

"Del, Robert and I are splitting up. I found out about some pretty horrible things he's been hiding. When I confronted him, he said it was none of my business, and if I had a problem with it, I should leave. So I did."

I was shocked. I felt her sadness, even through the phone and miles between us.

"Oh, honey! I'm sure you did what you felt was right. It would have to be pretty terrible for you to walk away. I know how much you wanted this to work. Are you okay?"

"I am now. It's going to take some time, and I have to get reestablished but, you know, everything had been a fight with him lately, and now I know why. I'll tell you more about it next time we're together. Right now, I just needed to hear your voice."

"Anytime, you know that. Where are you staying? Can you get out here? I've got a great place. We'll put on our jammies, watch movies and eat chocolate anytime you want."

She hesitated, and I heard her sniffling. "Actually, Del, I just might take you up on that. I'm on a five-day trip that ends in Dallas on Thursday. I could catch a flight to Fayetteville from there and spend the weekend with you. It would be really good for me to get away from here for a while, and I'm dying to see your new digs and, um, the new guy you dig...ha ha."

It was so good to hear her laugh.

"Dig. That's a good one."

She cracked up. "Wait. I wouldn't be interfering now, would I?"

"Absolutely not. You are never interfering. I'll need some girl time after this first week of school. Damien will actually be gone this week on business and should come back Saturday. You'll get to meet him, but you and I will have plenty of time together.

We worked out plans, and I made a note to myself to speak to Nigel about her visit. It would give me an excuse to visit his beautiful home. I probably needed an appointment to see him but hey, I'd make it work.

I stretched out on the bed and looked at the clock. It was almost lunchtime, and my stomach was rumbling. I decided to take a quick shower and head over to have lunch with the kids. I was sure they'd be anxious about classes starting tomorrow, the new ones anyway. The students who had been here for a while seemed as though they were at home. I wanted to be sure I touched base with Sergei, Nate, Matteo, Hazel and Joanna for sure. I figured I should also chat with Raven to see where she was with her research.

When I finished my shower, I walked back into my bedroom and stared at my bed. It hit me that I had actually spent the past two nights sleeping with Damien. Fully clothed, of course. But we'd definitely enjoyed each other. Thinking of this morning filled me with joy.

I walked around and sat down on "his side" of the bed. I picked up the pillow he'd been sleeping on, and I brought it to my face, inhaling deeply.

God, he smelled good. It wasn't a cologne or aftershave kind of smell. There was a hint of tea tree oil and freshly cut wood. Hard to describe but it was incredibly sensual.

I closed my eyes and remembered his touch and his kiss. I wondered what he had in mind for later and thought about just how far I was comfortable taking things at this point. I wasn't afraid to be intimate with him, I was simply unsure and nervous. He had a way of kind of overwhelming my senses when I was with him that led me to believe I would only be aware of him.

And he was falling in love with me…

SIXTEEN

FIRSTS

THINGS WERE BUSTLING IN THE COMMONS. I STOPPED TO CHAT WITH SKYE and Justin. He was still following her around like a lost puppy and she was enjoying the attention. They were laughing about the latest viral videos. Sounded contagious to me.

"Hey guys. Are you all ready for tomorrow?"

Skye exploded into action. "Oh Delaney, is everything okay? I was so worried about you when you left the commons last night and I heard someone had been shot and then I didn't see you come back to your place and with classes starting tomorrow I was hoping everything was okay and—"

I placed my hand on her shoulder and reassured her that everyone was fine, that Jackson was resting and would be back on his feet soon. She grasped my hand and offered her services if I needed anything. She asked if I wanted to join them.

"No thanks, I'm actually looking for Raven Parsons, have you seen her?"

Justin choked a little on his food. "Is she really back this year? Last year with her was an exercise in futility. She made us all pay for her unhappiness."

I tilted my head and gave Justin a look. "Not all of these kids are going to be grateful now for the services they're receiving. It's our job to make sure they all get what they need, whether they like it or not. In her case, I think her bark is worse than her bite. We just need to find out what she's into, you know? I actually got her working on some research for me and she's quite adept with the computer. Did you know that?"

He shook his head and looked guilty. "No. I guess I never really bothered to find out. She's probably in my tech class. Maybe I can work with that. I could use a kid who's got some skills. Some of these kids start looking around on the floor for furry things when you tell them to grab the mouse."

Skye cracked up at that, and he looked pleased that she found him amusing. I smiled at the two of them and thought maybe I wasn't the only one experiencing some joy.

"Well, keep me posted, Justin. Have a nice day, guys." I headed off and the two of them put their heads closer together to continue their conversation. I looked around and saw my new boys sitting together, so I decided to plop down with them for lunch.

"It depends on whether you're talking about money or reputation, know what I'm saying? If you're talking top-grossing acts, Drake, Lil' Wayne and Kanye are all top money makers. Jay-Z even. And A$AP Rocky be killin' it. But when you consider cultural impact, you can't leave out Tupac and Kendrick Lamar, you know, the dudes who are out there preachin'."

"Yes, but you are leaving out greats like Ice Cube, Dr. Dre, Public Enemy and Snoop Dogg," Sergei answered. "They have been around long time. And things are different in other parts of the world. In Europe, we are listening to other artists."

Nathan and Sergei going head-to-head on GOAT had me smiling.

"Do you listen to rap, Miss Frost?" Nathan asked me.

"Sure do. Eminem, Yelawolf, Busta Rhymes, Tech N9ne. And you can't forget the Beastie Boys. But most of the time I listen to metal."

I took a bite out of my grilled cheese sandwich and looked up to see all three boys gawking at me with their mouths hanging open. Playing along, I said, "What? I can't have an opinion about rap? Is it because I'm a chick? Because I'm old? Because I'm white?" I smiled at them, and they relaxed, still looking at me in wonder. "I mean, I prefer my music with loud guitars and crashing drums, but I do like to dance and can enjoy a quick wit."

"You really listen to rap music?" Matteo frowned at me in disbelief.

"I listen to all kinds of music. I love show tunes and I'm a huge Elvis fan as well. It's good for the soul to have an eclectic taste in music. Seriously, you'll get more chicks if you listen to Sinatra or the King. But I don't think any of you are going to stall out in the chick department."

"Miss Frost, you are genius. When we are needing dating advice, can you give us more, how you say, pointing?"

"Pointers, sure. And one more thing, if you can dance, you'll steal her heart."

"Oh, like Mr. Preston doing that Hokey Pokey? Is that what it takes?" asked Matteo.

Now it was my turn to blush. "Well, the fact that he wasn't afraid to embarrass himself to have fun shows his confidence, so yeah, I think that would work for a girl."

"Ah yeah, and he's got an accent too," Nathan said. "We need to hit him up for some advice, he's probably got a lady on each arm, right?"

I snorted at that. "He better not. I mean, I doubt it. Uh, I'm going to see how the ladies are doing. See you guys around."

I heard them debating on whether Mr. Preston had "swag" and I suppressed a laugh. I couldn't wait to tell him, although it might give him an unfair advantage.

"Hmph." I spotted Hazel and Joanna together again, and I breathed a sigh of relief. I'd had a feeling those two would be good for each other.

"You know you're not going to save them all."

The voice came from the booth I was passing. Raven sat there alone. I knew I needed to talk to her but that was absolutely not the way I wanted to start.

"You're right. At this point, I'll be happy if everyone is safe and sound." I slid into the booth and took a seat, which seemed to surprise her. "But that's not really in my control either. Part of life's lessons is to figure out what you have control over and what you don't."

"So, you think people should be control freaks? Isn't that, like, totally against what counseling is supposed to be about?" She was looking at me with her arms crossed, one eyebrow raised.

"There's a difference between trying to control things and accepting that there are things you can't control." I tried to tread lightly with her. I didn't want to make things worse.

"You should tell that to my parents. They can't accept that I have no control over this...thing I do. They avoid talking to me because they don't want to hear what I have to say."

"It's not easy for parents to accept that their children are different sometimes. Certainly doesn't make it easy on their kids though, and frankly, when you have kids you kind of have to be willing to accept come whatever may, true?"

She looked at me for a long minute. "What about you? Are you always willing to accept 'come whatever may'? Like when Joanna's father shows up here? Like if Mr. Preston doesn't come back? Will you be able to accept those?"

I thought about what she said for a minute before I spoke. "I will *never* accept that it's okay to use a child for gain or to hurt them in any way."

I realized at that moment that confidentiality was going to a problem at this school with so many of the children who could See things. But again, I wanted to be as honest as possible, so I kept going.

"As for Mr. Preston, I can't control what he does or how he feels. I can only trust that he's honest with me, right? That's what you do when you become involved with someone. If you can't trust them, then what kind of a relationship can you have?" I laughed for a moment. "Unless you can always tell what they're thinking or what they're afraid of, but that's just a whole other situation, isn't it?" I smiled at her, hoping she took that last statement as only the truth and not an attack.

"You know, Miss Frost. You don't have to try to make me like you. You don't have to sit here and pretend to be interested in my feelings. You're free to go anytime you damn well please." She looked down at her plate and picked at her food.

"Raven, you don't have to like *me*, and yes, I can leave. But I hope you might use that gift of yours to look inside me and tell me whether or not

I'm pretending with you. I'd really love to see you use that energy in a way that doesn't push people away from you."

She just shrugged and continued to look down.

"Thanks again for the research you did for Sociology. If you want, I'd be happy to make your work-study title be my Research Assistant. Think about it and let me know, okay? And enjoy the rest of your day." I'd said my peace, so I stood up to leave.

So quiet I almost missed it, she said, "You're welcome." Her tone was more sad than anything. I really hated for her to be hurting. I wanted to pull her into a hug and take that pain away for her. But she had to be ready.

Lunch had stretched to two hours for me, and by then the commons were mostly empty. I went by to check on Jackson, who was as ornery as ever but pleased to have his X-box moved into his room so he could play against several of the kids. I warned him about too much excitement and he actually stuck his tongue out at me.

I had one more thing I wanted to do before I returned to my cottage, and that was to figure out how to set up Joanna with Morgan for some training. I went by the library and as I entered the stacks, I heard hushed voices arguing. I cleared my throat so as not to catch anyone off guard but they continued arguing.

As I rounded the corner, I heard Morgan saying, "If we don't sever the link he will never stop coming for her. He's already got a breakout plan in place. I say you send Damien there first to check on his security, or we're going to have more blood on our hands." Morgan's face was red as she glared angrily at Nigel, who remained composed as always.

He turned to smile at me in the doorway. "I believe you were coming to talk to Morgan about Joanna, so you might as well join us." He motioned for me to take a seat on one of the leather couches. Morgan was pacing with no intention of settling down.

"We need more security, with Damien leaving and Jackson down. Elijah, Vincent, and George are all powerful, but when he comes, he will not be alone." She stopped and put her hands on her hips. Her low-cut, long-sleeved dress had flowing sleeves that almost reached the floor. I saw her tapping her bare foot on the floor to keep from losing it.

"Morgan, I am quite aware of our needs, and I was going to discuss that with Delaney as well. Dear, isn't it true your cousin James has experience with security and intelligence?"

"Yes, sir. He spent time in Bosnia and parts of Africa in the nineties gathering intelligence for NATO, among other things he's not allowed to talk about. Do you think he would be a good fit? I'm sure he would be willing to assist us. It would likely give him something to keep his mind off his own troubles."

"Very well. Please call him and ask him to come see me at his earliest convenience. And as for your other guest, she is absolutely welcome to visit provided that she not be privy to our current situation, nor the 'special circumstances' of our students."

The man never ceased to throw me with his pronouncements.

"Thank you, sir."

"Is there anything further I can do to ease your mind, Morgan? I'm afraid I can't undo certain things once they have been set into motion. Joanna is meant to be here, and here she will stay." With that, he gave a small bow and left the room.

"Goddammit, that man is infuriating sometimes," Morgan shouted. A book flew across the room and crashed into her row of unlit candles. "I simply want him to have a less lackadaisical attitude about our security. I can do some things, and yes, there are many of us with similar powers here. But without Damien and Jackson, we're basically sitting ducks. The local authorities can't help with someone like Mr. Rains."

"What do you know about him, Morgan?" I asked. "Are his powers similar to hers?"

She shook her head. "Not really. His are more about getting in your head and seeing what motivates you and then using it against you. It's not total mind control, but you get the picture. He can get to anyone, at any time here who doesn't know how to guard against that. He could coerce someone to open the gates, for goddess' sake." She started pacing again.

Her anger wasn't helping us problem solve, and I wished she would relax.

I decided to experiment. I took a couple of deep breaths and focused on her. I pictured her calm, the tension bleeding out of her. The air around her grew distorted, like heatwaves rising from a blacktop.

She stopped pacing and turned to face me.

"Are you doing what I think you're doing?" Her eyes grew wide, and she smiled knowingly. "You are, you little snot. When did you figure that out?"

"Um, just now? I've kind of figured out how it feels, and what I have to do, and it just kind of works I guess." I shrugged at her and smiled innocently. "I did it with Jackson after he was shot, and with Damien after he healed him. I've also done it for Joanna. It sort of feels like an exchange of body heat or something. Maybe it's getting stronger, because I didn't have to touch you to do it."

"Well, I'm really glad. Just think what you can do with that little trick. You'll be able to calm people with just a few breaths. That will come in handy, especially with things to come." A dark shadow crossed her face, and she turned away, heading over to her desk.

"What is it, Morgan? Have you Seen something?"

She kept her back to me as she spoke. "This visit was only the beginning. I'm afraid Damien's trip will be in vain and that more violence is heading our way, but I can't make out the particulars."

She turned and her eyes had gone dark again, the whites barely visible, as if the pupil had completely taken over her irises. "His power grows, and he will be able to penetrate the minds of anyone here. The students will need to be warned. I'll want you to practice your new trick and see if you can keep them all calm while I talk to them about what's going on, or at least as much as they need to know."

"I don't know if I can but I'll try." I wanted to help, but I was afraid to disappoint her.

"Don't be nervous, Delaney. You've come a long way already, and you've barely scratched the surface of what you can do." She smiled and gestured me over to where she was standing in front of her altar.

"From the first time Nigel told me about you, I've tried to See you, and I've Seen many things in your future: the good, the bad and the ugly. You'll need to be strong, for all of us. And I will send you my powers whenever I can." She looked at me sideways. "Do you trust me? Do you trust in what we do here?"

"More than I ever thought I would."

"Would you trust me to do something with you? I know we haven't had much time for working together, but I think you're ready to take the next step."

"Whatever I need to do, Morgan, I'll do it. I just want to help. "

"Very well, close your eyes and give me your hands."

I did as she asked and tried to relax, not sure of what I was about to do. She began chanting in a low voice at first, and then the sound reverberated around the room. My pulse sped up in my veins, the blood flowing through in a rushing motion. The air began to circulate faster and faster until we were standing in the middle of a twister. Behind closed eyes, I sensed the lights flickering. I heard Morgan panting over the rushing sound of the wind.

She squeezed my hands one last time and the room went quiet, all except my pounding heart.

"You can open your eyes now," she said breathlessly. Her red hair was wild and there were papers strewn all about the room. All of the candles had been blown out.

I stepped back and brought my hand up to my chest, my heart finally slowing down. "Wow," I said softly. "That was intense. But Morgan, I thought we were supposed to go to the basement in the case of a tornado."

She chuckled at that and eyed me curiously. "How are you feeling?" She started to pick up items that had blown out of place. I helped her pick up the papers and placed them on her desk.

"I don't really know," I replied. "Kind of buzzy, kind of wired. How am I *supposed* to feel?"

She raised an eyebrow at me. "Just like that." She laughed and took my hands, leading me over to sit next to each other on the couch. Her smile made me think I'd finally done something to please her.

"Did I do something right?"

She laughed at me again. "Really, Delaney, you need to relax. Whatever gave you the feeling you were doing something wrong? You've handled all of our eccentricities extremely well. I'm just so pleased that this trance we did worked. I think we've gotten a little deeper into your psyche. You have such untapped power! It's exciting to me. Now when you use your gift, you'll truly be able to connect with a person's pain or area of trauma and draw it out."

Morgan got serious for a minute, and I leaned in closer to hear what she had to say. "You may find that you start to get drained the more you use it, and I don't want any flare-ups with your asthma. If you start to feel winded at all, stop and be sure you see Damien or myself, although I'm guessing you'll enjoy the kind of healing *he* can give you a bit more." She smirked knowingly at me and my face got hot.

"Ah, about that. Things have, um, progressed a little and...I, er..." I was stammering like an idiot.

"I know you guys have gotten closer, and I'm really happy for you. Why are you worried?"

"I don't want anyone to be uncomfortable, or to break any rules or anything. I'm just not sure how to proceed." She laughed and I started to giggle. "Damn, I haven't been this way about a guy since forever. It kind of makes me feel like a teenager again." I rubbed at my face as if I could really make the blush fade that way. "I just don't want to screw it up, you know?"

She nodded seriously. "You have a precious thing with Damien, and it needs to be nurtured. If you start to feel like things are going astray, just talk to him. And if you need to work out the words, come to me. Like I said before, anything you tell me stays with me. Even the counselor needs a counselor sometimes, right?"

I reached over and gave her a hug. "I'm so happy to hear you say that." I sat back and gave her a smile. "I have a tendency to get all up in my head and not deal with things, and I don't want to do that with him. He's..."

"Hot, I know."

We both burst out laughing. "Man, is he ever. And he has a way of putting me off guard that's scary and exciting at the same time. Most of all, I don't want to hurt him or make things more difficult for him. He's very important to this place, and to me."

She squeezed my hand and smiled. "And that is why I'm happy for you. Damien is a special person, and not just because he's a healer. Damien always puts everyone else first. Havenhart has been his priority for years now. I'm not saying he's been unhappy here, but he's certainly lit up since you've arrived. Actually, since he returned from California, always with that dreamy expression. Of course, if you called him on it, he'd immediately be all business and talk about how 'Delaney will be good for the students, she'll be an asset to the academy, blah blah blah.'" This last part was spoken in a mocking British accent.

I couldn't believe she was telling me this, but I didn't want her to stop talking.

"I just hoped," she continued, "that Jackson wouldn't be a problem. He had an unnatural fixation on you, even for him. Whenever he's made a connection with someone, he can always call upon it. For some reason, he was determined that with you, it was different."

I nodded solemnly. "We had a long talk the other day and thankfully he was able to get some perspective. I'm really happy he's in my life, but I don't feel anything more for him than friendship, and I wanted him to be okay with that. I think he will be."

"So do I, and I think he'll come to terms with it. He and Damien have never been super close, but I saw them after the shooting, and there was a bond that formed that night."

She drifted off and looked away for a moment.

"You better go, Delaney. Call James. See if he can come as soon as possible. I'm really concerned..."

She had a far off look in her eyes so I said my goodbye and crept quietly away.

As I walked back to my cottage, I felt energized and a little hypersensitive. Everything my skin came into contact with was intensified. The heat burned, the breeze was like sandpaper, the rocks under me pushed up through my shoes and poked at my feet. Not that it hurt, exactly. I was just more aware. I walked inside and immediately called James.

"Yo, FC. You get my message?" he answered, speaking quickly as always.

"Yes, and thanks. We've had, um, a situation here. Was there anything you needed to tell me?

James blew out a breath. "He's solid, at least as far as my sources could tell me. Good soldier, good guy, saw some shit as a kid, saw some serious shit in Afghanistan and Iraq. Did his twenty with no problems, only commendations."

"Thank you. I'm actually not surprised given some things that have come to light. I'm not concerned about Jackson any longer. But that's not the reason I called. Can you, uh, come out here? There's someone I want you to meet and something I need you to do."

He assured me he'd arrive in thirty minutes.

I puttered around my place for a few minutes, throwing in some laundry, cleaning the cat box and feeding the little monsters. I straightened up my paperwork for class tomorrow. I chose the outfit I would wear for the first day and smiled approvingly at my choice. In twenty minutes, Vincent called from the front gate to tell me James was approaching. I thanked him and asked him to let the headmaster know.

I jogged up to the gate, energized by my session with Morgan, and also by the thought of James working with us. I knew this would be good for him. The students' safety would rest in more than competent hands.

James was decked out in his leathers and his barely legal helmet as he rode his Harley onto campus. I'd lectured him before about the lack of benefits to his brain bucket but he'd always reply, *"Cousin, I'm more than three times seven, I can do what I want."*

He was all business when he got off the bike, storing his helmet in his saddlebag and stripping off his leather riding gloves before hugging me tightly.

"You call, I come, FC. That's the arrangement."

I kissed him on the cheek and led him over to the gatehouse to introduce him to Vincent. As always, our Vincent was the man of few words, shaking hands and telling us the headmaster would like us to go to the house. I waggled my eyebrows at James and we thanked Vincent. When we were a few yards away, I whispered, "Yes! I've been hoping for an excuse to check out the house. It's gorgeous."

"What's going on here, FC? Why's the big man want to talk to me?"

I wasn't sure how much I was allowed to tell him, so I stuck to the facts.

"We have some additional security needs, and he asked me if you would be available. We had an incident yesterday and one of our staff was injured."

"Injured how?" He stopped me and raised an eyebrow. He didn't appreciate my pussyfooting around the issue.

"That's what the headmaster wants to talk to you about. I'm just really glad you're here."

We had reached the steps of the glorious house and he took a minute to check it out.

"This is some serious money here. Who is this guy?"

At that moment, the front door swung open, and Nigel stood there looking approvingly at James.

"I am a man in need of your services, Mr. Morton. Thank you so much for coming out here. I hope it was no trouble. Please come inside."

He waved us in the door and we stepped into an immaculate foyer. A huge chandelier hung in the center and a rounded staircase led up to the right. Nigel led us to the right into a parlor with Victorian-era furniture. I was afraid to sit on anything, so I looked around for the sturdiest piece.

"Nothing in here is so fragile that you present a danger. Contrary to your belief, my lady, you are quite graceful and do not weigh nearly enough to cause damage. Please sit."

James stifled a laugh, and I gave him the stink eye.

"Very well. I'm sure you're curious as to why we asked you out here this afternoon. Are you aware of what we do here at Havenhart?"

"No, Mr. Hart, I'm not. I've heard stories in town but I'd rather hear it from you."

"Of course. I know that Delaney was unsure of how much to divulge to you."

I shivered. I was glad I hadn't said more but I was still weirded out by him. Not in a major way, but still...

"I founded this academy over thirty years ago to meet the needs of a very special group of children. These children, in most cases, have experienced severe traumatic events and have come away from them forever altered. In some cases, they had been exceptional prior to the tragedy, but many of their gifts are a result of their experiences."

"Exactly what do you mean by 'gifts'? Are we talking ESP, mind reading, moving things?"

I was glad to see that James was taking this seriously, not scoffing at what he was hearing.

"For some, it is what you would call Extra Sensory Perception. For others, it is more an innate intuition about things. For example, your dear cousin Delaney. Do you know why we brought her here?"

James turned to look at me with a startled expression. "Delaney?"

I took his hand and closed my eyes for a minute. I sensed his anxiety and discomfort at what he was hearing. He stared at me, confused. I took a deep breath, and I wished his anxiety would melt away.

When I opened my eyes, his expression had changed to one of wonder.

"What's happened to you? What was that?" He turned fiercely toward Nigel and stood up. "What did you do to her?"

"We have only helped her to realize a small portion of the power she holds. Tell me, James. Haven't you ever wondered why she is so gifted as a counselor? How it is that she can instantly tell when someone is in need of comfort?"

James looked down at me, frowning. "You mean that creepy thing that happens when she gets you to talk about shit that you never meant to?" He sat back down, still staring at me in disbelief. "Did you know about this?"

He was trying to understand, but this was out of his realm of belief.

"I swear, James, I had no idea it was anything other than me trying to make people feel better. They've showed me things here, and I've worked with Morgan, our librarian. She's helping me get stronger. I don't make people do things they wouldn't do on their own, I just make them feel more at ease so they can let it out."

I looked down at my lap, hoping he wouldn't be angry with me. I couldn't bear it if I hurt him.

"Delaney, you have nothing to worry about. Your gift is to be treasured. It is very rare and is essential to the work we do here. James, there is nothing malevolent about your cousin or anyone else on this campus. However, there are forces out there that would bring us harm. That is why I have asked you to come."

James looked at me, and I saw him come to a resolution. "What can I do?" He looked intently at Nigel and took my hand in his.

I squeezed it reassuringly, and he glanced at me quickly before focusing on the headmaster.

"One of our new students here, Joanna Rains, is being hunted by her father and his associates. Mr. Rains is a powerful man, and he uses his powers for illegal pursuits. He has dragged his daughter all over the country, using her gift of Sight to make a small fortune, which he plunders almost as quickly as he makes it. He has big plans, however. Deadly plans.

"She stopped cooperating with him and he became increasingly violent. When Delaney and Mr. Preston took her into our custody in Florida, she was beaten severely, with cracked ribs and a collapsed lung. He knows she's here. He is currently incarcerated in Texas, but his powers can reach beyond prison walls.

"He sent a private investigator out here last night and, unbeknownst to us, this investigator was accompanied by two armed associates. One of my staff members, Jackson Howe, was attacked with a knife and shot. He is recovering, thanks to Mr. Preston, but that leaves me shorthanded. Mr. Howe is a former Ranger with excellent skill in security—and these men were able to overcome him. I now have to send Mr. Preston to collect two new students and now he must also go to Texas to deal with Mr. Rains. With Mr. Howe incapacitated, I am in need of your services. I have read your military file, and I'm aware of your level of expertise in this area. What will it take to persuade you to come work for me?"

I was startled at his admission. Damien was going to see Rains? I had a very bad feeling about this.

James looked at him for a moment, reading him for ulterior motives. He'd always been excellent at gauging people. It was like watching two chess pros in the final round of a high-stakes tournament. Then James laughed.

"My military record was classified. You must know some powerful people if you got ahold of it. And yes, I've got experience in recon, intel, weapons and protection. But all you needed to tell me was that my cousin was in danger to get me to stay. If there's *any* chance she's mixed up in this, of course I'm going to stay."

Nigel grinned in satisfaction. "That settles it then. I will have Vincent set you up in one of the carriage house apartments—"

"If it's all the same to you, I'd rather stay with Delaney. I want to be close by in case she needs me."

"James, you'd be close by, and all I have is a pull-out couch..."

"That's fine. Or I can sleep on the floor. I'll need to run home and pick up some of my things. I can be back here in a couple of hours." James stood to leave, all business.

Nigel stood and shook hands with him. "I'm very glad to hear you'll stay and see us through this situation. Do you need me to contact your employer?"

James shook his head. "I'll let him know I'll be taking a leave. I've been thinking of moving on to something else anyway."

"Excellent. I shall see you to the door. And don't worry, Mr. Morton. You will be amply compensated for your time here. You're welcome to stay as long as you'd like." He touched his arm with his other hand and lowered his voice. "And if you're in need of assistance in the matter of your daughters, please do not hesitate to ask. I have extensive knowledge and experience in that area, not to mention my connections." He gave a sly smile at that.

James nodded, looking grim. "Thank you, I appreciate it. I'll stay as long as you need me." He turned to the door.

I walked over to give him a hug. "I'm so glad you came, FC," I whispered in his ear.

He put his hands up to my cheeks.

"Will you be okay until I can get back?"

"I'll be fine. I'm meeting up with Damien for a bit and Vincent will let me know when you've returned." I turned to Nigel. "Actually, can Vincent drive him, so he has a car to bring his things?"

He nodded. "I was going to mention that. James, you can pull your motorbike into one of the bays under the carriage house. Vincent will drive you and see you back safely." We said our thanks and I walked him back to the gate as Nigel picked up the phone.

"What the hell have you gotten yourself into, Delaney? I thought they were taking care of you at this place. I never would have wanted you mixed up in this shit."

I turned him to face me.

"I'm completely fine here. They've taken wonderful care of me. I feel stronger and healthier than I have in a long time. I haven't even had to use my inhaler in a couple of days. And wait 'til you meet the kids. They're fantastic. But they need me. They need someone to advocate for them and to help them heal, James. You can understand exactly why I'd want to be a part of that. And that was great what the headmaster said, that he can help with the girls."

James' face softened, as if he might tear up. His voice was weak when he continued. "You know how many people have said they could help me? I've given up hope on that. I just wish I knew if they were okay."

I pulled him into a hug and he slumped a little, the agony of the separation weighed heavily on him. I held him tightly and focused on easing his pain.

"Always lovely to see a family reunion."

I turned around to find Damien smiling brightly at us. The boys shook hands and Damien said, "I'm very glad you'll be here. I really don't want to leave, but it is crucial that I see what Mr. Rains is up to."

I turned to him, surprised. "So, you're going to see Rains?"

He nodded. "I am. I need to see that he's secured. Nigel can't have both of us gone. I would have told you, but he wanted to talk to you about it himself."

"I'm going to head over and pick up my things. I'll see you in a couple of hours." James kissed me on the cheek, and a look passed between him and Damien.

"Thank you again," Damien said.

James nodded and entered the gatehouse.

"I feel a lot better about leaving knowing he'll be here. I take it he's going to stay with you? I was ready to tell Nigel to go himself if James wasn't agreeable."

I looked up at him and smiled. "I wish you didn't have to go, but I know how important it is. I hope you'll be safe."

He kissed the top of my head, and I relished the feel of his arms, knowing it would be several days until I would be close to him again.

"Well, Mr. Preston. I'm at your disposal for the remainder of the evening. What's your nefarious plan?"

He grinned wickedly. "Ah, yes, I have you all to myself. But first I must feed you. You will need your strength."

My eyes closed to suspicious slits and he laughed.

"Depends on what you consider nefarious. I simply want to have dinner with a beautiful lady and then whisk her away for a moonlit walk. Does that meet with your approval?"

I knew better than to take him completely at his word, so I grabbed his hand and led him to the commons. "Come on, oh devious one. Let's get some grub."

We walked hand in hand in the paling light. Dinner was chicken Caesar salad and fresh sourdough bread that almost rivaled what I'd grown up with in San Francisco. I knew there was magic involved, because you can't get bread like that away from home.

We ate quickly, sitting with some of the other staff. Jared and Isaac debated about the lack of leadership in the Democratic Party and their chances in the next election. Damien chatted with Justin and Skye about their plans for their first week of classes.

Morgan and Elijah sat at a table near the back of the room, and when I caught her eye, she nodded approvingly. I smiled back at her but when I met Elijah's glance, something dark was there, and it made me shudder.

Damien looked at me, concerned. "Are you alright?"

I nodded and motioned for him to continue his conversation. When I looked back over, they were gone.

George sang along with the music behind the counter. When the kids were finished eating, they headed over to the lobby of the dorms for a Just Dance competition and board games. Marcia, Moira, Isaac, and Jared were leading the activities tonight to get the kids relaxed before classes started in the morning. Jackson was still in the infirmary, and I told Damien I wanted to check on him before we left. He needed to speak with Morgan, so we went our separate ways and agreed to meet back at my cottage in a few.

Jackson was doing much better and hoped the Waldens would give him clearance to go back to his own bed that night. Grace checked his vitals and was going to talk to George about it after dinner was finished.

I told him about James coming, and he said he was looking forward to meeting him. I told him I'd be sure to bring him by in the morning so Jackson could catch him up on our current security status. He nodded and closed his eyes to get some rest. I smiled, grateful that he'd be back to himself in a few days. The world just wasn't right without his crazy energy.

I walked back to my cottage, listening to the cicadas and the crickets. Their symphony was beginning to really appeal to me. I stopped to look at the sky. I was in awe over the amount of visible stars in the night sky.

A sharp pain stabbed the back of my eye, and my skin was suddenly tight and twitchy. A faint scent that was similar to sulfur wafted near me. I strained my eyes, but even if I could see anything, there was nothing there.

The darkness closed around me, and I quickened my pace. I knew if I reached my cottage, I would be safe. As I rounded the corner of my cul-de-sac, I saw Damien standing on the porch. He hurried down to meet me, looking concerned at my approach.

"Hey, what's gotten into you?" he asked worriedly. "You're freezing. Let me get you inside."

"I'm fine, I'm fine," I insisted. "I just had a weird pain in my eye and then my skin was crawling. It was freaky. But it's gone now. Maybe it was just some creepy swamp creature watching me. Isn't the Black Lagoon somewhere close to here?"

"Very funny. No deflecting me here. Let me look you over."

I giggled and said, "Why, Doctor, should I put on a gown? Where are your instruments?" I gave him my best eyelash batting and he growled at me.

I cooperated while he checked my pulse, looked at my pupils and tested my reflexes. Then he put his hands on the sides of my head and closed his eyes. A familiar warm sensation traveled over my scalp and down my neck. I turned to putty in his hands.

"You keep doing that and I'm going to be a useless blob. Then we won't be able to take our walk." I pouted up at him.

"You are incorrigible." He bent down and kissed me.

I lit up like a firework. Warmth immediately flooded my limbs. Any wooziness I had was gone. I kissed him back with feeling.

"Mmm, I think my patient has made a full recovery. Shall we take that walk, milady?" I tried to hide my hope that the walk would lead to my bedroom. I looked longingly at the bed as we passed through my cottage to the back porch.

"Are you tired? Would you rather just go to sleep?"

I detected a hint of disappointment in his voice.

"No, I want to go," I hurried to reassure him. "I was just thinking of the last time we were here."

That heated look crossed his face once more and he pulled me to him, kissing me amorously. My arms circled his neck, and I twirled my fingers in his hair. He pulled back and looked as if he were reconsidering his plans.

"Delaney, I'd—"

I put my finger to his lips. "It's fine. There will be time for that when you return, right?"

A wave of energy pulsed through us, and I gasped. We looked at each other, surprised.

"What is it you do to me, Damien? I feel you all over even when you aren't touching me, and when you do, it feels like electricity is flowing through me."

He shook his head. "It's not me, love. I think when you, um, are feeling a certain level of excitement it, ah...sends out energy. I don't know what it is, but it's most certainly coming from you. Dear *Lord*, is it good."

I searched his eyes and sensed what he was feeling: Pleasure, longing, and—the best part—love. Another wave went through us, and he gasped this time as well.

"If I don't get you through that door, I'm going to have you undressed and under me in seconds. I don't want to push you. I want you to be ready."

While it might be the most amazing experience of my life to this point, he was right. I was still leery of taking that final step. I'd only been close to him for a short time and as much as I trusted him, I wasn't ready for any form of rejection. I was still somewhat self-conscious around him.

I smiled graciously and took his hand, opening my back door with the other.

"C'mon. I'll take a rain check. I hope you honor it."

He bent down and kissed my hand. "I always keep my promises, Delaney." He winked at me and motioned for me to step out ahead of him.

We walked in silence, enjoying the sounds of the night around us. He led me to the same bay I'd found him in so many nights ago. It seemed like forever since that night I'd surprised him working on his bike. I never would have guessed the next time I'd return, he'd be holding my hand and looking at me so tenderly. All traces of hesitation were gone from him.

I took a good look at the Mustang parked in the far corner. "Who does this belong to?"

He gave me that devilish smile that made me squirm in a delicious way. "It's mine. I bought her when I came back here and I've been fixing her up. She's a beauty, but quite temperamental."

"Do all the women in your life fit that description?"

He narrowed his eyes at me. "You may be on to something there. But I know that when I get under her hood, I can make her purr."

That salacious statement made me wobble on my feet as heat gathered just below my navel. I had a mental image of parking that bad boy off the road with the top down and having him show me just how he liked to tinker. It appeared he was thinking something along the same lines. He sighed and tugged on my hand.

"One more thing for us to look forward to, love."

We passed his bike and James's, which was parked right next to it, and he led me through another doorway. The smell of hay and alfalfa grew stronger.

"I thought you might enjoy visiting the horses."

A huge grin spread across my face. I hopped up and down, I was so excited, and he chuckled at my response.

I'd always loved horses, but had only limited experience with them.

When I'd heard they had them here, it was definitely one of the selling points.

He led me down a row of stalls showing me the ten gorgeous horses that lived there. My eyes rested on a beautiful black and white Paint who nosed his way over his gate to say hello. His muzzle was one of the softest things I'd ever touched. He nudged me playfully with his broad head. I petted him gently between the eyes and he chuffed happily. Damien handed me a sugar cube and I offered it to the horse. He gently lifted it from my hand and worked it around his mouth.

"This rascal here is Storm. He likes to act sweet with the ladies, but as soon as he's out, he's all but uncontrollable for even our resident horse whisperer, Paco."

"Not you, you sweet boy. You'd never give anyone trouble, could you?" Storm shook out his mane, agreeing with me. I looked over at Damien, who gazed intently at me.

"I think we may just find your talents affect more than *our* own species. I think this guy likes you."

I smiled back at him and rested my forehead against Storm.

He immediately stilled.

Surprised, I stepped back.

Damien smiled in satisfaction. "You are exquisite." He came up behind me and wrapped his arms around my waist, holding me close.

I laid my head on his chest and we stood together for a long time, just watching the horses.

"When I return, I want to take you for a ride."

I smiled up at him and touched the new white streak in his hair.

"What's this about? I know you had one from before, but this one is new. Was it from healing Jackson?"

He nodded solemnly. "The first one happened after the loss of my wife and child. I didn't even notice it right away." He let out a small laugh. "I thought about dying it but I was told it added character." He was trying to be funny but there was sadness in his voice.

I twirled his hair in my fingers. "You have character regardless. You are so beautiful." I smiled when he looked perplexed.

"I don't believe anyone has ever told me that before."

"Believe it." I tucked his hair behind his ear and he bent down to kiss me.

"¡Hóla, Señor Preston." A boy of about twelve came around the corner with a wheelbarrow full of hay. Damien spoke to him in Spanish and reached over to ruffle the boy's hair.

"Miss Frost, this is Paco. He and his family care for the horses. His father was a preeminent horse trainer until he retired. The headmaster brought them here to care for the grounds and the horses. They've been with us for several years, and Paco is one of our students."

I raised an eyebrow and smiled at the young man. "¿Qúe es su caballo favorito?" I thought I would try out my Spanish and hoped what I said made sense.

Paco beamed at me and answered, "Probablemente es Florita." He motioned for me to follow him down to the end stall. There was a lovely roan mare pacing a bit, looking quite restless. "¿Quieres mirarle en la fuera?"

I nodded enthusiastically. "Yes, please." I wanted to see the horse move.

He entered her stall, speaking softly to her in Spanish while he put on her halter and led her out the side door. Behind the carriage house there were two spacious outdoor arenas and a covered one a bit farther beyond. He led her into the first of the two arenas and unhaltered her. She shook out her mane, and we watched her from the rail as she trotted and kicked out her legs playfully. She altered between a canter and a full run. The moonlight shone brightly on her coat as she frolicked.

"Ella es muy guapa, ¿verdad?"

"She is beautiful."

Damien placed his hand on my lower back. "She's a rescue horse. We brought her here, almost like what we do with our students. She had been mistreated in her previous home. The local animal services called us. Paco has nursed her back to health and she loves him dearly for it."

We watched for a bit longer and said our goodbyes. Paco gazed at her dreamily as we left. Damien took my hand and walked me back through the stables.

As I realized our night was coming to a close, I felt a profound sense of uncertainty. Damien was leaving tomorrow for a week, partly to go and check on a very dangerous man. I didn't know where he was going to pick up the children. I didn't know if we would have any more visitors. I was nervous about the beginning of a school year in a new place where I wasn't totally sure of the rules and procedures.

I must have let my mood show, because Damien stopped us outside the doors of the garage.

"Delaney, what's troubling you?"

I snorted at him. "What's not to be troubled about? I try not to be a Negative Nelly, but there are a lot of unknowns tonight. I'm a little afraid." He pulled me close to him and held me tightly against his body.

"How about we have some aquatic therapy? We seem to have missed a few of our nightly swims." Damien looked at me hopefully.

"I don't know. I don't think I have the appropriate swimwear. Will that be a problem?"

That hungry look was in his eyes again. I ran for the motorcycle and grabbed my helmet. A satisfied smile crossed his face as he joined me on the bike. He draped his jacket around my shoulders and I slid into it. I loved the smell of the leather and his unique scent.

"Hang on then." He kicked the bike to life and I held on tight. We pulled out the doors and sped along the path toward the gates. On the way past, he let Vincent know that we'd be at the reservoir for a bit.

"James is settled in your house, Miss Frost."

"Thank you, Vincent." I was pretty sure that was the most he'd ever said to me.

I thought I detected a hint of a smile on Vincent's always-stoic face. It could have just been the lights moving across his face.

SEVENTEEN
TRUTH OR CONSEQUENCES

THE RIDE WAS SHORT. MY HEART RACED WITH THE FEELING OF THE WIND against my skin and also in anticipation of being in the water with Damien again. A lot had happened since our first swim. I wondered if he would enforce his boundary this time.

When we arrived, I jumped off the bike and stripped off my clothes as I dashed toward the water. I heard him laughing behind me. This time, I watched as he stripped off his shirt, his boots and then his worn jeans. He walked to the edge of the water in his boxers and paused for a minute. He was truly breathtaking, and as I stared, my eyes welled up. I had such hopes for where we were going. In this moment, my heart was so full of love for him I thought it would burst.

He moved toward me in the water and dove in. I waited a few seconds and then he surfaced directly in front of me. The water glistened on his skin and his eyes sparkled.

"Is this okay?" he asked hesitantly. I shook my head and he looked concerned. Before he had a chance to speak, I moved forward and wrapped my legs around him. He pulled me in tight and kissed me quickly.

"Are you sure you're comfortable with this?"

I nodded and kissed him again.

I was a bit more daring this time as I'd only left on my panties. His hands were quickly all over me, caressing my breasts eagerly. He moved his hands down to my thighs and lifted me up out of the water enough to capture my nipple between his lips. The sensation was so intense.

A moan escaped my lips and I grasped onto his shoulders. I felt a rumble in his chest, the vibration reverberating against my core. He kissed me and ran his teeth along my neck. One hand slid down to cup me over my panties, and the heat from his touch sent waves of desire throughout my body, making the muscles in my legs contract involuntarily, pulling him closer.

He rubbed his thumb over my panties in just the right spot. My hips met him stroke for stroke. I knew that at any moment, I was going to come apart.

Then he slid one finger under the elastic band of my panties, touching me so softly. Our eyes met and held. He slid his finger inside of me, continuing the pressure with his thumb until I cried out with pleasure. My head fell back and I saw stars behind my eyelids.

"God, Delaney, I'm right there with you. You're so beautiful when you come for me."

We held each other, panting, and I noticed steam rising off the water. It lapped gently against us, mimicking the waves of my release as they worked their way through my body. The night was so silent, the only the sounds to be heard were our breathing and the movement of the water. The peacefulness was so soothing that my tension drifted away. For once, I didn't feel the need for a snappy remark to break the silence.

"I want to be inside of you, Delaney. I want to make you feel as good as you deserve. I want to spend a whole night worshiping this amazing body of yours. Would you let me do that?"

I looked him in the eye as his desire enveloped me. "I want that, too. Very much. I know it'll be incredible when we spend the night together... no time constraints, no stress. Just us."

He smiled and kissed me gently, his lips and tongue mingling with mine. He laughed softly and rested his forehead against mine.

"I suppose I'll just have to keep my memories of this night to get me through the next week." His smile warmed me even as I began to shiver.

There was no shame, no fear, only comfort and anxiousness for the next time our bodies would meet.

"Mmm, Damien. You are so good to me. I'd like to return the favor but I don't think I could even come close to making you feel this good."

He shook his head in protest. "You really have no idea what you do to me, woman."

We separated just a little, and I felt the chill in the air around us for the first time. The water was delicious against my skin. I thought now would be a good time to break through that stoic veneer of his.

"There are a few things we haven't covered yet. I think it's Truth or Consequences time."

He raised an eyebrow at me. "What is Truth or Consequences? I'm not sure I've been introduced to this game."

"It's simple, really. You ask a question and the other person answers with the truth or faces the consequences. I'll start. What's your most embarrassing moment?"

Damien looked perplexed. "My most embarrassing moment? Hmmm. Other than the Hokey Pokey?"

I nodded and he reluctantly went on.

"I'd have to say it goes back to my days as a student here. We had a professor at the time, an old friend of the headmaster's father. We all figured he was about a hundred years old. Anyway, his desk was in the back of the room, and he often sat there while we completed our arithmetic.

"One afternoon, I felt a tingling at the back of my neck and I turned around. He had slumped over in his chair. My sense was still new to me, but I was afraid he was going into cardiac arrest. I jumped up and ran to the back of the class and I placed my hands on his chest. He woke up with a start and slipped out of the chair and we both fell to the floor. The whole class turned around and laughed riotously. He dragged me by my ear to the headmasters office, berating me the whole time. I was so afraid I'd be in terrible trouble, but when Mr. Henry explained what had happened, the headmaster just 'tsked' at him and said, 'Oh William, what did you expect to happen when you fell asleep? The boy thought he was saving your life.' Mr. Henry was not pleased. He glared at me for the rest of the term. The headmaster did not ask him to return and so he left the academy at the end of the year."

"What happened to you?" I imagined him as a schoolboy and knew he was probably a heart breaker even back then.

"The headmaster laughed off the whole incident and assured me that he wasn't angry, that I had only done what I was meant to do. Unfortunately for Mr. Henry, he'd been ignoring medical advice for too long and shortly thereafter, he did have a heart attack. I always felt terrible about that. Eventually I learned how to better assess situations."

"I think that was probably more embarrassing for him. I'm not sure if that counts." We were facing each other in the water and he shrugged at my comment.

"Maybe it doesn't seem embarrassing to you, but I was a proper English gentleman. Tackling a defenseless old man was pretty horrific."

I sighed. "I guess, but mine can totally beat yours."

His eyes lit up at the challenge. "Do tell, love. Do tell."

"Did your spies tell you that I was a cheerleader in college?"

He blanched at that but then got very intrigued. "College, too, hmm? I rather enjoy picturing you in the whole short skirt outfit, shaking your hips." In a husky voice he asked, "Do you still have that uniform?"

I splashed water at him and then continued.

"One night, I kind of got a little overzealous while cheering at a basketball game and the crowd got more than they bargained for from their entertainment. It was the start of halftime, and we planned to run out onto the court to do our routine. I was super pumped, so I took off running for a round off and, well...I kinda kept going and landed on my rear, sliding across the court in front of about three hundred people. For weeks, I answered to 'the cheerleader who fell on her ass.' Not my proudest moment."

Damien smirked and pulled me closer. "It's such a beautiful ass. You should definitely take better care of it." His hands cupped said part of my anatomy. He kissed my neck and before I was completely lost, I pushed away and dunked under the water, swimming around to his back. I popped up and he turned with a start.

"Now, Mr. Preston, we aren't done with this exchange."

He actually pouted. He was too damn sexy. "I think I'd rather we share a more intimate kind of exchange." He swam toward me, and I dodged his grasp. He looked flustered, and I was so pleased to finally be able to get under his skin.

"Alright, what's next?"

I thought for a moment. "How about your first kiss?"

He thought a little too hard about that one.

"Hey, I know there were probably hundreds of girls in your past, but you *have* to remember your first."

"I'm insulted. The number's actually in the thousands, my dear."

My shocked look brought an evil smile from him, so I took the liberty of dunking him under the water. He came up behind me this time and grabbed me around my waist.

"Now we'll have no more of that, young lady, or I'll have to put you over my knee."

"Oooo, I love it when you sound so Corporal Punisher." We both laughed, and I reached back over my head, linking my hands behind his neck, stretching my body out to lazily kick my feet. "Do go on, you were saying... Thousands?" He ran a hand down my side and it brought on another layer of goose bumps.

"I hate to destroy the myth, but I was actually quite a clod as a teenager. It's true. I know you'd never think this dashing man would be so uncouth but I'm sorry to say, it's a fact. My first kiss was not until after I'd graduated from Havenhart. I was at Richmond University in Virginia at the time, and she was my tutor for Calculus." He looked at me cautiously, worried about my reaction.

"Ah. How'd that go for you?"

He put his head down but not before I saw a grin.

"It turned out she was trying to make her boyfriend jealous. He just happened to be my professor of Physiology *and* faculty advisor. He made things a bit rough for me after that, but he couldn't deny my talent and made sure that I made it into the medical school of my choice. Or maybe that was because he was afraid of a sexual harassment suit."

We both laughed at that. Then he got serious. "Alright, Frost. Your turn to confess."

"I was much younger than you when I had my first experience with kissing. It was fourth grade, to be exact. Logan Whitley on the playground at lunch recess. He was dared by the other boys to do it. He mustered up all his courage to approach me while I was waiting for the swing. It was over fast, but I knew we were in love and would be married as soon as we were old enough."

Damien laughed heartily at my confession.

"It's true. I even knew we'd live in my house with my parents and get matching Huffys. Big plans I had, I'm telling you. Alas, it wasn't meant to be. The next week I caught him kissing Cassidy, and I was devastated. There went my dream wedding." I faked some tears and Damien held me supportively.

"There, there. Schoolyard crushes can be tough. But I'm sure it's good material when you're counseling."

"Oh the memories," I continued wailing. "And the children we never had together…"

He stilled for a moment, and I realized what I'd just said. I hoped I hadn't just crossed a line.

"I'm sorry, Damien. I didn't mean—"

He shushed me gently. "No, love, don't worry about that. I'm really fine."

I looked at him over my shoulder to be sure and found him smiling warmly at me. It made me curious.

"Do you think you'll ever want to try again?"

He looked thoughtful for a moment. "I love children. If it's meant for me to have them, I will be the best father I can be. But I've really left it in the hands of fate."

"I kind of feel the same, I guess. I love them, too. The idea of being pregnant and taking on that huge responsibility is scary as hell, however, I think it would be kind of exciting too. I always said if I were with the right person and it was meant to happen, I would welcome it. Apparently that hasn't happened yet, and I'm not too sure I'm physically up for it any longer."

"Well, some of us are getting older."

I splashed him again and he chuckled in my ear.

I let my legs sink down, bringing my body up against his, and leaned back to kiss him. It was a slow sweep of tongues this time. They danced over each other in a smooth caress. His lips left mine and traveled down my shoulder, attending to the back of my neck. His hands stroked my breasts and splayed across my belly. The temperature of the water warmed, the steam once again rising and swirling around us as it floated up to the sky.

"I wish I never had to go without your touch. You have the most talented fingers."

He chuckled softly in my ear as his equally talented tongue joined his superbly talented lips in a gentle stroking of my earlobe. He sighed against me sadly and said, "But I need to get you back before your lips turn blue. Shall we go then?"

"Give me just a minute?" I pushed off and swam toward the middle of the reservoir. It was invigorating to be moving against the water. My lungs worked as they should with no weakness. I tried out my breast-stroke and butterfly and they felt great. When I stopped and looked back at Damien, he was just a speck. I swam toward him at a faster pace. I stopped between him and the shore.

He smiled at me brightly.

"Feel better now?"

I nodded. "But it's really time to go. I can't stop my t-t-teeth f-f-from ch-ch-chattering."

He laughed and swam toward me. I jumped out of the water and hugged myself. He grabbed his shirt and dried me off with it.

"Always the gentleman."

He looked longingly at me.

I raised an eyebrow. "It won't be any fun if I become hypothermic, right?"

I so desperately wanted him to take me down right there on the ground and make love to me until we were both wrung out. But part of me worried about what would happen if we took that step. So much had been happening in the periphery, I didn't trust myself to make the right decision. I was having so much fun with him. Standing there with his wet hair, his beautiful torso glistening in the moonlight, and smiling down at me, I imagined how it would be...the two of us... But not tonight.

Damien helped me into my clothes and threw his jeans and boots on hurriedly, wadding up his shirt and putting it back in the saddlebag. He had a second sweater stuffed in there and he handed it to me. When I protested, he grabbed my hand and put it against his naked chest.

"Do you feel that? That's you, love."

His skin was burning, almost feverish. I looked closer and saw what appeared to be steam rising off of him.

Before I could ask him anything else, he started up the bike and I climbed on behind him, nestling in close. I loved the feel of his muscles shifting beneath my hands as he steered the bike. I knew there would never be a better place in this world than pressed against him.

We returned reluctantly to the academy and, after parking the bike, Damien walked me back to my cottage. The lights were on inside, so I assumed James was on sentry duty.

We got to the back door and I hid my face in Damien's shoulder. "You'll be careful, won't you? I just have this sick feeling about you leaving."

He lifted my chin with his finger and kissed me gently. This temporarily put that worried feeling out of my mind, replacing it with the desire to take him to bed with me. He stepped back and almost stumbled off the steps. We both laughed, and the door flew open behind me.

"Oh, it's just the lovebirds. You better get in here before you wake the whole compound."

We were still snickering as we came inside and James shut the door, noticing the state of our attire.

"Funny, I don't remember a downpour occurring in the past hour."

"We, uh, went for a swim. It's my therapy."

I looked to Damien for support and he backed me up.

"Yes, of course, her therapy. You know, swimming is an excellent form of stress relief and a perfect way to strengthen one's lungs." He was trying to be serious but James just rolled his eyes at us.

"Whatever. You should really take towels next time and probably some condoms."

We froze, totally busted.

"Okay, *Dad*," I threw back at him. He turned with a snort and flopped on the couch. He'd obviously gotten into my meager movie collection and had fired up a good one.

"Ooo, is that *Evil Dead 2*? Awesome!" I turned to look at Damien, who was staring in disbelief.

"Do you mean you actually watch this madness?"

"Of course. Sam Raimi and Bruce Campbell are true geniuses of cinema. Haven't you seen these films?"

He shook his head in disdain. "I'm afraid I missed these on the list of important film classics."

I narrowed my eyes at his sarcasm and said, "You better not be a film snob, Damien Preston. I'll have you know that *Evil Dead 2* and *Army of Darkness* are required watching in this house."

"Hail to the king, baby." James threw that last one in from the couch and we slapped five.

"On that note…"

I knew it was time for him to go. I didn't want the evening to be over, but I also knew he needed his strength for the trip. I grabbed his hand and walked him over to the door.

"Hey Preston, don't worry. She's in good hands."

Damien looked over my shoulder. "Thank you, James. I have no doubt. I can't tell you how much better I feel knowing you'll be with her."

James held up a hand and waved, obviously not wanting to miss the crucial scene where Ash must put the head of his beloved in a vise to keep her from killing him.

"I'll call you when I arrive and keep in touch while I'm gone. I'll be in Texas tomorrow, and on Tuesday I fly to Toronto and then to Massachusetts. I'll be home Saturday morning early." He held my hands and looked at me seriously. "I hope I don't have to tell you that if anything weird happens, you must call me, and if you start to feel out of sorts, please go see Morgan. Will you promise me?"

"Of course," I assured him. "I'll be so busy this week I won't have time to get in trouble. And Cassidy is coming in Friday, so you'll get to meet her Saturday. That is, if you aren't too tired."

He pulled me to him and kissed me sweetly. "I'll sleep on the plane. Mrs. Walden will meet us when we land and help me get the new students settled into the dorms. I'll go directly home and sleep so I can meet you for dinner, how does that sound?"

I grinned so wide my cheeks were starting to hurt. "I can't wait."

"Del, you're going to miss the best part. Hurry up," James yelled from the sofa, and I looked back at Damien sheepishly.

"It really is a great movie."

He kissed me on the forehead. "I'm sure it is. I'll even watch it when I return so I can make an informed judgment. Will that do?"

"Definitely. Now go to sleep. I…"

I wanted to say more, but I hesitated. Later, I'd kick myself for not telling him I loved him, but I wasn't sure if the timing was right.

"I know, love. Me too. I'll be back before you know it." He winked at me and stepped out into the night.

I shut the door behind him and sulked my way into the living room. I plopped down on the couch next to James and let my head fall back. The events of the past few days were swirling around me, and I needed to just make everything stop.

"You're leaving a puddle on the couch."

I elbowed him. "So what? It's my couch."

He elbowed me back. "Where I have to sleep. Why don't you go change?"

"I'm too tired to move," I said, laying my head on his shoulder.

"Gross. Get your slimy hair off me." He frowned down at me. "What are you wearing?"

"Damien's sweater." I went to pull it off and realized I hadn't exactly grabbed all of my clothes from the water's edge.

"Something wrong?"

I scurried into my bedroom as he laughed at me.

"Hey," he yelled. "You forget something?"

I'd shrugged out of my wet stuff and grabbed a towel. When I peered back into the living room, he had my wet bra hanging from a finger.

I ran over and snatched it from him as he continued to laugh.

"It must have been balled up in my shirt."

"Uh huh."

I smacked the top of his head and ran back to my room.

"Better make that a cold shower," he said as I shut the door.

I made faces at him behind the safety of the door and then sighed.

I did need a cold shower.

EIGHTEEN
SCHOOL BEGINS

THE NEXT MORNING, I WAS UP BY SIX TO SHOWER, DRESS, AND GET A GOOD breakfast of Multi Grain Cheerios and OJ in me to face the day. I made sure to throw a protein bar in my bag for Second Breakfast and a yogurt for Elevensies. The hobbits had the right idea.

James grumbled his way into the shower after I'd finished, and when we were both ready, we stepped into the bright sunlight. It was already eighty degrees out. I was ever so thankful for air conditioning as the temperature and the humidity were overpowering.

"You'll be meeting Jackson this morning, and he'll update you on what's been going on. Then you'll need to hook up with George in the commons, as he'll be working with you on a schedule. You tight with this?"

"A-ffirm," he nodded. "I'm always tight. You, on the other hand, better keep me posted on how you're doing. If anything weird happens, you tell me. This Rains guy sounds like big time trouble."

"That's why I'm worried about Damien going to see him." I had to push that fear out of my mind, but I couldn't help the nagging feeling things were going to get much worse. I didn't want James to freak out and get all *James* on me, so I let it go. "I'll meet you for lunch around noon, sound cool?"

He shrugged. "I know you're going to be busy so don't worry about me. Just do what you gotta do, dig?"

We entered the courtyard between the dorms and my office. I directed him toward the middle set of doors. "Jackson supervises the boys' dorms, and he's right through this way." Damien had let me know they let Jackson go back to his apartment last night, and I was pleased for him. I knew he hated being laid up and the sooner he was back to normal, the better for him.

When we approached his door it was open a crack, so I stuck my head in. I tapped lightly on the door, but his music was up loud again.

He answered me by turning the corner in nothing but a towel.

"Dammit, Delaney! Why is it that only *you* can keep sneaking up on me? And Dayam! Can I tell you how good that shower was?" He stepped forward and offered his hand to James. "Sorry about the informal attire, but your cousin here has a knack for catching me at interesting times." He winked at me and invited us in while he went to dress. I noticed he was still moving pretty stiffly and hoped he wasn't in much pain.

"I've got to split. I want to be ready for the kids this morning. I'm on meet-and-greet duty while they enter classes, and then I'll be making the rounds and checking to see everyone has what they need. I told James I'd meet him for lunch. Why don't you join us?"

"I'll be glad to, Counselor. Have a good one."

I said my goodbye to James and tried to make sure he was okay, but he and Jackson had already started gabbing, so I knew they'd be fine.

Classes started at eight, and as it was just before seven, many of the students were heading over to the commons. When I entered the lobby of my building, I looked over at Damien's door and sighed. It was definitely going to be a long week.

I climbed the steps and found Diana already at her desk. "Hey Diana. Feels like forever since I've seen you. That spa trip did me wonders. How are you?"

She smiled and came around her desk to give me a hug, and then stepped back to admire my outfit. I had chosen a lavender sleeveless dress and strappy sandals.

"Turn and give me the full view."

I blushed but did as she said. When I turned back to face her, she was nodding in approval.

"Excellent choice for the first day. Are you comfortable?"

"I guess as much as I can be." I was trying to combat the gremlins that had taken up residence in my stomach. I needed to calm them before the day began.

"You'll be great, Delaney. Now why don't you take a few minutes to get situated, and then you and I can go down and herd the masses to their classes."

I smiled at her in appreciation and turned to head to my office.

I smelled the roses as I opened the door. A large bouquet of the darkest, reddest roses, all perfectly formed, sat in a beautiful square vase on the table with an envelope leaning against it. My name was written in a masculine script across the front. I stared at it for a moment, savoring the scent of the flowers. There was also a small, rectangular box.

I sat down on the sofa and reached for the envelope. I slid a finger under the flap and pulled out a cream-colored piece of stationary. A huge smile bloomed across my face as I saw whom it was from:

Delaney,

I regret that I'll not be with you on this first day. I was so looking forward to watching you with the students. Someday soon I hope you'll realize just how much of what you do as a counselor is all about the tremendous capacity to love that's within you. Bringing you here for our students is one of my greatest accomplishments for Havenhart Academy.

I have never been as completely connected to another human being as I am with you. Your energy warms the deepest part of me, and I can still feel it surrounding me. I love that you were so willing to share that sacred part of you, and I will cherish that for the rest of my life. I have such hopes and plans for us when I return. I'll savor the memories from last night while I'm away, and I'll be searching for the words that will do justice for my feelings for you. I had this small gift made for you. Please wear it next to your heart and know I am with you.

You will be fantastic. You are *fantastic. I'll be counting the minutes until you're back in my arms.*

Love, Damien

I WAS BREATHLESS AFTER READING HIS LETTER. HIS WORDS EXUDED SO MUCH of what I had come to love about him. He knew exactly what to say to ease me, knew exactly what I would be worried about. I didn't know whether to laugh or cry. I probably did both.

My hand shook slightly as I reached for the box. Inside the lid I found tissue paper closed with a wax seal featuring the letter P. I carefully pulled the tissue paper away, preserving the seal, and my breath caught.

A pendant with a dark stone lay in the center. The stone was surrounded by delicate metal work in swirls and loops. A silver chain lay beside the pendant and I lifted both, cradling the gift in my hands. Engraved within the loop at the top of the pendant was an H. I recognized the script as being similar to Damien's ring. What a lovely gift. I slipped the chain over my head and the pendant rested on my chest just above my heart. I placed a hand over it and sighed.

"It's really not fair that he left with the last word," I said to myself, but then I was so all over the place with my feelings that I knew I could never have written anything as poignant. I wiped at my tears and sat back against the couch. I needed to center myself for the day. Damien and the headmaster were counting on me to make things run smoothly.

After collecting myself, I stepped out into the hall. I noticed a young woman sitting in the waiting area near my office with her back to me.

"Is there something I can do for you?" I asked as I walked around to face her. She had beautiful brown skin and her hair was styled in perfect ringlets. She appeared to be around fifteen, and she was dressed in the Havenhart uniform; a green and blue plaid jumper with a white blouse underneath and navy blue shoes. Her eyes were wide and terrified.

"Are you Miss Frost?"

If I'd said "boo," she would have fallen over. I stepped around and knelt down in front of her.

"I am, darlin'. Are you looking for me? I promise I won't bite. Are you a new student here?"

She nodded again but was too afraid to speak. I reached my hand out slowly and touched her hand resting on her knee. She jumped and started to move away from me but then something stilled her. My gift, I guessed.

She gulped back her terror and said in a voice barely above a whisper, "My mama said I should come find you if I was nervous before school." She had a drawl I placed in the Louisiana neck of the woods.

"Well, you've come to the right place. The first day of school is always a tricky thing, especially when you're new. Can I tell you something funny?"

She nodded yet again, and I was finally starting to see less of the whites of her eyes. I sat down next to her on the couch and while she didn't take her eyes off me, she seemed to be relaxing a tad.

"When I started my first day of high school, I was *so* sick. I threw up my breakfast all over the place. My mom said it was just nerves and made me go anyway."

She stared in disbelief.

I continued, "She said it would be better once I got there, and she was right. But then the next morning it was back. And the day after that, and the day after that... For two whole weeks this went on, and I was getting pretty tired of throwing up every morning. She finally took me to the doctor, and he said, 'Yes, it's just nerves.' I thought they were ridiculous but you know what? The next day it was gone."

Her look of disbelief was now sheer doubt.

"But how come it took so long?" she asked skeptically.

"Well, I reckon I needed to hear it from someone else. Not my mom, because at that time I thought she was just saying it because she was, you know, my mom. I didn't want to admit she was right." I smiled at her, hoping she'd give a little.

"My mama told me this place would be different. I don't want to have another bad school year, Miss Frost. I'm scared. At my last school, the kids all stayed away from me and called me 'freak.' I can't help what I am. I can't even control it! My mama said things would be different here, but I just can't believe her." Huge crocodile tears slid down her slim cheeks. She was so slender, just a wisp of a girl. I tried to concentrate on taking that worry away from her.

"I can absolutely understand. Can you tell me your name?"

"My name is Ebony, ma'am." Her shoulders relaxed just a smidge. "Is this really a place for kids who, um, are different than other kids?"

"Absolutely, Ebony, and I've met some pretty incredible kids so far. How about I walk you to class, would that be okay?"

An ever-so-slight smile touched her lips, and I stood up from the couch, offering her my hand. She frowned at it but stood to follow me and we walked together down the hall.

"Mrs. Sinclair, Ebony and I are off to class. Wish us luck."

She gave us a wave. I had my bag with me so I was ready to start my meet-and-greet.

"To tell you the truth, my dear, I am probably just as nervous as you. I know you might not believe me, but this is my first day of school in a new place, too. Up until about a week or so ago, I'd never met the people here and had no idea that I was different."

She stopped and looked at me, puzzled. "But how..."

I gave her a nudge to keep us moving, and I continued talking. "Mr. Preston, the Director of Student Services, came to see me and told me that I had a way of helping people other than just being a counselor and talking to them. I totally didn't believe him and I almost didn't come. But then again, life is about taking risks, true? Even when they're scary."

She seemed to ponder this. When she stopped again, she turned to face me.

"It's that thing you did back there, huh? I thought I wouldn't be able to say nothing and you got me to talk."

I smiled at her, trying to gauge her reaction. "It's not something that I really understand. I just want people to be at ease, that's all. I don't want them to be upset or afraid, so I do what I think will make them feel better. I guess there's more to it but I'm still learning." I wanted to see just how comfortable I was making her. "Do you want to tell me how you feel different from the other students?"

A look of horror filled those ethereal brown eyes.

"You don't have to, of course. But if you ever want to, you know where I am, okay?"

She looked at me intensely, then reached out to touch my arm with a shaky hand.

My heart immediately began to race and I gasped for breath, staggering back from her. Her touch made me feel as though I'd just received a shot of adrenaline. What on earth could cause that?

"Wow," I said, trying to keep my composure. "That's quite a touch you've got there. I guess that's gotten you into a tight spot before?"

She nodded, still trying to see if I was angry with her. "If I'm not careful, I can really hurt people. I don't like to touch people. I'm afraid." She got that look in her eye as if she was going to run for it.

I decided to try what I'd done with Morgan. I closed my eyes and sent a wave of energy at her, releasing her fear.

It was her turn to stagger back.

"Did it work? I just learned how to do that. If I can learn how to control my energy, I bet you can, too. I know just the person to teach you."

She looked hopeful for the first time.

"How about you come to my office after class today and I'll take you to meet her?" She nodded and looked more confident.

"Alright then. So you're off to Science this morning? Perfect. The teacher is Miss Livorna, and she's wacky. You'll love her. She kind of fits the California Hippy stereotype."

She giggled for real this time, and I patted her on the shoulder. "You're going to be great. I'll see you this afternoon, unless you need me first."

We were at the door to the Science Building, so I pointed the way and she waved goodbye. I took a deep breath and made a mental note to get this young lady to Morgan or Elijah ASAP before she truly *did* hurt someone. I also wanted to check with Marcia about who she was rooming with.

Kids were milling about, most looking as if they knew where they were going. I answered a few questions and chatted with some of the students I'd met already. When the bell rang, the courtyard was empty. I waited to see if any more students were lost. When the coast looked clear, I walked over to the library.

Morgan had a class in the morning, and so I hung out in the back to listen to just what she was going to be covering. She was discussing some of what she called the "alternative disciplines" in our world. I listened keenly to her clarification between Wicca and Voodoo, and I knew I'd be coming back when she mentioned the ancient druids and Paganism.

The rest of the first day flew by. I visited more classes, got to watch more of the teachers in action and was energized by what was happening. I saw Hazel and Joanna at lunch. They were deep in conversation, so I didn't disturb them. When I joined James and Jackson, I immediately realized my mistake in putting those two together. I was now the sister for them to nitpick and tease. They flat out tormented me.

Okay, some of it was funny, but sheesh.

I stopped by Morgan's table on my way out and asked if I could bring Ebony by later that afternoon. "She's really powerful and really afraid."

Morgan agreed they should meet. I also told her I wanted to take her morning class. She laughed.

"I'll give you the reading list and you can follow along. It'll be good for you. I'll even test you."

That night, I ate a quick dinner and returned to my cottage alone. I was elated by the day's events, but I was tired. James' shift at the gatehouse started at two and went until ten, so I had the place to myself. I decided to try out the lovely claw-foot tub and relax with my newest Adriana Herrera novel. I turned on some mellow tunes and poured in some fragrance-free bubble bath.

"I think I earned this," I said to my four-legged friends. All was right with the world. I soaked until the water was cold and then I got out and toweled off. I went straight for my bed and noticed I'd missed a call.

"Good evening, love. Not sure what you had on your agenda tonight, but I wanted to say hello. My trip has been uneventful so far. My visit to the prison was rescheduled for first thing in the morning. I will try to ring you when I'm done there. I hope you're relaxing and taking care of yourself. I can't seem to stop thinking about you... Sleep well, and I'll talk to you tomorrow."

I listened to the call while lying on my bed. It was the sweetest sound I had heard all day. I must have drifted off thinking about Damien because I woke several hours later when I heard James coming in, and I was still in my towel.

"Del, you awake?"

"What's up, dude? I must have fallen asleep after my bath."

He stood in my doorway snickering. "Long day, I take it?"

"It was a really good day, but I'm pooped. You cool? You need anything?"

He shook his head. "Nah, but I think I'll skip breakfast in the morning. How about I meet you for lunch?"

"Sounds great, FC. How did everything go tonight?"

He hesitated. "I hate to use the 'q' word because you know what that can do, but it was cool. Jackson told me there was a miscommunication at the prison and Damien won't get in to see that Rains guy until tomorrow."

I nodded. "Damien left me a message and said he was seeing him in the morning. I really hope that goes well. The guy scares me. I've never even seen him, but I've seen what he did to his own daughter." I shuddered and got up to put on a nightshirt. "Anyway, I just want this to be over, you know?"

"Abso. I'm going to grab a snack and watch a movie. I'll try to keep it down."

I held up a hand. "Not to worry, I'll be out like a light in a few minutes. I'm pretty drained. All that smiling and being professional takes it out of me." He laughed and said good night.

I flopped back down on the bed and barely had the energy to pull the covers back over me.

The dream was back, but this time it was slightly different. I ran through the woods and Damien followed behind me, trying to stop me. For some reason, I ran toward the Shadow Man...I had to get to him. I needed to let him in—

"Delaney, DELANEY!"

Strong hands grabbed me by my arms, shaking me. I screamed and fought to get away before I realized it was James.

"Damn, girl. Wake up! What the hell are you doing?"

I looked around and found myself in the kitchen, with no idea *what* I was doing.

"Since when are you a sleepwalker?"

"I'm not. What happened? I remember you coming in when you got home from the gatehouse…how did I end up here?"

James grabbed his penlight and looked in my eyes, the light like a spear straight into my brain.

"Ahh, God, get that out of my face. I'm fine."

He didn't seem to buy that but after a few more tries, I got him to let me go back to bed. I glanced at my alarm clock and noticed it was 3:54 a.m. I hoped getting back to sleep was possible, but I was wired, as if I'd just swam a race.

It took some time but I did get to sleep. When the alarm woke me at six, I was only a little groggy.

I showered and quietly crept out of the cottage so I wouldn't wake James. I decided to eat a more substantial breakfast than Cheerios to help me clear my head. Grace was sitting at the counter talking to George and drinking a cup of coffee.

"George, I need a huge slab o' protein this morning if I'm going to function."

"What's the matter, Delaney? Have a rough night?" Grace was teasing but she looked concerned.

"Just a weird dream woke me up in the middle of the night. I'm fine, really. I'm craving some of George's awesome cooking."

"You've come to the right place, pretty lady." George went back to his grill and was back in minutes with a plate of bacon, eggs over easy, and toast. My mouth watered profusely. He set down a large glass of fresh-squeezed OJ, and I turned to Grace.

"Mind if I kiss your husband? This looks amazing."

She laughed ,and he leaned his cheek over for me to plant a big one on. It was so nice to feel like part of a community here. It made everything taste better.

We gabbed about the previous day for a bit until the students started to trickle in. I helped them get things set up for the buffet-style breakfast. I saw some new faces and introduced myself. When it was time to start heading to class, I followed the students out and went to my office.

Raven was waiting for me with her notes for the Sociology class that was to start the next day.

"I found some articles on the institutions of education, religion and family. I also found the research you wanted on Zimbardo's Prison Study. That was halfway interesting, I guess. And I plan on getting some information on mob mentality next."

She had done great research. I thanked her and asked her if she wanted to make copies for the class. She shrugged a "whatever" and followed me to the machine. According to my schedule, there were ten students in my class, all between tenth and twelfth grades. I was hoping at least a few of them would be talkers.

At nine-thirty, it was time for her to go to class so I thanked her again and watched her walk off.

I went out the doors to the courtyard and thought about my first day on the job. I looked over to the bench where Damien and I sat that morning and remembered the encouraging words he spoke to me. I was warm inside just thinking of him. I wondered if he'd already spoken to Mr. Rains.

A couple of students looked lost, so I showed them to class, which happened to be in the Arts building. I had been told Elijah was covering Jackson's classes until Thursday, as well as continuing with his music program. I sat in the back of the theater and listened to the beautiful melodies they were making. Some of the students were really talented.

I noticed Ebony up on the stage sitting at a piano. Her fingers stroked the keys, playing softly, and she seemed lost in her thoughts. My buddy Nate was looking at her with a lopsided grin on his face. I decided to wait and see if he'd try to get his "swag" on. He must have felt me looking, as he glanced in my direction. I gave him a thumbs-up and he grinned at me.

I watched him get up, saunter over, and sit next to her on the piano bench. She kept her eyes down but she slid over to give him room. He sat with his back to the keys and watched her play. I smiled at him, pleased to see his confidence. I hoped his charisma and charm would make her feel comfortable.

Just as I was feeling cozy and happy in the back row of the auditorium, the stinging pain returned with a vengeance in my left eye.

I held my head for a moment, willing the pain to pass. After a couple of minutes, a sensation like hot breath landed on the back of my neck.

I flew out of the chair and turned to face it.

There was nothing there, and the door was closed. There was no explanation for what I'd just experienced.

I turned to face the stage, hoping that no one had seen my little freak out. Unfortunately, Elijah was very aware I was having a moment. His eyes burned into me, and he started to approach me up the aisle. I smiled and waved and turned to make a quick exit. Out in the hall, I tried to catch my breath. I shook myself to be rid of that creepy feeling. It was similar to the other night, but it had really seemed as though someone was behind me.

Okay, I was really freaking out.

I wandered down the hall and heard familiar music coming from the art studio. Jackson was there with a few students, so I stepped in the door to watch. The students were doing some sketching exercises and a large still life display had been set up in the middle of the room under a skylight. It was a combination of Asiatic lilies and long blades of grass, very colorful and with lots of textures. Jackson walked around, looking at their work and giving them some pointers. He made his way over to me and leaned back against the workbench near the door.

"Are you spying on me?" He wasn't looking at me but the playfulness was there in his voice.

"Should I be?" I whispered back. "Shouldn't *you* be in bed like a good boy?"

"Can't stand to be cooped up anymore. Don't have any more pain, been off the meds for twenty-four hours, so I'm good to go. I'm drinking my liquids and taking it easy, and as soon as you're out of my hair I'll sit down, alright lady?"

I punched him gently in the arm, making sure it wasn't the one that had been cut.

"Ouch! Abuse from the counselor," he protested loud enough for the students to hear.

"That's what you get, Mr. Howe, for not following doctor's orders. Students, let me assure you that while your instructor is an amazing artist and teacher, he is a bad patient and should be resting. I'm counting on all of you to be sure you make him feel guilty and irresponsible for being up and around before he should."

I glared at him and he mocked me. The students all giggled. I looked around and noticed Matteo in the far corner, oblivious to our conversation. I strolled over to glance at his work. When his easel was in view, my breath caught by what I saw there.

"Oh Matteo, that's amazing. Have you been drawing long?"

I noted that he had not only drawn the flowers impeccably, but he'd also drawn a lovely woman standing behind them, smiling sadly. It brought a tear to my eye, and I wondered if it was—

"Es mi madre, Senorita Frost. Whenever I am drawing beautiful flowers such as these, I know she is looking at them with love. She was as beautiful as a flower." He was so composed and open. I ached for him. This young man had lost so much, and yet he created such stunning work.

"You've captured her so lovingly. She looks very proud of her son."

He smiled at me appreciatively and went back to his work, adding fine lines and details.

I smiled at Jackson and pointed my finger at him to watch himself before I left the room.

I hadn't been to my office for a while, so I wanted to check email and see if Diana had any news from Damien.

I had a few emails from parents asking me to check in with them about their children. I began making a list of students I wanted to meet with and go over their plans for post-high school. I created a schedule of appointments for the third week of school.

I was so involved in my work that I didn't hear Diana come in.

"Delaney, you missed lunch. Are you feeling alright?"

Startled by her voice, I jumped and spilled the last bit of water from my cup.

"Ahhh, gotta catch that before it hits my keyboard! I'm a mess."

She rushed over and tried to help me. "I didn't mean to disturb you. I just kept waiting for you to come out of here and when I noticed it was so late, I figured I'd better be sure you ate."

"Thanks, it is sooo not like me to miss a meal." I tried to laugh it off but she looked concerned.

"Have you spoken to Damien today?"

I shook my head, curious to know why she was looking so grave.

"I haven't. I wasn't sure of his schedule, so I thought I'd call when I was finished here. Guess I just didn't finish."

She told me she'd pick me up a sandwich from the commons and bring it back. I tried to protest but she wouldn't hear of it.

"Why don't you call Damien, and I'll be right back with your lunch."

I turned to thank her but she was already gone. I grabbed my cell and dialed his phone. Suddenly anxious to hear his voice, I dialed his number and waited impatiently for him to pick up.

"Hello, you have reached Damien Preston, Director of Student Services at Havenhart Academy. Please leave your number and I'll call you just as soon as it's possible. Thank you and have a great day."

I pouted just a little and then left him a message.

"Hi. It's, uh, Delaney. So...hi. I hope your day is going okay. Things here are great. I've been so busy I forgot to eat lunch. Anyway, I just wanted to hear your voice, preferably not just your outgoing message. I...I miss you. Yeah, just wanted to say that. And I hope you're being careful. So... Bye."

Ugh, I felt like such a teenager. But there was no do-over function in his voice mail system so I left it as such. Besides, I had no hope to sound less gawky.

Diana came back a bit later and I thanked her for my sandwich. I ate it as I worked, looking over my notes for tomorrow's class. The phone rang, and I answered it clumsily, almost knocking my water over again.

"Hey, beautiful. What are you still doing in your office?"

My heart raced at hearing his voice.

"I'm just doing what you brought me here to do. Work."

"True, but my dear, it's six o'clock. I tried your cottage thinking you'd be there. Is everything alright?"

How did it get so late?

"I wanted to be ready for my class tomorrow, and I guess time got away from me." I frowned, looking at the clock. I'd been sitting here for five hours and it seemed like only five minutes. "Wow, I guess I was just being uber-productive. But what do you know? My lesson plans are done for the next three weeks, and I've already scheduled several graduation update meetings."

"That's fantastic. But don't overwork yourself. I want you to be ready for some fun when I return." His voice lowered an octave, and I shivered as though it was caressing me.

"I'll absolutely be ready when you get back. But that's not for four more days. I have to keep myself occupied until then."

All of a sudden, I felt kind of spacey and twitchy. I started to pace and move things around. I was restless, and I missed something Damien said.

"I guess I did work a little too hard today. I think I'll head back to my cottage in a bit. But first, how did the meeting at the prison go?"

Damien was quiet for a minute. "I'm afraid that wasn't successful. Mr. Rains refused to see me at first until the warden forced him from his cell. He didn't have much to say to me…other than no one can keep him from his daughter."

"Do we have grounds to keep her? I mean, obviously her father should never have custody, but can Nigel really keep her here?"

"I would hope so, Delaney. I don't want to see a child hurt like she was ever again. I will do all that is in my power to keep that from happening. But we're safe for now. And I want to hear about your adventures. Have you been staying out of trouble, Counselor?"

I giggled at that. "I suppose. I haven't cut any classes or caused any mischief, yet. I may have been out in the halls without a pass, though. Will that get me detention?"

He groaned softly in my ear. "Oh yes, you will definitely have to pay for that. Now listen, I want you to go home and get some rest. I was serious about you being ready for some fun on Saturday."

"But Saturday is so far away," I whined.

He laughed and gave me a few more reasons to be anxious for it to arrive.

After we hung up, I shut down my computer and packed up my things. Diana was long gone so the building was extremely quiet. As I passed by the headmaster's office, I listened for a minute to see if he was in. I couldn't remember when Damien said he'd be back. I barely remembered what day it was.

Dusk was beginning to be my favorite time of day here. It was cooler than the daytime. I'd grown to love hearing the nighttime creatures start to come alive, and the sky was incredible, all purples and pinks and fluffy clouds.

I have no idea how long it took me to get home, but when I arrived, I was greeted by two yowling cats. I fed them and gave them some scratches behind the ears.

I laid out my clothes for the next day and must have somehow ended up in bed, because the next thing I remembered was trying to open the door.

"Dammit, why won't this thing open?"

"Delaney, what in the hell are you doing? It's four in the morning. Where are you going?" James had jumped off the sofa bed where he'd been sleeping soundly.

"I...I have somewhere I have to be?" My senses came online with my hand still trying the doorknob.

"Del, sit down. What's going on with you? Have you talked to Damien today? Does he know about your late-night activities?"

I shook my head. "I talked to him today but I forgot all about last night." Something very strange was going on, but I couldn't put my finger on it. It was almost as if there had to be some connection but I couldn't think...

"I'm sorry I woke you, James. I'm going back to bed."

He asked me again if I was okay, and I told him I was fine, just needed more sleep. He let me go reluctantly but watched from my doorway to be sure I went back to bed.

When I awoke the next morning, my alarm was beeping like crazy and James was yelling from the living room for me to turn it off. It was almost seven-thirty. I barely had time to shower, change, and grab a protein bar before heading out the door.

I rushed to my office to grab my things and jammed over to my class-room off the second floor of the library. Morgan called out to me on my way, and I assured her I'd be by after class and I had something important to talk to her about. She frowned and waved me on, wishing me a good first class.

I was totally discombobulated and relieved that the students hadn't arrived yet. I had come over previously and arranged the desks into a circle. Morgan had put some lush green plants in each of the windows, so the room had some life to it.

I heard a bustle behind me and turned to see the students arriving. Three girls arrived first, followed by Sergei, my Russian friend. The only other students I recognized were the couple I had seen on one of my first days here, and Hazel. A couple more boys came in to round out my ten students and they all took their seats.

I smiled nervously at them, and they all looked up at me expectantly.

"Good morning," I said cheerily.

They mumbled some good mornings back.

"Are we all here for Sociology?"

They nodded, looking around at each other.

"Before we get started, maybe you can all go around and tell me your name, where you're from, and one thing you are happy about this morning. I'll go first. My name is Delaney Frost. I'm from Fremont, California, and I am happy that all my clothes match today."

There were some giggles, and then all eyes turned to the girl on my left.

"My name is Simone, I am from Bogota, Colombia, and I am happy that I don't have Calculus this year."

I smiled at her and agreed that was a pretty good thing to be happy about. We went around the circle until reaching the student to my right, Sergei.

"Hello, I am Sergei Revyenko and I am from Kiev, Russia. I am happy to finally be here at Havenhart Academy."

I said in response, "Me too. How many of you are happy to be here?"

They all raised their hands hesitantly.

"It's sure been a wild ride so far. I've met some amazing people and I've been really excited to come and teach this class. Sociology has always been a love of mine since college. How many of you know what Sociology is all about?"

Not a single hand went up.

"Wow, talk about going in blind. Well, have you ever wondered why people act one way when they're alone with you and another when they're in a group?" Some eyes perked up at that, and a few of them sat up straighter. "How about, why is it that people often hold on to religion in times of distress?" A few more looked up enthusiastically. "Or, one of my favorites, why is it that people will blindly follow a charismatic leader, even if it means giving up everything, including their lives?"

That old thrill I used to get from turning on the light bulbs in their minds cleared my own, and my mental fog lifted.

"Basically, Sociology is the study of how people interact in groups, how they organize their societies and develop the rules that people are expected to follow within them. Sometimes it's harmonious, sometimes it's ugly, but it's all human nature. Does that make sense to you?" They nodded and a few even opened up notebooks to start writing.

"We're going to cover a lot of ground this semester, but besides giving you the basics, I want this to be an open forum where we discuss what you want to discuss and apply it to Sociological theories. How does that sound? "

They murmured enthusiastically. I took a deep breath and continued.

"My research assistant, Raven has gathered some reading material for us to start with, so I'll hand that out now." I gave them their reading assignments and asked them to be ready to discuss them on Friday. With that, the class was over and I said goodbye. I noticed a few of the students lingering and chatting with each other about the course.

"Miss Frost?" I heard a familiar male voice call out.

"Yes, Sergei?"

"I think this is good subject for me to study. I am wondering how it is that people in my country have struggled so much, and why they have made the choices they have made. Can you teach me?"

"Of course. I find the history of Russia and the former Soviet Union fascinating. I'm sure we can get into it. We can talk about Stalin, the Bolsheviks, and we can even get into Rasputin. Talk about a charismatic person."

He thanked me and left with a smile on his face, his chin a little higher.

I packed up my bag and headed downstairs to Morgan's office. Some students were just leaving, and she was putting away some of the books they'd had out. I followed her into the stacks. She waited patiently for me to begin.

"So a funny thing happened around four a.m. today. Wanna take a guess?"

She looked at me impatiently. "I hope you don't think this is funny, Delaney. I know why you're here. I sensed something last night, too." She looked at me with narrowed eyes. "Something is trying to get in, penetrate us. I warned you this would happen."

"You did, but what am I supposed to do? I was asleep both times it happened. I don't know what would have happened if James wasn't there."

She thought for a minute. "I need Elijah."

My stomach dropped. Something about Elijah unsettled me. I didn't want him to know what was happening, but I doubted Morgan would change her mind. She picked up the phone and called him, asking him to come right over.

I sat down heavily on the couch and put my head in my hands. I was suddenly very tired, and that spacey feeling was invading me again. I knew I had somewhere to be but I couldn't think straight.

"Miss Frost, I need you to look at me."

I hadn't even heard Elijah come in but when I looked up, he was crouched in front of me. Morgan stood behind him, tugging on a wild curl. My heart started to pound. I wished she would give me some reassurance.

He stared at me for a long time. An icy feeling started crawling up the back of my neck, and I swiped at it with a hand, trying to make it stop. I started to pant and tried to move back into the couch to get away from his stare. The freezing tendrils curled around the front of my neck and moved upward, toward my face.

I scrambled over the back of the couch and fell to the floor on the other side. I clawed at my face, screaming to make it stop. Morgan rushed around and picked me up, holding my hands.

"Delaney, it's okay. It's over. It's okay, you're okay. Just breathe with me...breathe with me."

I gasped and started coughing violently. I couldn't get enough air in. She put her hands on my shoulders and closed her eyes, whispering rapidly while her eyes rolled back in her head. The oxygen finally reached my brain and my senses came back online.

I pushed Morgan away and wrapped my arms around my midsection. "What the hell was that about? Are you trying to make me crazy? I fucking trusted you people, and this is what you do?"

I ran out the door with Morgan yelling behind me. I glanced behind me to see if anyone was following. I was petrified.

When I turned back, Elijah was in front of me—and everything went black.

The next thing I knew, I was lying in Morgan's office with Elijah, Grace, Jackson and Nigel. I tried to get up but there were many hands holding me down.

"Jackson, what the hell is going on?"

He looked frightened. Helpless. His eyes darted back and forth between the people around me, searching for words. When no one else spoke, Elijah stepped forward.

"You're completely open, Miss Frost, and he knows it. He's trying to use you to get inside, to get to his daughter. You must learn to shut him out, or he will take you over."

Everyone looked frightened by his words, and it dawned on me what he was talking about.

"Rains? But how? He's in prison."

"There are no walls that can stop him, not now. He knows where she is, and he will not stop until she's with him again. She's marked you as her Protector, so he will use you to get to her if he can." He leaned in closer to me, and I trembled in fear. "We have to make it so he can't."

"What do you plan to do with me?" I didn't really think I wanted to hear what he had planned.

Nigel spoke up at this point. "You must know we would never do anything to hurt you, Delaney. Young lady, we have worked extensively to bring you home to us. You belong here, and Joanna needs you. We simply must remove this threat."

He knelt down and took my hand. "Delaney, you are so powerful but you don't know how to control what goes in or out yet. I'm afraid this has left us all vulnerable. It is time for you to learn. Will you trust us?"

"Do I really have a choice?"

Jackson put his hand to my cheek. "Del, you said once that you thought I was like a guardian angel. I would never let anyone hurt you. Not for anything." At that, he looked around at the others. "Whatever you have to do, I will be present. Delaney is not to be harmed, do you understand me?"

"Jackson, are you questioning me?" Nigel looked slightly perturbed. "You of all people should understand her importance here. Now please, both of you, we do not have time to lose. I received a call from the prison. Rains escaped from maximum security and his current whereabouts are unknown. He's likely on his way here now. There is no time to waste." He stood and moved to close the doors.

I froze at that bombshell. "What do you mean, he escaped from maximum security? Isn't that supposed to be impossible?"

He sighed. "My dear, Rains has the power of persuasion. How difficult do you think it would be for him to motivate the guards to let him out? We've explained before, he knows what people want and uses that to bend them to his will."

If what Nigel was saying was true, how in the hell were we going to be any match for him?

"Morgan, Elijah. We must prepare."

The three of them moved away and toward the rear chamber, where I had come across Morgan's rituals before.

I was still shaking, but Jackson had not let go of my hand. Somehow I knew he wouldn't let anyone hurt me. He stood up and helped me to my feet.

We followed the others into the Morgan's inner chamber. Jackson kept a hand on my lower back, guiding me and yet also keeping me from running. In the center of the room, Morgan, Elijah, and Nigel stood clad in dark robes. Candles burned all around, casting shadows on the stone walls. Incense filling the room and the smoke added to the hazy feeling.

"Delaney, please."

Morgan held out a hand. I took it and then Vincent came from behind me and took his spot in the circle along with Jackson. The five of them stood around me and slowly began chanting. My heart raced in my chest. I knew I should try to relax, that fighting this would only make it worse, but the sharp pain was back, and then a bright light.

"Delaney, tell me everything that is happening."

"The pain," I gasped. "It's so bad. I have to…I have to get there, I have to open…something." I covered my eyes, blinded by the light. "It's so bright, but I have to get there—"

"Where do you need to go?" I thought it was Nigel speaking to me, but the sound of cicadas buzzing in my ear drowned out most of his voice.

"The gates. I need to open the gates. I need to find—"

The shadow man stood before me, but I still couldn't see his face. His eyes glowed in the darkness and I could make out a voice whispering…

I felt hands on me, so many hands, and the pain grew so much more intense in my head.

"Morgan! It hurts…my head…Jackson, make it stop." I pleaded with them. I opened my eyes enough to see Morgan's face. She was chanting, her eyes completely black. I turned from person to person and they all were chanting. I screamed and tried to break free until I felt arms around me.

Elijah.

"She is ours."

Elijah's eyes went from golden to black and the pain in my head turned to that freezing sensation.

"Please…" I begged of him.

Elijah placed his hand over my face and everything went black once more, but this time I was still aware. My body floated in the darkness. It was a similar sensation to floating in water. The pain in my head began to subside as flashes of memories began to appear. Morgan and I in her study during the first trance. Joanna in the hospital bed. Damien on my front porch. My last day at my last job. My parents at my high school graduation. The fire.

My lungs burned with the need to breathe as flames danced over my body. I smelled burning hair and smoke and heard the screams. Children clung to my legs as they burned…And standing there in front of me was the Shadow Man. With a lighter in his hand.

. . .

I CAME TO HEARING JAMES SPEAKING RAPIDLY IN HIS MILITARY VOICE. TWO other male voices spoke softly with him. Something furry and warm was pushing into my hand.

I realized I was in my bed and Ramses was curled up against me, nudging me with his nose insistently. I got up and used the restroom, noticing I wasn't in the same clothes. Through my window, I saw bright, sunny sky. The last thing I could remember was the late afternoon. This was more like high noon. I splashed cold water on my face and dried it off with a sigh.

I wandered into the living room, and all three voices silenced.

"Hey FC, you alright?"

I nodded. I was okay, just very tired. I had a hollow kind of a headache. I sat down next to James on the sofa and leaned my head against his shoulder.

"I feel as if I've had an out-of-body experience inside my body, and it's not agreeing with me. Anyone have a clue how that happened?"

Jackson cleared his throat and came to sit on the other side of me.

"Darlin', you've been put through the ringer. We, uh, weren't sure when you were going to wake up." He looked away guiltily.

"What do you mean, when I would wake up? What time is it?" I searched around frantically for my phone or a clock or—

"It's noon. On Friday. You've been out for almost forty-eight hours."

Stunned, I fell back against the couch. I'd lost almost two days and I didn't remember what happened.

"I was in Morgan's office..." I tried so hard to remember but the brain fog was dense.

"They attempted to break the link Rains had formed through you, but it was a lot more involved than anyone thought it would be." Jackson hesitated to go on, but he apparently needed information from me. "Has anything else weird been going on?"

"Define weird. Jesus, Jackson! This whole experience has been completely insane." I was starting to get angry. It sounded as if I was being blamed for something. "Are you trying to say this is my fault?"

"No! Absolutely not, Delaney. It's just, we're trying to figure out how he's linked so strongly with you."

I took a deep breath and tried to recall the events of the past few days, prior to my mini-coma.

"It all started with the nightmares. Then, I got a really bad headache, almost like a migraine, and I felt like my skin was crawling. I've been kind of spacey, I guess. I'm sure James told you about my early-morning walkabouts."

Jackson exhaled. "He told us."

"So, did whatever you tried to do work?"

Jackson frowned. "We don't know for sure. You passed out. Did you remember anything else? You were screaming, and your nose started to bleed—"

"Jackson made them stop, thank God," James said, shooting a glare in Jackson's direction. "But we don't know if it worked."

"Okay," I said, feeling deflated. All of that for nothing. The dream I'd been having lingered in my consciousness, and whatever it had been felt urgent, but I couldn't make my brain give it up. There were just pieces. If I tried to think too hard, the pain came back.

"I'm sorry. I know there's more...I can't get to it."

He nodded solemnly. "I'll share this information with the others. There's still no word on Rains or his location. We've got the entire campus monitored, and it's not likely anything can get in here without us knowing, but we have to be prepared in case that happens."

"Uh, has anyone told Damien?"

They all looked uncomfortable. Vincent, who had remained silent as usual up until this point, spoke up.

"He's on his way back, Miss Frost. We couldn't get ahold of him. His phone wasn't working. We finally reached him after he left Texas. He should arrive late tonight." He looked down at his feet.

"Needless to say, FC, he's pissed at us and worried sick about you. I talked to him and assured him you were resting, but he's not going to be satisfied until he sees you."

I relaxed a bit at that. Knowing he would be here soon put me at ease. But then something occurred to me.

"What about Cassidy? She's supposed to be coming in today. Has anyone heard from her?"

James nodded. "She should just be landing in Fayetteville. My guess is that she'll be here in about an hour. Vincent is going to pick her up?"

He nodded and stepped out.

"Now that that's all settled, can I get some chow? I mean, really? Two days without food? I'm ready to gnaw my own arm off here." I tried to make light of the situation because I honestly couldn't keep it together much longer in this current mood. I was still trying to figure out what all I'd seen...

"That sounds like my FC. I'll call Grace and have her bring you something from the commons."

I shook my head. "Actually, can I just shower real quick and then we can all go over there?"

He shrugged and looked to Jackson. "Well, *I'm* not going to say no to her. Care to step in here?"

Jackson laughed. "I try never to get in the way of a woman and food so by all means, let her do what she wants."

"Hmph. That's better. I'll be out in ten. Neither of you better leave without me because I still want answers."

They both held up their hands and tried to look innocent.

Thank goodness for short hair. I was ready in fifteen minutes. I grabbed both of my guards and dragged them out the door.

When I thought about them being my guards, I got a bit more confused. Were they protecting me, or were they protecting others *from* me? If what they were saying was true, Rains could somehow control me to do his bidding. I had a painful thought about poor Joanna. Would he use me to hurt her? I couldn't bear that.

We ate in silence. Some of the kids stopped by the table to check on me so I assumed the story was that I had taken ill. I tried to be my cheery self, and I think they bought it.

I ate until I was full to bursting and then we went to the gatehouse to wait for Cassidy. "So what's the story? What are we telling Cassidy about all this? She has no idea what the hell is going on here."

"The headmaster thought it would be prudent to let her know that we had a security concern because of a high-profile student, which is true, of course." Jackson was trying to sound convincing, and I scoffed at him.

"But nothing about her best friend psychically freaking out, is that right?"

He nodded and I shook my head.

"Great. Well, I guess I'll stick to the story. You know she's going to know better, James. She can always read me."

"We'll deal. We'll do what we have to do. The cottage next to yours is unoccupied, so she and I will crash there once Damien returns. He, uh, said we're not to leave you alone at all."

I swallowed hard. "I guess I can't be trusted, so that's probably good." I'd moved beyond scared and angry to feeling guilty. Didn't exactly fit the five stages of grief but it was the best way I had to relate.

A few minutes later, the school van rolled up and Cassidy bounced out the door.

"BESTIE!" We both shrieked and ran at each other. Of all the times she'd been there for me after shit had hit the fan, this time, I needed her most of all. I held on so tight to her, she had to tap out before I cut off her oxygen.

"I know we're excited, but I can't breathe over here."

I stepped back and tears streamed down my face.

"Oh, honey, what?" She looked worried and glanced over my shoulder to James questioningly.

"We've had some excitement around here and Delaney's been a little under the weather." He gave her a hug, but she never lost eye contact with me.

"It's cool, I've just been a little out of it. One of our students has a psycho dad and he's trying to get in touch with her. James is here to help out while Damien is out of town."

She looked at both of us as if we were toying with her. "Okay—and you can tell me the rest after you show me around. I can't believe how beautiful this place is. You weren't lying, friend."

I glanced over at Jackson—and found him staring at Cassidy in wonder, as if he were seeing the sun for the first time. If I were in a better place, I might have recognized it for what it was. Instead, I just took the opportunity to introduce them.

"Cassidy, I want you to meet my colleague and newly appointed guardian angel, Jackson Howe. Jackson, my best friend since second grade and all-around amazing woman, Cassidy Mackenzie."

He took her offered hand and shook it gently, his touch lingering.

Cassidy's other hand went to her chest, and her face lit up in an enthusiastic smile. Neither said a word.

James interrupted the moment and asked, "So Cassidy, did you get dinner or are you hungry?"

Jackson dropped her hand, flushed and stepped back, keeping his eyes on her.

"I'm good, actually. I had some time to kill before the van picked me up so I grabbed some food. It was actually pretty good."

We linked arms and headed to my cottage. James picked up her things and Jackson followed along, studying her closely.

"Boys," Cassidy called over her shoulder. "Delaney and I need some girl time for a bit. Can we meet up with you in a while?"

The guys looked nervously at each other.

"It's okay, James, you can put us under surveillance but no bugs. Girl talk is private, dig?"

"I'll, ah, just come in and grab my stuff to take next door. Cassidy, do you need your bags, or would you like me to put them in your room? The headmaster has given us use of the cottage next door, so we can all sleep more comfortably."

It was kind of lame but it made sense.

"Sure, you can take this bag. Let me just grab a change of clothes." She looked at me with a raised eyebrow but followed along.

It wasn't long before we were in our jammies and had popcorn and sodas going. I'd even managed to find some chocolate to top it all off. I told her about some of the wonderful people I'd met, like Diana, Grace and George, carefully avoiding talking about some of the others who were involved with my little situation. I told her about the kids and my awesome first class. She was thoroughly happy for me. I wanted to turn the focus on her, though. She wasn't happy in her own life and that pained me.

"Sweetie, how are you holding up with all of this?"

She lost her smile a little and let me take her hand. I didn't consciously do my trick but she opened up regardless.

"I found some financial records at the hangar and discovered he'd been taking money out of our account to pay for some gambling debts. He owed over one hundred thousand dollars to a shady character, and he'd been spending increasing amounts of time with various women he claimed were interested in taking flight lessons. You know we had been trying to build a business together as flight instructors—"

"Yeah! You were so excited about it."

"Well, I told him I was frustrated that he hadn't been doing his part. I told him I was going to take on more hours with the charter company to make ends meet, and he accused me of backing out of our plans. He got more volatile the more I confronted him.

"It seems like such a hopeless situation, Laney. I don't know whether to just cut my losses or try to make it work. I feel like I'm giving up but he's just blown my trust so much, not to mention I'm tired of taking the brunt of his frustrations and temper."

"Do you feel like there's enough left to salvage? Those were some pretty big things he was keeping from you. Do you think he could make you happy once again?"

She thought about that for a minute and shook her head. "I don't know that he *ever* made me happy. I think I wanted to believe I would be happy being married to him. Funny how that doesn't just fix everything, does it?"

I took her into my arms and held her while she cried softly against my shoulder. I wanted to take her pain away, wanted her to follow her heart and move away from this toxic relationship. She took some deep breaths.

"Laney, why is it I always feel so much better after I talk to you?"

"Because I love you and you're my best friend. And you deserve the best there is, always. Honey, I will always be here for you, and I will support you in whatever you decide is best, okay? And my boss has already said you're welcome to stay as long as you need. He even mentioned you doing some work for us, if you want to. He's got a plane and everything. As he says in his nifty English accent, 'we are at your disposal.'"

She sat up and wiped at her eyes, growing wary. "You ever think this place is too good to be true?"

I laughed out loud, which I don't think was the response she was expecting. "I do, and there are definitely some things about this place that are not what I thought. But I do feel as if I've joined a community here that really cares for each other. And no, not like a 'hey, drink this here Kool-Aid' kind of community."

We cracked up at that and helped ourselves to more snacks.

It had been such an emotionally exhausting week, so we decided that we didn't need to solve all of the world's problems at that point, but that we needed a dose of Dave Grohl and the Foos to ease our troubled minds. I popped in their Live from Wembley show and we talked girl talk and bounced around the couch.

Around ten, she decided she couldn't keep her eyes open any longer, so I walked her to her cottage. She carried on about how adorable the places were. This particular cottage had two small bedrooms, so she and James would get some real rest. I assured her we'd meet for breakfast and find some way to occupy ourselves the next day. I hugged her good night and headed back to my cottage, my feet dragging.

A vague discomfort nagged at me but I was beyond caring. All I could think of was my comfy, cozy bed, and the fact that I'd see Damien in a few hours.

It was nice to come back to quiet. I crawled into bed and hugged Clio close to me as she had made herself comfortable on my pillow. I drifted off to sleep and for once, my dreams were quite pleasant. I dreamt that Damien had come in and crawled in bed with me, stroking my hair and gently dragging his nails across my back. He whispered to me how sorry he was that he had been gone, and that he'd never leave again if it meant that I'd be safe.

I shushed him and snuggled in close thinking that I never wanted to wake up from this dream. Life was infinitely better when he was lying next to me.

"Shit, it's Saturday!" I slammed my hand down on the alarm clock as it began its incessant beeping the next morning. I rolled over and almost fell out of bed when I saw what—or who—was next to me.

"I thought I was dreaming," I whispered and reached out to touch Damien's hair. His silky locks were heavenly. I leaned down to breathe in his scent.

A smile crept across his lips. With his eyes closed, he said, "Let's pretend we're still dreaming and that we get to stay here forever."

I lay my head on the pillow and he gathered me close. For the first time since he'd left, everything was as it should be.

A little while later, the phone rang. It was Cassidy asking if we could pass on breakfast. She wanted to sleep in, and I wholeheartedly agreed. I told her to call me when she was ready to face the day.

I hung up and rolled over, snuggling closer to Damien. He started kissing my neck. I needed more of him. I reached down and grabbed for his shirt, trying to haul it over his head. He apparently had the same idea.

Our sleepy eyes held each other as we undressed. When our lips met, there was no hurry, no desperation, just a silent communion. We kissed each other as if we were making a vow. Our naked bodies met and we held on to each other lovingly. He placed slow and gentle kisses along the inside of my arms and across my breasts. I took his nipple between my lips and nibbled delicately, nuzzling against the soft hairs on his broad chest.

I looked up into his eyes and saw so many emotions there, it startled me. When I started to speak, he put his finger to my lips. I held his gaze as I kissed the pad of his finger and sucked it into my mouth. This man who always seemed so composed gasped and began to tremble, his hands becoming greedier in their caresses. I wanted this. I wanted *him*.

I rolled over on top of him. His eyes searched mine, looking for any sign that I wasn't totally with him. I wanted to reassure him that this was where I longed to be.

"If I learned anything from this time away from you, it's that I love you even more than I thought possible." I smiled down at him and kissed him deeply. "I want this."

His arms wrapped firmly around me, and I knew in that moment that I had everything I'd ever wanted right there.

He slid inside me, breaking any barriers left between us. His face tightened in ecstasy. I had never seen anything more beautiful. He more than filled me as I moved against him. All inhibitions were gone. I couldn't get close enough. He felt it, too. He suddenly flipped me over and slid an arm under my thigh to penetrate me deeper. I cried out and tears stung my eyes. When I opened them again, his gaze was full of adoration.

"You are so very precious to me. I love you so much, Delaney."

I clung to him as his words intensified my need. He was exquisite above me, his powerful frame all tension and strength. Heat radiated from our bodies as he began to move faster and more insistent within me. His head kicked back and his muscles strained. All of my senses were heightened. A burning sensation began deep inside. It was so hot, it was like we were bathed in flames. They licked at my skin and drove me closer and closer to the edge.

When I felt myself going over, I lifted up to look into his eyes. We slammed into each other and held on tightly as the waves broke through us both. I clung to him to keep from washing away. The bliss was just as overwhelming as the fire. I wasn't sure which was more powerful.

We were both panting and covered in a layer of sweat. Every time he moved, it lit up my nerve endings and a new round of shivers racked my body. He collapsed on top of me, kissing my face. I felt safer than ever as his body covered mine.

We lay there in each other's arms, quietly listening to the late-summer rain fall gently outside. Nervous thoughts threatened to snake their way into the room, but I silenced them, determined to stay in this bliss.

"I knew once we came together it would be incredible, but I never..." His words drifted off and I looked up at him.

"Yeah, me neither." We laughed together, and the rumble from his chest tickled my cheek.

"Damien, I've never...It's never been like that for me."

He looked at me, puzzled. "What, you've never completely destroyed a man with your touch? I find that hard to believe."

I bit him on his stomach and he protested loudly.

"Hey, I'm serious. I'm so spent right now, I'm not even sure I could move even if this place were about to explode."

I laughed and kissed the spot I had just bitten. "Speaking of... Was it just me or did it feel as if we would spontaneously combust?" I laughed but he gave me a slightly sinister look.

"I told you, you just didn't believe me. I'm not giving you a line when I say you get me hot. I think I genuinely have a fever."

"Come on, be serious. What is it?"

He paused to think for a minute. "I don't really know, love. It's just that whenever you touch me intimately, your power seems to focus and it's like a roaring fire. Not that I mind. It's quite intoxicating." He waggled his eyebrows at me, and I fell back groaning.

"So being with me is like, what, pyrotechnics?"

He murmured in agreement. "Yes, you are like special effects at a rock concert." He bent down and kissed me sweetly.

"Do you think it's dangerous?"

He frowned for a minute. "I should think not. But perhaps we should be sure your fire extinguisher is charged." He held me close again, and I smiled against him. My next thought made that smile disappear.

"So...hear any funny stories lately? Like the one about the counselor who started wigging out and ended up practically in a coma surrounded by folks in bathrobes? Let me tell you, it's a kick."

Damien sat up and leaned his elbow on his raised knee, the sheets pooling at his hips. "I have spoken to Morgan, Nigel, and Elijah and made it very clear I was not pleased that they had gone ahead without me here. However, as something or someone seemed to be interfering with our communication, I'm not sorry they did. Delaney, you were seriously in danger, and I can't believe I wasn't here." He turned away from me and moved to get out of bed. I reached for him and he sighed.

"Hey, you don't get the blame here. Don't you dare be angry with yourself. You were doing your job. Now that I know what to look for, he's not going to get the drop on me, all right? Now, if you have pertinent information to share with me, please do—and do it quick because I'm not quite finished with you."

He stood from the bed and held out a hand for me. I took it and walked into his arms. He held me like that for a moment and then led me to the bathroom.

I had been so focused on how incredible the claw-foot tub was for taking a bath that I hadn't dreamed of how soothing a shower with Damien would be. He washed every part of me, lingering on his favorite spots of course, assuring himself that he'd done a thorough job.

I had probably never been this clean in my life. He was so attentive, almost as if he were memorizing my every feature. He paid close attention to all of my scars, asking me about each of them. He was particularly entertained by the story of me getting run over by a bicyclist, which left a nasty scar down the side of my knee.

"What? I was roller-skating. I tried to get out of his way and we both rolled to the same side of the walkway. His friends came unglued, accusing my eight-year-old self of trying to knock their buddy off his ten-speed. I had to skate the rest of the way around the lake bleeding and sniffling."

His bottom lip poked out, and he made sure kiss my old booboo and make it better. That led to kisses up the inside of my thigh until I melted into the corner of the tub.

Damien worked his way over my belly, scraping his whiskers so very gently before looking up at me, green eyes hooded passionately. My head fell back on my shoulders and I ran my fingers through his hair. He gripped the sides of my thighs and pressed a gentle kiss just above my core. My body jerked, and I dug my nails in, holding on for dear life while he deepened his kiss.

When his tongue snaked out, I moaned and reflexively held his head a little closer, taking what I needed from him. He deftly supported me, never losing his pace. He groaned against me and the added vibration tore me apart. I tensed as every muscle exploded deliciously, the waves running through me like water down the side of a mountain after a downpour.

I panted hard while Damien continued to hold me up. He was on his knees before me, arms around my waist, dropping feathery kisses across my chest. I lifted his head and kissed him deeply, stroking his tongue with mine until he breathed as hard as I did.

I helped him up and I guided him under the stream of water. Without a word, I grabbed the shampoo and squirted some in my hands, motioning for him to wet his hair again. I sighed happily when he dropped his head back, his eyes closed and his biceps flexing as he ran those long fingers through his wavy locks. I gently massaged the shampoo into his scalp and he murmured contentedly.

"That feels heavenly."

Little did he know I was far from finished massaging him.

Using the suds from his hair to wash him, I ran my hands over his shoulders and chest, rubbing in circles as I worked my way down. I crouched in front of him and his gaze followed me heatedly.

"God, Delaney...I... *Oh my Go—*"

His words cut off as I ran my hand between his legs, cupping him gently. I caressed his length and sighed at the feel of his smooth skin stretched tautly over his arousal. I teased as long as I could stand it before I took him into my mouth.

He hissed and shifted his weight, grabbing desperately for something to hold on to. He moaned and began to tremble. I knew he was right there when he grasped my shoulder and cried out.

Just as he released...*crash.*

"Bloody hell!" he shouted as the shower curtain fell down.

I fell on my ass in the tub, laughing hysterically.

"Are you hurt? I swear I'll fix that. Are you sure you're all right?" he questioned nervously. He helped me to my feet and as we both tried to catch our breath.

"I never thought playing in the shower was so dangerous," I said in between giggles. I grabbed for a towel and stepped out.

He was still shaking his head. "Statistics do show that a high percentage of accidents occur in the bathroom. I just never quite pictured this being the cause. Damn, Delaney. I can't feel my legs."

I giggled some more and wrapped us both in the towel. I rested my head against his chest and his heart beat wildly. I sighed and held on to his sheer perfection.

After our shower, we sat in the kitchen, me drinking ice water in shorts and bra, and he in his boxers with a cup of tea. Damien explained that he'd made it to the next leg of his trip and realized no one had checked in with him or returned his calls. He tried again from the hotel phone and finally reached Vincent, who told him everything that had transpired. He had the jet refueled and flight plans filed to return as soon as possible but there were complications at the airfield and traffic...delay, delay, delay. Almost as if someone was deliberately trying to sabotage his flight.

"Then was it wise to get on a *big flying hunk of metal in the sky*? Seriously. What if the plane had been tampered with, Damien?"

His look of resolve cooled me down. The thought of losing him now was unacceptable.

"Inspections were done and everything was fine. The pilot was on alert and the weather was clear. I wouldn't have taken any chances."

He leaned across the counter to kiss me again. I knew I'd never tire of him touching me, and his kiss, well...

We talked about what I remembered of my first week, and he was tickled that everything went smoothly.

"I'm so glad to hear it. I knew I'd made the best decision leaving you in charge. I knew you'd be fantastic." The devious gleam in his eyes had returned, so I sat back and squinted at him.

"Oh really? Well, I'm glad I passed your test, Mr. Preston."

He came around the bar and lifted me off my stool and kissed me heatedly. Damien backed me up against my desk and ran his hands down my sides and slid his fingers into the waistband of my sweat shorts, cupping my behind. His kisses took my breath away. I steadied myself by grabbing his biceps and holding on.

He started kissing down my neck and along the lacy edge of my bra. My head fell back, suddenly feeling too heavy for me to hold up any longer.

Just then the phone rang, and it was Cassidy. I knew it was time to greet the public.

I was sure the goofy smile on my face was permanent, and I knew that Damien wouldn't lose his flushed look soon either. His skin was still hot to the touch. It mirrored my insides when I looked at him. He was so beautiful in the afterglow.

"Hmmmm, the things we could get into without that bloody phone interrupting us." Damien's voice was husky. We stood holding each other for a moment.

"If only the world would just leave us alone for a while. Think that will ever happen or is it just a taste of what's to come?" I asked the question playfully, but I knew that the nature of our jobs and where we lived would necessitate being ready to go in a moment's notice. I sighed.

"As long as I know our spare moments can be spent like this, I'll survive." He sighed then, too. "I will treasure our times, Delaney. My God, I so desperately wanted to touch you before. Now it's like severing a limb to let you go. I love being with you." His words, spoken in reverent tones, brushed against my neck.

I looked up at him and saw my own feelings reflected there.

"I love you, Damien."

He kissed me with his eyes open, and the heat began building once again as I looked deeply into them.

"And I love you. But I don't know that our companions will love us if we cause them to miss another meal."

We dressed quickly, sneaking glances at each other as we walked out the door. I couldn't wait until we returned.

We ended up meeting Cassidy, James and Jackson for a late lunch. She looked better after a good night sleep, and I was so happy she and Damien finally got to meet. They talked like old friends. Damien held my hand against his thigh, and I loved the lazy way he drew interlocking circles on my hand. He'd done it before on the plane. As I thought back to that night, I felt so lucky to be holding his hand. Anything might have happened to keep us apart this week.

Jackson watched Cassidy curiously. It was shocking to see him so quiet, his joking nature silenced for the first time since I'd met him. He listened to her talk to Damien intently, and I thought about his gift.

It finally dawned on me that perhaps he had made a connection with Cassidy. *My* Cassidy! How was I going to keep her out of the loop knowing that Jackson was now going to be able to basically tune in to her wherever or whenever he had the urge? I'd have to speak to him about it when we were alone. I had no idea how she would react to any of this.

Cassidy had been raised by conservative parents who'd done their very best to shelter her from the evils of the world. When she moved out at eighteen, she'd tried to crawl out from under that shelter and find herself. That led to some painful relationships before she'd followed her heart and applied to flight school. We were both sad when she had to leave, but I'd been so proud of her.

It took her years of patience and perseverance, but she got her license and was hired by the airlines. She'd finally settled down at a charter company, flying the rich and/or famous to fancy destinations. She was a tremendously skilled pilot and businesswoman. That was part of the reason I believed Robert was so drawn to her. After a whirlwind romance, they'd eloped, and, well…

She was here now, and I hoped she'd make a clean break. I knew how hard this was going to be on her. I vowed I would care for my best friend as she had looked out for me all our lives.

Damien was speaking to us both and when I tuned in, I heard, "What do you say, ladies?"

Cassidy raised her eyebrows. "Did you hear that?"

"Actually, no. Sorry, what did I miss?"

Damien frowned at me. He put his arm around me and asked if I was okay. I nodded, so he continued.

"That One Band is going to play a show tonight," Cassidy said. "You didn't tell me there was a house band at the school."

"Oh, uh, it's a well-kept secret," I said with a shrug. I yawned and tried to cover it. I was still a bit tired and distracted.

"So the BBQ begins at four and then the band will play. The head-master has alumni coming in to do some activities with the kids this evening. There will be extra security on hand."

The guys looked like they needed to talk.

"Guys, Cassidy and I are going for a walk."

They all stood up and looked at us with concern.

"We'll be fine," I said, specifically to Damien. "We'll stay close."

I gave him one last kiss on the cheek and stood to bus our table. I grabbed Cassidy's hand and we dashed off for some girl talk.

When we stepped back outside, she put her arm around my shoulder.

"Friend, that is one amazingly *hot* male specimen. And you *even considered for a moment* not taking this job? You get *paid* to look at that?"

"Mmmm, I know." Then I got serious. "Cassidy...I am *so* in love with him."

She looked at me, surprised but pleased. "And he better deserve it. Lord knows *you* do."

"He does, Cass. He's been alone for a long time. We both have our demons. I think Fate decided we both needed a kick in the ass. He's been so attentive and supportive since I've been here. And once he decided not to keep things professional, ah, it's been..."

She laughed knowingly, and I left it at that.

We kicked back in my cottage for a bit, just catching up. But I wanted to check on her wellbeing. I reached over and took her hand.

"Cassidy, I'm so happy you're here with me, but I know you're hurting, honey. Is there anything I can do?"

She took a steadying breath and kicked up her chin a bit.

"I really don't want to expend any more energy on Robert. I've cried buckets, gone without sleep and food, and I've worked so very hard to make things right...but I'm not the problem. I've kicked myself over and over. I think I've finally accepted that I couldn't have known what he was doing short of hiring a private investigator. If I had to go that far to find out whether he was being truthful with me, it wasn't meant to be. I filed for divorce this week. We're going to put the house on the market. I'll put my stuff in storage until I figure out where I want to end up. With my job, I can apply to transfer. I'm not sure I want to be in SoCal anymore."

She stopped speaking for a moment, and a small smile crept up on her face. "It's kind of liberating, you know? I can start over. The sale of the house will give me some startup money. Who knows? Maybe I'll finally be able to be close to you again. I hate that we've been apart for so long." She cleared her throat and a sparkle found its way to her eye. "But Arkansas? Really, Frost? I'm not sure I can do it. Has it been horrible? The weather? The bugs?" She shivered in mock disgust.

"It actually hasn't been as bad as I thought it was going to be, and believe me, I'm a huge wimp when it comes to heat. It's so beautiful here, and the work...Cassidy, I'm finally doing what I've always wanted to do.

And with Damien..." I think the dreamy look on my face explained it all. "It's the whole package."

We hugged and laughed together. I was glad she seemed better than when we'd talked on the phone. I knew part of it was being here. She even remarked how much better she'd felt since getting such a good night's sleep. She mentioned the comfort of the cottage, the bed, and my thoughts drifted off to the previous night's activities...

"You okay?"

I realized I must have spaced out on her. "Yeah. I'm sorry. I was sick this week. I guess I'm still a little tired. If it's okay with you, I think I'm going to take a nap before dinner."

She laughed. "That sounds like heaven." She hugged me and kissed my cheek. "I'll come by to get you for dinner, okay?"

"Sounds great."

She headed back to her cabin and I was alone for the first time in who knows when.

A shiver of anxiety creeped up on me, and I thought about Joanna. Was she safe here? Were all of the kids safe? Would Rains come here?

Was I still a weakness?

I crawled into bed and was out as soon as my head hit the pillow. My dreams were full of smoke, fire, bright lights, pain. So much pain.

And the Shadow Man.

When I woke, my entire bungalow smelled like fire. I took a shower, stripped the bed, washed the sheets, opened the windows, but I couldn't get the smell to go away. I closed my eyes and tried to pull on my inner calm, the place Morgan showed me in our work, and was able to at least put on a façade by the time the guys and Cassidy came to get me for dinner.

I hoped I could keep it up. I didn't want to give this damn man and his agenda one more ounce of my energy. I would do whatever I needed to keep my friends, the kids, and the man I loved safe.

NINETEEN

THE LIGHT

THE BBQ WAS A BLAST, AT LEAST EVERYONE ELSE HAD A GREAT TIME. I WAS able to get out of my head enough to enjoy having my best friend with me while we watched the band play and then listened to speakers from the headmaster's alumni pool. There were all kinds of success stories to be heard. None of them spoke openly about their powers, but if you were aware, you'd pick up on hints. Cassidy was impressed and by the end she'd even teared up.

"This is such a great place, Del," she said, giving me a hug when it was over.

"It really is."

At the end of the presentations, it was near dark. We helped get the kids back to the dorms where Marcia, Jared, and some of the other teachers had set up some games for the kids.

Jackson, Damien, Cassidy and I strolled along the path at the back of the campus, talking and laughing.

"So you were really a student here?" Cassidy asked Damien.

"I was. A loooong time ago."

"And what did you love most about it?"

Damien thought for a moment. "Actually. I loved the campfires we would have on weekends. There's a fire pit just behind the commons that we use sometimes. I'm surprised the headmaster didn't have the program out there tonight. Perhaps he thought our guests would be more comfortable inside."

I raised an eyebrow. "A campfire circle? Like for s'mores?"

Cassidy and I gasped and looked at each other. "That sounds soooo good."

Jackson rubbed his belly. "I think we could manage some s'mores. I've got room for dessert."

I turned on Damien. "Can we please?"

He gazed at me with that smile I knew meant he'd let me get away with whatever I wanted. "Yes, we can have s'mores."

Cassidy and I cheered.

"I'll just go grab the fixings," he said and he turned toward the back doors of the commons.

"Ow," I said, bringing my hand up to my eye. The stabbing pain was there, not nearly as strong as before, but Damien was right beside me in an instant.

"Are you alright?"

I nodded. "It's not as bad."

"Here we are," Jackson said, carrying a brown paper bag. "George said he's already got the fire pit set up so I grabbed some matches for us and —shit."

Jackson dropped the bag and it ripped open, spilling our supplies all over the ground. The matchbox burst open and matches went everywhere.

Damien bent to help him along with Cassidy and they tried to catch every last match—

The pain flared behind my eye and I gasped. My heart beat rapidly, and I had some place I needed to be, if I could just clear my head.

Run.

My feet carried me at a sprint down the path where Damien and I had our first kiss and beyond. I barely heard Damien calling after me as I ran deeper into the woods behind the commons. Damien and Jackson followed me, I knew they were there, but I was compelled to move faster than I'd probably ever run in my life.

I had to get there. I was needed.

I'd worn my flat sandals this afternoon, but that didn't impede my progress. I only slightly recognized that I was cutting my feet on the twigs and stickers as I ran and ran.

I sensed what was pulling me forward, and I slowed just a bit, still faintly hearing Damien's voice over the sound of my heartbeat roaring in my ears. Just ahead there was a man in the shadows.

In the back of my mind, I registered that this was my nightmare becoming reality, but I couldn't resist moving toward him.

"That's right, Delaney. Come to me now and there will be no more pain."

The stabbing hit me in the eye. I grabbed at my head to make it stop—and in that moment, I missed him raising his arm and the metal gleaming in his hand.

"Delaney, no!"

Damien's words were the last thing I heard before a blast of light hit me in the chest, and then I was falling.

The pain was loud, like standing too close to the rush of a jet engine. Everything else was muffled. I faintly heard screaming. Hands grabbing me, jostling me.

Then, I heard it. Maniacal laughing. It reverberated in my head.

You belong to me. I had you once before and I'll have you again. No walls can keep me. I'll have you and I'll have my daughter and no one will keep me from my plans, not even your precious Healer.

Breathing hurt, and I was so tired, so cold. I just wanted to lie there. Why wouldn't they just let me lie there? Warmth licked at my shoulders, like flames spreading over me, and I smelled smoke. I wanted to scream, but my lungs had given up. As I drifted away, I heard Damien's voice.

"Don't take her. Please, God. Don't take her, too."

The next thing I was aware of was major cottonmouth. My head was so heavy and there was at least a full pallet of lumber parked on my chest. I tried wiggling my fingers and toes and that worked, so I attempted to open an eye. It felt glued together. It was very quiet, wherever I was, but I heard someone breathing heavily.

"Dude, you need to get some sleep. Let me sit for a bit and you go rest."

Was that James? He was here? I wiggled my fingers again.

"I'm not leaving, as I've told you." Damien's voice sounded cracked and weak.

I tried unsuccessfully to open an eye again.

"I'll call you when she's awake. You really need to rest, Damien. You need your strength." Ah, Grace.

Let me open my eyes, I don't want him to go.

"Grace, how could I have let this happened? It's my fault. It's all my fault. I promised I would keep her safe. I couldn't get to her..."

The heavy breathing I heard had to have been him crying. *Oh, God, Damien I'm okay. I'm here. Just take my hand. See? I'm wiggling my fingers. Why won't my eyes work?*

"Damien, he got past our cameras. I've got enough on my hands with James beating himself up that he wasn't there and Jackson angry he couldn't keep up. This is not anyone's fault."

A chair scraped the floor, and I heard footsteps. "Why the hell I— I never should have brought her here."

The door slammed, and it reverberated through me. I tried again to open my eyes and got one this time. I barely made out Grace standing in the middle of what had to be the infirmary with her head in her hands.

"Grace," I croaked.

She turned to me, alarmed, and rushed to my side.

"Oh Delaney, you're awake! We were so worried. Can you move, are you in pain?"

Tears pooled in my eyes. "Damien, please."

She nodded and moved quickly for the door. At that moment, James came in and knelt next to the bed, his eyes red and his face white.

"Dammit, Del, what the hell! Are you okay? That motherfucker!"

I tried to lift my arm but it wouldn't work. My other eye decided to join the party and I looked down at myself. I was decked out in hospital gear, my left shoulder bandaged. The pressure around my head must have been gauze.

"What...James?" I could barely get any words out, and the tears were running down my face. "Water, please," I said as a coughing fit took over. Wow, that was painful.

"You were shot, dammit, by that fucker Rains! He got in somewhere around the rear of the perimeter. I had just been by that area and saw *nothing*. What the hell were you thinking, running into the woods?" The anger in his voice was making it hard for me to breathe. He gripped my hand so hard, and I felt him shaking. I tried to squeeze back but I was so weak.

"Anyone, hurt, else? Joanna!"

He shook his head, and then looked toward the door. Nigel and Morgan approached. Nigel put his hand on James' shoulder.

"My dear, I'm so glad you are awake. Are you in any pain?" he asked.

All I could do was blink. Moving my head was impossible. It was so heavy.

"No one else was hurt, Delaney. Joanna is safe in her room asleep, with Marcia looking over her. You took off so fast, by the time Damien caught up to you, the two of you were far into the woods. Jackson tried to chase you down, but with him just recovering from being shot himself, he couldn't keep up. Grace needs to check your vitals, my dear."

"Rains?"

"Apprehended, and in police custody."

"Damien." Talking was like rubbing sandpaper across my larynx. Grace held up a cup with ice chips and slid one between my lips. I looked at her and tried to thank her with my eyes.

"George has gone after him. He tried to heal you but you were losing a lot of blood. He carried you here and kept trying until we finally stepped in. He's quite distraught." Nigel looked so worried.

Morgan looked angry.

"Not his fault." I became agitated and tried to sit up. Grace gently pushed me down. Morgan came over and placed her hands on me, and I began to slip away again.

"No, no—need Damien, please!" And then all was black again.

THE NEXT DAY, I WOKE TO FIND CASSIDY AND JACKSON SITTING NEXT TO MY bed. They asked me if I needed anything.

"Damien," was all I said.

Jackson just shook his head and stood to look out the window. He cursed to himself.

"I'm sorry, Delaney." Cassidy held my hand and wiped away my tears with a tissue.

Why had he left? Why had he left me? I squeezed my eyes shut and drifted off again, being awake too painful.

Later, I heard Nigel and Morgan talking, and I tried to listen.

"His motorbike is gone and no one has seen him. I sent Elijah. Hopefully he can track him. He's blaming himself for all of this, Morgan. Maybe I pushed him too soon with her. I thought they were both ready. I've mucked things up this time, haven't I?"

"Nigel," she said in a low voice. "This hasn't played out. But we have to find him, soon. If he gets too far, it might be years before we find him again."

I couldn't bear to listen anymore.

He'd left. I felt horribly guilty for having put him in this scenario again. It had to have taken him back to losing his wife and son. I should have been stronger, should have resisted Rains.

The other side of my brain was so very hurt that he would leave me. I just wanted to hold his hand one last time.

ONE WEEK LATER...

James and I sat in my living room eating dinner he had brought from the commons. I spent three days in the infirmary, and then he brought me back to my bungalow. I hated him playing nursemaid, but he was pissy when I didn't let him.

"James, I am taking a shower by myself today, and you can't stop me!" I glared at him across the table and waited for him to argue.

He glared right back. "Girl, you watch yourself. You can shower when I say you're damn good and ready. You've only been up and around since this morning. You do too much, you'll be right back in the infirmary." He took a drink of his milk and kept glaring, daring me to talk back. What he didn't realize is, he had a major milk mustache and some was even hanging on his goatee.

A giggle bubbled up. Before I could help myself, I was belly laughing hysterically, and then crying because uh, gunshot. He stared at me as if I'd just grown a pair of horns.

"Cousin, have you just finally lost it?" He was so alarmed, I laughed even harder, until the tears were pouring down my face.

Between gasps for air, which hurt my shoulder tremendously, I got out, "You should see the look on your face right now."

The phone rang right then.

"Auntie. Yea, she's right here, laughing at me. ... Damn if I'm going to let her wobbly ass take a shower by herself... Uh-huh, I got the package. ... Grace said she's healing fine and will be back to work next week."

I had the hiccups by now, and when he tried to hand me the phone, I signed that I'd call her back. The laughing subsided, leaving a hollow feeling in my chest.

I walked to my bedroom and heard James hang up with my mom. I looked at myself in the mirror. The stitches on my forehead came out this morning. After I'd been shot, I fell and hit my head, further causing blood to exit my body at a rapid rate. The bullet nicked my collarbone and went through my muscle, so I was still bandaged up and in a sling but I was more than functional.

"I'm going back to work tomorrow, James. If that means I have to let Grace help me shower one more time, so be it. You'll just have to deal with it. I need to get back to the kids." I swallowed hard. I didn't want to sit here in this house any longer reliving what had happened and blaming myself.

Before I left the infirmary, Joanna was brought to see me. She told me she'd known what I'd dreamed would come true but that I would make it out of it. She also told Nigel she Saw where Mr. Preston was. He sent Elijah in the direction of the Gulf Coast, but by the time he got there, Damien was gone.

She also said her father had gotten in touch with an associate and ordered him to try to gain custody of her by legal means. An attorney and a man in a greasy suit with equally greasy hair had come to the gates, asking to speak with Nigel. Apparently, this attorney had filed a custody order on behalf of Joanna's "godfather" that, due to the violence on our campus, she was unsafe and should be remanded to his custody.

Nigel's attorney contacted the judge, who promptly rescinded the order.

Rains was still in custody, but was scheduled to be sent back to Texas, which had Nigel worried since they'd failed to keep him before.

It was a lot to take in. I was numb. Cassidy stayed until I was out of the infirmary, but she had her own affairs to settle so she promised she would be back soon and would stay in touch to make sure I was okay. Jackson drove her to the airport to see her off safely. He'd been by daily to check on me, and Skye had brought food and taken care of my cats while I was out of it.

James was back on my couch, refusing to leave my side. I was grateful he was here and grateful he wasn't saying anything about Damien. He had no idea what had really transpired. He was livid that this man who was supposed to love me had abandoned me. He didn't have a lot of patience for people who took off. He'd been married to one. When she left, she took his precious daughters and disappeared.

Nigel agreed I was able to return to work, so by Monday morning I was ready to be back in action. I still hadn't received word from Damien, and I was worried, but I wouldn't let it paralyze me.

Diana was not happy to see me out of bed, but she saw the determination in my eyes and didn't say anything. I spent the day checking messages and visiting with kids during breaks. I called Nate's mom. She was worried he'd experience some culture shock. I assured her that he'd already made friends and seemed in great spirits. I saw him and Matteo at lunch and sat with them for a bit. They were both overwhelmed with their classes, so I hooked them up with Sergei for nightly homework sessions. The three of them made such a comical trio. They always made me smile.

Jackson came by and told me he and I would start physical therapy the next day.

Around four, I was just about to shut down my computer after getting my plans together for my next class when the phone rang.

"This is Miss Frost."

There was silence on the other end for a moment. My heart kicked into overtime as I waited.

"Delaney." His voice sounded hoarse and tired.

"Damien? Where are you?" My eyes filled with tears but I didn't want to scare him off.

"I needed to hear your voice, needed to know you're okay."

"I'm better. I'm not in much pain. A little itchy, but I'm good. Are *you* okay?"

"I'm tired. I just…" He trailed off.

It took everything to not cry out how much I missed him and wanted him here with me.

"I really made a mess of things. I failed you."

"Damien, no." My heart was breaking for him. He sounded devastated. "You saved my life. I'm fine—"

"You were shot, Delaney, in a completely preventable situation. I blew it. I just wanted to keep you safe, and I thought if I was by your side, if we stayed on campus and with other people…"

"Where are you? Let me come to you, please, Damien. I've been so worried. I just need to see you—"

"You need to be safe, not with me. The kids need you. I should have known better." He cleared his throat. "When I saw him in Texas, I never told you…he knew. About us. He taunted me, said there was nothing I could do, that his will was inevitable. I lost my temper. I told him I would never let him get to you. This is my fault."

"Blaming yourself for this isn't going to change what happened. It isn't going to fix anything. You need to come home, Damien. We need you. *I* need you."

It hurt to tell him that, knowing that in his state of mind, he was just going to pull away further. The counselor and the woman in love were at war. He was hanging on the edge of a cliff. If I shifted my weight, he would tumble into the abyss, gone from me forever. At least if he were in front of me, I could possibly read him, but even then he was so difficult to read.

"Delaney. I should never—"

"Don't say that to me." My internal battle was about to get bloody. I was angry now. "You asked me to accept a lot of things when I got here. Why can't you accept that you are *not* responsible for this? The actions of a sick man caused this, not you." I tried to keep my voice low but I was screaming inside.

"You should go back to your cottage. You need your rest. Good night, Delaney. I… I'm sorry."

The click on the other end was so anticlimactic. I wanted to scream. I wanted to throw the phone and break stuff. Dammit, how could I get through to him?

Sitting at my desk had me feeling impotent. I stood up and stomped out the door. A plan was forming with one of my internal generals, and I needed reinforcements.

"Morgan, we need to fix me so I can go find that stubborn man and bring his ass home!"

I stood fuming in the doorway of her study. She eyed me warily. We stood that way for a beat before she picked up the phone and dialed without taking her eyes off me.

"I need you. Delaney is here. It's time."

I was thrown, but I was determined. I needed to unlock what was inside of me, and learn how to control it. I needed to be impenetrable to Rains' persuasion. I needed to be strong enough to find Damien and convince him that when two people love each other, they are both responsible for themselves and each other.

Elijah came in then, and we got to work.

Over the next few hours, we made a lot of progress, but it ultimately took days of meeting with them before I felt ready. They explained that—like everything else—learning how to channel the power inside of you comes easier when you're younger. I didn't care how hard it was, I was going to master my gift if it took every last breath from my body.

Elijah was less scary to me now. I understood his gift was different from mine in that I *gave* energy and he *took* it. I gained energy from being around others and from helping, he pulled the darkness from those who needed—and were deserving of—his help. Our gifts balanced each other. Once I figured that out, how each of us functioned with the others in

Havenhart's inner circle, I not only felt stronger, but I understood my purpose.

I was meant to be a Healer. An emotional Healer. Damien was a Healer, but his gift, like Morgan had explained before, involved manipulating the body's organic chemistry and working with what already existed. My healing was only limited by my own perceived boundaries. My gift and Elijah's were closer than mine and Damien's. It also explained why Damien had limitations. He had a finite amount of energy to work with, and that was why it drained him so. He needed my healing as much as I'd needed his when I'd been shot. And since he'd left without being healed, he wasn't operating on all physical, mental and emotional cylinders...and he was in danger. He was operating from his "lizard brain"—the limbic system. Fight or flight were the emotions ruling him at the moment, and would continue to do so unless I found him. Soon. Morgan told me she'd Seen him in dire straits. This knowledge made it all the more urgent that I figure myself out...and find him.

I spent time with Joanna daily. She told me everything—about the abuse, the death of her grandfather and her mother's disappearance, and the insanity that her father had made her a part of for years. She was so strong. She had developed a shell around her sacred self that she never let him break through. She also spent time with Morgan and Elijah and learned to focus her Sight.

Between the four of us, we located Damien and plotted to bring him home. Nigel was on board and assured me that he and the others would hold the fort down while I went after him.

It took more persuasion to get James to agree to let me go alone.

"Cousin, you just got shot. You're nuts if you think I'm letting you—"

"James, Rains is still a threat. The kids need you. I can't do this without knowing they're safe. I'll be fine. I'm stronger every day. My physical therapy with Jackson has given me back some strength in my arm, and the work with Morgan and Elijah has me feeling stronger than ever."

I was fierce inside. I knew I could take on the demon when next we met, and I was certain we would meet again. I was no longer afraid of Rains. If he managed to escape, if he tried anything again, I would fight him—and I would win. He wasn't getting Joanna, and there was no way in hell I was going to let him hurt anyone I loved ever again, including myself.

I packed a bag with some clothes and necessities to get me through a few days. Skye agreed to take care of my cats. James was pissed at me. He was even more pissed at Damien because I was going after him.

"He left, Del. He couldn't handle it, and he left. As far as I 'm concerned, he should be history. He made his bed."

I shook my head and knew I had to share what happened to make him understand.

"James, Damien has suffered more than you know. He's lost everything, time and again, and he blames himself. Tell me, if you had watched your wife and child die, and you thought you should have been able to save them, how would *you* deal with that the next time you were faced with losing someone you loved?"

He was taken aback but he heard the determination in me. He nodded. "I get it. Fine. But dammit, Del, if he hurts you—"

"This is *my* choice. If I get there, and he decides he can't handle it... well, that will be *his* choice. I won't like it, and I intend to fight dirty if I have to. But bottom line, he's either going to see the truth or he isn't. And then we'll deal."

He walked me to the gatehouse, where Vincent had the car ready for me. I hugged James and made him promise to take care of everyone, including himself. He just nodded and walked over to stand by the gate, his arms crossed over his chest, just daring anyone to get past.

I drove south with my GPS guiding me. Joanna had seen Damien near lots of water in an old place. Nigel recalled Damien having once had a flat in the French Quarter of New Orleans, but thought he'd sold it years ago. A quick search told us that he still, in fact, owned it...and with the address in hand, I set off on a sunny, muggy Saturday morning, three weeks since the night that had sent Damien seeking haven elsewhere.

TWENTY

RESCUE MISSION

I drove through some beautiful country on my way through Southern Arkansas and Northern Louisiana. I vowed to return when I had more time to explore, maybe even bringing some kids with me on a field trip. When I turned onto Interstate 10 headed for New Orleans, my pulse sped up. I went over my plan in my head, what I would and would not say to him when I found him. I took the Esplanade exit and followed it down to Chartres.

The building was a brick collection of apartments near St. Philip. I drove past once and circled the block looking for a place to park. It was late afternoon, and there were lots of folks milling about. The heat was much more stifling than it had been in Arkansas. I was grateful for my light skirt and tank with sandals.

I entered the quaint courtyard and immediately understood why Damien had fallen in love with the place. I looked for the correct number and knocked on the door. I waited a beat, and then heard a little voice behind me.

"He's not there. He comes out in the evening. He likes the water." An adorable little girl with braids on both sides of her familiar-looking tawny cheeks smiled up at me. She had a jump rope with her and was beaming at me. "Wanna jump rope, lady?"

"Why, that's a kind offer, darlin', but I'm not much of a rope jumper. My big 'ol feet get in the way. You sure look like you can do it well."

She moved a few paces away and demonstrated for me. She started reciting a rhyme while she jumped, and I sat down on a chair to watch her. I admired her innocence and prayed she'd be able to keep it for a long, long while.

Just then, a woman stepped out of the door across from Damien's. She had a basket of laundry balanced on one hip.

"Ella, did you finish your studies?"

Ella dropped her rope and her smile at the same time. She trudged dramatically into the house, taking a moment to glance back at me while the woman shooed her inside. The woman then looked appraisingly at me. "You the woman from Havenhart?"

I blinked and nodded. "I'm Delaney Frost. Is Damien staying here?"

She looked me over again and seemed to take my measure. "That depends. Are you here to heal him or cause him more pain? Cos, chére, he doesn't need any more pain."

Her eyes were kind, and I wondered what kind of relationship he had with her. She appeared to be in her mid-to-late forties and she had the most beautiful hazel eyes...eyes that reminded me of someone I'd met recently.

"You seem so familiar to me."

The woman's look became even more intense. "You met my daughter? Ebony? She come see you up there?"

I nodded. "I did. She's such a poised young lady. She's doing very well. She seems to like Havenhart." The puzzle of this situation was coming together for me. "And she plays piano beautifully."

"Mr. Preston taught her. I'm Letitia."

I walked over to her and held out my hand. She took it firmly, turned it over and looked down at my palm. Her brows creased together in the middle for a moment and when she looked up into my eyes again, I felt those cold fingers snaking up the back of my neck, just like when Elijah had looked at me the same way.

I steeled myself and concentrated on those fingers, warming them from that place inside of me.

It was her turn to blink. Then she smiled a slow, mischievous smile. "You got yourself figured out, now didn't ya?"

I smiled, but I was desperate to learn of Damien's well-being, not to discuss this psychic interaction.

"How is he? I need to find him." It was full dusk. The foot traffic on Chartres grew louder and jazz music had started up somewhere down the block.

"Not well. Every evening he goes down to the water, and then he shuts himself back up in there." She gestured with her head. "He needs to find his peace. You gonna bring it to him?"

I took a deep breath. "I sure hope so. I've come to take him home."

She nodded and started for the doors at the other end of the courtyard. She called to me over her shoulder. "Keep heading down Philip. You'll cross the market. Head downriver and you'll find him."

"Thank you, Letitia," I called back. I turned on my heel and stepped out onto the street. Even though it was getting darker, the heat persisted, but it seemed a gentle breeze was coming from the river. I passed some of the most beautiful old buildings and colorful people along the way. I gathered in the energy of the place, making myself stronger. There were musicians playing outside the French Market and lots of folks had stopped to listen. I smiled as I walked past, some of my fears falling away.

The river walk was less inhabited the further I went. The families and tourists must not venture down this far.

I found Damien sitting on a fallen log under a tree, elbows resting on bent knees. He stared out over the water and didn't appear to notice me coming.

I sank down next to him and tried to see what he was looking at.

He looked over at me in surprise. Several emotions crossed his face—sadness, longing, anger, regret—before he looked away. He sighed and continued to look at some point across the river. His eyes were dull. Hopeless.

"Why did you come here, Delaney?" His voice was so quiet and sad.

I wanted to gather him up into my arms, but he was so fragile I was afraid he might break if I wasn't ever so careful.

"Why do you think I came here? Have you forgotten what I said to you weeks ago?"

A muscle worked in his jaw and he frowned. I didn't want to push. I let that sit for a moment. And so we sat for what seemed like years on the banks of the Mississippi.

"I've been so cold without you." Tears threatened in his voice.

I took a chance and reached over with one finger. I traced the infinity symbol on his biceps, just as he'd done to me. His eyes closed tightly and he let out a shaky breath, looking down at the ground beneath us.

"I saw you crumple to the ground in front of me, and there was so much blood. You...died. I almost couldn't bring you back." His shoulders were shaking with the effort it took him to hold back his sobs. "I touched you, and I tried to stop it, but there was so much blood..."

I took his hand and led it to my shoulder, where the wound was now just a pink scar.

"And here I am, sitting next to you. You saved me, Damien. And not just that night. You took me away from my miserable, static life, and brought me to the most wonderful place I could ever imagine. You brought me out of my protective shell and showed me that I could trust a man with my heart." My own tears pooled in my eyes but I had to finish saying what I needed to say. He still wouldn't look at me.

I moved to kneel in front of him, taking his hands in mine. I concentrated on my center, and I let the warmth spread down my arms. As soon as it reached his hands, he pulled away and looked at me with the most pained expression yet.

"Stop it, Delaney. I don't deserve it. I don't deserve *you*." His eyes were red. He hadn't shaved, probably since he'd left. Thick black hair sprinkled with gray and silver covered the lower half of his face. I winced when I saw that he had a third white streak through his beautiful hair, right down the middle.

I reached out and touched his disheveled hair. He closed his eyes. I ran my hand down around his cheek, letting my nails scrape through the coarse hairs.

"One of the things I've learned from this experience is that I'm no longer going to let others dictate what I believe is true for me. Not Rains, not my detractors…not even you."

He glanced up cautiously. I continued in the toughest voice I could muster.

"I've let others decide for me long enough. I let the fire rule my actions, I let the school district convince me I wasn't doing a good job with my program, and then I let you talk me into getting on an airplane and come to Havenhart, sight unseen. That was the second-most intelligent thing I've ever done. The first was letting you into my heart.

"Damien, you've been so good to me, and you've shown me the strength I didn't believe I possessed. I'm grateful to you. I'm even grateful that you left."

With that statement, he looked taken aback. "How can you say that?"

I smiled at him and scooted closer. I leaned on his knees, and he sat back, holding himself up on his shaky arms. "Because if you hadn't left, I never would have decided it was time to unlock what's inside of me."

I placed my hands on either side of his face and looked into his eyes. I willed the love I felt for him into his body, I willed my healing into him and he immediately stiffened. Then he closed his eyes…and an almost peaceful look came over him.

When he opened his eyes again, they were full of wonder.

He leaned forward, placing his legs on either side of me and cupping my face in his hands. "Delaney, what happened to you? How did you…?"

He couldn't stop touching me, and when I pulled him closer he didn't resist. I placed my lips on his, and he groaned, wrapping himself around me.

I focused my energy on warming every part of him. He kissed me back in a frenzy. Tears streamed down his face. I let my tears fall with his and we stayed there holding each other, our cheeks pressed together, as the night grew darker around us.

When we finally collected ourselves, he stood wordlessly and took my hand. He kept watch of me while we walked back down the river walk, the brightness back in his gaze. We reached his apartment and he opened the door, pulling me forcefully inside. He backed me up against the door and buried his face in my hair.

I kissed his throat and the taut skin over his collarbone. Then I covered his shoulder with more kisses. I pulled back and looked into his eyes. He grazed his knuckles down the sides of my face, and then reached for my hand. He led me to a small staircase at the back of the room. At the top, we entered what I assumed was his bedroom

The room had exposed brick walls, hardwood floors and vaulted, exposed wood ceilings. It wasn't as warm inside his place. The ceiling fans kept the air moving. When we reached his bed, he pulled me to him and held me close. I inhaled his scent and opened the top buttons of his shirt to kiss his chest. I climbed up and knelt on the bed, taking his hand to lead him to me. He hesitated, but I insisted. We lay facing each other on our sides.

A pained expression filled his face. I pulled him to me and cradled his head to my chest. I just held him there.

He finally sighed deeply. "I'm so tired."

I kissed his forehead and sent more calming energy his way. Soon, he was breathing steadily and his body relaxed against mine.

I spent a long time lying there, stroking his beard and his hair. Finally, I closed my eyes and prayed he would get the rest he needed.

Sometime in the night, he stirred, and I woke. He sat up and took his shirt off. I disrobed, dropping my clothes off the side of the bed. We watched each other undress and then curled up together, kissing softly. He turned me over to spoon with me, and he kissed my neck.

"I just want to hold you, love. Can I hold you tonight?"

I nodded and brought our linked hands up to kiss his knuckles. We stayed like that until the morning light shone through his window.

When next I woke, Damien was kissing the back of my neck. He moved his knee to nest between my thighs. His hairs tickled me as I pressed up against him. His body tensed behind me, and a growl rumbled in his chest.

"You feel so good, Delaney. I can't help myself. I want to be inside you."

I looked at him over my shoulder and touched his face. "I want that, too, Damien. I want you."

He kissed me hard and reached down to touch me, finding me ready for him. He groaned again in desperation. He rolled me onto my stomach and spread my legs enough to enter me from behind. He was inside me with one deep thrust, his body shuddering and his breathing shallow.

We both cried out with the pleasure of being together once more, as we were meant to be. He moved as if he were trying to crawl inside and penetrate all of me. I pushed against him as he pulled my hips back to meet his thrusts. His weight sank me deliciously into the mattress with each movement of his hips. Our faces were next to each other, and I felt the heat of his skin. I wanted to warm him even further. I didn't ever want him to feel cold again. I reached back and held his head while his hands reached forward to grab the edge of the mattress as he thrust even deeper.

We came together, and it brought tears to my eyes again. Damien continued to move within me, all of his muscles straining and shaking.

He rolled over onto his back and I curled up against his chest. His eyes were closed. I was pleased to see the peaceful look was still on his face.

"Now, that's what I wanted to see. No more scowling or frowning."

He chuckled softly. I loved that sound and prayed I would hear it again and again.

He leaned over to kiss me, and it warmed my heart. I was physically tired but emotionally recharged. I hadn't known what to expect when I found him, but he'd clearly still been in survival mode. My healing kick-started his higher functioning, but Morgan had warned me that might kickstart, ah, other base needs. I certainly wasn't complaining about that little side effect. In the morning light, I saw that he really hadn't been well. He'd noticeably lost weight. His hipbones jutted out and I knew once he shaved, the hollows under his cheekbones would be more prominent. At that thought, I scraped my nails through his beard again and giggled.

"Something tickle you?" he asked, amused.

I nodded. "I'm just hoping this is really Damien and not his mountain man cousin, Daniel Boone."

He flipped me onto my back and rubbed his whiskers across my breasts. I squealed and tried to wiggle away, but he wrapped his body around mine, keeping me close.

"I think I kind of like this look on you, Mr. Preston. I'm not sure how it'll go with your wardrobe, however. I understand the academy employs some stylists who could determine that for you."

More tickling and giggling occurred until we were both breathless. Then he looked at the time.

"We need to get you fed, Miss Frost. Breakfast is the most important meal of the day. And although I'd love to eat it off of you, naked in my bed, I have absolutely no food in the house. We'll have to actually get up and get dressed." I pouted, and he bit my lip gently then sucked on it.

Damien climbed out of bed and stretched out his arms and back in the middle of the room. The sunlight illuminated his glorious body and sadly accentuated the weight he'd lost. His muscles were more defined and stark. His lightly tanned skin was covered with fine black hairs that met in the center of his chest and ran more thickly down his torso. His shoulders were heavy and curved like a swimmer's, his arms and legs delicately defined. Even his feet were perfect. I realized I hadn't yet tasted his toes.

He turned to look at me over his shoulder and seemed unsure of himself for a minute.

"You are truly breathtaking. Do you know that?"

That seemed to bother him. I sat up and frowned. "What's wrong, Damien?"

"I just can't believe you're really here. I was afraid I wouldn't ever see you again. Definitely not in my bed."

I looked down at myself. The sheet was draped across my thighs, my hair disheveled, my breasts bare to him. I looked at him a long time before I stood and approached. I stopped in front of him without touching. He looked down at the floor. He seemed to be silently warring with himself; angry he left, angry he'd made love to me this morning when all he'd meant to do was hold me one last time, maybe before sending me away again.

I tipped his chin up with my finger and got right in his line of sight. "You're pulling away from me." He tried to look away but I was persistent. "If you don't love me, and don't feel this is where you want to be, then I'll accept it and leave you here."

He looked up angrily but before he could speak, I put my finger against his lips. "If you love me, but feel you should stay away from me out of some misguided sense of chivalry, I'm going to be angry. If you know me even just a little, you know that I'm an optimistic person who believes people can make just about anything work when they love each other. And I love you, Damien. For all of your pigheadedness, I love you." I paused.

He dug his fists into his hips and his mouth fell open in shock. "Pigheaded? Of all the... You're the one who's stubborn."

I squinted my eyes and got even closer without touching my body to his. "You're right, I am. So what's it going to be? Are you going to work this out with me, come home with me? Or should I get dressed and go?"

That pained expression was back, and he dropped to his knees in front of me, his arms wrapping around my waist. He buried his face in my chest.

"God, Delaney. Can you really forgive me? I panicked and left you while you were wounded. I'm disgusted with myself." He fought the tears I knew were there. I cradled him to me and held on. He whispered in a pained voice, "I love you so much, it scares me."

I bent down and kissed the top of his head.

"I know. It scared me, too. In the beginning. But Damien, I'm not afraid anymore. I know what I want, and I know what we can do together. You need to forgive *yourself*. Will you promise me you'll try?"

"I will try."

"Good. Now can we please eat some breakfast? I don't know how much longer I can hold off my tummy growls."

He pulled me down onto his lap and kissed me gently.

"I'm so glad you came, Delaney. And I'm terribly sorry. I love you so much." His green gaze was fragile but steady. We'd get past this, I was sure. I just hoped that he would forgive himself and put *his* past behind him.

We showered quickly, and he went out to the car to get my things. I heard him talking to Letitia outside, and I peeked out the window. She nodded approvingly and smiled at him. I heard him say, "Thank you, Letitia. She means everything to me."

A little while later, we walked down Chartres Street and ate breakfast at the cozy Café Fleur de Lis. New Orleanians sure know how to do breakfast. It was heavenly. Damien watched me contentedly, touching and kissing me between bites. He wiped away my powdered sugar and syrup messes, laughing lovingly at my dining foibles.

"Now do you see how brave I am that I took you to Zachary's? Look at my atrocious table manners."

"Yes, I see you do have some issues with getting food to your mouth. But I seem to recall you have other very special oral talents."

I blushed, but then realized two could play his game. I reached under the table and ran my hand over one of my favorite parts of his anatomy, which twitched appreciatively. His lids lowered and he sucked in a breath.

I smirked and whispered, "If we can take some of this powdered sugar and syrup with us, I'd be glad to show you those talents again."

He grabbed my hand hard and the heated gaze he gave me said I'd better finish my breakfast, because we had other things to do. I smiled coyly and finished eating while he hoarsely asked for the check.

Once we got back to his cottage, we were naked and all over each other for the remainder of the afternoon. We had so much fun discovering new and better ways to make each other feel good.

He dozed off after several rounds of play, and I snuck out of bed to call Havenhart and let them know that Operation Rescue was going smoothly. Morgan was pleased to hear it. I also spoke briefly with James. He pretty much grunted.

"Hurry and getcha ass back here, FC."

I smiled and blew him a kiss through the phone.

When I curled back up next to Damien, I, too, fell into a peaceful sleep.

We woke as the last lights left the sky. "I can see how folks become night owls around here. It's much more bearable in the evening."

He kissed my nose. "I always seem to be here under less than favorable conditions and have yet to truly experience all the city has to offer. Perhaps someday, when I'm ready to let you out of my bed, we can explore together."

I grinned up at him just as my traitorous stomach started growling again.

"Oops," I giggled. "Guess breakfast can only tide one over for so long."

We went for a late dinner and ended up on Bourbon Street at Turtle Bay. I had some delicious alligator sausage and fried crawdads. It was a crazy scene outside. The music was great and we had a nice little corner from where we did some people-watching for entertainment. When the band took a break, I curled up into the crook of his arm and asked him how he'd ended up here.

"After I traveled in South America, I thought I should try to get back into shape for human interaction. I came back through Haiti, and so it was the logical next stop to land here in New Orleans. I fell in love with the place and found the property for a good price. I got to know Letitia's family, who had been tenants for quite a while. When I realized what Ebony was doing, I knew it was no coincidence that I'd landed here.

"I told Letitia about Havenhart, and she was very interested in pursuing it for her daughter when she was old enough to go. I called Nigel, who was very patient with me, wanted me to come when I was ready and take my place as his right hand. It was too daunting at first. I just wasn't sure I had it in me to be responsible for anyone yet. But watching Ebony struggle while trying to figure out what to do with her gift, I knew I couldn't delay. Letitia agreed to take over as property manager, and I gathered my things and left. I haven't been back here since. I knew she'd kept it up for me. It just felt like the right place to come."

I was so sad for him. I imagined the torture he had been putting himself through all this time. "I'm glad you have a place to go where you feel safe."

He smiled down at me and kissed my forehead. He was quiet for a long time and then he clasped my fingers in his. We looked down together at our hands.

"Have I ever told you how much I love your fingers?"

He frowned at me. "Fingers? I've never thought about fingers as being particularly alluring. Although, now that you mention it, I'm quite fond of yours."

"Yours are long and strong. Very masculine. They're so talented...the guitar, the piano—which I haven't heard you play yet, by the way. And when you draw those circles on my leg..."

He smiled down at me. I had so missed the crinkles in the corners of his eyes.

"It makes me think of how completely I love you."

He pulled me into his arms and held me close.

"As beautiful as this place is, and as much as I'd love to just stay here in your arms... Have you thought about coming back with me?"

He nodded solemnly. "It's time, I think. There's something I need to do tomorrow before we leave. Is that all right with you?"

"Of course. Do you want me to give you some space?" I didn't want to crowd him.

He took my hand and kissed it, and then we stood together. "The only space I need from you is right in here." He lightly brushed his knuckles against my chest directly over my heart.

I beamed up at him. "It's yours, always."

The next day, we woke late again, and this time we did enjoy our breakfast all over each other. We took a lazy shower together and dressed, stopping to kiss and touch repeatedly before we actually got out of the house. We walked down to Jackson Square. I admired the artists' works hung around the bars of the park. There was so much talent in this city.

Damien paused in front of the St. Louis Cathedral and took my hands in his. He looked down at me gravely.

"You said I needed to forgive myself. I don't know how completely I can let go of this, but I think I might know how I can make amends. Will you come with me?"

"Whatever you need from me." I kissed him on the cheek and we went inside the cathedral. Just inside the foyer, Damien approached an altar covered with candles. He lit two and knelt down before them. He closed his eyes.

I joined him and said a prayer for his wife and child. I said a prayer for him, asking that he find the strength to let go of his regrets and his feeling of responsibility for their deaths. I said a prayer for his parents, thanking them for bringing such a precious man into this world. And I thanked whoever was listening for bringing him into my life, and the lives of the children he'd touched at Havenhart and elsewhere.

I glanced over at him, and he was trembling, his eyes closed tight. I reached over and touched his hand, focusing my warmth to flow into him. He entwined his fingers with mine and gave a faint squeeze. I heard him take in a deep breath and let it out. We knelt in silence for a bit, watching the candles flicker.

When we left the cathedral, he gave me a hug so intense, he lifted me off my feet.

"I loved them both. I often think of what our lives would've been like if they'd lived. I hope Siobhan gives us her blessing. And I pray she understands. I've tried to live my life doing right by others. Now I want what's right for me, and that is you, Delaney."

"You have me."

TWENTY-ONE

COMING INTO POWER

We departed New Orleans in the late afternoon. Damien was rested enough to drive us into Shreveport, where he'd made us a reservation for the night. We tried to call the school, but his phone was on the fritz again. He mumbled about technology and needing a new one when we returned.

We pulled into a Hilton, Damien checked us in, and we headed up to our suite. The elevator ride seemed to last forever. We got off on the fifth floor and quietly entered our room, putting out the "Do Not Disturb" sign. We dropped our things in the bedroom and fell on the bed, fully clothed. We talked until we couldn't hold our eyes open anymore.

I woke with a start less than an hour later.

Something was very wrong, but my brain was so foggy from the short amount of sleep, it was difficult to focus.

Rains was standing at the foot of our bed with a woman from Housekeeping. Who was pointing a gun at us.

Damien woke and cursed when he saw our captor.

I don't know what I was expecting, but this small, plain man with a thinning, sandy-blond combover was not it. He stood a full head shorter than Damien, shorter than me, even. His pale skin was blotchy and he looked unwell.

When he spoke, his voice had a slight Texas drawl and the pitch was much higher than it seemed it would be. There was absolutely nothing remarkable about him physically. But he more than made up for it in psychic power. It ran over me like the touch of an unwanted suitor.

"You should have kept running," he said with a sick smile. The housekeeper pointed the gun at Damien. "And you," he said and the gun moved toward me. "You are so predictable. It was easy to figure out where there was smoke," the woman pointed the gun at Damien. "There's fire."

The woman pointed the gun at me once more, her hand shaking as tears poured down her face.

"This stops here," I said to Rains, my voice shaky at first but growing with strength. "You won't hurt me again. You won't hurt anyone I love ever again."

"You sound so sure of yourself, Miss Frost. But you see, that's where you're wrong. I will hurt you. I'll hurt you and anyone else who gets in the way of my plans. You got lucky the first time, but that won't happen again."

I pushed up slowly on the bed and got to my knees.

"A bullet won't stop me."

"I know that," he said, his disgusting laugh nearly caused me to shudder, but I would show no weakness. "Fire won't stop you either. I learned that a long time ago."

I couldn't hide my shock at that statement.

"They called it faulty wiring, but, you know, I helped." His thin, scarred lips split into a horrible grin revealing yellowed, crooked teeth.

I shook my head. "But...how?"

"I hated the nursery. My daddy would never let me come to big church even though that's where I longed to be! I knew that was my destiny, leading the services. My Maker, he talked to me, even way back then. But Daddy refused and left me with some teenaged girl who knew nothing about the Maker and his plans. I'd been...experimenting...with my thoughts. I knew I could influence things around me, so, why not fire?"

Oh God. "You caused the fire? You killed those children."

He cocked his head to the side. "Yeah, but not you, though." He shook his head and then spit onto the floor. "The girl who wouldn't burn."

"Yeah, well I'm still here. And I'm not going to let you hurt—"

"You said that, but who has the gun? You think your Healer can heal himself?"

The housekeeper pointed the gun at Damien and fired, hitting the bed next to his leg. The housekeeper screamed.

I had to think. If I used too much energy, I'd kill him and likely hurt the poor woman. If I didn't use enough, he'd—

"I've frankly had enough of the two of you. I will *not* be incarcerated. I will *not* be kept from my daughter. And I will not be kept from my plans.

"The End of Days is near, and Joanna is the key to our salvation. You are interfering with something you cannot possibly comprehend!"

He reached out his hand and Damien rose from the bed. He had no control over his actions. He placed Damien in front of the woman and her gun. I reached out with my senses and felt how much Damien struggled to free himself of the man's Influence.

"It would be much easier and cleaner if you simply took yourselves out of the equation, but if I can't make that happen, I'll do it for you. Or, Renee will do it for me."

In that moment, a feeling of calm descended over me.

I knew I was ready for this.

"It's such a shame you won't be rejoining your colleagues at Havenhart. I need my daughter back, and without you two in the way, I *will* have her." He seemed so confident.

I fueled my quiet rage with thoughts of what Joanna had shared with me about the torture she'd endured at his hands. The temperature in the room raised subtly as I gathered the energy around me, just as Morgan and Elijah had taught me.

"I thought about making it appear that the two of you died in a lover's quarrel. It would certainly take all suspicion off me, and further discredit Hart and his academy. 'He knowingly let unbalanced and deviant characters supervise our children,' they'll say. It's really better that you don't see what I have planned for the rest of your colleagues. But no, Renee will be just fine. No one will suspect I had anything to do with this. Hell, they don't even know I escaped."

Rains twisted his hand and Damien screamed as his arm was bent in an unnatural way. He looked at me, alarmed. He was unable to fight the man's innate force.

That's all it took for me to end it.

I funneled my fury into the hottest source I could find within myself. Just as Damien had shown me that my passion caused his body to heat, my anger and rage ignited a heat much more powerful than ever before. Elijah had taught me well just how to project that heat, and while I didn't know how I was going to deal with the aftermath, I desperately wanted there to be an after with the man I loved.

When I spoke, my voice was gravelly with the barely contained rage.

"Mr. Rains, I am *not* sorry to inform you that you have *completely* overstepped your bounds. Besides the unforgiveable pain you have caused your daughter and your family, the families of your victims, and my friends, you're trying to interfere with something that is so filled with good and promise, your twisted mind cannot possibly comprehend its importance. I'm going to give you one more chance to cease and accept your punishment. If you choose to proceed, I will end this here and now. Permanently."

He looked surprised and supremely entertained.

He even laughed as he forced Renee to lift the gun again and fire at Damien.

Before the bullet even left the chamber, I sent a small taste of what was to come to the handle of the weapon, heating it so intensely I knew she would drop it instantly, and prayed no permanent damage would come to her or my Damien.

"*What did you do?*" he screamed, furious. He pulled out another weapon —and I unleashed my fury in his direction.

His skin turned bright red, blisters swiftly following, and he screamed again before he crumbled to the floor, convulsing.

Damien and Renee both collapsed as well, exhausted from trying to fight back.

Security pounded on the door and then rushed inside.

I hurried to Damien's side and helped him sit up.

"Ma'am, are you okay?"

"I am. This man held the maid at gunpoint and forced her to let him in.

He tried to shoot my boyfriend, but he dropped the gun. Then the guy had some sort of seizure."

Damien was so stunned, he could only stare at me in wonder.

Within minutes, the room was full of police. The paramedics came in then and checked Damien first, then Rains, who was in serious trouble. They rushed him out, handcuffed to the gurney. Renee was treated for the burn to her hand and then questioned by the police.

We would later find out that he'd appeared to the paramedics to have an extremely high fever that had made him delirious. The police believed that's what had caused him to enter our room and pull a weapon. However, Damien told them about Rains, Joanna and Havenhart Academy.

After we answered everyone's questions, it was quite late. I didn't think I'd be able to sleep in the same room where everything had just transpired, but it was surprisingly easy, given the energy I had just expended. I fell asleep listening to Damien relay the incident to Nigel over the phone.

The next morning, we ordered room service and, over breakfast, he questioned me about everything.

"How did you know you could do that? Did it hurt you? How were you able to control it?"

"I wasn't sure what would happen. It didn't exactly hurt, just made me feel as though I'd run a marathon while smoking a pack of cigarettes. Elijah taught me how to focus it. I just hoped it would work." I shuddered. "For a minute, I thought I'd killed him. I didn't know how to feel about it. Ending a life is anathema to what I do."

"You're incredibly brave, Delaney. I was horrified, but I had no control over my limbs. You knew exactly what to do, though, didn't you?"

"It's what I had prepared for. Otherwise, I would have come straight for you as soon as I got out of the infirmary and was able to locate you." He seemed surprised by that. "I knew why you left, and I couldn't bear it that you were blaming yourself. But I didn't want to be a liability to anyone anymore. I hope you understand."

He held me and assured me that he was unbelievably proud of me, and grateful for all I'd done.

We arrived at Havenhart in the late afternoon and were met at the gates. Everyone was so happy to see Damien back and looking well.

James checked me over for damage and then approached Damien menacingly.

"You're lucky she's in one piece, you son of a bitch. You do that again, and I will make you wish you'd never been born. Do you understand me?"

Damien put his arms around me and said, "James, if I am ever that stupid again, I hope you'll keep your promise."

James wasn't quite sure what to think of that, but when Damien held out his hand, he took it, then punched him in the arm before turning back to me.

"I understand your lessons came in handy. Care to debrief?"

"Actually, James, I want to go home and savor the idea that we're all safe for now, and that everyone is okay. Can I please do that?"

He nodded and smiled. "I'll be next door if you need me." I hugged him and thanked him for being there. He waved all my thanks off and walked away, shaking his head.

The well-wishers left us to walk back to my bungalow alone.

Damien stopped me at the porch. I looked at him with an eyebrow raised questioningly.

"I'm not sure how to proceed here. One school of thought says I take you inside, tuck you in and leave you to your space and rest. That would be the noble thing to do. The selfish thing to do would be to take you inside, love you, and sleep curled up around you tonight and every night after. What are your thoughts, love?"

I gave him my most winning smile. "Can we discuss it in the morning over breakfast?"

THE END...

Stay Tuned for Havenhart Academy Book Two in Winter 2021

AUTHOR'S NOTE...

Healer is the first book I ever wrote. Like Delaney, I'd been working in a program for kids with learning and behavior issues and I loved them all. I'd experienced the most difficult two years of my professional life, lost students to gun violence and incarceration, and my body gave up on me. I ended up on disability with pneumonia and a sinus infection that required surgery.

That was 2009. I began writing this book in August of that year and finished it in June 2012. I had no idea what I was doing. I'd never thought I'd be able to finish a book, but when you hit rock bottom, sometimes writing is the best way to heal.

I wrote Haunted, then The Rock Season and then the Teacher Trilogy and... I've never looked back. I'm grateful to those of you who have been with me from the beginning and hope to bring you many more stories. Writing still soothes my soul and helps me process all of the difficulties life flings my way.

I really did attend Graceland University. There really is a Cassidy and a James, although their names have been changed to protect the innocent-ish.

As for whether Havenhart exists...I sure hope it does somewhere. It's exactly the kind of school many of our kids need; a safe place with caring staff who are given the freedom to actually teach and counsel students rather than all of the limitations and constraints our current education system places on those of us who want the best for our kids.

Thanks for taking this journey with me.

ACKNOWLEDGMENTS

To my editor Kelli Collins The Magnificent! I could never have done this without you. Thank you for helping me clean up this beast and for challenging me to make the changes necessary for this book to be the best it can be.

To the real "Cassidy," thank you for always believing in your bestie and cheering me on.

To Agnieszka, thanks for never giving up on this story! I'm so happy to be releasing it FINALLY.

It only took eight years…

To my Roadies…You guys rock and I couldn't do this without you.

Thanks to my family for supporting me no matter how cuckoo my dreams are. I promise, I'll get my chores done. I swear. I love you.

If you enjoyed Healer, please leave a review wherever you are inclined. Let other folks know about the books you love. I'd also love for you to sign up for my newsletter-y thingie at www.rlmerrillauthor.com for all the latest news from the world of Rock 'n' Romance.

COMING SOON

Breaking Bread – The Dark Divinations Anthology published by HorrorAddicts.net releases May 2020. When a young newlywed seeks guidance from the town matron, her quest for the truth may lead her down the path of no return.

R.L. Merrill returns to the Magic and Mayhem Universe in June 2020 with Gator Me Twice, the third book in the Shifted series. Layla knows mating means babies, so why is it that everyone and their gator seems to be knocked up but her? And have they seen the last of the river god Brad and his soggy wenches? Return to Terrebonne Parish for more hijinks and tomfoolery with our friends from Assjacket, West Virginia.

And much, much more! *Stay Tuned for more Rock 'n' Romance...*

www.ingramcontent.com/pod-product-compliance
Lightning Source LLC
Chambersburg PA
CBHW030638260626
47157CB00007B/2383